san Car
got a bad grade
TV until the grade had im
with books. Now, having turne
into a love for writing romance, sh
She loves castles, travelling, afternoo
voraciously and hearing from her readers.
newsletter at SusanCarlisle.com.

Julie Danvers grew up in a rural community surrounded by farmland. Although her town was small, it offered plenty of scope for imagination, as well as an excellent library. Books allowed Julie to have many adventures from her own home, and her love affair with reading has never ended. She loves to write about heroes and heroines who are adventurous, passionate about a cause, and looking for the best in themselves and others. Julie's website is juliedanvers.wordpress.com.

Also by Susan Carlisle

Pacific Paradise, Second Chance
The Single Dad's Holiday Wish
Reunited with Her Daredevil Doc
Taming the Hot-Shot Doc

Also by Julie Danvers

From Hawaii to Forever
Falling Again in El Salvador

Discover more at millsandboon.co.uk.

FROM FLORIDA FLING TO FOREVER

SUSAN CARLISLE

SECRET FROM THEIR LA NIGHT

JULIE DANVERS

MILLS & BOON

First Published in Great Britain 2021
by Mills & Boon, an imprint of HarperCollins*Publishers* Ltd,
1 London Bridge Street, London, SE1 9GF

www.harpercollins.co.uk

HarperCollins*Publishers*
1st Floor, Watermarque Building,
Ringsend Road, Dublin 4, Ireland

ISBN: 978-0-263-29786-7

12/21

MIX
Paper from
responsible sources
FSC™ C007454

This book is produced from independently certified FSC™ paper
to ensure responsible forest management.
For more information visit www.harpercollins.co.uk/green.

Printed and Bound in Spain using 100% Renewable Electricity
at CPI Black Print, Barcelona

FROM FLORIDA FLING TO FOREVER

SUSAN CARLISLE

MILLS & BOON

To Michelle.

You were always the nurse angel we needed.

CHAPTER ONE

"You want to place the Skintec so that it just covers the incision joint but doesn't overlap the vessel more than necessary." Dr. Lily Evans demonstrated for those standing around the operating room table. She handed the tissue forceps back to her assistant and took the tiny brush filled with liquid. Using another set of tissue forceps, the fellow, the doctor who was finishing his advance training, who stood across from her folded back the corner of the patch. Lily applied the glue before the fellow laid the Skintec into place again. She continued around the square until it was secured.

The microphone of the OR observation room clicked on. A deep male voice filled the room. "If you also brush along the edges from the top, it'll give it a more firmly fixed seal."

Lily's breath caught. Her hand stilled. She knew that voice. It may have been fifteen months since she'd heard it, but she remembered the warm tone too clearly. Dr. Maxwell James. His voice had been the same one that had whispered in her ear as he kissed along her bare shoulder, up her neck, to find her lips.

She shuddered, heat washing through her. Max still had that effect on her after all this time. With heart beating faster, Lily raised her head to view the observation room with its large window. She swallowed hard. Max stood tall in a well-fitting dark suit with his white shirt open at the neck, in front of the two other people sitting there. With a hand stuffed in his left pocket, his body language screamed devil-may-care as he looked down at her.

His brilliant blue gaze met hers. She remembered it well. It appeared in her dreams often to haunt her. The man had intrigued her from the first moment she saw him years earlier at a medical conference. The problem was he had that effect on most women. Therefore, she'd always kept her distance. She wanted a special someone she could trust, that would be there for her for the long haul, a soulmate, not just a conference fling. Max was known as the playboy of the liver-transplant-surgeon conferences and that type of man didn't fit her life plan. Despite the one night she slipped up…

The corner of Max's mouth quirked upward.

Lily had hoped never to face him again. Mentally, she shook herself. Her patient waited. She had a transplant procedure to finish. Closing her mind to Max and that night when she'd lost control and humiliated herself beyond belief, she calmed her shaking hand and returned to her surgery. The transplant on this teenager would be completed to the best of her ability. Despite her desire to show her defiance and disregard Max's suggestion about the glue, she did as he said and brushed the edges. After all, he had developed the adhesive.

They may not have meshed in their personal lives, but their work had done so. She'd developed Skintec and he'd created Vseal, which together had revolutionized reattachment of vessels during a transplant. In honor of that, they were being recognized with Medical Invention of the Year Awards in the area of renal surgery. That must be why he was in town. But why so early? The ceremony was ten days away.

Lily wanted to groan. Ironically, her most significant professional achievement would forever be linked to the one man with whom she'd completely degraded herself. All because of her ex-boyfriend turned jerk, Jeff, who had picked that week to dump her. A coldness still flowed through her when she thought of that time. Now she just hoped Max didn't drag up what had happened between them and ruin her joy over her achievement.

She shook off those shameful memories and refocused on what she needed to do. "We should be able to reinfuse the liver now. Let's check for any bleeding and get this patient out to ICU." Lily removed a clamp.

The students standing around the table refocused their attention on her.

Lily watched the vessel-reconnection point carefully for bleeding. "With this new process, it has cut down on bleeding by 90 percent." Her intervention had done so by 50 percent, but paired with Max's, it had become even more effective.

She would put Dr. Max James out of her mind and get this patient closed. Maybe she'd see him only today and then not again until the awards ceremony. The least interaction she had with him the better.

An hour later, Lily spoke with the family of her patient, telling them the transplant had gone well and the liver was already working. "But," she reminded them, "the next forty-eight hours are critical. If Taylor does well during those, I fully expect him to live a long life."

The boy's mother wrapped Lily into a full hug. "Thank you, Dr. Evans."

This was what Lily found the most rewarding. Making a patient or their family happy. The feeling of knowing she made a difference in someone's life. "You're welcome."

A few minutes later, Lily headed toward her office. If she hurried, maybe she wouldn't have to see Max. Him just showing up had her nerves strung tight. She'd known he'd probably be coming to town at the end of the next week. By then, she would have been mentally prepared for him. Not now, not yet. There hadn't been any communication between them after their night together. Instead, he'd just appeared in her OR wearing a sexy grin.

By the time the awards ceremony came around, she'd have her act together. Be able to face him. Something she'd promised herself she'd never do again. She'd stopped going to conferences where she thought she might run into him. Instead, she'd sent a colleague or viewed the seminars online.

Her phone buzzed. Lily looked at her screen. It was Dr. Lee, head of transplant services at Miami University Hospital and Lily's boss. "Hello."

"Lily, can you come to my office for a few minutes?" Dr. Lee asked.

"I'm on my way to do rounds. Can it wait until after?" Lily had her fellows waiting, as well as patients.

"It won't take but a moment." The statement sounded casual, but Dr. Lee's firm note implied Lily didn't have a choice.

Minutes later, she entered Dr. Lee's office. A thin, tall woman with salt-and-pepper hair sat behind the desk. Max lounged in a chair across from her. As Lily stepped farther into the room, Max came to his feet and faced her. She clutched her hands in front of her until they hurt.

He still caused her heart to pick up its pace, the traitorous organ.

Max stood close enough for her to really study him. He hadn't changed much since she last saw him. His dark wavy hair had a little more silver at the temples. It didn't make him look older, just more distinguished. What hadn't altered were those deep blue eyes that twinkled with mischief as if he saw humor in everything. The laugh lines might be a little deeper, but they only added to his charisma. She shuddered to think he saw her as ridiculous after what had happened between them. She'd been pitiful on so many levels. The shame almost swamped her.

He grinned.

That crooked smile on his full lips shot a stream of warmth through her, despite her best effort to resist it. Lily clinched her jaw, determined she wouldn't let on what seeing him again did to her. Thank goodness he'd be in town for only a short time. As soon as the ceremony was over he'd be on his way again.

Lily drew in a deep breath, straightening her shoulders. She could handle this. Him. Max had stepped into her world. A place she felt comfortable. One she controlled. In it, she could cope with him.

"I believe you know Dr. James," Dr. Lee said. "He's going to be in town until after the awards ceremony. He has asked if he might join the liver transplant team this week. See how we do things. I told him you'd show him around."

Lily's lips tightened. Dr. Lee wasn't asking her but telling her she'd be responsible for Max. Lily forced a smile and put more cheer in her voice than she felt. "I'll be glad to."

"Thank you, Lily." Dr. Lee's phone rang, and she picked it up. "Dr. James, I'll leave you in Dr. Evans's capable hands."

Max nodded at Dr. Lee and grinned at Lily. "Thank you. I look forward to that."

Lily's mouth thinned in aggravation at Dr. Lee's unintentional statement, which Max had turned into a sexual innuendo. There would *not* be anything personal between them again.

Max followed her out the door. In the hallway, she turned to face him. "I'll see you tomorrow. You can find me in the clinic seeing patients." She pointed to the left.

"Aren't you on the way to do rounds now?" Max moved up beside her.

"Yes. And I'm late." She turned away from him, being as dismissive as possible.

He matched her steps as she walked away. "Then, I'll just tag along with you, if that's okay?"

She looked back at Dr. Lee's door. Why must Max be so insistent? He'd made it clear to her at the conference he didn't really care for her company. So why the interest now? "Sure."

Max kept pace beside Lily down the wide, glossy hallway. She acted as if she wanted to get rid of him. He hadn't expected her to jump into his arms when they met again, but he'd at least thought he'd get a friendly reception. Ice-cold would be more like what he was receiving. But why? "It's nice to see you again, Lily."

She jerked to a halt and glared at him. If she used that look on her fellows, he had no doubt they toed the line. "Look, I'm sorry about that night. I made a fool of myself. What went on between us shouldn't have happened." Her gaze dropped to the floor. "I was upset and drank too much." She shook her head. "I never drink too much. That wasn't like me, and I shouldn't have come on to you. I never do that. It was unprofessional. Can we just forget it and move on?"

He stepped back and put up his hands, palms toward her. "Hey, hey. I didn't mean to bring on a tirade. I was just making polite conversation. Saying hi."

A stricken expression came over Lily's face, making him want to give her a big reassuring hug. Was that night they'd spent—almost spent—together really still that raw for her? He gave her a coaxing smile. "Let's start over. Can we do that?"

Lily looked at him with her glossy green eyes.

Seeing him again had really upset her. That hurt. More than it should have. Their time with each other hadn't ended as he would've liked but he had no wish for her to react with tears to seeing him. When she didn't say anything he dared, "You did good work in the OR today."

"Thanks," she muttered and continued down the hall.

He joined her. "I'm sorry if I stepped on your toes by suggesting how my glue should be used."

"No worries. I want what's best for my patients." She pushed the door to the stairwell open and started to climb.

Finally, her voice had evened out once more. He wanted to keep it that way. "I couldn't agree with you more. By the way, congratulations on your medical invention award."

Her shoulders relaxed. "You too."

If he kept their discussions on medicine, Lily acted as if she could handle it. When the talk became personal, she started becoming undone. Was she really that sensitive?

As they climbed the stairs, Max took a second to appreciate the woman in front of him. Ever since he saw her at a conference five years earlier, he'd been attracted to her. There hadn't been a chance to really get to know her until their last conference together, and it hadn't gone as he had hoped. Apparently, she didn't have the best of memories about it either.

He'd never thought he had a chance with the soft-spoken, so serious-looking Lily, until she came on to him that last evening of the conference. Unfortunately, that ended with her passing out in her hotel room and him receiving an emergency call and having to leave. Since then, she'd not been at another conference he had attended. Then, of all things, he'd learned they were both receiving an award for a medical invention. When his father had asked him to approach Lily about allowing The James Company to package their products together, Max had viewed it as an opportunity to get to know Lily better.

"Kind of ironic that we're both getting the same recognition in the same year."

She glanced back at him as she made a turn to take another flight of stairs. "That's not what I'd call it."

Before Max could question her further, Lily opened the floor door and stepped through it. Ahead of them were three people wearing white lab coats, standing in a group in the hallway. They all faced her and smiled. Had his fellows ever smiled when he joined them?

Lily waved a hand toward him dismissively and started for the nearest patient door. "Hey, everyone. This is Dr. Max James. He'll be joining us today,"

Max didn't miss the look of surprise on the faces of the two men and one woman when his name was mentioned.

"Sara, how's Mr. Truman doing today?" Lily asked in an all-business tone.

"Recovering. His output is normal. His numbers on his blood work are within the normal range, and he's able to walk the hall unassisted."

Lily nodded as she looked at her computer pad. She knocked on the door and paused. At "come in," she entered. "Hello, Mr. Truman. I heard you're our star patient."

The older man grinned from the chair he sat in.

"Dr. Locke, would you like to tell Mr. Truman the good news?" Lily looked at the fellow she'd called Sara.

The doctor nodded and said to the patient, "You'll be going home tomorrow morning."

The man smiled. "Thank you. My wife will be glad to hear that."

Lily placed her hand on his shoulder. "I'll see you in my office in six weeks. No dancing until then."

Mr. Truman grinned. "I'll save that until the wedding. My daughter won't thank you for her sore toes."

Lily laughed. Max liked the sweet melody of the sound.

"I can't help with that." Lily said. "I'm a surgeon, not a dance instructor. And for that, you should be grateful. I'm an awful dancer. Dr. Locke will get you discharged. See you soon."

Their group moved out into the hall. They strolled to the next room, which was located down a few doors. Lily led them through the same process, except this time a different fellow was responsible for the patient. They all stood around the bed as Lily examined her.

"You should be getting out of here in a few more days. You're doing very well," Lily reassured her.

At the next stop, Lily's expression changed to one of

concern. She looked to the fellow who hadn't had a patient yet. "How's Mr. Roth doing today?"

The fellow glanced down at his notes, but Max had the impression he knew exactly how the man was doing, without looking at them. The fellow shifted through his papers. "He's still running a low-grade fever, with no presenting reason to be doing so. He's had a CT scan, X-ray and a battery of blood work."

Lily looked at each fellow. "Any ideas about what should be done?"

"I think a MRI should be ordered," one fellow suggested.

Lily nodded and waited.

"I'd consider a biopsy," another fellow offered.

"I agree," the last one said.

"All good suggestions, but first, I'd like to examine Mr. Roth before we decide." Lily pulled her stethoscope out of her pocket.

Minutes later, Max along with the fellows were all standing beside Mr. Roth's bedside, watching Lily.

She listened to Mr. Roth's heart rate and respirations. Lily straightened and stepped back from the bed, then studied his chart. "I see you're still running a fever. Do you ache anywhere?"

"Nope." The man shook his head.

"Mr. Roth, I'm Dr. James. I'm working with Dr. Evans. Do you mind if I have a look at your incision site?" Max asked.

Lily's look met his. She hesitated a moment before she spoke to Mr. Roth. "Dr. James is visiting us from New York. He's a liver transplant surgeon, as well. Would it be okay for him to examine you?"

"I don't care who looks at me. I just want to feel better," the middle-aged man ground out.

Lily patted Mr. Roth on the arm. "We'll figure this out."

Max stepped closer. Mr. Roth pulled up his hospital gown so that his middle showed, with its large, V-shape incision. There were no obvious, outward indications of infection, such as redness or swelling. "I'm going to look at your incision site. And touch around it. Let me know if you feel any pain." Max pulled the hospital gown up farther. The incision site looked like it had healed well. He gently pushed on the skin around the scar. He could clearly feel the edge of the liver. All seemed as it should.

"Mr. Roth, would you mind rolling to your right?" The man did so, and Max applied pressure to the lower back but got no reaction from the man. "Now to the left." The man rolled and Max repeated his examination. "Thank you, Mr. Roth. You can rest back again."

Lily spoke to her patient. "We'll see that you get to feeling better soon. Try to rest."

One of the fellows pulled the door closed behind them as the group returned to the hall.

"May I see the blood work?" Max asked the fellow. "How far out from transplant is the patient?"

"Eight weeks," Lily answered.

The fellow handed him the computer pad. "Looking at his white blood count, there's no reason to believe he has an infection. I'd suggest lowering the antirejection meds and changing the IV antibiotic to a stronger one. Get a CBC again in twelve hours. I've had success doing that with cases like this."

The group looked at him. He returned the pad.

Lily paused for a moment, then nodded. "Sounds like

a sound plan. We can reevaluate over the next two days. Before we consider something more invasive." To the fellow responsible for Mr. Roth, she said, "See it's done right away."

Max watched Lily. "I think you'll notice a difference quickly."

She nodded. "I hope so."

Over the next half hour, Max stayed with the group as they finished their rounds. Max couldn't help but be impressed with how quickly the transplant patients were recovering. Lily ran a good program. Maybe it stemmed from the positive rapport she had with her patients and the staff. Hers made him want to improve on his.

Finished seeing the last patient, the fellows left him and Lily.

She faced him. "Thank you for your help back there with Mr. Roth. We were running out of ideas."

"I hope mine works." Max couldn't deny he liked having Lily's praise, despite it being unexpected.

For once, she met his look with a direct one of her own. "Do you really plan to spend all your time in Miami in a hospital?"

"Not all the time, but I wanted to see how your program works. See if there's something I can take home to mine in New York City."

She started down the hall toward the stairwell door. "I'm sure following me around must be dull. Wouldn't you rather go to the beach?"

Max liked she'd become comfortable enough with him to ask a personal question. He grinned. "Is that an invitation?"

Lily stopped and gave him a piercing no-nonsense look. "No."

"Come on. I think we could find some time to spend on the beach." Max gave her a teasing smile.

She opened her mouth to speak, but he raised a hand. "I know. You have clinic tomorrow."

"Yeah, and it's held in the building next door. Just ask the receptionist at the front desk and she can tell you where to find me."

"I'll see you then." Max lifted a hand and walked to the bank of elevators.

The next morning, Lily entered the building to find Max leaning casually against the front desk, talking to the woman behind it. She looked pleased to have such a handsome man's attention. Lily even heard a giggle. Max hadn't changed.

Even before they had gotten together that dreadful night, Lily had heard the talk about Max being a big flirt with little substance. Lily was looking for someone who would be her partner through life, not someone looking for nothing but a good time. She'd watched him from afar at conferences for years. No different than most women, she'd been drawn to him like the proverbial moth to the flame. Max just had something about him that interested her. With his easygoing personality, he had a way with people, especially women. She fallen for his charm, despite knowing better. Weak, she'd just been weak.

"Good morning," he drawled and handed her a cup. "It's tea. I didn't figure you for the coffee type."

Max had already placed her in a *type* pool? She wasn't sure how she felt about that. Taking the paper cup with the cap on it, she said, "Thanks."

He shrugged. "No problem. So, is there any special case you're seeing today?"

"Most are post-op patients." Lily headed down the hallway toward the wing of the building where she saw them. "But I do have one that's coming in that might interest you."

"Good morning, Dr. Evans," the nurse standing in the hall said. "Your first patient is waiting in room one."

"Thanks, Carol." Leaving the tea on a corner of a counter, Lily took the electronic tablet from the nurse.

Disappointed to leave his hot coffee behind, Max did the same and hurried after Lily.

Going to the closest door, she knocked and entered. "Hello, Mrs. Sandoz. How're you feeling?"

The middle-aged woman, her black hair liberally streaked with white, smiled. "I feel much better than I did before the transplant."

"Thank you so much, Dr. Evans. It's so nice to have my wife back," Mr. Sandoz said.

"I'm glad to hear it. Mr. and Mrs. Sandoz, this is Dr. James. He's visiting with us this week."

Max gave Mrs. Sandoz one of his charming smiles. The woman's eyes warmed, and she returned it. Was there no end to Max's appeal to women?

Lily scrolled through Mrs. Sandoz's chart on the pad, then took the chair next to her. "May I give you a listen? Your X-rays look great." Lily pulled her stethoscope out of the pocket of her white lab coat.

Max took the pad from her and brushed the screen, looking at Mrs. Sandoz's chart as Lily listened to the woman's heartbeats and respirations.

Lily stood. "Now, if you'll lie down on the exam table, I'd like to look at your incision site."

Mrs. Sandoz went to the table.

Max stepped up and offered his hand to the older woman. “Here, take my hand and I’ll help you lie back.”

“Thank you.” The woman placed her hand in his and the other on his forearm, steadying herself as she stepped up and sat on the table.

Lily couldn’t help but soften toward Max for his consideration for the older woman.

Placing a hand at her back, he gently supported Mrs. Sandoz as she eased back. “I’ve seen enough of my patients struggle to lower themselves after surgery to know it isn’t always comfortable.”

Mrs. Sandoz settled on the table. She pulled her full blouse up beneath her breast, revealing the large pink incision that went from one side of her body to the other.

Lily studied the area. “It all looks good. You’re healing well.”

“It still feels tight when I move.” She brushed her hand over the area.

“It’ll take a while for things to get back to normal. But overall, you’re doing great. You can start driving again. I’d like to see you back here in three months. Don’t forget to have your lab work done.”

Mrs. Sandoz pulled her shirt down. Lily helped the woman sit up.

“Thank you, Dr. Evans,” Mrs. Sandoz said with a large grin.

“You’re welcome. See you soon.” Lily smiled over her shoulder as she opened the door.

Max followed Lily out into the hall. “She looks great. I read in the surgery notes you used my glue on her.”

Lily rolled her eyes. He would pick that out of the record. “Yes, Vseal does work.”

He grinned. "It's always nice to hear admiration from such an esteemed surgeon."

Lily huffed and walked to the next examination room.

CHAPTER TWO

MAX COULDN'T DENY the more he was around Lily, the more impressed he was with her and her transplant program. Spending the morning shadowing her only confirmed what he'd heard and read. She was a consummate, caring professional. That being the case, maybe she would agree to his proposal. If they were to package Vseal and Skintec together, they could make a lot of money and help his father's company in the process. This was Max's chance to impress his father for once. He'd been a disappointment for so long, but if he could pull this deal together with Lily, maybe his father's view would change. Alone, his and Lily's products were good, but together, they were outstanding. The James Company could move up the ranks of medical manufacturing if he could work this out with Lily. Would she consider his suggestion?

Even after spending some time in the last twenty-four hours together, Lily remained cool toward him. Why, he couldn't figure out. Nothing had happened that night. He didn't take advantage of drunk women. When he'd seen her sitting alone at the table by the pool, drinking, his protective side had won out. He had to admit he'd been tempted to stay after she invited him to her room, but one of the many things his father had insisted Max be was a gentleman. And only in one area had he gone against his father's wishes, and being a gentleman hadn't been it.

"So, what now?" he asked as they walked back to the clinic's nurses' desk. "Lunch, I hope. I'll buy."

"You don't need to do that. I have to go over to the hospital and check on a patient." Lily handed the charting pad to the nurse and smiled.

Max wished she'd offer him one of those smiles, at least once. They were going to have to get what had happened between them—or hadn't—aired out. "How about lunch, then I'll go with you to see Mr. Roth?"

She studied him for a long moment then sighed. "Okay."

Max smiled at the nurse. "It was nice to meet you." He turned back to Lily. "Have you seen Mr. Roth's morning lab tests yet?"

Lily started down the hall toward the front of the building. "I have. They look better. But I'd like to see him myself."

"After lunch. I'm starving."

"I usually eat in my office or skip it." She sounded as if he'd invited her to a funeral.

"I don't like to eat by myself. Join me. I don't even know where the cafeteria is. And you're supposed to be taking care of me." He grinned at her like a cartoon character.

She huffed and walked ahead of him. They continued through the building, took the outside door and started across a garden area with a softly bubbling fountain, a brick walk and palm foliage all around.

"It feels so good here." Max looked up at the sky. "I could get used to all this warmth and sunshine."

Lily chuckled. "You think that, until it's blistering hot in the middle of the summer."

"I'd like to try it at least once." While they had a few moments together, he intended to straighten things out between them. If he didn't, he'd never get her to agree to a partnership. There was too much at stake for them not to at least trust each other. "I haven't seen you at a conference in the last few months."

"I watched them online. I've been too busy to get away." There was a hard, sad note in her voice.

"I've looked for you."

She glanced at him but didn't slow her pace. "Why? So you could humiliate me again?"

He touched her elbow. "Why would you say that?"

Lily gave him a pointed look and stepped away from his touch.

That hurt for some odd reason. "I think we need to talk. Come over here." He pointed in the direction of a bench secluded in the greenery, where they wouldn't be overheard or disturbed. "Please."

"I thought you were hungry." She looked toward the door as if she were a mouse preparing to escape a trap.

"I think it can wait five minutes. The way you've been gigging me, my guess is you'll never have time. I'm going to be here for a week, and I don't want a misunderstanding standing between us the entire time. Please."

Lily shielded her face from the sun with a hand as she watched him. "I don't have time to talk about this right now." She shook her head. "Anyway, I just want to forget it."

He met her gaze. "My feelings would be hurt if you did forget. I haven't."

Lily's lips pursed as she gave him an exasperated look.

"There's nothing to talk about. I understand completely. I was the one who woke up alone. I was your conference good time!"

A nurse exited the hospital and gave them a curious look. Max stepped toward the quiet spot, and Lily followed. "Listen, nothing happened between us other than I took a tipsy woman to her room and put her to bed. Call me decimating, but I don't have sex with women who won't remember it."

Her eyes widened. "What? We didn't…?"

Max shook his head. "No, we didn't. Not that I wouldn't have enjoyed it, but like I said, the time wasn't right."

"But I remember you undressing me. Kissing me," she said so softly that he had to lean close to hear.

He kept his voice low. "I did. Then, the next thing I knew, you were curled up in the middle of the bed asleep." He grinned. "Snoring, I believe."

She gasped, turning her back to him. "I didn't!"

"Yep. You did." He felt sorry for her in her embarrassment. "I think you already had had a few when I came to sit with you by the pool, then you insisted you wanted another."

Lily hung her head. "I had. And I don't usually drink. I hate being out of control."

"That doesn't surprise me."

She glared at him. "What do you mean?"

"Just that you're a woman who likes to keep a tight hold on her world and emotions." He met her look.

She returned it without blinking. "You don't know me well enough to make those assumptions."

Max shrugged. "Maybe not. But that's not what we were discussing. That night after you passed out, I put you to bed. I didn't think you'd appreciate me going through your things to find whatever you sleep in. I'd have been there when you woke, but I had to leave. I was called in for emergency surgery. But you were already down for the count."

Lily put her head in her hands and groaned. "And to think I was humiliated before."

Max chuckled. "Hey, you shouldn't feel that way. I was flattered. I knew enough about you to know you aren't promiscuous. So, are we good now?"

Lily shrugged. "I guess. Please forgive me for being so, uh, unwelcoming to you."

"I understand. Don't worry about it." He smiled. "In that case, could we maybe start again? After all, you're the only person I know in Miami."

"I guess so." Meeting his look, she said, "I promise nothing like that'll ever happen again."

For some reason, that disappointed him. Especially since he'd thought more than once of the shapely curves and silky skin he'd seen and touched briefly that night in the hotel. Lily had interested him. She still did. "Come on. Let's have lunch and then see Mr. Roth."

Lily nodded.

He stepped ahead of her and opened the side door leading into the hospital. They went to the nearest elevator. After entering, Max watched Lily as the door closed. Her scent wrapped around him in the closed space. She smelled of sunshine, tropical flowers and a fresh rain. The women he usually dated wore the latest popular, expensive cologne. None smelled as lovely as Lily. In fact in most ways, they were nothing like Lily. Why, then, did he find her so appealing?

"You know your glue is really brilliant." Lily spoke as if trying to fill the silence between them.

"Thank you. Have you had offers to sell Skintec?"

"You know I have. Just like I'm sure you have had offers for Vseal."

Max grinned. "A few." The door opened and they stepped off the elevator. "I want to talk to you about that…"

Lily's phone buzzed and she answered it. "Hey there."

Max looked at Lily. Her entire demeanor had changed. Her voice took on a sweet note as if she were speaking to a child. "Yes, I'll be on time."

Did Lily have a significant other? In almost two years, a lot could change.

"Yes, yes we'll have tater tots and chicken strips. I know they're your favorite." She turned her back to him.

Was she talking to her child?

"I have to go now. See you soon." Lily pocketed her phone and turned to him. "The cafeteria is down this way."

"I had no idea you had a child." Too curious not to find out.

"It was my sister."

Lily looked up to see Max take a huge bite out of the hamburger he'd ordered from the cafeteria grill. "You were hungry."

"Yeah. I had to leave the hotel before they had breakfast laid out in order to meet you on time." He continued eating.

"Where're you staying?" She watched, fascinated by the movement of his throat.

"In South Beach."

"Oh, I love those retro hotels. Which one?" She couldn't help her interest.

Using a napkin, he wiped a dot of ketchup off his chin. "Hotel Blue Sea."

"I know the one. It has the neon-blue waves along the side. Right across the street from the beach." She would love to explore the lodging.

"That's the one." He gave her a long look.

"Nice place." She'd never been inside, but she wouldn't be saying that to Max. That would be far too suggestive. She needed to change the subject. It seemed she had to do that often around him. "Are you still at New York Central Hospital?"

"I am." Maxwell picked up his cup and pulled his drink through the straw.

"You've a big program there." She pushed the lettuce of her salad around.

Max set the cup down on the table. "We do, but there still isn't as much work as I'd like."

"Our program here is almost overwhelmed. There aren't enough doctors to handle the need."

Max nodded. "That's what I've heard."

Who'd he heard that from? Had he been checking up on her? The program? Why?

He lifted his chin toward her uneaten salad. "Are you saving room for tater tots and chicken strips tonight? Interesting menu."

"It's what Ivy likes." Lily poked at a lettuce leaf again.

"Ivy? That's your sister's name?" Humor circled his words.

"Something funny?" She dared him to laugh.

"No. Just interesting. Ivy and Lily. It sounds like a garden."

Lily watched as he tried to cover his smile with the hamburger. She glared at him. “It isn’t polite to make fun of people’s names.”

He looked around innocently. “I’ve not said a word about anyone’s names.”

Lily leaned forward as she continued to glare. “No, but I know what you’re thinking.”

He finished his bite. “What? That your names make me think of springtime.”

“They’re awful.” She sat back, a grin on her lips. “Not so bad apart, but when said together, they’re pretty bad.”

“I wouldn’t say *bad*, just ear catching.” He returned her smile.

She smirked. “Thanks, that’s a nice way of putting it.”

“I guess Ivy lives nearby, since you were talking about dinner together tonight.” Max returned to his hamburger.

She didn’t talk about Ivy much, especially to strangers. Wasn’t that what Max was? “Yes.”

“Do you have other siblings?” He took another bite of his burger.

“No. Only Ivy.” She watched him chew and swallow. Why did Max fascinate her so?

“I’m guessing you two are close.”

She shifted in her chair aware of him watching her. “Very. I’m Ivy’s guardian.”

“Guardian?” Surprise rang clear in his voice.

She met his look with a direct one. “My sister is mentally challenged. Has been since birth. She has been my responsibility since my parents died in a car accident five years ago.”

He placed what was left of his burger on the plate and wiped his mouth. “I’m sorry to hear that. About your parents. That’s tough.”

Lily appreciated his sentiment, but she didn't need his pity. "It has been, but Ivy and I have adjusted."

The expression in his eyes had turned from teasing to kind. "I'm sure it hasn't been easy."

"Nothing's easy all the time. We just keep moving forward." How many times had she told herself that? Hadn't she said that when Jeff dropped her just before they were supposed to spend the week together at the fated conference? Again, after Max had left her in bed alone. After her parents died. Yeah, she'd just kept moving.

"I guess you do." Max returned to his sandwich.

"Do you have brothers and sisters?" She wasn't sure why she wanted to know more about him, but she did.

"One of both. Jessie, my sister and her family live in Atlanta. Rob and his family live in Chicago where I grew up." There was fond note in his voice as he used their names.

"Are you close?"

He nodded, a softer look coming over his face. "Yeah. We enjoy being together. I wish it was more often."

"And your parents?" She really wanted to know more about the people important to him.

"Still alive and kicking. Mom's involved in every charity in town." He made it sound more indulgent than critical.

Something about the fact he said nothing further concerning his father felt odd, especially compared to the warmth in his voice regarding his mother.

"Are you finished?" Max abruptly dropped his napkin on the tray. "I want to see Mr. Roth, then I have to go to the hotel and return some phone calls this afternoon."

"Yeah, sure." She stood and picked up her tray, heading toward the disposal area. Did his sudden urge to leave have anything to do with not wanting her to question him about his father?

With their trays put away, they walked out into the hall.

"Hey," Max said, "I like where I'm staying, but I really don't want to sit around the hotel the entire weekend. Since I'm from out of town and this is your regular stomping grounds, how about showing me around? I'd love to see some of the city."

"I can't." She shook her head. If she could, would she agree? She and Max might have moved beyond what had happened that night at the conference, but she hadn't forgotten it.

"Or won't?"

Why was he pushing her? "I promised to take my sister to the beach."

His face brightened. "My hotel has a dedicated area on the beach. Why don't you bring her there?"

Lily looked at him, her eyes wide with surprise. "Are you serious?"

He returned a frank gaze as if he thought his invitation wasn't the least out of the norm. "Sure, why not?"

Max's look of anticipation made her say against her better judgement, "I, uh… I guess we could do that."

Max wouldn't have been shocked if Lily had texted him the next morning to say she wouldn't be coming. Yet it was time for her to arrive and he hadn't heard from her. Remaining optimistic, an hour ago, he'd reserved two cabanas. He looked toward the street again, hoping to catch sight of Lily.

Two women holding hands crossed the road. There Lily was. He walked through the soft white sand to meet her. A large-brimmed hat sat on her head, and dark glasses covered her eyes, but he recognized her walk. She wore a flowing cover-up with a pointed hem, which floated around her ankles. A small cooler was in the hand not clasping her sister's.

Ivy looked very much like Lily. The hair color, the shape of her face. Were Ivy's eyes the same? They were covered by sunglasses, as well. Despite their similarities, their demeanors were different. There was something childlike in Ivy's actions.

"Hey. I was wondering if you were going to make it." Max pulled off his glasses and smiled briefly at Lily and longer at Ivy.

"It, uh… It, uh, took us a few minutes to find a parking place," Lily seemed to struggle to say.

Even with the glasses covering her eyes, Max had the distinct impression her focus remained on his bare chest. "I didn't think to make arrangements for your parking. Sorry. I will next time. Let me take that cooler for you."

Lily released it but not before their hands brushed. She quickly pulled hers away. "No problem. Max, I'd like you to meet my sister, Ivy. Ivy, say hello."

Ivy looked at the sand she kicked with the toe of her shoe. She said a shy "hello."

"Hi, Ivy. I'm glad you came today. Would you like me to take that bag for you?"

"No. It is mine." She pulled it tighter to her.

"Okay." Apparently, he'd have two Evans women to win over today. Why it mattered so much, he wasn't sure. "I have us some cabanas right down here." He started back toward the bright yellow umbrellas with blue waves that matched the one on the wall of the hotel. Double lounges sat beneath them. He pointed to theirs. “You may have whichever you want.”

“I like this one,” Ivy stated and plopped the bag down on the cushion, then looked around. “I don’t know this beach.”

“I told you we were going to try a new one.” Lily pulled a towel out of a bag that had been over her shoulder and spread it on the lounge next to Ivy’s.

“Where are we?” Ivy asked, looking panicked.

Lily placed her hand on Ivy’s arm, gaining her attention. “We’re in front of Max’s hotel. He wanted us to come to the beach with him today.”

“Oh, this is Max’s beach.” Ivy peered around again in awe.

Max chuckled. “Something like that.”

“I’m not used to such luxury at the beach.” Lily settled on the lounge next to Ivy’s and looked around.

Max dipped his head under the umbrella and sat on the lounger next to hers. “For somebody from New York City, I thought it best my skin wasn’t out exposed all the time, even wearing sunscreen.”

Lily laughed. “You’re probably right. The sun is strong here year-round.”

A ripple of heat ran through him that had nothing to do with the sun. “You need to do that more often.”

“What?” Lily faced him.

“Laugh. It’s a nice sound.” Max watched as a pink tint traveled up her neck to her face.

“I want to go to the water,” Ivy announced.

“Okay, but first you have to make sure you have on plenty of lotion. You don’t want to burn.” Lily sounded like a mother hen talking to her chick.

“I know. I can do it.” Ivy dug into her bag.

"I was working on the same thing when you got here." Max picked up his bottle of sunscreen. "I still need some on my back. Lily, would you mind?" He offered her the bottle.

Lily looked at it as if it were a snake. Her mouth formed a circle. He could almost see the wheels turning in her mind. She slowly took the tube from him.

He presented her with his back. Lily took so long to start the job he glanced over his shoulder to see if she was still there. Her hand hovered over his right shoulder. He turned around and waited. Finally, there was a faint brush of something cool against his back. Her fingertips shook for a moment then became bolder as she smoothed the lotion around. His chest tightened while his breathing quickened. As she worked her way over his skin, his muscles rippled beneath. He experienced every movement in slow-motion detail.

Lily's fingers wrapped his shoulder, then moved to the center of his back. Her hand left him. He held his breath until it returned. This time she rubbed one way, then the other—with purpose, as if she were trying to get the job done as soon as possible.

Too soon and not soon enough for his body's relief, she said with a shake in her voice, "Done."

Max needed to put some distance between them. If he'd had any idea he'd react like a teenager to a girl's first touch when Lily stroked her fingers over him, he'd have figured out some other way to get lotion on, or done without.

"I'm ready," Ivy announced.

Lily cleared her throat. "Go on, but wait on me before you get in the water."

"Hurry," Ivy threw over her shoulder as she headed toward the water.

Max found the interaction between the sisters interesting. Lily's mothering instinct was clearly in overdrive with Ivy. He didn't have much experience with adults with learning disabilities, so he couldn't question Lily's protective attitude. "I'll go down and join her."

A look of relief washed over Lily's face as she picked up the lotion again. "I'll be there as soon as I finish putting this on."

Max almost offered to help her but thought better of it. He feared that once he started touching Lily, he wouldn't stop. Instead, he worked his way out from under the umbrella. "Is it okay if we go ahead and get in the water? Can Ivy swim?"

"Yes. And yes."

He started walking away.

"Thanks, Max."

Lily watched Max and Ivy as they splashed water at each other. His large shoulders glistened in the sunlight. The muscles of his back tensed and relaxed as he played and laughed with Ivy. He really was a gorgeous man. He didn't have the body of a thin young man but had one of maturity that made her think of steadfastness, security. One that could shelter.

For a few minutes earlier, she'd forgotten herself and enjoyed rubbing lotion on Max. Her attraction to him had taken over and led her down a trail of desire she'd not intended to travel. She couldn't let that happen again. He was here for only seven more days, and then he'd be gone again. Being left behind once more wasn't something she wanted any part of. She needed to find the man who she was enough for that he would stay around. Max wasn't that type. They would be friends and nothing more.

What would it hurt for her to enjoy watching him while she could?

"Let's splash Lily," Ivy yelled.

She and Max turned to Lily, who had been peacefully bobbing with the waves. "You better not gang up on me. I don't get mad. I get even."

"We're going to get you," Ivy said.

The words were hardly out of Ivy's mouth when Lily was hit in the face with a shower of water. Lily wiped it away from her eyes to see Ivy and Max grinning at her. "Now you've done it."

Over the next few minutes, they had a water fight, laughing and having a good time. Max acted as if he was in his element. Jeff had cared nothing about Ivy. In fact, the less interaction he'd had with her, the better he'd liked it. Ivy had been a bone of contention between them from the beginning. Jeff had accused Lily of thinking of Ivy more than she did him. Lily had tried to overlook his attitude in the hopes it would improve with time. Now she could see it for what it was—immature jealousy. He'd never shown Ivy the interest that Max had in just these last few minutes.

Max moved closer to her. "Ivy, I think Lily has had enough."

Lily agreed. She hadn't been on the prevailing end of the splash fest, but Ivy had enjoyed it.

Max pushed water at Ivy as he turned his head to protect his face from the water coming at him. "It's been too long since I've done this. I'd forgotten how much fun it can be."

Lily smirked. "It depends on who's on the winning side."

"My brother and sister used to always be against me." Max gave her a self-satisfied smile. "But I still always won."

"Why am I not surprised? I don't imagine you lose often." Lily pushed her wet hair out of her face.

He grinned. "Not if I can't help it."

"Did your family live near the lake?" For some reason, she was curious about Max's past. Even when she shouldn't be.

"No, but my mother made sure we went to the beach for a week every year." He looked off toward the horizon.

Was there a sadness there? "Your father didn't go?"

"He didn't have time. Too busy building the business." A bitterness surrounded the words.

"What does your daddy do?"

"He's the head of The James Company." Max continued to look into the distance.

Lily's eyes widened. "I know that name. That's one of the largest medical supply companies in the world. They want me to sign a contract with them."

"Yeah."

"I hadn't put your name and the company together." Lily couldn't get over Max being the son of one of the most well-to-do men in that industry.

Max moved toward Ivy. "Hey, Ivy, do you want to see if we can see some fish?"

Max had certainly put an end to that conversation. The James Company was a huge outfit. They manufactured all types of equipment. She'd read the name on her surgical instruments, even had a contact number for them.

They stayed in the water for a while longer before Max said, "I don't know about you ladies, but I could use something to eat."

"We brought some snacks." Lily started toward the shore.

Max joined her. "I need something more substantial after that water battle, don't you, Ivy? How about pizza?"

Lily couldn't help but admire his gorgeous physique of broad shoulders, thick muscles, sleek skin that tapered to trim hips as Max moved ahead of her through the waist-deep water.

"I love pizza," Ivy squealed.

Max grinned over his shoulder, a grin that came close to taking Lily's breath away. "I thought you might. I was told a pizza truck parks only a couple of blocks away. I was going to walk down there and get us a pie."

"Can I go with you?" Ivy asked.

Max stepped out of the water. "Sure you can. We'll let Lily stay here and lie in the sun, and we'll deliver."

"Max—" Lily moved toward him.

His eyes narrowed as he gave her a meaningful look before his voice turned soft. "I've got this."

Lily pushed her nervous concern down. "Ivy, you stay close to Max. Do as he says."

"I will." Ivy happily pranced off beside Max.

Lily stood there in wonder before she mentally shook herself and followed them out of the water.

They gathered around the lounges.

"You need your cover-up on, Ivy." Lily picked up a towel to dry off.

"I know," she said in a sharp tone.

"Will you hand me the T-shirt on that bag between the chairs?" Max asked Lily.

She picked the garment off the top of the carryall. As she handed it to him, the rich scent that was Max's fluttered beneath her nose. She stopped herself just short of bringing it up to her face and inhaling.

Ivy had her cover-up on. “Let’s go.”

“We shouldn’t be long.” Max leaned closer to Lily. “By the way, you look gorgeous in a swimsuit.”

Lily’s breath caught as heat shot through her. She watched as Max’s strong legs with thick thighs carried him through the sand while Ivy chatted happily beside him. What Lily intended not to let occur was happening. Her attraction to Max was growing.

Settling on the lounge, Lily closed her eyes, enjoying the warmth and a few moments when nothing was required of her. They were rare between work, Ivy and her research. Slowly, she drifted off to sleep with thoughts of rubbing her hands across Max’s shoulders.

She woke to Ivy lying on the lounger to her left and Max stretched out on the one to her right. His head rested on his hands, clasped behind his head.

“I wondered how long you’d sleep.”

Max’s low rumble rippled through her. She jerked her head around to look at him. “How did you know I was awake?”

“Um, a good guess?” Humor filled his voice.

“You’ve been watching me?” She raised her sunglasses to glare at him before letting them drop into place again.

“I don’t remember you being so sensitive.” He sat up, turning to face her, giving her a clear view of his chest. Grateful for her dark glasses, she took full advantage of the vista in front of her.

“You remember something about me?”

“I remember a lot about you. I’ve paid attention to you at conferences and followed your career for years.”

Lily wasn’t sure what to make of that. Somehow it made her sit straighter.

Some time passed before he said, “I like the name Lily. It’s soft and sweet-sounding like you.”

“My name might imply that, but I assure you I don’t fit your definition.”

Max chuckled. “I don’t think that’s true. I’ve seen you with your patients. With Ivy. The only person I know of who you don’t have a soft spot for is me.”

Little did he know. “We agreed there would be nothing between us.”

“If I remember correctly, it was you who said something like that.” He shifted on the lounge, resting his knee against her chair.

“I did.”

He shook his head. “But I made no such statement.”

“Max don’t start.”

“Okay, okay. We’ll keep it a happy family day.”

She glanced at Ivy, who softly snored beside her. “That’s what it should be.”

“You hungry? We left you some pizza. It’s not hot, but it shouldn’t be too bad. If you’d rather, I can order something from the hotel.”

Why must he be so considerate? It made it hard not to like him. “Pizza is fine.”

Max picked up a paper plate with a napkin over it. “Your drink is right here.” He pointed to a soft drink can in a cup holder beside him. “Ivy told me what you like.”

Lily grinned as she took the plate from him. “I bet she did. She likes to be the one who has the answers.”

“She’s a sweet girl.”

“She is.” Lily took a bite of her pizza.

“Does she live with you?”

Lily picked up her drink and took a swallow. “No.

She lives and works in a group home about thirty minutes from here."

"I figured you must have some help, otherwise it would be hard for you to work."

"Sometimes it still is, but I've managed." She replaced her drink, making sure she didn't touch Max's leg in the process.

He placed his elbows on his knees, leaning in closer. "You're a good sister, Lily."

Max watched Lily's body relax. She had appreciated his compliment. He could only imagine how difficult it had been to realize she would be responsible for her sister for the rest of her life. That had to have been life changing.

"I'm hot. I think I'll get back in the water," Ivy said.

Lily looked at Ivy. He silently watched them.

"Sure. I feel like a swim too." Lily stuffed her half-eaten pizza into an empty plastic bag she pulled out of her carrier. Without a backward look at him, she pulled off her cover-up. His chest tightened as her feminine curves came into full view. Her beautifully rounded breasts that he remembered from months ago still temped him.

Before Max knew what had happened, Lily and Ivy were leaving.

Ivy said, "Are you coming, Max?"

Lily took her hand. "Max may want to take a nap. We can swim without him."

Ivy looked perplexed as she glanced back over her shoulder while Lily tugged her away. Max took his time joining them. They were treading water and laughing as waves slapped against them.

"Hey, Max." Ivy waved.

"Hi, Ivy. You look like you're having fun."

"We are. Lily and I like the waves."

Max looked at Lily and grinned. With her hat pulled low and her sunglasses on, he couldn't read her reaction.

"Ivy, watch for the waves. You don't want one to knock you over." The words were hardly out of Lily's mouth when a wall of water struck her and carried her under.

Her body hit his. Max reached for her. His hands went to her waist as he struggled to remain standing. He pulled her back against him, but the sand shifted under his feet and they fell backward. Lily twisted to right herself before the next wave hit them, while he worked to stand. Her hands ran over his chest, finding his shoulders. His hands tightened on her waist and supported her as she stood.

Lily's hat drooped and her glasses sat askew as she stammered, "I'm sorry. I didn't mean to knock you down. The wave…"

His thumbs brushed over her waist. "Hey, I'm not complaining. I like it when a beautiful woman grabs me."

"I didn't—"

He grinned. "That's not how I remember it."

"Ivy!" Lily turned.

Max let his hands fall away. "She's fine. She fared better than you."

"That wave got you good." Ivy laughed. "Better than when Max and I splashed you."

Lily pushed away from him.

He was tempted to pull her back.

Lily moved toward Ivy. "Yeah, it did. We need to think about going."

"Do we have to?" Ivy whined.

"Yeah, it's getting late." Lily started toward the shore.

Max hated to see her leave. He'd had a good day,

something he couldn't recall happening in a long time. What would Lily say if he begged them to stay longer? Too soon they were walking toward the loungers.

Ivy had moved ahead of Lily and him. "I know that today was family day. Do you have plans with Ivy tomorrow night?"

"No, I'll take her home tomorrow afternoon."

He touched her arm. She stopped and turned to him. "Then, how about having dinner with me? I have something I'd like to discuss with you."

"We can't do that now?"

He looked at the crowd on the beach. "It's related to our innovations, and I'd prefer we aren't interrupted when we discuss what I have in mind. Why don't we have dinner here at the hotel restaurant, where it'll be less public?"

"I don't know..."

He grinned. "Come on, Lily. You can trust me. I thought I'd proved that."

She sighed. "All right."

"I'll pick you up at eight."

Lily started walking again. "No, I'll meet you in the lobby at eight."

CHAPTER THREE

LILY ADMIRED THE retro waterfall-chandelier's light reflecting off the black-and-white tiled lobby floor of Max's hotel. Orange sofas and yellow chairs and ocean-blue pillows with the signature wave imprinted on them were arranged in groups around the large space. A reception desk constructed of clear glass blocks with a wood top, creating a curve, was located to the right side of the entrance doors. On the walls were black-and-white pictures of beach days from the 1950s. The hotel was all Lily thought it would be and more.

As she walked farther inside, Max rose to his feet from where he had been sitting in one of the chairs. He looked as if he belonged there, attired in a white button-down dress shirt, cream-colored jacket and navy slacks. Everything about him screamed suave male.

The grin on his lips appeared sincere and made her middle flutter. How could she resist him? Despite their understanding about their failed night together, she remained unsure about him. She had a sense there was more to his interest in her than he'd let on so far. Maybe she'd find out if she was right tonight.

He stopped in front of her. "Hi, Lily. I'm glad you came."

"I said I would."

"You did. The restaurant is this way." Max's fingers touched her elbow long enough to direct her toward the elevators.

When the doors opened, Max's hand came to rest on the small of her back as they entered, then it fell away. Another couple joined them in the small space just as the doors closed, crowding her against Max. She could feel his heat along her back. The old elevator jerked as it started up. She stepped back to steady herself. Max's hand found her waist again and remained there. The evening had already turned into more than she had prepared for emotionally.

To her relief and disappointment, the warmth went away after they stepped out of the elevator onto the hotel rooftop. An attractive young woman stood beside a slick podium. "Hello, Dr. James. We have your table ready for you."

The area was like a tropical oasis, with palm trees and foliage set so that they created small alcoves with tables neatly tucked between them. Blue, pink and white lights were laced under and around the greenery and fixtures. A small candle with a frosted globe glowed in the center of each table. It reminded her of a nightclub she'd seen only in movies.

Max held her chair while she settled in at the two-person table in the corner where they could look out at the ocean. She'd never been to a more romantic spot. Wasn't this a business meeting?

Max took his chair. "I hope this all suits you."

Lily couldn't picture anywhere that she would've liked more. A trio played softly in the distance. She looked around, then back at him. "Are you kidding? This is the most amazing place I've ever been."

"I'm glad I get to share your first time here with you. I would've thought you'd come to a restaurant like this regularly."

"I work most of the time, and when I'm not doing that, I'm with Ivy." What she didn't say was that she watched her finances closely because she carried a content fear that if something happened to her there wouldn't be enough money to care for Ivy.

"You haven't been on dates to places like this?" His look didn't waver from her.

"My ex didn't like going anywhere fancy. He was more of a pizza-and-TV kind of guy."

Max's brow rose. "Your ex? Husband? You've not mentioned him before."

"Ex-boyfriend. It was a long time ago. In fact, we broke up the night before I came to that fated conference."

Max pursed his lips and nodded his head thoughtfully. "So that's why you were drinking by yourself and had a sudden interest in me."

The gentle breeze off the ocean rustled the palms around them, cooling her heated cheeks. "Yeah. I wasn't in a good place."

"Why's that?" He wanted to know, to understand her. For a minute there, he wasn't sure she would answer him.

Finally she said, "For weeks, Jeff and I had talked about him coming with me to the conference. It was supposed to be a shared vacation. He didn't care for Ivy going places with us, so it was to be our time away. The night before we were to leave, he dumped me because he said I wasn't worth taking on all my baggage, which meant Ivy. But he also didn't like that I wouldn't give him an answer about Skintec. See, he was a salesman for a biotech company. He wanted me to give them the rights to my invention, with him a leader of the project. I told him I wasn't ready to do that. I wanted to have my lawyer look at contracts first. Jeff didn't like that. He said the only reason he'd been interested in me in the first place was to get a chance at Skintec.

"Things blew up. There I was, stupidly thinking he was going to ask me to marry him while we were away." Lily shook her head. "I'm sorry. You didn't need to hear all that."

"I don't mind, and it sounded like you needed to say it."

She appreciated his tone of compassion. "I hate to admit it, but what Jeff did still stings. Worse, it made me act like a fool in front of you and others who I value their respect. I never do that sort of thing. I'm so ashamed."

Max smiled a smile that reassured her. "We all have people who make us say and do things we wouldn't otherwise."

A waiter came to stand at their table.

"What would you like to drink?" Max asked.

"Something fruity. With an umbrella."

Max chuckled and told the young man, "Make that two."

Lily studied him for a moment. "You don't strike me as a fruit-drinking man."

"Normally, I'm not, but it sounded kind of fun."

She looked out toward the ocean. "You like to have a good time."

"I do. I think life is too short to take it too seriously. My job is serious enough for me."

She wished she had the pleasure of not seeing life so seriously, but that wasn't the case.

"It gets hot in this part of the country in the summertime, but I do love living near the ocean. Tell me why you picked this particular hotel to stay in?"

"My father stays here when he comes to Miami. He recommended it."

She picked up her drink. That's the father he didn't talk about yesterday when he spoke about his family.

Max fingered the candle shade. "Did Ivy have a good time at the beach?"

"You know she did. She thinks you are the best thing since sliced bread. As usual, you have a way with women."

His expression turned thoughtful. "That would be with every woman but you."

He affected her. Too much so. She couldn't afford to show it.

"At the risk of making you angry, I want to apologize again for what happened at the conference."

"I might have overreacted." Of that, she was sure. But she still had a hard time working past her embarrassment.

"It's okay. I understand."

"I doubt you really do." What would a man like him know about his pride being damaged? Who wouldn't be pleased with him?

"Why do you say that?"

"I can't imagine that a woman has ever managed to humiliate you."

"Humiliate me? Maybe not." His look remained fixed on her. "Disturb me, concern me. Stay in my thoughts. Yeah."

Was he talking about her?

"I think you're a very special person, Lily. Especially where your sister is concerned."

She twisted her fingers around each other in her lap. It made her nervous to have Max's complete attention. "I appreciate that. Few people understand the challenges of what it's like to be responsible for a mentally challenged adult."

He leaned back in his chair. "Yes, but that doesn't mean that I don't sympathize."

"I appreciate that. Sympathy is fine. Pity is not."

"No one said anything about pity. Ivy is a sweet girl. I enjoyed getting to know her."

"She is." Her pride in her sister, she didn't try to keep out of her voice.

"Was it difficult growing up? I mean, did kids say ugly things about her around you?"

"Not often. Mostly it was questions. When we were teens, it was harder. Sadly, I was her only real friend." Lily kept the times she resented Ivy to herself.

"Teenage years can be difficult."

Lily bet Max's weren't. "Even now, I wish she had a wider social circle."

"Ivy is a lot of fun."

With every word, Max made it more difficult to keep her distance from him. Ivy was her soft spot. "Thanks for that. Truthfully I wasn't sure how you would react to her."

"Apparently you've had more than one poor reaction to Ivy. I'm sorry for that. It's not fair to you or her."

"I'm just supersensitive where she is concerned." After all, Ivy needed her to take care of her.

"With your tender heart, that has to be difficult at times." Max took a sip of his water.

Again, he'd impressed her with his observations. "I can be tough when I need to be."

Max grinned. "I don't doubt that. I've been on the receiving end of that toughness."

Why did everything have to circle back to their night—almost—together? Thankfully, the waiter returned with their drinks and to take their meal order.

"What did you want to talk to me about?"

"Why don't we wait until after we eat?" Max suggested.

The waiter arriving with their salads answered the question for her. They ate for a few minutes.

Lily looked around. "I like this place. I'll have to come again. Maybe bring Ivy. She would love the lights. If it were up to her, I'd have to leave the Christmas strands up year-round."

"She'd love my mother's house, then. She has them everywhere. Inside and out."

"That does sound like a place Ivy would appreciate." Lily could imagine the look on Ivy's face.

"What about you?"

"Me?" She met his gaze.

"Yeah. How do you like to decorate for Christmas?"

"I like a real tree with little blue lights, shells and starfish ornaments with little orange beach-chair ornaments here and there."

He chuckled. "That, I hadn't expected. You have a bit of whimsy in you."

Lily halted her fork halfway to her mouth. "Is that your way of saying you think I'm crazy?"

Max's eyes locked with hers. "The last thing I think you are is crazy."

Lily started to ask what he did think of her but was

afraid he'd answer too frankly. "Does your family get together every Christmas?"

He lifted a shoulder and let it fall. "Not as often as my mother wishes."

"Most moms feel that way. I know I would."

Max finished the last of his well-prepared steak. He'd enjoyed his meal and Lily's company. They'd settled into small talk about movies they liked, TV shows they watched when they had time, and books they had read. She had an intelligent and quick wit. Something he admired.

Too often the women he went out with were interested only in fashion and how nice his car was. What did his choice in dating partners say about him? Had he become as shallow as they were? He'd spent years trying to grow his career, which left him little time for a real relationship. In truth, he wanted a bond like his parents had but hadn't found the right woman.

His parents were busy people, but they loved each other. As demanding and uncompromising and relentless as his father might be, he'd been a good and devoted husband to his mother. Max couldn't fault his parent in that. It was something Max hoped he'd inherited but feared he couldn't live up to. Maybe that's why he'd always sabotaged his relationships by picking the wrong women—the concern he wouldn't measure up to his father in that area. After all, he was nothing like his father where business was concerned.

Then along had come Lily and her quiet, easy ways, who made him think more about his life. Less about bright lights and more about nights spent at home. Just that quickly he started to dare to peruse the future he hoped for.

People thought him more a playboy than he truly was. He just hadn't found the right person to get serious with. Could Lily be the one? Too many of his friend's marriages had ended in divorce. He didn't want that to happen to his. Especially if it involved Lily. Did he have it in him to make her happy?

He studied her. She was a real woman. Someone who cared deeply for others and was furiously loyal. He wanted a partner to share his life with who fit her profile. Lily was rare. He recognized that. With her, maybe he'd have a real chance.

Max leaned back in his chair, his hands in his lap. "Would you like dessert?"

Lily shook her head. "No, thank you. I've had plenty and it was wonderful. I'm curious. What did you want to talk to me about?"

He looked around at the tables filled with people. It was best their conversation wasn't heard by anyone. "Why don't we go for a walk? It's a nice night."

"Okay."

As they exited the hotel, Max said, "Let's cross the road and take the beach sidewalk."

"All right. I'm really curious now."

Max grinned. "It's not that big a deal." Or at least he hoped he framed it that way. He had to present the suggestion so Lily didn't think he was doing the same thing Jeff had been trying to achieve. "I guess more of my father has rubbed off on me than I wish to admit. I just don't think our conversation needs to be overheard."

Her eyes narrowed and she leaned in close. “Are we going to discuss the answer to world peace?”

Laughter rolled out of him. He chuckled loudly. When was the last time he'd laughed like that?

Lily's eyes twinkled.

“No, it's not that large.” He grabbed her hand and tugged when there was a break in the four-way street. At the walkway on the beach side of the street, he let go of her hand.

“Okay.” Lily looked behind and in front them as if they were spies. “I think it's safe to talk now.”

He glared at her. “You're making fun of me.”

She grinned. “I might be. What's going on?”

He strolled down the walk and she joined him. “It occurred to me that it might be beneficial for us to consider packaging Vseal and Skintec together.”

Lily watched him. He looked at her. A suspicious tone filled her voice. “Why's that?”

“Because our products work well together. More often than not, they're needed at the same time. And I believe we can get a better deal if we do.”

“I still haven't made any decision.” Lily's voice had turned thoughtful.

He stopped. “Good. Please don't until you've talked to me first.”

She continued to walk. “Business isn't really my thing. Can I think about it?”

“Sure you can. But just don't take too long. I think it would be to our advantage to announce our decision at the award banquet.” Max came up beside her.

“You do?”

“Yeah.” At least Lily was hearing him out.

“Do you have someone in mind to package it?”

She asked all the right questions, yet he didn't want her to take his answer wrong. "My father's company has a lot of experience in this area. We'd have more control going with him, I think."

"Wouldn't that be a conflict of interest for you?" She studied him a moment.

Lily might have more business knowledge than she wanted to admit. "No, because I expect to handle working with my father just as if I were doing business with anyone else. He may be a demanding businessman, but he's fair and honest."

"I just need to think about it." She pushed her blowing hair out of her face.

"I don't blame you." They had reached a bench facing the ocean. "Enough about business. Let's sit for a while and watch the sunset."

"That sounds nice." She took a seat beside him but not too close.

The sky had gradually turned orange as the sun moved toward the horizon. They sat in silence a few minutes. He glanced at Lily and saw her shiver. Removing his jacket, he placed it around her shoulders.

She settled into it. "Thanks."

Why did he wish she'd huddle into him like she'd done with the coat?

"Do you watch sunsets often?" Lily said without looking at him.

"No. I can't even tell you the last time I did."

"So why now?"

He laid an arm across the back of the bench but made sure not to touch her. "I don't know. Maybe it's the pace of life here that begs people to slow down enough to do so. Or I just thought it would be something nice to do with you. Does it matter?"

"No. I was just wondering. I've watched you at conferences too. Heard others talk. Just watching a sunset with a woman isn't what you're known for."

"I think you might be surprised to learn that not everything you hear is the truth." His reputation had never bothered him before, but somehow now, it needled him.

"I also have good eyesight."

He chuckled. "I'm not ashamed that I like women."

"From what I've seen, they like you too."

"Is that a note of jealousy I hear?" Max turned so he could better see her.

"Why would I be jealous?" Her tone of innocence didn't ring true.

Max sat a little straighter and gave her a cheeky grin. "I hope because you find me, uh, interesting."

Lily looked at him for a while before she said, "Maybe a little bit."

His hand slipped down to her neck as his head moved toward hers. He couldn't resist the chance to experience Lily. "Enough that you'll let me kiss you?"

Her lips met his. At first, it was a tentative touch, but she soon showed signs of hunger. He pressed his mouth firmer against hers. She shifted closer as his mouth found the perfect angle to better seal his lips to hers. He restrained his desire, not wanting to scare her with how badly he desired her, had wanted her for too long.

His coat fell from her shoulders as her hands reached to pull him closer. The tip of his tongue brushed the seam of her lips. At her whisper of a sigh, he entered, touching his tongue to hers. She shuddered. Her hands gripped his shoulders. His went to her waist to bring her close. He wanted so much more of sweet Lily.

At the honk of a horn, they broke apart.

Lily quickly shifted away. “Um, I’m…um.”

He felt a slow grin came over his face. “That was as nice as I remembered. I’ve wondered over the last months if I had imagined how great it was.”

Lily eyes flickered to meet his. “You have?”

“I have. And I’m not disappointed.”

CHAPTER FOUR

LILY DIDN'T KNOW what she had been thinking. She'd returned Max's kiss. She hadn't intended to, but she'd become caught up in the pleasure of kissing him. Her heart still leaped when she thought about his lips meeting hers.

They'd had an agreement. She'd stepped over the line. Those honey-sweet moments of Max kissing her kept running through her mind. There was an attraction between them. One she couldn't let get out of hand by repeating the embrace, even though she wanted to.

There had always been something simmering between them. Even before she really knew him, she'd felt it. He'd drawn her attention, even when she'd stood well across a large room he'd just entered. But she couldn't let that affect her. Becoming enamored of Max James shouldn't be part of her life. It could be her downfall in more ways than one.

Did she dare consider a personal relationship? Their being emotionally involved while joining in a business deal wasn't a good idea. Still, she couldn't help but wonder what it would be like being Max's love interest. In a perfect world it might be possible, but she had Ivy's future to consider. She needed a clear head.

She couldn't spend any more time on worrying about

Max. Despite not sleeping much the night before, she managed to get to the hospital early enough to see Mr. Roth before she was due in surgery. Lily headed to his room. She'd almost arrived at the door when she stopped short. Max leaned casually against the wall. "What're you doing here?"

"Good morning to you too."

"I'm sorry. I was just surprised to see you." Her mind had been so focused on Max, she'd not noticed him standing there.

"I came to do rounds. Remember, I'm part of the team for the next few days."

Lily hadn't forgotten. She'd just hoped for a little breathing room, time to think away from him. When he was around, he swallowed up all her thoughts. Now he was doing the same when he wasn't there.

"I wanted to see how Mr. Roth was doing."

"I'm headed to see him right now." She unlocked the office door.

Max followed her in. "I called and checked on him last night. He seemed to be doing a little better."

Wouldn't it be nice if she had someone who cared enough to check in on her? She missed her parents. Her best friend had taken another position out of town six months earlier leaving Lily to her work and Ivy. Maybe it was because she was feeling lonely that Max had such an effect on her. Still, it would be nice to have someone to help shoulder her decisions and worries. What made her think Max would volunteer for that type of position? After all, he was just in town for a few more days.

Lily put her purse away and grabbed her stethoscope off the hook by the door on her way out. "That's good to hear. I only have a few minutes before I'm due in surgery."

"Do you mind if I watch you in action?"

She did, but she wouldn't let him know how much his presence affected her. "I get the feeling you're going to do what you want to anyway."

His mouth went down, creating a comical face. "That hurts my feelings. You know that's not true." His gaze lingered on her. "You'd be surprised by the restraint I have."

His words sent a ripple of awareness along her spine. Thankfully, the elevator door opening gave her an excuse not to comment.

After seeing Mr. Roth, Lily headed to the surgery locker room. By all indications, her patient was improving. Soon she had her gown on and had entered the OR. She glanced up to see Max sitting in one of the eight seats in the viewing room.

He smiled.

She nodded, squared her shoulders and stepped to the table where her patient waited. Minutes later, she became so involved in the surgery, she forgot about Max and was focused on her job. Confident in her abilities, it still made her nervous to have him watching. For some reason it mattered to her what he thought.

As she prepared to use their products, she thought over what Max had said about joining their marketing strategy. She looked to where he should have been and found him gone. Moving away from the table, she allowed the fellow to close.

While the patient was on the way to recovery, Lily left the operating room, fully expecting to find Max waiting for her in the changing room. He wasn't there. She went to speak to the family, and still no Max.

She returned to her office. Until she was expected

in surgery again, she intended to take care of some issues. She had to pay for Ivy's next month at Palm Plantation, the complex where she lived. Lily wanted Ivy to remain there. She had a warm, sheltering place to live, with caring people around her. The problem was that it was expensive. Her parents had left some money, but it would soon run out. Lily had a good job, but not one that would handle paying for her home and Ivy's specialized care. With Max's suggestion they co-market their products, the financial gain might be the answer to her money concerns.

Hours later, she'd finished her straightforward, second surgery, done rounds and was headed home early for the first time in weeks. She'd yet to see Max since that morning. One of her fellows had mentioned he'd seen Dr. James in ICU with Dr. Lee. Other than that, Lily had no word about what Max had done all day. She should've been happy not to have him hanging around all the time. Instead, not knowing where he was made her wonder about him more. It came close to making her angry she not seen him after he been constantly there the last few days.

At home, Lily prepared a salad with the few items she had in her refrigerator and settled in to watch a TV show. Thoughts of Max kept swimming through her head, ruining what should have been her peaceful evening. Lily picked up her phone. He hadn't even bothered to call or text. With a huff, she set the cell on the table. She should be more concerned about keeping her professional distance than with seeing Max again. No doubt he was out doing what playboys did, picking up women. Why did that idea make her sick to her stomach?

How, in such a short time, had Max managed to make

her crazy? Instead of thinking about Ivy's needs and what she should do about Skintec, she was spending all of her time on wondering about Max. It had to stop.

Max couldn't help but grin when he saw the surprise on Lily's face when she found him standing beside Mr. Roth's door the next afternoon. Had she missed him? He sure hoped so.

She nodded and entered Mr. Roth's room, then went to his bedside. "How're you doing today?"

"Okay, but I felt better yesterday." The man's coloring wasn't as good as it had been the day before.

"What's different from yesterday to today?" Lily removed her stethoscope from her neck.

Mr. Roth grimaced. "I don't know. I just don't feel right."

Lily put her charting pad down on the end of the bed. "Let me have a look at you. Your fever seems to be down, and your blood work is looking better. Can you sit up for me?"

Mr. Roth leaned forward.

Lily used her stethoscope to listen to his respirations, then his heartbeat. "All sounds good. I'm going to add another antibiotic. That should take care of your problems."

"I sure hope it does," Mrs. Roth said. "He's starting to be a bad patient."

Lily gave her an encouraging smile. "I'm sure that'll improve when you get out of here. Which I hope is soon."

"Me too," Mr. Roth whined.

"Thanks, Dr. Evans," Mrs. Roth said, patting her husband's shoulder.

Their group moved out into the hall. "Mark," Lily said to one of the fellows, "increase the current antibiotic and add IV erythromycin bid. Let's see if that kills off the problem. That's it for today. See you all tomorrow."

As Lily turned to leave Max fell into step beside her. "How have you been?"

"Fine."

That was a short, curt answer, almost too much so. Was she angry at him? They walked a little farther in silence. "Have I done something wrong?"

Lily faced him. "Nothing, other than you show up one day wanting my time and attention, then disappear for a day without a word."

He grinned, sidestepping in front of her to see her face clearly. "You missed me, didn't you?"

"I did not." She raised her nose higher. "I just thought it was rude not to let me know you wouldn't be around yesterday." She truly sounded miffed.

"Rude. I'm sorry. I didn't mean to be rude."

"It's just that I wondered at your disappearance. Dr. Lee told me I was to see about you."

They stepped into the elevator. "See about me? I was with her most of yesterday, so she's aware you weren't shirking your duty. This morning I had an appointment."

When the door opened, Lily quickly exited. She threw over her shoulder, "That's good to know. Since you've done so well on your own, then I'll leave you to it. I have work to do."

"One of the fellows was telling me about a restaurant in Little Cuba. I'd like to try it, but it would be so much nicer with company. How about going with me tonight?"

"I don't think I should—"

He wiggled his brows. "Are you afraid you can't resist me?"

Lily's shoulders dropped, and she gave him a disgusted look. "I've had a long day and have an early one tomorrow."

"You have to eat sometime." He gave her his best pitiful look. "You wouldn't want a visitor to your city to eat alone, would you?"

She took a deep breath and released it slowly. "You're not going to take no for an answer, are you?"

"Not about this. I really hate eating alone." He did. Because of that, he'd had too many of his meals at the hospital. It was one of things he missed about not being in a relationship. Not that he was planning a relationship with Lily. He snorted. Like she'd even give him a chance. Yet that kiss had him daring to hope. "Nope, I don't think that'll happen. When will you be done here?"

"In an hour."

Max grinned. He had her now. "Okay. Why don't I pick you up at your place in two hours?"

"I can drive myself."

He recognized Lily's plan for an early getaway. He wasn't going to let that happen. She needed some fun in her life, and he was going to see to it he provided it. Doing so would let her get to know him better. In turn, she would learn to trust him. That would give him a better chance of convincing her to go along with his plan of packaging their products together.

There might even be a chance of finishing what they'd started at the conference or with that kiss at the beach. Too often, he'd thought about what could have been. He'd like to find out if they would be as good together as he dreamed. "We don't need to take two cars. Just give me your address."

She sighed, then told him what he wanted to know. "Now, let me get my notes added to patient's charts."

"Okay, I'll see you soon." Max left Lily with a bewildered look on her face, while he wore a satisfied grin on his.

For the last two hours, Lily had tried hard to resist the idea that she and Max were going on a date. Yet everything she'd done led only to that conclusion. She'd left the hospital earlier than she'd intended in order to dress for the evening. That had turned into an ordeal. She'd changed four times, finally settling on a simple dress and low-heeled shoes. She'd taken special pains with her hair and applied more makeup than she'd worn in years.

She'd suggested that she drive since she knew the way, and it also gave her some control over the evening. As she pulled up to the front of Max's hotel, she found him waiting. With a quick look in the rearview mirror, she opened the car door to greet him.

A casual grin rested on Max's lips. "Hello."

"Hey." Lily couldn't help feeling shy. An odd emotion, since she was used to running her world. Around Max, she seemed so unsure. On the occasional, casual dates she'd had since Jeff, she'd known she had no real interest in the men. But for some reason, it mattered too much what Max thought. Why, of all men, did it have to be him?

"You look lovely."

Lovely. Of all the adjectives he could have picked, somehow that one pleased her more than any other would have. Men had told her she was cute, pretty, even beautiful on occasion but never lovely. Coming from Max it seemed more important that the other adjectives. "Thank you. You look like you have gone native."

He glanced down at himself. "I went shopping yesterday. Too much?"

She giggled. Max self-conscious? "I like the beach-shirt-and-shorts look. You fit right in."

"I have to admit I'm a little surprised to see you. I was afraid you'd still be putting up arguments about going with me this evening."

Was she really that easy for him to read? "I decided if I had to go, then I might as well enjoy it."

"Ouch. Come on." He led her back to the driver's door. "I'm hungry."

"You're always hungry."

He grinned. "I've been saving up for this sandwich all day. I heard it's that good."

She asked, "Do you mind if we put the top down? It's a nice evening."

"Are you kidding? I'd love it. I begged my parents to buy a convertible when growing up. They always said we needed to live in a warm place. As an adult, I understand that. I've resisted buying one too. It isn't practical in Manhattan either."

With the top lowered, they settled in the car.

"What's that look for?" She glanced at him as she put on her safety belt. His brow had wrinkled and his lips had thinned.

"I'm just not used to the woman driving when I take her out." He gave her a chagrined look.

Her heart picked up a beat. "This is a date?"

"When you look like you do, you bet it is."

"Oh, okay." The thrill of having Max say that made her pulse beat faster. "Do you think your self-esteem can stand to have a woman drive you around?"

Max grinned the sexy grin that always pulled at her heart. "I'll try to hold it together."

As she drove Max casually laid his arm along the door and lifted his head into the wind. “This is as good as I imagined.”

Lily laughed. “This can’t be the first time you’ve ever ridden in a convertible.”

“No, but it’s the first time I’ve been in one with a lovely woman driving.”

There was that word again. Lovely. She smiled. “I’m glad you’re enjoying it. Tell me where we’re going?”

He did, and thirty minutes later, Lily pulled into a parking place near the Máximo Gómez Park. “Give me a sec to put the top up. The restaurant is just across the park and down a block.”

As they strolled, Max asked about the people sitting at tables under the trees. “What’s going on here? What’re they playing?”

“Dominoes.”

“Interesting. I’ve never played the game.” Max stopped to watch a moment.

“If you lived around here, you’d have to learn. It’s almost the national pastime.”

He glanced at her. “Do you know how?”

“Yeah. My grandfather taught me as a child.” It had been so much fun playing with him.

“Nice. All these people come here just to play Dominoes? Is it like this all the time? This must be a tournament.”

“Nope. All the time.” She led him out of the park across the street. “This is the famous Calle Ocho.”

“Eighth Street,” Max said, more to himself than to her.

“Correct. This is as Cuban as it gets outside of Cuba.

Here's where you can pick up a cigar and a thick cup of black coffee."

Lily inhaled the smell and the sounds. She didn't come here often, but she loved taking it all in when she did. It was like being in another country. As the sidewalk became more crowded, Max's hand came to rest at her waist. When they reached the restaurant entrance, he removed his hand. She missed it immediately. The sense of belonging and security evaporated.

After they were settled at their table and had placed their orders, Max asked, "Have you been here before?"

Lily looked around the courtyard with the bright, festive pennants and small different-colored lights that hung from the palm trees to the building and around the privacy fence. Tall outdoor heaters were stationed in various spots around the space. "No. I've never been here, but I've heard it's very good. I don't get down to this area very often."

"I'm glad I could be the first. I thought some guy might have already escorted you here."

She brushed her hand across the red tablecloth with its blue and yellow stripes. "I don't have much time for a personal life."

Max looked at her long enough that she squirmed in the chair. "Why?"

"Because I have my work. My sister."

He continued to watch her. "Okay, but don't you need more than that? When do you have fun?"

She leaned forward until her chest pressed against the table. "You know, I could ask you the same thing. Or have you got someone who's special who doesn't know you're out with me?"

He followed her move, bringing them almost nose to nose. "I don't cheat. There's no one in my life."

Lily grinned, feeling unusually pleased. "Why not?"

Max leaned back. "Because the right one hasn't come along."

"So you're out for a good time until then?" She had no interest in being another in his long list of women.

He shrugged. "Something like that."

They were interrupted by the server placing their thick Cuban sandwiches in front of them.

"This looks great." Max looked as if he were a dog who hadn't eaten in a week, ready to pounce on the food.

"It's enormous." Lily studied the Cuban bun with so much sliced meat, pulled pork and Swiss cheese piled on that she wouldn't be able to get her mouth around it. "How am I supposed to eat all this?"

Max chuckled. "You can always get a to-go box."

She laughed. "Yeah, and eat it for the next week."

Lily gave up on her sandwich well before Max. She watched as he finished his off. At twilight, a mariachi band took the small stage in one corner of the patio and began playing a rhythmic tune. It floated in the gentle breeze around them. A few couples moved to the open area to dance.

Max took a sip of his drink, then stood and offered his hand. "Will you dance with me?"

Lily's middle tightened as she glanced at the salsa dancers and shook her head. "I'm a horrible dancer. I can't do that."

"Come on. Live a little." Max's hand didn't move.

She pursed her lips. "I'm not making it up. I've never been a good dancer."

"Come on, Lil. I'll take care of you." His gaze urged her to take a chance.

With a roiling stomach, she gave him her hand.

Max pulled her to him and whirled her out to the floor.

"Wow. You do know how to do this."

He gave her wry smile. "Yep. My mother told me one day a girl would be glad I could dance."

"And my mother told me that if I ever found a man who could dance that I better hang on to him."

"Could it be we were meant for each other?" He pulled her close, then whirled her away.

Should she hope that was true? If she didn't live here and Max didn't live thousands of miles away, would they have a chance? If they weren't considering being business partners, maybe? If she could trust him to be the stable man she needed in her life and not a playboy. If, if, if… *Ifs* were too scary. She needed to keep her mind on her career and Ivy. Max was just moving through her life with no intention of staying.

Max enjoyed himself like he never had before. Dancing with Lily was fun. Her head was thrown back, and a smile filled her face as he twirled her away from him and then close. Holding her against him, he rocked back on a foot and she followed as if they had practiced their moves. They seamlessly shifted into a slow song.

"Who told you that you couldn't dance? They were wrong."

"My ex. I never had any training, but I loved to dance until he told me I wasn't any good at it."

Max murmured a harsh word. "Let me assure you he was wrong. He's wrong about other things, as well."

He let his hand dip lower on her waist and brought

their hips together. She didn't resist as they moved around the floor in a rocking step. Other couples had joined them, making them have to stay close. Lily's hand on his arm tightened as he led her to the beat of the music. Lily's face was flushed, and her body pliable. His body reacted to her sensual moves. What he wanted from her couldn't be achieved on a dance floor.

The song ended. Lily's dazed look told him she'd felt their sexual attraction too. Max's first impulse was to kiss her, but the crash of a dropped dish jerked him back to where they were. He turned her toward the table. "I think we should be going."

Lily blinked. "Yes, I think that would be a good idea."

Max guided her back to their table. While they waited for the bill, he said nothing and neither did Lily. Not soon enough for him, they were out of the restaurant, away from where the sound of the music urged him to take her into his arms again.

"Let's walk for a while." This was the second time he'd suggested a walk, and he didn't take walks. Somehow, Lily had him wanting to do things he rarely did.

"Okay."

Max took her hand and started down the street in the opposite direction from where her car was parked. The area had become more crowded while they were having dinner. That gave him a good excuse to continue to touch her.

Ahead of them stood a large cream-colored building with a tower on the top. The neon sign beneath read Tower in huge letters. "This looks like an old 1930s theater."

"You are close. It was built in 1925 or 1926. They have redone it. I've not been inside, but I've heard it's nice. Very retro. They show old movies and have film festivals here."

"According to the marquee, The Maltese Falcon is being shown tonight. It's one of my favorites, but I haven't seen it in a long time." He glanced at his watch. "What to go?"

"Go?"

"Yeah."

"I really should get home." Lily gave the building an unsure look.

"Come on. It's still early." Why couldn't she let go some? Do something spontaneous.

"I guess I could. I usually see movies with Ivy. It would be nice to see something a bit different."

He gave her hand a tug. "Then, let's go."

A few minutes later they were seated in the center of the theater, waiting on the movie to begin.

"This is one of the best noir films." Max continued to study the brochure he'd picked up on their way in.

"Noir?"

He dipped her voice low. "You know the dark, brooding man and the sultry woman he loves, but she is bad flick. A crime or mystery film."

"Sounds exciting," she said drily.

"Have you ever seen the Maltese Falcon?" He stuck the brochure in his pocket.

"Parts of it."

Max turned so he could see her more clearly. "What? I can't believe it. You've missed part of your education."

She grinned. "And you're planning to correct that."

"I am." The houselights lowered. "Right now."

As the first scene developed, he took Lily's hand and rested his on his thigh. Pleasure filled him when she didn't pull away. Two-thirds of the way through the movie, he felt the weight of Lily's head on his shoulder. She'd fallen asleep.

Something about Lily feeling comfortable enough to nod off on him seemed right. Too much so.

As the credits rolled, he gently shook Lily awake. "Hey, it's time we get going."

"Oh. I didn't mean to nap on you literally and figuratively."

"Not a problem." He chuckled. "I could tell you were glued to the movie."

Lily winced. "I'm sorry. What I saw was good, but I just got so sleepy..."

"I'll try not to take it personally. Let's get you home." He directed her toward the exit.

Half an hour later, they were back in Lily's car, headed toward her house.

Max didn't want to apply pressure, but he needed to know if Lily had given any thought to his suggestion they merge their products. His father had always been good at pushing for what he wanted. Max normally didn't like to, but his father was expecting an answer. "Have you thought about my proposal?"

She stopped for a red light. "Proposal?"

"About packaging our products together."

Lily studied him for a moment with a piercing look. "Is that why you've been cozying up to me? To get me to agree?"

"Cozying?" He raised his brows.

"Yeah. Inviting me to the beach, out to dinner. Being sweet to me. Especially after the fool I made of myself at the conference."

"There was nothing sweet about that kiss we shared.

Hot, steamy, unforgettable, maybe, but nothing I'd call cozy." Her soft intake of breath brought him a sense of satisfaction.

"That may be so, but the question still remains. Was tonight about getting me to go in with you to make more money?"

Disappointment filled him. He didn't want to be thought of in the same vein as her ex. "You don't have a very high opinion of me."

"You're still dodging—"

Her phone rang. She pushed a button to use hands-free mode in her car.

"Hello. It's Dr. Evans."

A male voice came through the speaker. "All of Mr. Roth's vitals are out of line. His white count is up, and he's in pain. Has developed a fever."

"Prep him for surgery. I'll be there as soon as I can."

CHAPTER FIVE

LILY HURRIED DOWN the hospital hall toward surgery. Max kept pace beside her. When she'd offered to let him take her car to his hotel, he'd said, "No, I'm coming with you."

A nurse was busy checking the IV pump attached to the line leading into Mr. Roth's arm when Lily and Max entered the patient-holding area of surgery.

Lily stepped to his stretcher. "Mr. Roth, I'm sorry you're having to go through this. I promise we're going to make you feel better. Hang in there with me. May I have a quick listen to you and have a look at your incision site?"

"Dr. Evans, what's going on?" the man moaned.

"I don't know yet, but we'll soon find out." Lily pulled the stethoscope out of her pocket. Moments later, she listened to his heart rate. "Now, may I see your incision?"

Max stepped up beside her. The area had turned red and was distended. Lily palpated the area.

Mr. Roth grunted.

"May I?" Max asked. "I'll do my best not to hurt you, Mr. Roth."

The way he moved his hands around the man's midsection showed Max's experience. As he touched the same spot as she had, Mr. Roth reacted.

Lily put a hand on the man's shoulder, giving it a gentle squeeze. "When I see you again, the plan is to have you feeling better." She spoke to the nurse. "I want the latest CBC, electrolytes and liver panel report. I'll be ready to start as soon as I change. Have you seen Dr. Marsh? He's my second tonight."

"He's caught in traffic. Won't be here for another half an hour."

"I'll scrub in," Max said. "I can assist. The board granted me privileges, after all. I might as well take advantage of them."

Relief washed through her. "I'd appreciate it. I don't want to wait any longer. Mr. Roth doesn't have that kind of time."

Max followed her out of the room. As quickly as possible, she and Max were gowned and scrubbed, then standing beside the patient.

"Scalpel, please," Lily said.

The nurse beside Lily confidently handed it to her.

Max stood on the other side of the patient. "My guess, there's a bleeder somewhere."

"But where and why now?" Lily kept her eyes on what she was doing. She efficiently reopened the area, making an incision just to the side of the original in order to not have to deal with scar tissue. She needed to get in quickly.

"We should know soon enough." A few minutes later, Max positioned the retractor holding Mr. Roth's incision open for their viewing. "Now the hunt begins."

"Yeah." Lily gently shifted a lobe of the liver, looking for the problem.

Minutes crawled by as their heads bent over the open abdomen of Mr. Roth. Lily continued to search as she moved her probe in different directions.

"Wait a sec." Excited notes surrounded the words as Max leaned closer.

"What?" Lily searched but saw nothing.

Max's voice stopped her moment. "I thought I saw something. Lift that spot again. Just as you did before."

Lily did as he said.

"There," he barked. "Got it."

Lily frantically looked. "Where? I don't see anything."

"I only saw the perforation for a second as you moved the vessel." He tilted his head as if trying to find the right angle.

"Mirror," Lily snapped, and the scrub nurse placed it in her hand. She held the glass so that she could see the area Max indicated. "I'm still not seeing anything."

"Let me have the probe." Max put out a gloved hand.

She released the instrument.

"Now, watch." Max shifted the organ to the right.

Joy and relief filled her. "I see it. Just large enough to cause a problem. Let's clean the area and patch it up."

Max's blue gaze met hers over the top of his mask. "I take it you're going to use your patch and my glue."

Her jaw tightened. Was he making a point that once again their products should be packaged together? "I am. Skintec, please."

The nurse presented it in a sterile pan.

"Max, will you hold the edge of the liver just as you have it so I can get this into place." Slowly and carefully, Lily positioned the patch where she wanted it. "Max, hold the flap right there. Glue."

The nurse handed it to her.

Lily sealed the patch. Studying the area carefully, she watched for any indication the repair wasn't secure. She straightened and rolled her shoulders. To Max, she said, "You can relax now."

He stood, as well. "Looks good."

"Yeah. Now let's see if we can find anymore issues." She returned to probing the area. A few minutes went by, then Lily declared, "I'm ready to close now."

An hour later, as she removed her gloves and threw them in the trash outside the OR, Lily said to Max, "Thanks for your help. That was a good spot. I was glad to have you in there."

"You're welcome. I'm sure you would've found it on your own."

"Maybe so, but I still appreciate your assistance." She had. He had been an extra set of excellent eyes.

They finished stripping out of their OR clothing down to their scrubs.

Max threw his soiled garments into the cloth disposal bag. "Not to start a fight, but our products came through again."

"I know, but that never was the issue."

Max pushed the swinging door to step out of surgery. "It's too late and we're both too tired to get into it now. It'll save."

Lily followed and covered a yawn. "I agree. I'm glad I got that nap during the movie."

Max chuckled. "If I'd realized I was going to be in surgery most of the night, I would've joined you in getting some sleep."

"It has been a long day. Give me a few minutes to speak to Mrs. Roth, and I'll drive you to the hotel."

Max looked at the lightening sky of a new day. Most people had been sound asleep in their bed for hours, but he and Lily were just driving away from the hospital. "You live closer than the hotel. I don't want you driving there and back at this hour by yourself."

"I do it all the time." Lily turned right at a light.

"Not with my knowledge. I couldn't in good conscience let you do all that driving. Let me get a couple of hours sleep at your house, then I'll get a taxi to the hotel. I'll be a gentleman. I'll use the sofa. I won't take no for an answer."

"And I'm too tired to argue with you." She yawned.

Insisting he sleep at Lily's might not have been one of his best ideas, but he'd never forgive himself if something happened to Lily on her return trip from the hotel. He'd always taken for granted the women he dated didn't need his help. Lily, he was sure, didn't need it either, but she brought out the desire to protect in him. Something he'd have sworn, up until she came along, wasn't well-developed. He'd spent most of his life being single-minded and career driven, trying to prove he was the best in his field, just as his father was the best in his. Lily made him think of a softer side to life, a less ambitious one.

He was worn out too. Maybe after a hot shower and finding a comfortable spot with a pillow, he'd forget about Lily being under the same roof. Maybe.

Soon, Lily turned into a short drive beside a yellow bungalow. It looked as if it was straight out of the 1950s, with its small porch on the front, wooden siding and coral-colored tropical shutters that stuck out from the house at an angle. Lush flowers bloomed in the front and near the back door. Luxuriant greenery filled the backyard. The place fit Lily perfectly.

In silence, he followed her through a side door into the kitchen. "Nice home."

She placed her purse on the tile-covered counter. "Thanks. It's close to the hospital and is large enough for Ivy and me." She covered another yawn with the back of her hand. "The bath is down the hall. First door on the right. The door across from there is Ivy's room. You're welcome to it. The sheets are clean. You can have the bath first. I have to feed the cat and let the hospital know I won't be in until this afternoon."

A tabby cat wandered across the white-and-aqua tile of the floor to circle Lily legs.

"This is Poppy. Ivy's cat."

"Hello, Poppy," Max was unsure how to respond, not being a cat person.

"The towels are under the cabinet, along with a spare toothbrush. Make yourself at home. Good night."

He took the hint and headed toward the bathroom. Fifteen minutes later, he stepped across the hall into the bedroom, wearing only his unbuttoned pants. Flipping on the light, he almost groaned out loud. The room's walls were painted a little-girl pink, and a ruffled spread covered the bed. He shouldn't have been surprised. It had to have been picked out by Ivy. As he pulled back the spread, he remembered he'd left his shoes in the bath. Stepping into the hall, he bumped into Lily.

"Ho." His hands held her arms to steady her. "Sorry. I wanted to get my shoes out of your way."

Despite a night in the OR, she smelled like sweetness and the salt of the outside. His gaze met hers. Held. Even in the soft light coming from his room, he could see the interest and insecurity in her eyes. If he kissed her, would it lead to more? Did she want that? Could he afford to have her think he was taking advantage of her? Tonight wasn't the time. He couldn't scare her off.

Stepping back, he put distance between them and let her go, even though his real desire was to pull her against him. "I'll get them when you're done. See you in the morning."

Lily slipped into the bath, and he watched as she gently closed the door behind her. With a lingering look, he closed the bedroom door behind him. He climbed into bed but didn't sleep. Instead, he listened to the water running, then the quiet as he imagined Lily's wet, naked body as she dried off, then put on her nightclothes. Finally, the sound of the door opening and the patter of soft, bared feet going along the wood floor told him Lily was secure in her room.

With a deep sigh, Max punched the pillow beneath his head. He willed his body to relax and tried not to think about his body straining to go to Lily.

By midmorning, Max was cooking breakfast while the stove and the sun heated the cheerful kitchen. He could get used to living in a place like this. No gray days, cold or snow. He'd been restless for some time, but somehow, being in Lily's home eased his soul. His days had consisted of long workdays, unfulfilling relationships and rare trips to Chicago to see his family. Something about being a part of Lily's life made him want to have someone to commit to, invest in. To care about and have her care about him. Maybe it was time for him to stop drifting through his existence.

Max sensed rather than heard Lily behind him. He continued the rhythmic clink of the fork against the side of the ceramic roll. "I hope I didn't make so much noise I woke you."

"No, I smelled the coffee."

He glanced over his shoulder to find Lily standing in

the entrance from the hall. "I have some water hot. I figured you'd prefer tea, based on the amount in the cabinet."

"Thanks. I'll get some after I've checked on Mr. Roth."

Max turned to the eggs. "I've already called. He's stable and had a good morning. The respiratory therapist has already removed the breathing tube. Vitals and labs look good."

Lily had stepped toward him, based on the closeness of her voice. "You've been busy."

Max stiffened at her tight tone. This time, he turned around to completely face her. Lily's hair was mussed, but he could tell she'd tried to push it into some form. She'd pulled on a short housecoat that showed too much leg for his comfort. Her feet were bare. "I'm sorry if you feel I stepped out of my lane. I was just curious. I won't do it again."

She came toward him. "It's okay this time. I should've been up earlier, and then I would've been the one doing the calling."

Max poured the eggs into the hot pan.

Lily reached for a cup and saucer. "So you cook?"

"I do, in fact. Haven't you figured out I'm a bit of a foodie?"

She pulled a tea tin out of the cabinet. "Mostly, I just thought you were hungry all the time."

He grinned. "That too. It helps if you're a foodie."

"I guess it does." She looked over his arm. "What's for breakfast?"

With complete confidence, he said, "My world-famous omelet."

"World famous. Um, isn't that what they all say?"

Max lifted his jaw. "I don't know what others say, but I know what mine tastes like."

She sniffed loudly. "It smells good, but I really should be getting to the hospital."

"I think you've time to eat. It's almost ready anyway. And I promise you don't want to miss this." He held up a spatula. "Please sit down and I'll serve you."

Lily studied him a moment, then finished preparing her tea before taking a chair at the table.

Max kept his satisfied smile to himself as he slipped the omelet onto a plate and presented it to her with a flourish.

"This is good." Lily held up a forkful of omelet.

"Don't sounded so surprised. I'll have you know I have a number of talents."

Lily's eyes widened. She knew that well. Max was certainly a good kisser. She'd experienced that firsthand, but she couldn't say that. Why did he get to her so? No matter what her mind said, her heart refused to listen where it involved Max. Lily couldn't control her emotions. She liked Max. Admired him, even. She continued to look for ways where he failed, but he always came out being a stand-up guy. Feelings were just feelings. She'd learn to deal.

For now, she'd try to ignore them. "I know you're a smart man. Your glue alone proves that."

Max nodded. "Thank you. Coming from you that's high praise."

Lily held her tongue about them joining sides in marketing their products. She had a sense that he wanted her to say more, but she couldn't. The idea required more thought. Her decision affected Ivy too much for her to make it lightly. Hooking her wagon to Max had too many ramifications to make a snap decision she could regret.

She still wasn't convinced it would be her best financial move. Ivy's long-term care would be expensive, and she needed to know she would be taken care of into her old age.

Poppy wrapped around her legs and then around Max's.

Max sat down his coffee mug. "Tell me about Poppy. You said she belongs to Ivy."

Over the next few minutes, they talked about the cat.

Lily put her fork down on the empty plate. "I'll clean up since you cooked, then I've got to get to the hospital. I have surgery that was pushed back to this afternoon. I hate having to do that to my patients. At least it doesn't happen very often."

"You go get ready. I'll take care of the cleanup. I'm dressed. All I have to do is put on my shoes. There isn't much to do anyway. I'll put it all in the dishwasher and start it."

"Thanks." Lily stood. "And thanks for breakfast. You really could be a chef."

He chuckled. "Now you're laying it on a little thick."

Lily wore a smile as she walked out of the room. Who knew it could be so much fun to share breakfast with Max?

Half an hour later, they left her house.

"Would you like me to drop you off by the hotel before I go to the hospital? I've got just enough time to do so."

"I was hoping you'd let me scrub in with you," Max said from the passenger seat.

Lily glanced over at him, her brows drawn together behind her sunglasses. She couldn't imagine him regularly wanting to take a back seat to her or anyone else in the OR. Surgeons by nature were territorial. Max had played sidekick more than once to her, but how long could it continue? Yet she didn't know how to tell him no. "That's fine, if that's what you want to do."

"Afterwards, I need to speak to Dr. Lee, so I'll get my own way back to the hotel."

"Have you and Dr. Lee known each other long? You seem sort of friendly."

"Friendly?" He grinned. "Actually, we worked together in Chicago a few months before she moved to Atlanta and then took the administrative job here."

"I see."

"See what?"

She felt more than saw him looking at her. "Just that you're colleagues."

"Did you think we were involved personally?"

Lily thought of bending the truth but thought better of it. "I might have wondered..."

"Let me set you straight. I wouldn't be going to dinner and a movie with you if I had something going on with Liz. I'm a one-woman man."

"But what we've been doing is about business and me being asked to show you around."

Even with Max wearing dark glasses, she felt his heated glare. "Let me make myself clear, since you haven't caught on. I'm interested in you. The person."

"After that fiasco at the conference, I wasn't sure."

"I thought I had explained that. That Jeff guy really played a number on your self-esteem, didn't he?"

She hated to admit it, but, yeah, he had. "You came along right behind him."

"Ouch. I'm sorry about that. Haven't I proved over the last few days that I'm not who you thought I was."

"Well, yeah. But I don't know how to tell for sure. I've messed up so badly before."

"You're right. You can't always know, but then you sure do miss out on a lot in life if you don't take a chance on people. Why don't you give me that chance? You might find out that I'm worth it."

She pulled into her parking spot at the hospital. "You think you're that good?"

He shrugged. "You'll never know until you let yourself go enough to trust me. Can you do that?"

"That's a tough request. But I'll try."

He patted the car door, then opened it. "Good. I promise not to disappoint."

"That confident?"

"Nope." He looked back over his shoulder as he got out. "Just willing to work hard to gain your trust." As they walked into the building, he said, "Tell me what's on for surgery this afternoon."

"I have to remove a tumor on a liver." Lily found it interesting that six days ago, it upset her to have Max in the viewing room and now she willingly let him into surgery. "Just remember who's the boss in my OR."

"Yes, ma'am."

An hour later they were in the operating room studying the patient's open midsection.

"This is large and more invasive than the tests indicated." To the nurse standing across from her and next to Max, Lily said, "Suction."

The nurse cleared the area.

"These two large tentacles will need to be cut simultaneously to control the bleeding." Lily looked at Max. "You good with helping with that?"

"Of course."

"I'm going to sever the smaller ones, then we'll do the larger ones last." Lily started removing the tentacles, cauterizing as she went. She felt Max intently watching her procedure. Finished, she handed the cauterizer to the nurse. Looking up at Max, she said, "You ready?"

"Yes." To the nurse standing beside him, he said in a clipped tone, "Scalpel."

She placed it in his hand.

Lily didn't look up. "We'll need to move quickly."

"Agreed."

"All right. Let's get this ugly thing out of here. On my mark. One, two, three." She cut through the vessel attached to the liver while Max did the same on his. Their nurses suctioned the area.

Lily scooped up the thick blob and placed it a pan. "Get it to pathology. Surgical glue."

The nurse handed her the adhesive Max had created.

"Let's get the seams sealed." She worked with speed and caution as she first covered her incision and then the one Max had made. "Now to watch for any bleeding."

An hour and a half later, after closing the patient and seeing her on her way to recovery, Lily and Max removed their surgical gowns.

Lily met Max's look. "I'm glad you were in there with me today. I needed the second pair of hands."

"Happy to be of assistance. I got worried there for a few minutes."

Lily tugged her gown off. "I didn't expect the tumor to be so invasive."

"I gathered that, but you managed the situation well. You did a good job in there."

Lily's phone buzzed. She picked it up off the counter. "Dr. Evans here."

CHAPTER SIX

MAX GRABBED LILY as her face went white and her knees buckled. He pulled her to him, supporting her. “What’s wrong?”

She shook her head as she listened to the person on the phone. “I’m on my way… Okay. Okay. Call me with an update every thirty minutes… Have the police been called?”

Fear shot through Max. What was going on?

“Call me immediately if you find her.”

His chest tightened. She must be talking about Ivy.

Lily hung up and she faced him, her face drawn with worry. “Ivy’s missing. She got mad when she was told she couldn’t work outside the compound. She’s run away.” Lily gulped.

Max tightened his hold.

She sniffled. “Ivy’s been gone three hours. They’ve been trying to phone me all that time, but I was in surgery.”

“You should notify the police.” He rubbed her back.

“They’ve already done that.”

“Then let’s go look for her.” Max eased away, ready to head out the door. He couldn’t stand the thought of Ivy out there lonely and scared. “We’ll find her.”

Lily clinched his shirt. "They want me to go home and stay put in case she comes there."

"Then that's what we'll do."

They hurried out of the hospital.

"I'll drive. You're too upset to do so," Max announced as they got into Lily's car. Minutes later they were leaving the parking lot of the hospital.

As they waited at a traffic light, Max glanced at Lily. Her hands remained clutched in her lap, the knuckles blanched of color. A single tear rolled down her cheek. His chest tightened. He laid a hand over hers. "They'll find her, or she'll come home on her own. Hang in there."

Lightning flashed.

"A storm is coming," Lily moaned. "What if she's out in dangerous weather?"

He squeezed her hands. "Don't borrow trouble. She's going to be all right."

"You can't promise that." Lily's voice wavered.

"No, I can't, but they're doing everything they can to find her, and we're going to do what they asked us to. There's no point in thinking the worst."

Lily's voice wobbled as she said, "All my life I've been told to protect Ivy, watch over her."

"Why was that your job?" Who put that sort of thing on a child?

"Because my parents said she doesn't have a good mind, so that's a reason not to waste mine. 'She can't take care of herself, so you need to help her.'"

Now he understood Lily better. "That's why you're so driven in your work."

"Yes. And I like helping people. Making them feel better. I haven't done a good job this time." She wiped her face with her hands. "I didn't go by to talk to Mr. Roth."

"He'll understand. I'll take care of seeing that one of the fellows checks on him and reports in when we get to your place. Ivy is the most important person right now. You worry about her, and I'll take care of the other stuff."

Max didn't make a habit of taking over a situation and telling anyone what to do, outside his OR or in regard to his patients, but this time, Lily needed his help. He certainly didn't get high-handed with women he was interested in. But it was obvious Lily was on the edge of hysteria by the time they arrived at her house.

He hadn't even turned off the car before Lily was out of it and running through the door, calling Ivy's name. He wasn't far behind. Lily hurried frantically from room to room. Her shoulders slumped with disappointment as she looked at him with watery eyes.

"Where is she?" Lily moaned.

She went down the hall again and back up.

Max's heart went out to Lily. When she reached him again, he took her by the hand and led her into the living room. In front of a cushioned chair, he gave her a nudge to sit. "You need to take a moment. You're going to make yourself sick."

At a rumble of thunder, she shook and looked out the window. "What if she's outside? I need to check the front porch and the yard."

He placed a hand on her shoulder when she moved to get up. "I'll do that. Where's your phone?"

Lily looked at him for a moment like she had no idea what he was talking about. "The kitchen counter. On the kitchen counter."

"Stay right here and I'll get it." He hurried out of the room and returned then handed her the cell. "You stay by the phone while I go out and look for Ivy." He squeezed her shoulder. "It's going to be fine. I promise."

Max stepped out the back door and searched the yard, looking behind the scrubs. He looked up and down the street of the neat neighborhood. He searched the front porch for any sign Ivy had been there and even double-checked the car in case she climbed in after they had arrived. No Ivy. Where was that girl?

Returning inside, he heard Lily talking. Had Ivy been found? Max stopped in the doorway, hoping he'd overhear good news. She clicked off. By the misery on her face and the way she clutched her phone, it hadn't been good news. "They still haven't found her."

At a crash of thunder Lily jerked, then shivered.

"Come here." Max took her hand, pulling her out of the chair. Wrapping his arms around her, he brought her close and rubbed her back. "Hang in there. You're not alone."

Lily buried her face in his shoulder and hugged him tight. They stood like that for a long time. The room dimmed as the storm approached. Max continued to hold her and whisper soft assurances in her ear.

A long time later, Lily stepped back. "Thank you. Thank you for being here with me."

"Wouldn't be anywhere else." Oddly, he meant it.

Lily returned to the chair.

He watched her wanting to help but not knowing what he could do. He settled for the practical. "I'm going to get you something to drink. Then I'll fix some sandwiches. All we can do is wait. We'll be here when Ivy comes home."

Rain tapped on the tin roof of the house.

Lily looked out the window. “She shouldn’t be out in the rain.”

“Ivy’s smart enough to find shelter. Don’t start imagining more than you know.” Max went to the kitchen and prepared Lily a glass of iced tea. He returned to find Lily slumped in the chair, her head lying back as she stared at the ceiling. After setting the glass on the table, he brushed a finger along her cheek.

“My father would be so disappointed in me for not taking care of her.”

Max had no doubt she spoke more to herself than him.

“I’m supposed to take care of her. I’m the one with the good mind. It’s my job to keep her safe.”

Max started to argue, but would Lily listen to common sense in the state she was in? Instead, he returned to the kitchen. Pulling items out of the refrigerator, he prepared them ham-and-cheese sandwiches. He looked through the cabinets and found a bag of chips. After placing a handful on each plate, he carried them into the living room. He sat one plate near Lily, who appeared not to have moved. The other, he put on the coffee table.

She didn’t open her eyes. “I’m not hungry.”

“No, I guess you aren’t. But I don’t know how to help other than to care for your practical needs. For my sake, eat two bites.” He’d never stayed around long enough with other women to become involved in their emotional issues. Had he been afraid he would fail them just as he’d failed his father? Lily had pulled him into an area where he wasn’t comfortable, yet he couldn’t leave her.

Lily gave him a weak smile. “That was some speech.”

Max shrugged. “But true.”

Lily looked out the window at the darkening sky.

He returned to the kitchen for his drink. When he

stepped back into the living room, he found Lily eating her sandwich. He took a seat on the sofa. They silently shared their meal. Lily dutifully took her two bites and munched on a chip before pushing the plate away. At a loss for what more to do, Max said nothing. When he finished, he gathered their dishes and set them in the kitchen sink.

Lily said something, but he didn't hear her clearly. Stepping to the door he asked, "What, sweetheart?"

"It's raining harder. She'll be wet and cold."

Max pursed his lips. He had the best education money could buy. Saved people's lives weekly. Even knew how to enjoy life, but he had no experience that would help him here. He didn't want to disappoint Lily by not being able to help her. "You don't know that." He took her hand. "Come over here and sit beside me."

She joined him on the sofa. He put his arm around her shoulders and brought her next to him. They sat like that for half an hour as the storm blew around them. At the ringing of her phone, they both jumped.

Lily snatched the device up. "Hello… Yes. Yes. Thank goodness… How is she?"

Max squeezed her shoulders, letting Lily know he was there.

She sighed. "Thank heavens. I'll be there in thirty minutes… What? But I need to see her."

Max watched the emotions wash across Lily's face.

"All right. If you think that's the best way. Tell Ivy I'll be there in the morning to take her for breakfast." Lily sounded excited and exhausted as she hung up.

Max turned to face her. "What did they say?"

"She's fine. Wet and cold but fine. She was just outside in the gardener's shed the entire time. She went to sleep."

"Really?"

Lily sighed and slumped back against the cushions, the phone dangling in her hand. "They have her back inside and warm and in her room again."

"Why didn't they want you to come see her?" The relief he felt could only equal Lily's. The Evans women had begun to matter to him a great deal.

"They don't want me upsetting her. She's calm and safe, and they want it to stay that way."

"I can understand that." He wanted Lily to feel the same.

"They have her settled. She was scared, as well. They're afraid it'll be too much if I show up. She might get upset again. Ivy knows they called me."

Max took her hand. "That makes sense."

"They suggested I come have breakfast with her in the morning. That's not all that unusual. I do it when I'm going in late."

Max hugged her and kissed her temple. "I'm glad she's home and safe."

"Me too."

He searched her face. "How're you doing?"

"I'm okay. Now." Her eyes still swam with tears. "It'll take a while for the adrenaline to settle. I'll drive you home in a few minutes."

"No hurry. I'll stay as long as you need me." He pulled her back into his arms. "We'll sit here for as much time as you want." The storm had settled into a steady beat on the roof. "This is nice anyway."

Lily turned so that she met his gaze. "Thank you for staying with me. I don't know what I would've done."

"You're one of the strongest women I know. You

would've handled it. But I'm glad I was here." Max found he meant it. He wanted to be there for her.

"I'm not strong where my sister is concerned."

"I don't think any of us are strong where our family is concerned." He certainly had a hard time standing up to his father. Even now, Max still felt he had to prove himself.

She laid her head on his chest and sighed. "You're a nice guy, Max James."

"Was there ever any doubt?"

"I had some for a while, but you've proven you're different than I first thought." She looked at him a moment before settling against him again.

"I'm glad you think so, but don't put me up on a pedestal because I get air sickness and it'll be easy to fall off."

"Sometimes you can't help how you feel," she said softly.

Max could certainly identify with that. He felt too much for Lily. Far more than he'd ever dreamed he could. What started out as a family situation was quickly developing into a personal one. A relationship that involved more than a one-night stand or getting her to go along with them packaging their products together.

Lily snuggled into him.

His breath caught when her lips touched his neck. He couldn't think of another time she'd voluntarily touched him since he'd known her. "Lily?"

"Yes?" Her lips continued along his skin.

"Don't play with me."

"What do you mean?" she murmured against his ear.

"You know exactly what I mean."

She kissed his neck again. "You mean this?"

"Yeah." He groaned. Did she realize what she was doing to him?

"I was just saying thank you." A teasing note circled the words. She kissed his jaw.

"You've just had a scare. You're not thinking like yourself."

Her hand came to rest on his chest. "I was thinking of celebrating."

"How were you planning on doing that?" He wasn't used to this aggressive Lily, but he found he really liked the idea of it.

"Before I tell you, I need to know if you'd be willing to celebrate with me." Her hand moved over his chest.

"I'd need to know what's involved before I answered that question."

"Such a careful man. I was thinking if it was all right with you, I'd like to kiss you."

Max sucked in a breath. "I think you need to be careful about what you're doing. There's a real chance I won't stop at a kiss."

Lily turned so their gazes met. "I'll take that risk."

Max looked around at the dimly lit room, giving his heart a moment to steady its beat and his mind time to think straight, because he had every intention of kissing her senseless.

Lily held her breath as she watched Max. Had she just embarrassed herself with him again? Was this his way of telling her he wasn't interested?

She'd made only a slight move when his arms tightened, and his mouth found hers.

Max's body remained tense, as if he were holding himself back, as if judging if he should take the kiss deeper. She suspected she'd made him question himself because of her attitude about what had happened between them before.

She wanted all his passion. Didn't want him to hold anything in reserve. Tonight, she needed to break out and feel alive. To forget her responsibilities. To be swept away by his touches and kisses.

Sliding her hand across the plane of his chest to the nape of his neck, she ran her fingers though his hair and nudged his head closer in encouragement as her mouth opened. Max took her invitation. His tongue brushed hers, causing a tingle to ripple down her spine. She shivered. Could anything feel better than Max's kisses?

His hand slid up her back and down again as his mouth left hers and skimmed over her cheek. To travel to her temple. "Lily, you taste as magical as I dreamed you would."

She leaned her head to the side, giving him better access to her neck. Her heartbeat tapped faster as he kissed behind her ear. She moaned, leaning closer to Max.

His arm scooped up her knees and he lifted her across his lap.

Lily pressed her chest against his as her hands cupped his face. Her mouth found his again. Being so forward wasn't like her, but Max's eager return of her attention made her bold. Kissing Max was all she dreamed it might be and more. She wiggled against him and wasn't disappointed to find the thickness of his desire pressing against her hip.

His arms tightened at her waist as he took over the kiss. With tongues in a tangle, he lay her on the sofa and bent over her. Her hands kneaded the muscles of his back as she returned his kisses. Her blood hummed through her veins. She'd never felt this heated need before. It made her confident. Had her wanting…more. Max. It all.

A large warm hand cupped her hip, bringing it more securely beneath him. His hand slipped under her shirt until his palm lay on her stomach. Her muscles tightened as his fingers worked their way upward. His mouth released her long enough to nip at her bottom lip.

"Mmm, I can't seem to get enough of you."

Lily squirmed. She kissed his chin, then his jaw, rough with its afternoon growth. It only added to his appeal and her appreciation of their differences.

Max placed light kisses on her eyes, forehead and found that sweet spot behind her ear that made her moan with delight. As his mouth worked its charms, his hand continued its exploration of her middle on the way to her breasts. One of his fingers followed the line of her bra from left to right before returning to the deep V where the front clasp was located. With a practiced flip of thumb and forefinger, he released her bra.

His mouth left hers and he looked at her with a flame of desire flickering in his eyes. "Okay?"

She wasn't sure whether he was asking about her feelings or if it was okay to open her bra, but the answer was the same for both. "Better than okay."

The hand that had stilled on her ribcage nudged her bra away. He cupped her breast. In a hushed tone he whispered, "So sweet. So perfect."

Air escaped her lungs in a whoosh. Her nipples tightened, and her breast tingled in anticipation of his attention.

"This shirt belongs somewhere else."

She raised her arms. Max pealed the material over her

head and dropped it unceremoniously to the floor. He brushed her bra straps away and looked at her.

Lily watched his eyes. They never left her. She couldn't remember being more exposed or desired in her life.

Max's gaze rose. Seconds later, his lips met hers in a gentle, controlled kiss that made her stomach flutter and her core heat. One of his hands supported her head, his fingers buried in her hair. His other hand eased over her midsection as if he were memorizing the dips and curves of her body. She quivered as he left a path of heat in his wake. Her breath came in puffs as she waited, anticipating him touching her aching breasts.

His mouth left hers. He kissed her cheek, the ridge of her shoulder, the top of a breast before his mouth found her nipple.

The breath Lily hadn't realized she was holding, rushed from her lungs. As Max's tongue tugged and teased, her center tightened and throbbed. Oh, what Max's touch did to her. The contact was electric. She whimpered.

His roguish look met hers. "You liked that?"

She nodded, unable to form a word.

He cupped and lifted her other breast. "Let's see if you like this better." His thumb grazed her nipple before his forefinger circled it.

Lily hissed from the heat swirling throughout her body caused by his attention. Why did Max, of all men, have such an effect on her? Her hands tightened on his shoulders, kneading his muscles as his lips followed the path of his fingers. His mouth continued its magic while her fingers moved to his waist and worked their way under his shirt.

At her admistrations, his body tensed. His skin rippled

as her fingertips drifted over his ribs and along his back. Lily kissed the top his ear. "I think this shirt should go."

He leaned back on his knees, jerking his shirt over his head. It quickly landed on the floor.

Lily wasted no time in running her hands across his chest, teasing the light dusting of hair there, before he lowered himself against her again. As her skin met his, Max's lips found hers. She joined his heated kisses with those of her own.

She wanted all Max could offer.

Max's mouth slanted across Lily's. He couldn't get enough of her. Her sweet kisses. Her sexy body. Her sinuous touch. Everything about her called to him. He'd known that night at the conference there was something different about Lily, something special. A piece he was missing in his life. He wanted to discover it, experience it.

As his tongue tasted hers, Lily lifted her hips to meet his thick and straining manhood beneath his pants zipper.

Headlights of a car from the next-door neighbor's drive arced around the room.

Max lifted his head. Lily's living room, with the large, low windows, wasn't where they should be when they took this to the next stage. He didn't mind being a bit of an exhibitionist, but he had no doubt Lily wasn't into it.

"I think we need to take this to a place a little more private." Max sat back and pulled her up beside him. He handed Lily the first piece of clothing he came to, which was his shirt.

Lily slipped it over her head. Standing, he looked down at her. Would she put an end to the direction they were headed because of the interruption? He wouldn't pressure her to go where she didn't want to go, even if it might kill him.

Her gaze met his and she placed her hand in his. "Would my bedroom work?"

"It would be a good start."

She giggled. "Did you have somewhere else in mind?"

He grinned and raised a brow. "The kitchen table?"

She tugged him toward the hallway. "I'm thinking someplace softer."

Max bumped into her when she stopped abruptly as they reached her doorway.

"Are you okay?" He looked over her shoulder and searched the room.

"I just wanted you to know I don't bring men here."

Max placed a hand around her waist. Pulling her back against him, he nuzzled her neck. He needed to get them back to where they'd been. "I'm honored to be invited. Would you show me around?"

"Huh?" Lily stepped farther into the room. "There isn't much to show."

What he was particularly interested in was the bed. "No hot pink and ruffles. I'm a little disappointed."

Lily gave him a silly grin. "Ivy and I don't share the same décor taste."

"And I'm glad." He glanced around.

A bed with an upholstered yellow headboard faced the door. A spread in light blue and yellow covered it. An antique-looking nightstand with a lamp was positioned to the right. That must be Lily's side of the bed. In front of a double window sat a desk with a floral-cushion chair in the same colors as the spread. An old-fashioned wardrobe that had been painted a cream color was positioned on another wall.

She went to the windows and closed the colonial blinds, shutting out the world. The only light in the room came from the hall.

He sat on the bed. "Lily, will you come here?"

She studied him a moment. That aggressive woman in the living room had turned shy.

Max waited, patient outside but eager inside. Finally, she stepped toward him. She stopped an arm's length away. He took her hand and led her to stand between his legs. "You're cute in my shirt."

Lily glanced down. "I should've put mine on."

"Why, when I'm just going to take it off?" His hands went to her waist and slid up under the garment, gathering it as he went. "You're too amazing not to admire."

Lily lifted her arms, and he removed the shirt. His hands went to her hips and nudged her forward. He needed to touch her. Seconds later, his mouth found a nipple. Her fingers came to his shoulders, the nails biting into him. She moaned and leaned her head back. His manhood went rock-hard.

Max moved his mouth to her other breast. Finding the button of her pants, he released it, then pushed the material down her legs. He continued exploring her body as he removed her panties, then guided her onto the mattress beside him. The dim light washed over her beautiful curves. Lily took his breath away.

"You are so lovely." His mouth found hers.

Wrapping her arms around his waist, she tugged him to her. She shifted beneath him, her center finding his hard length, and pressed against him.

"Lily, I don't want to rush this, but if you keep that up, I'll be done before we start."

She smiled softly.

He placed a hand on her stomach. "I want to touch more of you."

Her gaze locked on him as his hand slid lower. Her muscles tensed beneath his palm as it wandered over her. Her fingers traveled across his chest. He teased her curls, and she lifted her hips. Max moved his index finger between her legs. For a moment, her legs tightened, halting the advancement. His mouth returned to hers and she relaxed. Unable to stand it any longer, his finger found her opening and entered.

Lily quivered, which only increased his need. Yet only her pleasure was his concern at that moment. Max pulled away. Lily made a sound of complaint. He reentered her and she flexed to meet him. His mouth found a breast once more. As he suckled her nipple, he continued the push-and-pull motion between her legs, enjoying Lily's grip on his finger.

She squirmed, her hips lifting. Seconds later, her back stiffened and she whimpered her release.

Max gazed at Lily. His heart thumped against his rib cage. Pride filled him. He'd put that look of pure bliss on her face. Had he ever seen anything so beautiful? He could watch that every day for the rest of his life.

"Aren't you going to take your pants off?" Lily's hand moved to the button of his shorts, which were barely containing his throbbing flesh.

When her small hand grazed the bulge as she worked to release the button, he came close to losing his tentative control.

"I think I better do that." He stood. Pulling his wallet out, he removed a condom, then stuffed the wallet back into his pocket. He quickly flipped the button open, unzipped and pushed his pants and underwear to his ankles before stepping out of them. As he moved, Lily watched him with her eyes wide and her bottom lip between her teeth.

He rolled on the protection. "Honey, I don't think I can wait any longer. I want you too badly."

She leaned up, took his hand and gave it a tug. "I want you too."

Max came over her where she lay in the middle of the bed. His mouth found hers as his manhood touched her entrance. With a flex of his hips, he entered her wet, heated center. He pushed deeper. Lily lifted to meet him. He pulled back and slid in fully. Her legs circled his waist, fixing him more securely to her.

His world swirled around him as he forgot everything but Lily and the pleasure building like hot lava within him. Her fingernails scraped across his back as she wiggled closer, then tensed before keening her delight.

Max grasped for his release, plunging deep and steady. With a grunt of supreme satisfaction, he found an orgasm like he'd never experienced before.

The rain continued to fall outside, and night had settled in. Lily snuggled into the warmth of Max's side. Her head lay on his arm. At her movement, his hand came to rest on her shoulder.

He vaguely remembered pulling the covers back and helping her under them before he joined her, pulling her close. Did he dare wish for this contentment to continue? No, he couldn't think like that. He would be gone in four days.

"What're you thinking?" Max's husky voice rumbled.

"How do you know I'm thinking anything?"

"Because I can feel the change in your body." His words were matter-of-fact, as if his explanation was a given.

Was he that in tune with her? He never experienced that before.

"I was just wondering…"

An emotion resembling fear filled him. Max rolled so he faced her. Even in the dim light, she could see his eyes watching her. Concern filled them. "Do you want me to go?"

Her chest tightened. "I thought you might want to."

Max brushed her cheek with the back of his hand. "I don't want to be anywhere but with you. Right here."

"That's nice, but I can't get used to having this. You're leaving in a few days."

"Yeah, but there are airplanes and long weekends, and—" he grinned "—conferences. Right now, why don't we not worry about the future and just enjoy the here and now? I have other things I'd rather be doing." He trailed a finger over her shoulder and down to her breast where he circled her nipple.

He enjoyed Lily's sweet shivered. Was it wrong to wish for more moments like this?

CHAPTER SEVEN

LILY'S EYES POPPED open at the feel of warm flesh beneath her hand. *Max*. He was still there. She wasn't used to waking up next to a man, especially a naked one, but she had to admit she liked it. Too much.

She'd certainly appreciated his support while Ivy was missing. Living through that nightmare without his encouragement would have made the situation unbearable. Jeff would have never been there for her like Max had been. Could she let go and believe he could be with her for more than just sex?

Even her parents had missed the signals where her emotions were concerned. They had loved her, but their focus had been on Ivy so much of the time. Max seemed to see her, understand her.

A large hand brushed across her hip.

She stopped herself from purring like a kitten. She looked over to find Max watching her. "You're still here."

"I said I would be. I thought I had proven you can trust me."

She lifted a shoulder. "But after last time..."

"You can't blame all of what happened on me."

"I guess not." Some of it had been her responsibility. But at the time, she hadn't been able to see that. She's wouldn't think about him maybe not being all she hoped for. She subconsciously harbored insecurity issues where he was concerned. "What time is it?"

She'd always had a good internal clock, but somehow when she was with Max, she lost track of time and everything else. He was changing her. Was that good or bad?

"Somewhere around seven, I think."

She threw off the covers. She'd forgotten she wore nothing and quickly picked up Max's shirt and jerked it in front of her.

"You do know I've seen and touched all of you." His eyes held a wicked gleam.

Heat washed over her body.

"You fascinate me. You're this take-charge woman everywhere but where your personal life is concerned. I'm sorry I had a part in making you so insecure. That was never my intention. From the first time I saw you, I thought you were someone special."

Her heart opened and took him in. Max's words were balm to her aching self-esteem. "That's sweet of you."

He rolled toward her, the sheet going low on his hips. "I'm not being sweet, I'm telling the truth."

"Thank you." As much as she would've liked to crawl back into bed, she couldn't. "I've got to go. Ivy gets antsy if she has to wait, and I need to see for myself she's okay."

"I don't blame you. I tell you what, while you get ready, I'll call the hospital and check on our patients."

She pulled his shirt over her head. "I plan to go in after I see Ivy."

He pushed the covers away and sat on the edge of the bed. "Take the day off. You've done an all-night surgery and worried over your sister, back-to-back. Even you aren't superhuman."

She forced herself not to push his shoulders back to the bed and climb on him. A naked Max in her bed, saying words she needed to hear, almost made her forget her responsibilities. "I have patients who depend on me."

"Yes, they do, and from everything I can tell, you have good fellows. Let them handle today. There are excellent nurses and all the other staff there to take care of them. You're just a phone call away if you're needed."

She placed her hands on her waist. "Are you telling me what to do?"

"Uh, no." He shook his head. "I'd never make that mistake. I'm merely suggesting. Come on, Lily. Cut yourself a little slack for once. You've already left a message with your nurse to reschedule your patients. Let's do something fun."

She went to her dresser and gathered her underwear. He did tempt her. She had him only a few more days after all.

"I'd like to spend the day with you." His eyes held a wicked gleam.

Lily couldn't disagree, but she should be careful not to get used to such attention. She stepped to Max, placing her hand on his chest. "I would like to, but I don't play hooky from work. People depend on me."

He removed her hand and kissed the palm. "Neither do I, but I do think you need a mental-health day, and you've already taken off this morning."

She screwed up her mouth and shook her head.

"I tell you what. Why don't you take the rest of the day off, and we'll stop in and see your patients this evening. Would that work?"

"Deal." She put out her hand.

Max stood, in all his naked glory, his hands going to

her forearms. He looked into her eyes. "I'd rather seal it with a kiss."

Lily leaned into him as his lips found hers. She clung to his shoulders as he took the kiss deeper.

"How much time do we have before you have to leave?" He asked between nips on her lips.

"Not long enough." She pushed away.

Max wiggled his brows and gave her a sexy grin. "We could save time by sharing a shower?"

At eleven, Max parked in front of Lily's house. She'd dropped him off at his hotel on her way to see Ivy. She'd told him she'd call him when she started back to her house. Her car wasn't in the drive, but he expected her soon.

Their night together had been more than he'd ever thought it might be. Lily had been his dream lover, willing, responsive, caring and just a little timid. He wasn't the type of guy who spent the night with a woman, few in fact, but Lily had him wanting to hold her for hours. All through tonight and tomorrow night, forever.

Forever?

At one time, he'd thought of marrying but as time moved on and no woman fit his ideal of what he wanted or needed, he'd let the idea drift by. He had no interest in the women his father thought would fit the James name. Despite that, he'd continued to date the splashy, socialite type, hoping he'd find someone who would fit his needs and please his father. Then he'd seen Lily at a conference. Her quiet, easy ways interested him, but sensing her wariness, he'd not approached her until that night. He sighed. What would his life be like now if he'd gotten to know her years ago?

But now the idea of marriage had returned as something he could embrace. In reality, he just wanted Lily any way he could have her. The question was: Did she feel the same?

His phone rang. The screen showed his father's name. Max braced himself, then answered. "Hi, Dad."

"Max, I was just checking in to see if you have convinced that woman to package her product with yours. We have to start marketing it soon."

Max's mouth drew into a thin line before he took a deep breath. "I'm doing fine. Thanks for asking."

"This isn't the time to be joking, Max. This is a big deal and could send our company into Fortune 500 status."

"Dad, it's not my company. It's yours. I'm a doctor."

"You know what I mean. I could use your medical insight on this project if you'd give it, but first we have to get her product."

"That *her* has a name. Dr. Lily Evans." Max didn't like his father treating Lily as if she and her feelings were unimportant. He didn't appreciate having it done to him, and he sure wasn't letting his father do it to Lily.

"Max—" his father's voice held a whiff of irritation "—have you or have you not spoken to her about the partnership?"

"I have."

"What did she say?"

"She's thinking about it." Which Max had encouraged.

"Then, nudge her along. I need this deal."

"I've already agreed to let you have the production of my glue. You don't have to have Lily's patch."

Everything with his father was a transaction. The only deal he'd never been able to make was the one keeping his son from following in his footsteps. Max had been called to medicine, and his father had done all he could to stop Max from following that dream. Max had been groomed as next in line to lead The James Company. His father hadn't given up on pulling him into the business, even after all these years. The problem remained that Max carried guilt over disappointing his father. He'd hoped his discovery of the glue and giving it to his father's corporation for production would improve their relationship. Sadly, he wasn't so sure that could or would ever happen.

His father continued as if Max had said nothing. "Yeah, but with the patch we could triple the price and demand."

Apparently, once again, what Max had accomplished wasn't good enough.

"Dad, I get it, but I know Lily, and pushing her isn't going to make her say yes until she's ready. If she ever agrees."

"You're calling her Lily. That must mean you know her pretty well?"

"We're friends." More than friends. He was thinking about a future with her that had nothing to do with his father's aspirations. Max had no interest in hearing his parent's view of Lily.

"Then use some of that charm I've heard about with women and get me a positive answer."

Anger bubbled in Max. He would never *charm* Lily into doing something she didn't want to do. With her he wasn't that playboy everyone said he was. "Dad, it's been good talking to you. See you soon. Bye."

His father said something, but Max had finished listening.

A tap on the window drew his attention. Lily's face was framed there. Max stepped out of his vehicle.

"I was wondering if you planned to get out of the car. Everything okay?"

"Sure it is." Max pushed his father's words away and smiled. "You're here, aren't you?"

She huffed. "Now you're turning on the Dr. James irresistible charm."

He put his arm around her waist and gave her a quick kiss. "You think I'm irresistible?"

Lily laughed. "You aren't going to trick me into feeding your ego."

They started toward the house.

As she opened the back door, she asked, "Now that we have the afternoon free, what do you want to do?"

He followed her inside. "I hope you don't mind. I already have something planned."

"You have?" She placed her purse on the table.

"Yep."

She faced him. "What're we doing?"

"You'll see. Bring your bathing suit. We should have a chance to swim." As Lily started down the hall, he lightly patted her on the butt. "Hurry."

Half an hour later, Max pulled into a marina. He took Lily's hand as they walked down the long pier. He couldn't have asked for a nicer day. The sky was clear, and there was a light breeze. Something had broken in him, falling away while being with Lily. She brought an easiness to his life. Acceptance was what she gave him. It soothed his soul.

"What're we doing here? Are we getting on a boat?"

Max squeezed her hand. "So many questions? Don't you like surprises?"

"I do, but—"

He gave her a quick kiss. "Then, be surprised."

Six slips down on the right, they stopped beside a yellow cigarette speedboat. Max climbed on.

"We're going somewhere in this?" Lily's voice rose an octave higher as she looked in wonder at the watercraft with the long, sleek, V-shaped hull.

"We are. You coming?" Max lifted his hand.

She grinned and took it. "Sure I am."

Max chuckled. Lily had a bit of an adventuress in her. He liked that. It had shown some in the shower this morning, but it was increasingly coming out now. Was there more where that came from? He hoped to find out.

He helped Lily down. She came to stand between the two captain chairs and the bench seat behind them. Lily placed her hand on the windshield, which ran from side to side across the craft. "Wow. This is some boat."

"I'm glad you like it." Max climbed out and released the bowline, then the stern ropes before climbing back in. Taking the driver's seat, he started the engine, which roared, then settled into a purr. He had to agree the boat was a fine water machine.

Lily settled into the other seat with a look of amazement on her face. "I've never been on a cigarette boat."

"You've lived in Miami for years and never been out on one of these?" He maneuvered out of the slip.

Lily shrugged. "I haven't had a chance or anyone to go with. You do know how to handle a boat this powerful?"

Max stood to see the water around them as they moved at idle speed out of the marina. "I do. I own one similar at home. Happier now?"

"An ocean is a lot different than the Hudson River or the East River in New York." She looked at another boat passing them, going in the opposite direction.

"Big water is still water. We aren't going that far out. Settle back and enjoy the ride. You worry too much."

"Somebody has to think about these things." Lily eased back in the chair, looking more relaxed despite her words. "Since people like you don't seem to let anything bother you."

Little did she know. "Hey, I didn't mean to start an argument. The afternoon is too beautiful to waste bickering. But then again, I might enjoy making up."

Lily felt heat washed over her. She had no doubt from Max's grin that he'd been rewarded by her blush, which had nothing to do with the sun beaming down on them. Sex with Max had been… She had no words. Freeing, liberating, extraordinary, mind-blowing. Maybe she did have words, but they were inadequate. He'd been attentive, caring, tender. Max had seen to her pleasure before he'd considered his own. She'd had no idea what sex could really be like until Max. He'd made sure she felt desired and satisfied again and again.

She would have described herself as a conservative sexual partner until she'd had sex in the shower with Max. In fact, that had been another of Jeff's complaints about her. Max hadn't seemed disappointed. She smiled. From the way Max acted, she had satisfied him, completely.

But more than that he'd been there for her when Ivy had been missing. Jeff had been all about himself. His job, his problems and his pleasure. He would have never spent an evening with her if there had been a problem with Ivy. Max was so much more of a man than Jeff had ever been. She had wasted too much time mourning Jeff's leaving. Instead, she should be glad he wasn't in her life anymore.

Max had opened an entire new world for her. She looked at him. Even now, he had her body at a low hum. It excited her.

Despite her initial guilt of not going to the hospital, she was enjoying herself. The day couldn't be more beautiful, and she'd never felt better about life. She was having fun. When was the last time she'd been able to say that?

"Have you spent any time boating?" Max glanced at her, then looked back at the water ahead.

"What?"

"Boats. Do you know anything about them?"

Max had caught her daydreaming. Of him. "Not much, but I love them. I like being out on the water."

"When we're out into a less-congested area, how would you like to drive?"

A thump of excitement filled her chest. "Could I?"

Max gave the boat a little more speed. "Sure. Do you know why they call this a cigarette boat?"

Lily pulled a hat out of the bag sitting at her feet and put it on her head. "No. But by the look on your face, you do."

"I do. The boat design reminded the inventor of a cigarette. Long and sleek. Hold on to your hat. I'm going to give it a more speed." Max pushed the throttle forward.

They moved out into more open water.

Lily placed a hand on top of her head to prevent the hat from blowing off, then raised her chin, appreciating the wind and warmth of the sun. A thrill went through her as she they skipped over the water, the small waves making a thumping sound against the hull.

Max pulled back on the speed as they approached a wide inlet.

"Is something wrong?" she called to him.

"No."

"Then, what're we doing?"

He grinned. "I thought you might like a water tour of the rich and famous."

She stood up beside him, holding tight to the top of the windshield. "That sounds like fun."

Max slowed the boat to a crawl.

"How did you know where to come?"

He pulled a piece of paper out of his back pocket and grinned. "The marina master gave me some ideas. What did you think? I'd give you a cheap tour?"

"I never doubted you for a moment."

"Now, this house up here on the right belongs to a famous singer. The guy at the marina couldn't remember her name."

Lily laughed. It felt so wonderful to do so. For once, it was good to be alive. Think or not think about something besides work and Ivy.

"This next one belongs to a baseball player." Max pointed to one pale pink mansion whose bright green lawn came to the edge of the water, where an inboard motorboat rocked against a pier.

"It's gorgeous, isn't it?" Lily studied the place that reminded her of a gleaming jewel.

"How about this next one? A football player lives there."

She laughed. "How did you guess that, given the football goal in the yard?"

Max teased. "Hey, you have to give your tour guide some credit."

The wind picked up and Lily said, "Let me have that paper so you can drive."

He handed it to her as they continued to troll along the narrowing waterway.

Lily pointed to a house farther down. "I like this one. The yellow and cream. Let me see who lives there." She searched the list. "I can't find a name for this one."

"Apparently, someone rich but not famous." Max made a wide turn and headed back the way they'd come but staying to the other side of the channel.

"These are really beautiful houses with amazing yards, but they are too much..." She watched the houses going by.

"Too much what?"

"Too big, too much to clean, too many taxes."

Max looked at her. "You wouldn't like to live in one of these?"

Something about the way he asked the question made her think her answer mattered to him. "Heavens no, I really love my bungalow."

"I like it too. It feels much more like home than my apartment." His attention stayed on the water.

"I bet yours is in one of those ultramodern apartment buildings on the top floor."

His mouth quirked upward on one side. "It's on the second floor from the top. I don't spend much time there. Mostly, it's a place to eat, dress and sleep."

"I bet you're out on the town all the time." She didn't like to think of him with other women. It hadn't taken but one night with him to make her possessive.

He chuckled. "More like, at the hospital or in a lab."

"I thought you were a good-time guy." Lily tried to sound teasing, but her tone made her words fall flat.

"You can't believe everything you hear."

Her attention turned away from the houses to him. "Then, tell me something true about yourself."

"I like to think I'm a good guy. Dependable, honest and loyal."

She liked his answers. From what she could tell, they were true. "Those are all great qualities. If you weren't a doctor, what would you be doing?"

"I guess I'd be working in my father's company. That's what he groomed me for."

She noted the undercurrent of negativity in his voice. "But you didn't want that?"

"No, much to his disappointment. I've wanted to be a doctor since I was a kid and broke my arm when I fell out of a tree."

"You fell out of a tree? How far up were you?" Lily turned to see him clearly.

"In the top. It wasn't a supertall tree, but it was high enough."

She wanted to know about the boy he had been. "How old were you?"

"Eight, almost nine."

She could imagine a young Max with missing teeth, a grin and laughter in his eyes. "What did the doctor who set your arm do that made you decide then to become a doctor?"

"I don't know that it was him per se, but the idea that he could put something broken in the human body together again amazed me. I thought then I'd like to do that. There's a wonder to our work. Even today, I feel it."

Lily like this thoughtful side of Max. The one who was in awe of and had pride in his work.

"But not everyone sees it that way."

"Like whom?" Who wouldn't see how great Max was as a person and a doctor?

"My father."

"He doesn't like you being a surgeon?" She couldn't believe that. Max had too much talent to not be doing surgery.

"He'd rather me use my medical knowledge and clout to help expand his company."

She saw his hands tighten on the steering wheel. "And you have no wish for that?"

"Not even a little bit. I've never had any interest in business. I like the hands-on of operating. Of working with people. I hate paperwork, which I'm reminded of by medical records often. But my father can't seem to accept that, even to this day."

Lily shook her head sadly. His bitterness rang clear in his voice. "It would be a huge loss to the liver-transplant community if we lost you."

Max's bright smile brought one to her lips. "Thanks for that. It's nice to know someone has faith in me." He gave her hand a quick squeeze. "You better sit down. I'm getting ready to speed up."

She took her seat and held on to her hat as they sped across the water. When they were away from the boat traffic and in open water, Max slowed and stopped.

"Is something wrong?" Lily looked around. She could see boats only as specks in the distance.

"No. I thought you wanted a turn at being the captain."

Lily stuffed her hat in the bag and scrambled out of the seat. "I sure do." She moved over beside him. "Tell me what to do." She placed her hand on the steering wheel and one on the throttle.

Max chuckled. "I like a woman I don't have to ask twice."

She grinned over her shoulder.

"Okay, all you have to do is push the throttle forward and pull back to slow down. You have to get pretty fast to plane off."

"Are you ready?"

He moved back in the seat. She stood between his legs. "I'm ready."

Lily shoved the throttle and the powerful engine roared as the water rolled. The front end of the boat came up. She slowly gave it more gas. The long hull stood high, making it difficult to see.

Max put his hand over hers and thrust the throttle further forward. "You're going to have to give it more speed to get it to plane out."

The front lowered so she could see the horizon in the distance. Max's hands came to her waist. She liked his steady presence behind her.

As she entered a turn, Max put his hand on the wheel and eased them back into a wider arch. "You can't turn too tightly. We don't want to roll over."

"Aye-aye, Captain."

His hands returned to her waist, and she spent another half an hour enjoying the freedom of the water, wind and weight of Max's hands resting on her. Pulling the throttle toward her, the boat settled in the water.

"That was so much fun." Excitement still ran through her.

Max turned the switch off and the engine quieted. "Are you ready for lunch?"

"We're going to eat all the way out here?" She looked at the ocean surrounding them and the land in the distance.

"Sure, why not?" Max moved her hair away from her neck, kissed it, then nudged her out of the way.

She looked at the sky. "Don't tell me you're having our lunch helicoptered in."

"I didn't think about that, but it would've been impressive."

"Are you trying to impress me?" She studied him a moment.

He looked at her. "You know, I think I might be." Max sounded as surprised as she felt. "But I've messed up with the helicopter. I just had the hotel fix a picnic basket, and I put it and a cooler in when I rented the boat this morning. Not so impressive."

Lily stopped Max with a hand on his arm. She cupped his face in her fingers and kissed him. "Believe me, I'm impressed. This is the nicest day I can remember spending in a long time. Thank you."

"You're welcome." Max smiled, then pulled up one of the seat cushions on the back bench. He removed a basket and blanket, handing them to her. He set aside another cushion and lifted out a small cooler. Moving around her, he climbed the three small steps between the front seats and stepped over the windshield.

"What're you doing?"

He stood on the hull of the boat. "I'm going to set out our picnic."

"We're eating up there?" Had Max lost his mind?

"We are."

"We won't fall off?" She looked out over the water.

"I don't plan to." He offered his hand. "Give me your hand and I'll help you over."

Lily went up the steps and took his hand. As Max steadied her, she climbed over the shield and found her footing.

"This area up here is plenty big." Max set the basket down and spread out the blanket.

The breeze flipped the edges, and Lily carefully stepped to help him.

"Go ahead and sit on it." Max placed a foot at the corner.

Lily sat, smoothing out the area around her.

Max picked up the cooler and put it aside while he went after the basket. He returned and set it down in the middle of the blanket before he lowered himself beside it.

Lily watched as he removed their lunch. Shrimp cocktail, a tomato salad and crackers. "This looks wonderful."

"I figured you'd had a big breakfast with Ivy and would like something light for lunch."

"This is perfect." He was perfect. And thoughtful.

"Will you open things while I get the drinks?" Max pulled the cooler toward him.

Lily picked up the crackers. As she ate, she looked out over the blue-green water. "Thanks for doing this. It truly is amazing. I would've never dreamed of eating on the front of a boat like this. Or out here on the water."

He grinned. "What about being with me?"

She was grateful for her dark glasses. "Especially that."

Max chuckled.

Lily quickly said, "But I'm glad I am."

"Aw, and she says all the right things. I'm flattered."

Feeling contrite, she touched his arm. "I meant it."

Max kissed her. "I know you do. I'm glad I'm here with you. You didn't tell me how it went with Ivy this morning."

"Fine."

"Did you talk about her running away?" He dipped a shrimp in the sauce.

"She told me what'd happened. I reminded her that I worry about her. She cried. I did too. She promised not to ever do it again."

"Will she keep that promise?"

Max acted relaxed and nonchalant, but she had no doubt he watched and listened carefully. "I believe she will. We talked about voicing our feelings. Asking if she could call me."

He nodded. "Sounds reasonable. What did she get mad about?"

"She wants to work outside the compound at a shoe store. Some of the residents work off the property and she's asked to."

"So why doesn't she?" Max picked up his bowl of salad.

"Because I told the administrator I didn't think it was a good idea. I worry about her getting led astray by someone or taking the wrong bus." She shrugged. "Anything could happen."

"You're probably right." He shrugged.

Something in his tone made her think that wasn't all he thought, but the day had been too wonderful for them to fight, so she said no more.

They ate in silence for a while. Lily listened to the lap of the water against the boat and the sound of the seagulls above. Finished with her meal, she lay on the blanket with her hands behind her head and closed her eyes. "What do you see your future like?"

Max whistled. "Wow, you went deep with that question."

"I'm sorry. That's not really any of my business. I was

just thinking how often what we think life will be like doesn't end up like that at all."

"You're right about that. Mine hasn't turned out the way I thought."

"How's that?" Suddenly, she wasn't as sleepy as she had been.

"I thought I'd be settled down with a wife and family by now. Even a dog."

She liked listening to his deep, warm voice. "I'm surprised. You have never struck me as the kind of guy who thinks about those sorts of things."

"Just because I like to enjoy life doesn't mean that I don't want those things too. What do you want? Besides to take care of Ivy."

She sighed. How would he react if she told him? She given up on even thinking about having a man in her life after Jeff. She hadn't thought she could trust another guy. Wasn't sure she could take a chance on Ivy becoming attached to someone who would let them down again. Then came Max. She'd started to dream again. But she needed to put a stop to that. Except Jeff had used her. Max would never do that. "I want that, of course, but I'd like to have a baby."

"What about a husband to go with that baby?"

Was he volunteering? "Sure. I want what my parents had. I want to find someone who I can be happy with."

"I don't think happiness is something we plan for but something that happens. Everyone defines happiness by different guidelines. My father sees it as dollars and cents. You see it as a baby."

"And you?" She opened her eyes just enough to watch his expression.

He leaned back on his palms and crossed his legs at the ankles. He looked like he belonged to the world of fast boats and leisurely afternoons, as if he had no cares in the world. "I was thinking that right now. With you, I'm about as happy as I've ever been."

"Are you trying to sweet-talk me?"

His grin flashed, showing straight white teeth. "Do I need to?"

She placed her hand over her heart. "No woman wants to be thought of as easy."

"There's the Lily that I know so well. I assure you I don't think you're easy. It has taken me years to get to know you. Now I have, I want to know all."

"There's not much to know."

"I'm not sure that's true. Like, have you thought any more about us marketing our product together?"

She closed her eyes again. A trickle of caution ran through her. Was Max just being nice to her because he wanted something? "Is it really that important to you that I agree to packaging Skintec with your glue?"

"I wish I could say no, but yeah, it is. It means a lot to my father. It would make him very happy. But I want you to do what you think is right. That is the most important thing." He sounded encouraging and disappointed at the same time. What was going on between him and his father?

"You sure know how to apply the pressure."

He brushed a strand of hair off her face. "It isn't my intent to make you feel that way. Make the decision that you think you need to. I just wanted to answer you honestly."

She could appreciate that. The only thing about them going into business together is that they would forever be bound. What if something went wrong between them? "We would always be partners."

"Would that be so bad? I thought we had become friends."

For her, what she felt was more than friendship. She should have been more careful. "We have."

"You can trust me. I'll always have your best interests at heart. I never want to hurt you, on a personal level or a business one."

"That's a big promise."

"It is, but I mean it." He leaned over her, covering her lips with his.

Max did mean it. Lily had become too important for him to ever intentionally do anything that would hurt her. He'd been looking for the right woman for a long time, and he believed he'd found her in Lily. He wouldn't ruin what was between them, even for his father.

Her arms came around his neck and he held her tighter. He wanted moments like this one for the rest of his life. His hand slid under her tank top and over her belly to her breasts. Cupping one, he teased it until her nipple stood tight against the thin padding that covered it.

Lily moaned and wiggled against him.

His hand left her breast and traveled over her middle to flip open the button of her shorts. She pulled at his shirt. He leaned away long enough to pull it over his head. Lily wasted no time in moving her hands all over his chest. Taking her lips again, he pushed at her shirt raising it and pushing her bra away until she was bare to his touch. He took a moment to admire her in the sunlight before his mouth covered her nipple and tugged.

Lily arched to meet him as her fingers tunneled through his hair.

He reached around her and unclipped her bra giving him full excess to her breasts. "You're so beautiful."

"Mmm."

The sound of a boat in the distance registered, making him pull back to see if they were going to have company. He didn't see anyone, but he wasn't going to take a chance on them being caught unaware. She would never forgive him if she was put in an embarrassing situation.

"I think we need to take this to a place a little more secluded. I wouldn't want to share you with anyone who happens to come too close." With great effort, he pushed away.

Lily sat up, looking dazed.

Max brushed a finger over her cheek. "I like that look on you. It makes me feel good."

She tugged on her shirt, covering herself.

"Don't get too tidy. Because I don't plan to let you stay that way." He quickly gathered their meal debris and stuffed it in the basket before dropping the container into the passenger seat. He pulled her to her feet and gathered the blanket. Throwing it into the bottom of the boat, he stepped over the windshield and helped her follow.

"Wait here a moment." He let her go, picked up the blanket and spread it out over the floor. He lay down on his side, propped his head on his hand and patted the area next to him. "Join me."

Lily looked at him a moment before she lowered herself to her knees and leaned down to kiss him. She nudged his shoulders back and straddled his hips. His hands found her waist, fingertips gripping her tender skin. Her center moved lower, rubbing over his straining manhood.

Max pulled her shirt and loose bra over her head in seconds.

Lily, in an unexpected show of boldness, offered him her breasts like ripe fruit waiting for just him to enjoy their sweetness. He took her gift and feasted on the beauty above him. Lily with her head thrown back and the sun blazing behind her heated his blood. He had to have her.

She kneaded his shoulders as his tongue laved her breasts, first one then the other. His hand slid down to her thighs, moving under her shorts until his finger found her center, wet with want.

Her sweet mouth found his. He would have never guessed this hot, wanton woman lived quietly behind that subdued–Dr. Evans veneer. He liked this Lily. A lot.

Teasing her heated opening a moment, he then plunged inside her. She pushed down on his fingers wanting more.

"Take your pants off," she growled as she crawled off him.

As she removed her shorts and panties, he stood to do the same with his clothes. She looked at him with such brashness and admiration his chest swelled. They stood naked to the world as her hand wrapped around him, timid and testing.

To his amazement he grew at her touch. Hadn't he been harder than he'd ever been already? He caressed her hip to her thigh and back.

"I've never seen or felt a man like this. You are, uh, marvelous."

No other man had ever let her enjoy his body? What

selfish lovers they all must have been. He grinned. "I'm all yours for as long as you want."

She continued to grip him while stroking his chest. She kissed his shoulder, his neck on her way to his mouth. There she tugged his bottom lip with her teeth.

At this rate, Lily might kill him, but he would die with a smile on his face. He cupped her perfect behind and found her center. She spread her legs, letting him touch her freely. His finger located her special spot and Lily tensed, stopping her movements, and looked at him, eyes wide.

"I want to watch you come for me. I want you to see who's giving you pleasure." He wanted her never to doubt he was the one that could do so like no other.

She twisted and pushed down on his finger. Her gaze never waved from his. A wild look more beautiful than he'd seen ever before filled her eyes.

He pulled from her. She groaned displeasure. After he reached for his pants to pull out a packet he guided her to the blanket. Lily threw her leg over him, straddling him. Her hot center ran the distance of his manhood. It was his turn to groan.

"Lily, if you keep that up, I'm going to be a goner."

"I don't care," she murmured as she moved again, this time more slowly.

"But I want this to be about us, not just me." The truth of that shocked him.

She pressed against him a sassy grin on her lips.

"Stop teasing me, and let me get this on." He held up the square package.

Lily moved back and took the protection from him and slowly rolled it over his length.

"You are trying to be the death of me." He moved to

roll her beneath him, but she held steady and slowly slid over him, taking him completely.

Her look of supreme satisfaction filled him with hot desire, but he didn't act on it, preferring to let Lily have her way with him. She gave him painfully sweet pleasure like he'd never had before as she rose so high that she almost lost him before she dipped down to take him into her again with a deep rush.

Unable to stand it any longer, he rose up to meet her, then turned her on her back and plunged hard and fast. Lily's eyes flew open. She looked at him in surprise as her hands bit into his sides and her body shuddered.

She remained suspended a moment before she shook and relaxed. "Oh my goodness."

He gave her a quick kiss, then pumped into her like a desperate man. With a roar, he found a shattering release. He fell to his back beside her and pulled Lily to him.

How could he ever leave her?

CHAPTER EIGHT

LILY COULDN'T BELIEVE how easy and natural it was for her and Max to spend the morning getting ready for work together. It was what she believed it must be like for a settled couple. Hadn't it been the same with her parents? Jeff had never stayed over. In fact, more than once, she'd thought him too eager to leave. Would it always be this right between her and Max?

She feared she'd like it too much. They lived thousands of miles away from each other. What kind of relationship could they have? She needed to think straight. Less like a dreamy-eyed woman who'd just gotten out of bed after heavenly morning sex and more like the practical professional she was.

She looked at Max across her kitchen table.

He grinned. "What?"

"Nothing." Her heart whipped into race speed. Just like that, she basked in the warmth of having Max in her life.

That sexy grin she'd come to love spread across his lips. "I wouldn't look at me that way if you don't intend to keep your patients waiting."

"I'd better not." Lily stood and picked up her plate. She grinned down at him. "Even if I might like to."

He caught her by the wrist as she moved by him. He tugged her into his lap. "Being a few minutes late wouldn't be so bad."

She kissed him. "No, not so bad, but I really need to be on time. I'd like to see Mr. Roth before I go to clinic." Reluctantly she stood and continued to the kitchen sink.

"Then, I'll be ready to go in ten minutes."

She had to remind herself life wasn't all fun and games. More often than not, it didn't go the way she wanted it to. Didn't the fact Max was leaving soon prove that? It probably didn't even matter to him. The best she could tell, Max became truly serious only when he was in the operating room.

At the hospital, they went straight to ICU to see Mr. Roth.

"It looks like you're resting well." She looked at her patient's chart. "I'm glad to see it."

"Much better. Except for the new scar," Mr. Roth said.

"It won't be long before you'll be up and moving around." Max checked out the medicine pump behind Mr. Roth's head.

"Dr. James is right. You should go to the floor this afternoon and be home in a couple of days." Lily smiled at the man.

Mr. Roth gave her a wry smile. "I already feel better."

"That's what I like to hear." Lily handed the nurse the chart.

Mr. Roth looked from her to Max. "I have you and Dr. James to thank for that."

"I just happened to be along. Dr. Evans is a brilliant surgeon," Max assured Mr. Roth.

Lily couldn't deny she liked hearing Max's praise.

"Don't let him fool you. Dr. James is the one who saw the spot causing the trouble."

"Either way, I'm glad to have you both there to fix me up," Mr. Roth assured them.

"Glad to do it." She patted him on the shoulder. "See you later this afternoon." Lily walked out of ICU with a feeling of success, and oddly, she didn't mind sharing it with Max.

As they made their way to the clinic building, Lily couldn't believe that Max had been there just over a week. It seemed he'd been in her life forever. Carol, the nurse, was waiting on them when they arrived at her wing of exam rooms.

"I don't think I have a horribly long clinic today." She glanced at the printed list the nurse handed her.

"I'll have to leave you at ten-thirty. I have a lunch meeting with Dr. Lee."

"What's going on between you two?" This was his and Dr. Lee's second meeting. She walked to the first exam room door and Max followed.

"Is that jealousy I hear?" Matt's eyes narrowed.

"It is not!"

He leaned close and said for her ears only, "I like the idea of you being jealous."

Lily huffed. "You need to get that idea out of your head."

"You're saying you don't care?" He grinned, but his eyes held no humor.

Thankfully, she opened the door to the exam room, giving her an opportunity not to answer. Did she dare share with Max how much she did care? What would happen if she did?

She had seen five of her patients when she glanced at

the list to find Mr. Cruz's name next. She liked the man, but he could be too aggressive. Yet he did feed her self-esteem. He still had a difficult time with boundaries.

"What's the story on this next patient?" Max asked, moving around to look over her shoulder.

She handed Max the pad and knocked on the door. "Here, see for yourself."

Max took it.

She entered the room, leaving the door open. "Mr. Cruz, it's good to see you."

The young man, dressed in a sports coat, knit shirt and tan slacks, stood. "I've asked you to call me Miguel, Dr. Evans."

She quirked her mouth to the side and shook her head. "How've you been feeling?"

"Pretty good. That medicine you gave me last time really helped."

"I'm glad to hear it. How about sitting on the exam table for me and letting me have a look at you?"

"Certainly." He glanced at Max, who had just entered.

Lily nodded toward Max. "This is Dr. James. He's visiting with us this week."

"Hello," Max said.

"Hi. You're a lucky man to be hanging out with Dr. Evans. She's the best."

"I can't disagree with that," Max looked down at the pad. "How long have you had hepatitis C?"

"Aw, about ten years. It showed up when I was a senior in high school," Mr. Cruz said, but he watched her carefully as she listened to his heart, then lungs.

"Lay down for me and let me check your liver." She stepped away.

He removed his jacket and shirt then climbed up again putting his back on the cushion table.

Lily had to admit he was fit looking. "Are you still running daily?"

"Yes, but I only go in the early morning when it isn't so hot."

"Smart thing to do. Now, lie still for me and let me push around on you some." She rubbed her hands together, warming them. "They're going to be cold. Sorry."

"Cool hands, warm heart is what I've always heard." Mr. Cruz grinned.

Lily smiled as she pushed on her patient's middle, just below his right ribs. "I wouldn't count on that. Let me know if anything hurts." She felt for the ridge of his liver and around the sides. It was enlarged more than it had been six months earlier.

"I don't like that look on your face, pretty doctor," Mr. Cruz said.

"The disease is progressing. We're going to need to talk about a plan of action sooner rather than later."

As if she had said nothing life changing, Mr. Cruz teased, "Hey, doc. I don't like it when you frown. Put that smile back on your face. You'll figure it out."

Lily sure hoped he was right.

Max cleared his throat. "Do you mind if I examine you?"

Mr. Cruz's attention moved to Max and his demeanor turned more serious. "Sure, I guess."

Max moved in close as she stepped out of his way. Lily watched as Max efficiently palpated the same spot she had.

When he finished, he backed away. "Thanks, Mr. Cruz."

"You can get dressed now," Lily said as she took the

pad from Max and typed in her findings. "I'd like to see you back in three months. If you start feeling bad in any way, call me."

Mr. Cruz grinned. "Even if it's for a drink."

She chuckled. "I've already told you that I don't date my patients."

Mr. Cruz shrugged. "You can't blame a guy for trying."

Lily started toward the door. "I'll see you here in *three* months then."

Max entered the hall and closed the door. He hissed, "That man was flirting with you!"

"Ah, he's just teasing. He doesn't mean anything by it. His just one of those South Beach guys living off his father's money. He's harmless."

"Didn't look harmless to me." Max's face was all tight angles and clenched jaw.

Lily studied him a moment, then walked to the next examination room. The warmth of satisfaction rippled through her. She whispered, "Is that jealousy I hear?"

"You're damn right it is," he spat.

She liked feeling wanted by a man who could have anybody he desired. With a spring in her step, she entered the exam room.

Two patients later, Max led her into an empty room and closed the door.

"What's going on?" Puzzlement made her search Max's face.

"I have to leave, and I didn't want to do it until I've kissed you."

If he was looking for a way to make her puddle at his feet with a sigh of contentment, that had been the thing to say.

Max took her into his arms and gave her a kiss that had her clinging to him. He stepped back, his breath ragged. "I think that's enough in a public place and with you still having patients to see." He walked to the door. "Why don't I take you to dinner tonight?"

She missed his warmth already. Her mouth tightened in disappointment. "I'm sorry. Fridays are when Ivy comes to the house and spends the night."

"Chicken strips and tater tots are on the menu, then?"

She grinned. "Actually, she asked for spaghetti and meatballs tonight."

"That's one of my favorites."

Was Max fishing for an invitation? "Would you like to join us for dinner?"

He quickly said, "I thought you'd never ask."

She laughed. "You really do get excited about spaghetti and meatballs."

"I'm sure I'll enjoy the food, but the dinner company is what I'm really interested in." He took a step toward her.

Sadness washed through her. "You can't spend the night. Ivy wouldn't understand. I don't want to confuse her."

He nodded. "I understand. But I don't have to like it."

What Lily didn't say was that she didn't want Ivy to become invested in Max if he wouldn't be around permanently. The chances for that happening weren't great. She rarely included Ivy in her relationships, but Lily had so little time left with Max, she didn't want to give up any more than she had to.

"Call me when you're finished meeting with Dr. Lee, and hopefully, I'll be done with rounds. We'll head home."

"I'm looking forward to that part." Max gave her a quick kiss and opened the door.

* * *

Max waited only long enough to put the two bags of groceries he held down on Lily's kitchen table before he took her in his arms and kissed her soundly.

"What's that all about?" Lily watched him with bright eyes.

"I've missed you."

"We've been together the last hour."

"Yeah, but I didn't have a chance to kiss you and I missed doing so." He'd found himself thinking about her the entire time he was meeting with Dr. Lee.

Lily rewarded him with smile. Yes, he could stand having that expression in his life every day. Lily was looking at him like he was her favorite candy.

After they left the hospital, they had stopped by a bodega to pick up some items Lily needed for the evening meal. He had followed her around the small store, holding a basket while she placed pasta and vegetables into it. He couldn't remember the last time he'd done something so domestic. It must have been when he was very small, because for most of his life a cook had prepared the family meals. What made the activity particularly interesting was he'd enjoyed every minute of his and Lily's shopping stop.

Lily seemed as meticulous about buying her groceries as she was about everything else she did. He smiled when she picked up a brownie mix box and placed it in the basket. "I think I'd like to have these for dessert tonight. Maybe à la mode."

Max liked her mischievous grin. "That sounds good."

"Men like ice cream, I understand." She looked over her shoulder at him.

"I don't know about other men, but I do." He stepped close to her. "I like other things too."

Lily rewarded him with a blush and a shy smile. "Behave."

He liked teasing her. She always gave him such an enticing reaction. As if other men in her life had never done so.

Lily nudged him away, then stepped to the kitchen counter and began unloading one of the bags. "I need some space. I have to get the sauce started before I leave to get Ivy."

"I can do that for you, if you think Ivy wouldn't mind."

Lily stopped midmovement and looked at him. "Are you sure?"

"I wouldn't volunteer if I wasn't."

Lily didn't say anything for a moment, still watching him with a mixture of amazement and concern. Finally, she responded, "I'll call and ask her. She does know you, but I've never had anyone else pick her up."

"Why not?" Had her boyfriend never had any interaction with the sister Lily was so devoted to?

"Mostly because they never asked to."

Her ex must have been as self-centered as Max had gathered.

"Let me call. I'd need to do so anyway to let them know someone else is coming to get her."

Lily quickly spoke to Ivy. A smile reached her eyes after whatever Ivy said. Seconds later, Lily spoke to someone else, telling them Max would be by to get Ivy before she ended the conversation.

"I guess it was okay with Ivy."

Lily nodded. "Better than okay with her. It seems you've charmed another Evans woman."

Max pulled her to him. “Maybe so, but I’m only interested in kissing the one in my arms.” His lips found hers.

It took Max thirty minutes in light traffic to get to where Ivy lived. He shouldn’t have been surprised at the lovely place with its more decorative-than-restrictive gate and stucco walls. He requested entrance through a speaker. Soon, he drove along a circular drive, around a green manicured yard with groupings of furniture under low trees. He pulled in front of a low white building with lush plants and landscaping. If he hadn’t known better, he would have believed it was an exclusive country club or retirement center.

Lily must pay a great deal for Ivy to live there.

He parked beneath a portico. Sitting in one of the rocking chairs nearby was Ivy. She wore a big smile as she jumped up and waved at him. “Hi, Max.”

“Hello, Ivy. It’s nice to see you again.”

“I’m ready to go.” She picked up a bag near one of the large wooden double doors that were the entrance to the place.

“Shouldn’t we go inside and let somebody know you’re leaving?”

She thought for a moment. “Yeah, I’ll do that.”

“I think that’s the smart thing to see to all the time. You don’t want anyone to have to worry about you.”

Her face darkened. “I made Lily worry.”

Max patted her shoulder. “I know, but it’s all right now. The thing is to try not to do it again.”

Ivy’s face brightened. “I won’t. I’ll talk to someone about my feelings.”

Max grinned. “That would be the right idea. Now, let’s go tell someone you’re leaving. Lily has spaghetti waiting for us.”

"It's one of my favorites."

"Mine too." Matt opened one of the doors for her.

Minutes later, they were back at the car. Matt picked up Ivy's bag and placed it in the trunk.

"Can we ride with the top down?" Ivy asked.

"Sure, it's a nice afternoon." He pushed the button to lower the covering.

Ivy watched in rapt attention as the top slowly folded behind the back seat. By the time it settled, she had scrambled into the front.

Max scooted behind the driving wheel. "Buckle up."

Ivy did as she was told without question, then started talking and asking questions without pause. Max patiently answered them and, a number of times, chuckled at her reaction.

They were almost to Lily's house when Ivy's voice turned serious. "You like my sister, don't you?"

"Yes, of course I do." He smiled at her. "I like you too."

"I mean *like* like her."

A traffic light ahead had turned red, and he waited until he'd stopped before answering. His look met Ivy's. "Yes, I *like* like your sister."

"You kiss her?"

"I like kissing her very much." This interview made him almost as uncomfortable as the one he'd had with his first date's father. He had the distinct feeling his and Lily's relationship hung on how well he answered Ivy's questions.

"Jeff made her cry. He didn't like me."

"I promise not to make Lily cry." Max made sure to look Ivy in the eyes.

"Good." She nodded her head. "I like you."

Max chuckled. That might have been the highest praise he'd ever received. "I like you too."

As soon as he pulled into the driveway, the back door opened and Lily came to meet them as if she had been watching eagerly for them. She wore a large smile. It hit him in the chest just how much he did care for Lily. Somehow, she made the world brighter for him. He'd never thought he'd feel this way about anyone. This is what it felt like, being enough for someone. To measure up, to have them be proud of you for just being you. The feeling had eluded him until Lily came along. Wasn't this sense of belonging what he'd been looking for all his adult life? To arrive home to a greeting from Lily every day would be an amazing gift. It would be something he'd never take for granted.

Lily looked between him and Ivy.

Max gave her a reassuring smile.

Ivy popped out of the car and went to Lily. "Max put the top down. It was so much fun. He told me to buckle."

Lily gave her an indulgent grin, then a hug. "I'm glad to see you."

It crossed his mind that Lily would make a good mother. He'd never thought about a woman he was interested in being in that role. That was one of Lily's greatest attributes, she truly cared about people.

"Come on inside. Supper is almost ready." Lily started toward the back door. Once in the kitchen, she said, "Ivy, why don't you put your bag in your room." As soon as Ivy was out of hearing distance, Lily turned to him. "How did it go?"

"Just fine."

Lily's face softened and she gave him an adoring look.

"Thank you for being so nice to my sister. I've never seen her look happier."

"I don't find it hard to spend time with her."

Lily kissed him on the cheek. "You're a special guy."

Max reached for her and pulled her close. "I like that you think so." He gave her a tender kiss.

The rest of the evening was spent talking and laughing over dinner.

They were almost finished when Max said, "You know the one thing I haven't seen while I've been down here is an alligator. I've never been to the Everglades."

"I would like to see an alligator," Ivy said with enthusiasm.

"I tell you what. I saw a tourist pamphlet about an airboat at the hotel. We could go tomorrow morning."

"Can we?" Ivy looked at Lily with a pleading expression.

Lily's gaze met his. "I don't know. We have the awards banquet tomorrow night."

"We'll go early in the morning." He looked from Lily to Ivy and back. "We should have plenty of time. What do you say?"

"Please," Ivy pleaded to Lily.

"I guess we could do that." Lily didn't sound all that enthusiastic about the idea.

Max reached for her hand and squeezed it. "Come on. It'll be fun."

Lily's eyes narrowed. "How about safe?"

"It'll be safe. Think of it as an adventure."

She shrugged. "Okay."

They cleaned the kitchen and watched a movie of Ivy's choice. Max sat next to Lily on the sofa with his arm lying along the back of the sofa. He resisted pulling her closer, sensing she didn't want too much affection between them in front of Ivy. When the show was over, Lily sent Ivy to bed.

"I'm sorry you can't stay." Lily placed her arm around his waist and leaned into him as they strolled to his car, sitting behind hers in the drive.

Max put his back to the vehicle and brought her to stand between his legs. "Hey, don't worry about it. I understand. Ivy needs time to adjust to us."

"Thanks for understanding. I'll miss you." Lily wrapped her arms around his neck.

Max covered Lily's mouth with his and pulled her tight against him. She opened for him, and his tongue met hers in a dance he wished they were doing in her bedroom behind a closed door. His palms cupped her butt and brought her against his thickened manhood.

At Lily's groan, he nudged her away. He leaned his forehead against hers as he worked to settle his heavy breathing and get his desire under control. "Honey, we keep that up, and we'll be putting on a show for your neighbors."

She giggled.

Placing his hands on her upper arms, he directed her backward far enough he could open the driver's door. He slipped inside, started the car. Before closing the door, he said, "I'll miss holding you tonight."

Once again, because of Max's urging, Lily found herself stepping out where she never would've gone at all. Getting on an airboat and skimming across the top of swamp water was far beyond her adventure level. She'd lived in the Miami area her entire life, but had never been out into the Everglades. At least sitting on an airboat, she'd be more than three inches out of the water unlike some other tours.

Nothing about the Everglades particularly fascinated her. She knew people who thought the swamp was a wonderfully amazing place, with the animals and plants that were found nowhere else in the worlds. For her, the area always held a bit of terror. Snakes in the water and alligators that could eat her held no allure.

Ivy had been beside herself in anticipation since she'd woken. Lily wasn't feeling as happy or rested. She'd had a difficult time settling into sleep. She wanted to blame it on excitement over the award, to the warm weather and any number of other things running through her head, but what it came down to was she missed having Max next to her. How quickly she'd become dependent on him.

She and Ivy were dressed in T-shirts, long, thin pants and tennis shoes. Lily knew enough to prepare for mosquitos. They didn't need to return with bites all over them. Thankfully when Max arrived, he was dressed similar to them. Ivy ran to greet him while Lily picked up the bag she'd stuffed with sunscreen, hats and a few snacks.

Ivy settled into the back seat. Max gave Lily a quick kiss before he held the door for her to get in. On the hour drive to the border of Everglades National Park, Max and Ivy chatted about the alligators and snakes they hoped to see that day. Lily sat quietly and listened.

Occasionally, she glanced at Max. He would give her a reassuring smile and then return his focus back to the road or to whatever question Ivy had asked. Lily couldn't help but admire his patience and the attention he gave Ivy. Few of the men she had dated ever gave Ivy more than cursory hello. It was nice to hear the delight in her sister's voice.

Max pulled off the main road onto a dirt one. They traveled a short distance before they pulled into an open area with a small metal building. Tall cypress trees with masses of moss hanging from the limbs stood in the swamp behind it. An airboat was secured to the pier nearby. Max brought the car to a stop beside a battered truck.

As they stepped out of the car, a man exited the building and came to meet them. "Are you Max James?"

"Yes." The men shook hands. Max then introduced her and Ivy.

Hank, with a heavy beard, wearing a T-shirt that read Bite an Alligator Before He Bites You and well-worn cargo pants, looked intimidating until he smiled and spoke. He had a warm voice. "Are we ready to take a ride today?"

"Are we going on that boat?" Ivy pointed to the airboat.

"We sure are. Come on. I'll show you where to sit. Maybe you'd like to drive some today?"

Ivy looked at Lily. "Can I?"

Lily gave her a reassuring smile. "We'll see."

Hank led them down to the pier, built over the standing water. "Before we get on the boat, I need to go over a few rules. Number one, you must wear a life jacket. Two, I need you to remain seated at all times and, three, no hands outside of the boat. I don't want any alligators to be having lunch on us."

Lily shuddered.

She could do this. It would be for only a few hours. Ivy and Max were looking forward to it.

Hank stepped into the boat and helped Ivy to one of the four seats in the front. Ivy sat down.

Max stepped in the craft and helped Lily in. She took the seat next to Ivy, and Max settled in the one next to her.

"Your life jackets are under your seat," Hank said from behind them. "Put them on and then buckle yourselves in."

Lily got into her jacket, checked Ivy's, then she made sure Ivy's seat belt was secure and snapped hers on.

"All set?" Hank called from where he sat in a high seat behind them.

Max nodded. To her, he said, "You okay?"

Lily glanced at Ivy who had a smile and a look of excitement on her face. One like Lily hadn't seen in a long time. She gripped the edge of the seat and gave Max a nod. "Yeah, I'm sure I am."

The boat's huge fan roared to life. Lily jumped. Max removed her hand from the seat and held it resting on his thigh. Her heart settled with his reassurance.

Ivy looked at her. "This is going to be so much fun."

Soon the boat rocked, and the water rippled around them as Hank used the long-handled stick to put the boat in gear, then another to move the large wind rudders, sending them out into the water.

"Ivy, hang on," Lily called over the noise of the motor.

Despite her insecurities, Lily forgot them some as she looked at the intriguing landscape. The glimmer of the sun off the water on the beautiful cloudless sky. The tall grass blowing in the breeze held her attention. Birds flew as they moved across the water.

"How you doing?" Max asked, his lips close to her ear so he could be heard.

She nodded.

He squeezed her hand.

Ivy sat forward in her seat, her face in the wind.

Hank slowed the boat and cut the engine. They glided into a small glade of water. Before them lay a sea of white birds. Lily had never seen anything like it. Or more beautiful.

Ivy started to say something. Lily placed her hand on her leg. "Shh."

They floated without a noise, watching the amazing scene. At a squawk from one of the birds, they all took flight, creating an even more astonishing sight. Minutes later, the noise of flapping wings and screaming birdcalls moved into the distance.

Hank said, "I thought you might like this. You have to be here at the right time of day to catch the sight. Y'all were lucky."

"That was a lot of birds." Ivy looked at the sky in wonder.

Max chuckled. "That was an understatement."

"Beautiful," Lily murmured.

Hank started the engine once more, and they moved out into a different channel. They traveled up it until they had entered a wide lake. He turned off the boat.

"I wanted to tell you a little bit about the Everglades. There are a million-and-a-half acres of this swampland. It's really a large river. It starts with the Kissimmee River up in the middle of the state. The river dumps into Lake Okeechobee. The swamp is created by the overflow and creates a slow-moving river, which is all this water you see. It's sixty miles wide and a hundred miles long on its way to the ocean.

"There's no other ecosystem like it anywhere else in the world. Mangroves grow here, and there are pine flat-woods. Of course, the best known tree is the cypress tree with the knees sticking up everywhere and their tangle of roots.

"A number of endangered animals live here, like the leatherback turtle, the Florida panther and the manatee. Ivy, don't put your hand in the water."

Lily's head jerked to Ivy. "In your lap, Ivy."

She clasped her hands in front of her.

Hank continued, "You don't ever know what's in the water and if they're hungry. Now we're going to see if we can find one of those endangered species, the American alligator."

Lily flinched. Max gave her hand a squeeze of encouragement.

Hank restarted the boat, and they headed across the lake. Too soon for Lily, they slowed and eased into a narrow channel and under trees. A flop and splash of water draw their attention.

Lily saw the tail of an alligator disappear beneath the water.

"Oh," Ivy whispered.

As they continued to watch, another three alligators slid down the low, dirt bank. The water frothed just off to the right side of the boat.

"We can't sit here, because they'll start bumping the boat. We'll go on down. Watch the banks, and you may catch sight of some baby gators." Hank unhurriedly moved forward.

"Ivy, stay still," Lily reminded her.

"I am. They're scary." Ivy didn't take her eyes off the water.

"There's a baby alligator." Max pointed off to the left.

Ivy, with her voice full of excitement, leaned against Lily. "I see it."

"Let's count them, Ivy," Max suggested. "One, two, three..."

Fifteen minutes later, they came out into open water again.

"We counted twenty-three," Max announced.

"That's a lot," Ivy said with wide eyes.

It was plenty for Lily.

"Yeah, it is," Max agreed.

Hank increased the speed, and all talking stopped. Twenty minutes later, they entered a channel with low-hanging trees filled with moss that blocked out most of the sunlight. Hank announced, "Here is where you need to look for snakes. Pay attention to the low-hanging limbs. They'll be resting on them this time of day."

Lily was absolutely not interested in finding or looking for a snake. Somehow, it seemed to entertain Ivy and Max far more. They treated it like an Easter egg hunt. As they talked and pointed, she focused on the water ahead, hoping they'd soon be out in the open again.

Max looked at her, and his face turned serious. "Hank, I think it's time we head back."

"We have one more stop." The boatman continued at the same speed.

"Please take us in." Max used his firm OR tone.

At Max's stern statement, Hank turned the boat in a wide arc and headed into the sun.

Max had been so busy trying to give Ivy a good time and letting Lily see that he accepted her sister that he'd failed to give Lily the attention she deserved. When he'd glanced at Lily to find her wearing a sick, fearful look, he'd known he'd messed up. She'd been being strong to give him and Ivy some enjoyment. Once again, she'd sacrificed herself for others. Lily did that too much.

As they rounded a bend in the channel, Max looked ahead to see another airboat floating on the water. A man's head came up, and he waved his arm at them.

Hank eased back on the speed. They came to an idle beside the boat.

It was then that Max could see the man holding his bloody forearm.

"Help me," the man called.

Max released his belt and braced his feet. "Hold it steady, Hank, so I can get to him. I'm a doctor." He reached for the side.

Behind him Lily said to Ivy. "Stay put and don't unbuckle. Keep your hands in. Hank, where's your first aid kit?"

Max thought better of stepping into the other boat, in fear that the two would move away from each other and leave him in the water. Instead, he went down on his hands and knees and crawled across, rolling into the bottom of the other airboat. Hank turned off the motor. It was eerily quiet around them after the roar of the big engine.

"What happened?" Max asked the boatman.

"My arm got caught in the fan."

Max climbed over the metal bench seats. "When did this happen?"

"Just before you came up."

"Lily, I'm going to need something for a tourniquet," Max said over his shoulder. He had no doubt Lily was busy thinking through the problem, as well. The man had turned pale. "And a blanket. Something to treat for shock."

Max could barely make out the mangled muscle and

bone for all the blood. The craft bobbed, and he looked behind him to see Lily scrambling toward him. "You should've stayed on the other boat."

"You might need my help." Lily handed him a one-inch strap. "Use this for the tourniquet."

Max took it from her and wrapped it around the man's bicep. Pulling it tight, he watched as the flow of blood slowed. Done, he looked at the man, only to find he had passed out, which was probably the best thing for him. He must be in a great deal of pain.

Lily came up beside him. "We need to get this man in the bottom of the boat so we can get his feet above his heart, then we can see about his arm."

Max nodded. "Agreed. I'll get his shoulders and you take his legs."

Working together, they scooted the man into position. Lily rested his feet on the edge of the boat and efficiently laid an oily beach towel over him along with a couple of life preservers lying nearby.

Max returned his attention to the wound. It needed support and a covering to keep it clean. "Hank, call 9-1-1 and have an ambulance waiting for us. Also, we need a board, stick or something long and steady to secure this arm. Do you have a knife on you?"

"There should be a paddle in the boat somewhere. Here's my knife." Hank started to throw it.

"No, don't do that. We can't afford to lose it in the water," Max called to him.

"I'll get it." Lily scrambled to the front of the boat.

As she started back toward Max, the boat rocked from something bumping it. It happened again.

"The gators smell the blood." Hank's voice carried behind Max.

"Ivy," Lily yelled, fear filling her voice, "I want you to scoot—do not stand, scoot—over one seat to the middle of the boat. Hank, please see she does so and buckles up again. Keep your hands in your lap."

"I'll see she stays safe," Hank's gruff voice assured her.

Another thump against one of the boats reminded Max of how much more serious the situation had become. He pulled his T-shirt off.

Lily stayed low as she worked herself back toward him. She handed him the knife. "I'll get some vitals."

Max nodded and started cutting up his T-shirt into strips. "Before we start securing the arm, let the tourniquet go for a second. His fingers are turning blue."

She did as he requested. By the time she was finished, he had the strips of cloth ready to go.

Another bump rocked the boat from beneath.

Max looked around for a toolbox, spying one under the driver's seat. Stepping over the man, while being careful to hold on to the bar of the seat so he'd not get thrown out, he reached for the case. The last thing they needed was for him to go swimming with the alligators.

"Careful." Lily's hand gripped his pants leg.

He picked up the box, then quickly sat it down. The next nudge of the boat came harder and with a splash of water. Opening the toolbox, he located a screwdriver and went to work on the throttle stick in front of them. "Let's get this done and get out of here."

With the stick removed, he placed it under the man's arm. Max held the limb up and in place while Lily quickly and efficiently wrapped the T-shirt material around it.

The boat shook the next time, enough that water sloshed over the side.

Max called over his shoulder. "Hank, we're ready to get out of here."

"We need to tie up side by side. I can't pull you because of the fan." Hank handed Max some rope. "We have to loop around the cleat at the front of the boat and then at the frame of the fan."

"Will do." Max took the rope Hank pitched him.

He and Hank worked to pull the boats together. The thrashing in the water made the maneuvering difficult. After a couple of false starts, they managed to get them into position.

"I'll tie the back if you'll get the front," Max called to Hank.

Working his way to the driver's seat, he had to lean over to reach the bar he needed. It required he place his foot on the edge of the boat to keep his balance. His foot slipped. He straddled the side. Using all his upper body strength, he pulled his body upward.

Lily's gasp made him look down. An alligator's nose rose out of the water, just below him. Water spilled in. Her arms wrapped his waist, Lily leaned to the side, pulling him back with her bringing his leg out of the water. The boat steadied. Lily released him. He scrambled off her and searched the surface. Seeing nothing, he moved as fast and safely as he could to tie them off to the other boat.

With relief, he called to Hank. "Let's go."

"This will have to be slow and easy," Hank returned.

"Understood."

The motor started, and there was no more talking. Max took a seat next to Lily giving her a hug to show his gratitude. She returned it with tears in her eyes. He wished they could stay like that for a long time, but they had a patient to see to. They turned to check on him. Twice during the trip, he released the tourniquet while Lily did vitals. It took them three times longer to return than it had to come out.

The fellow woke when they were within eyesight of the pier. Lily reassured him. He settled again, a white line of pain around his lips. An ambulance waited in the parking lot. Max gladly handed over the care of the man to the EMTs. He gave a report about what happened and what he had done, and Lily told them about the man's vitals.

He stood beside Lily, watching as the ambulance pulled away. "This wasn't how I planned the day to go."

Lily placed a hand on his arm. "Hey, this wasn't your fault."

"Some of it was. You hated most of the trip, and then we had an emergency."

She faced him. "It wasn't all bad. I had a new experience to talk about. Some excitement in my life. And Ivy had a ball."

He shrugged. "She did. But I didn't want it to be at your expense."

"I had some time to think on the way back. We make a good team. In an emergency. In the OR. I think our products would make good teammates, as well."

"Are you sure? I don't want you to feel pressured." His father would have his way. This time, with Max's help. At least for once, he had a chance to please him.

She smiled. "I'm sure. Let's go get Ivy. I have an award banquet to attend."

CHAPTER NINE

LILY TWISTED AND turned in front of the mirror attached to her bedroom door. A sense of satisfaction flooded her. She looked her best.

She hadn't originally bought a new dress for the award ceremony, only planning to wear one of her nicest that evening. Instead, she'd splurged on an outfit from a boutique near her house. Time had been tight, but she'd worked it in. She and Max had dropped Ivy off at her place before he took Lily home. After she cleaned up, she'd hurried out on her shopping trip.

Twisting one way, then the other, she checked every angle in the long mirror. The knee-length blush dress swung around her legs. Its color matched the tint of her cheeks and nose where the sun had touched them.

She glowed like she couldn't remember ever doing. Normally, she didn't look forward to awards ceremonies. She tended to remain out of the spotlight. With the anticipation of Max being her escort, excitement hummed through her. How easily Max had become such a central part of her life. She refused to think about him having to leave the next day. They hadn't talked about the future, but she was sure there would be one for them.

She couldn't believe how shameless she'd become

where Max was concerned. It was completely unlike her. What was happening to her? Lily grinned. She was in love. Life had become more exciting with Max around. She'd come out of a shell she'd had no idea she'd been living in. The trip to the Everglades hadn't been her favorite outing, but she was super proud of herself for making it. Even more for helping Max. Saving a man's life had been rewarding. She felt alive. Happy.

When was the last time she could have said that?

All because of Max. What was she going to do when he left? Would she go back to living a dull, scared life once again? No, she wouldn't return to that person.

Her focus returned to filling her small clutch purse and putting her heeled shoes on. Max would be there in ten minutes to pick her up for the cocktail party before the banquet.

At the ring of the front doorbell, she hurried to open it. Max stood there, appearing more dapper than any man had the right to look or a woman's heart could stand. Lily couldn't believe he would be escorting her. Dressed in a blue dress shirt with the collar open, a navy sports jacket over it and cream-colored slacks, he looked like a model straight off a magazine cover. Max truly took her breath away.

Finally, she uttered, "Hey."

"Hi, beautiful. Don't you look lovely?" He studied her from head to toe. His arm slipped around her waist, pulling her close before his lips found hers. The tender kiss made her toes curl and her center heat.

Against her ear he murmured, "Why don't we just forget the cocktail party. Stay here and have our own celebration."

Lily giggled. "I think we'd be missed."

"How about we show up just in time to receive our awards and keep walking afterwards?"

She swatted his arm. "I don't think that would be good for either one of our careers."

"Maybe not, but I want you to know I'm going to spend the entire time thinking about how slowly I'm going to take that dress off you when we get home."

A honeyed warmth washed through her. She lowered her lashes. "If you go and behave, maybe I'll let you do that."

A sexy gleam filled his eyes and he held up three fingers. "I promise."

Max insisted they take his car. "I want this evening to be like a real date. Me driving you. You holding my hand."

Lily like that idea.

Max opened the car door for her and waited until she settled before going around and taking the driver's seat. "I'll put the top down on our way back. I'm sure you don't want to mess up your hair while getting there."

"I'd appreciate that." She patted her hair. "I did put some time into it."

As Max drove, he commented, "You really are beautiful. But especially tonight."

She took his hand and held it. "Thank you."

"You got a touch of sun today. I really do love the weather here." Max looked at her and smiled, giving her hand a squeeze. "New York can be so brutal during the winter months. It overshadows the rest of the year."

Would he consider relocating in Florida, and then they could really see where this relationship could go? "You ever think about moving your practice elsewhere?"

"Occasionally, I do."

"Life's too short to be unhappy where you are." Wasn't that something she'd just recently learned?

Max glanced at her. "Have you ever thought about going elsewhere?"

"No, I like the hospital, and Miami is a good place to live. Ivy is happy here, as well. I see myself growing old here."

He nodded. "I think this city suits you. And I can understand about Ivy."

"By the way, you were great with her today. I appreciate that."

Max glanced at her. "You act like that's a hardship. It isn't."

"Others have found it to be."

"That's on them." His thumb caressed the top of her hand. "I hadn't planned on us having such an exciting morning. I hope you got some rest this afternoon."

"Not exactly. I actually went out to buy this dress."

His hand released hers and he brushed it over her knee, leaving it there. "You made a nice choice. You look amazing. The other men are going to be jealous that you're with me."

Lily giggled. "Thanks. I'm not sure about that."

"I am." His emphatic tone made her heart expand.

"I'm positive the women won't be able to keep their eyes off you. They already have trouble doing that anyway."

"I don't care about what any woman thinks except the one who doesn't become crazy at the sight of blood, is devoted to her sister and kisses like there is no tomorrow." He rubbed his thumb along the side of her knee.

"See, there you go, being Mr. Charming. I wouldn't be much of a doctor if I couldn't stand a little blood."

He chuckled. When they stopped in traffic, he turned to look at her. "You have a problem with me being charming."

"No, I just have a problem with being part of a pack. I'd like to stand out among the crowd."

"Honey, you have no need to worry. You're special in general and to me in particular. In many ways." He squeezed her knee. "I'll be glad to prove that to you as soon as we get back your place."

If Max's fingers continued to caress her, she'd soon be telling him to turn around and take her home. She reached for his hand and brought it to her lap.

Half an hour later, she walked beside Max, her hand in his, as they entered the ultramodern hotel in downtown Miami. They were directed to the ballroom down a long glass-and-shiny-metal hallway. The setting sun created prisms of light around them. It made her think of being in a kaleidoscope. She sighed.

Max lightly squeezed her hand. "You okay?"

"Better than okay."

He gave her a sexy smile and a wink.

Heat washed through her. She stood a little taller, being with Max. His reaction to her appearance had her feeling like the luckiest woman in the world. With Jeff, she'd always felt like she didn't measure up. In hindsight, she couldn't figure out what she'd seen in him. The one part of his nature that stood out the most was his selfishness. Next to Max's personality, it was a glaring character flaw.

As they approached the people mingling around a high table over drinks, Max let go of her hand and placed his at the small of her back. The possessive action boosted her confidence. She was a winner tonight in more ways than one.

He leaned down and spoke into her ear. "I bet no one here would ever guess, that just hours ago, we were fighting off alligators and trying to save a man's arm."

"I wouldn't. I wonder how he's doing." She couldn't believe she'd gotten so caught up in herself that she hadn't called to check on the man.

"He was in surgery when I phoned. They think they can save his arm."

She placed her hand on his chest for a moment. "That's good to hear."

A short, squat man with thinning hair headed their direction with his hands outstretched. "Dr. James and Dr. Evans. It's so good to see you. I'm Dr. Molasky."

Lily recognized his name as the director of the awards ceremony.

"I'm glad to be here." Max shook the man's hand and passed her a sly glance.

She kept her features even, though she thought of what Max had said about he'd rather be taking her dress off. "Hi. I'm looking forward to the evening."

Dr. Molasky shook her hand, as well. "Please enjoy the cocktails. In a few minutes, we'll move into the ballroom. Your seats are at one of the tables up front."

"Thank you." Lily gave the nervous-looking man a reassuring smile.

As Dr. Molasky walked away, Max asked, "May I get you a drink?"

"I'll have some white wine, please." She needed something to settle her nerves.

Max's lips brushed her temple. "I'll be right back."

While he was gone, a number of her colleagues and people in her field approached her to say congratulations.

Max returned and joined the group. He handed her a glass, and his hand came to rest at her waist again. Obviously, Max didn't mind letting everyone know they were a couple. She wasn't sure how she felt about it, given his reputation and the fact they hadn't talked about the future. But she refused to let that ruin her evening.

"Maxwell," a woman called from behind them.

Max turned and she did, as well.

"Mom. Dad. You didn't tell me you were going to be here."

Lily had just gotten used to the idea of her and Max, and now she'd be meeting his parents. This, she would have preferred to have prepared for. She bravely raised her chin as Max excused them from the group and ushered her over to the older couple.

Max looked remarkably like his father, but there was a hardness to him that Max didn't have. Max had inherited his mother's eyes and smile. Petite, with a fashion forward hairstyle, Mrs. James's razor-sharp look told Lily she missed little.

Right at that moment, Mrs. James seemed to be summing up Lily and the way her son's hand touched her back. Lily decided she must have passed the test when the woman blinked and her smile widened.

Max handed his drink to Lily as he wrapped his mother in a tight hug. He shook hands with his father and patted his back in true male style, but it didn't look as affectionate between them as it should have. A tenseness vibrated off Max, as if he wasn't completely comfortable around his father.

Max put his hand at her back again and had her take a step forward. “Mom, Dad, this is Dr. Lily Evans.”

“It’s nice to meet you,” Mrs. James said with sincerity while curiosity rang in her voice.

“Dr. Evans? You’re the doctor who created Skintec.” Mr. James didn’t sound as if he was making pleasant conversation.

“I didn’t know you two were going to be here,” Max said before she and Mr. James could continue their conversation.

“Do you think I’d miss my brilliant son’s achievement?” Mrs. James sounded like a proud mother of a child in preschool who was receiving his first award.

Lily thought it was sweet. It made her miss her own parents. They would be proud of her.

“The James Company is a major sponsor of the event. It’s good PR for the company for me to make an appearance.”

Lily winced for Max at his father’s callous statement, but Max seemed unaffected.

“I realize that, but you usually send a representative to these sorts of events.” Max’s voice remained level as if this was a normal conversation between the two men, with no feelings involved.

“Max,” his mother took his arm, “of course, your father wanted to be here for you, as well. This is a well-earned award.”

Lily watched as Max plastered on a smile that didn’t reach his eyes.

His father added, “Of course, I did. You and Dr. Evans have both created wonderful products.”

“Thank you,” Lily said.

"I understand from my boy he has convinced you to package Skintec with Vseal."

Max had already told his father she'd agreed, when she'd done so only earlier this afternoon? Had Max been that sure of her going along with what he wanted?

Mr. James slapped Max on the shoulder. "I knew when I sent you down here you'd be able to get her to agree."

Her stomach lurched. The feeling of being ill washed over her. She'd been used. Again.

"Dad..." Max looked at her. His eyes begged for her to let him explain.

Lily swallowed hard. Had Max wanted to be a part of her team to get close to her? Had he pretended to like Ivy? Worse, had he taken her to bed to seal the deal? She looked around. Anywhere but at Max. She wanted to run, but she had to get through this evening somehow.

Mr. James continued to talk, completely unaware of the drama between her and Max. "I've been asked to say a few words. Tonight would be a great time to announce this partnership and the fact The James Company will be the packaging outlet."

The doors to the ballroom opened.

"We should go in," Max stated in a tight voice.

Lily placed their glasses on a nearby table and headed toward the entrance.

Max remained beside her as they made their way to the front of the room. She found the place card with her name on it. Max wasn't sitting beside her, and he deftly moved people around until he was next to her. His parents, not surprisingly, were seated at the same table. Max's mother's chair was next to her son, with his father on her other side.

Lily sat stiffly in her seat, wishing she could gracefully get out of the evening. This was the second time she'd been humiliated where Max was concerned. Why had she let herself believe? In him? What she'd hoped for? In happiness?

She knew who Max was. He was a player. She should have known he didn't really care for her. What made her think he would pick her out of all the women he could have? Once again, she'd acted like a love-struck idiot. He'd used her. Why was she so gullible?

It hadn't taken anything but that one statement from Max's father to squash her happiness. Somehow, the evening had taken on a different feel. One of betrayal.

Max had to fix this. What had his father been thinking? Only about himself. The look on Lily's face the moment she'd seen him again in the OR had returned. He could well imagine what she had running through her head. That she'd misjudged another man. That he had used her just as her ex had. In her mind, he was no better than Jeff. That was the last thing he wanted her to believe. It was the furthest thing from the truth. He had to convince Lily of that. He hadn't taken her to bed to get something from her. More important, he hadn't acted like Ivy's friend to get to Lily.

Somehow, he had to prove that to Lily.

The cool wind coming from Lily's direction made him shiver. It wasn't going to be easy. He put his arm around the back of her chair, blocking their conversation from others. She stiffened. "It isn't like it sounded. Give me a chance to explain."

Several people came up to congratulate them, ending any conversation that he and Lily might have. He'd have to settle for later. He feared that would be too late.

Their table filled. The servers went to work bringing them food. All the while, Max remained aware of Lily beside him. All the bloom had left her cheeks. This should be a big night for them both, and his father's greed and Max's desire to please had destroyed it. Max had never felt so low or inadequate.

Lily said all the right things to those joining them but not a word to him. She moved her food around on her plate, but little made it to her mouth. The one time he dared to touch her, she shifted her hand away and asked the woman sitting next to her a question.

He would make this up to her somehow.

Not soon enough, Dr. Molasky stepped behind the podium and started the awards portion of the night. The recipients in other disciplines were called to the stage before it was his and Lily's turns. His name was called first.

Max accepted his award and said a few words of thanks. As he returned to his seat, Lily stood to go get hers. He congratulated her and briefly squeezed her hand as they moved past each other. She returned a tight smile. With shoulders squared, she stepped to the podium and thanked her staff, Dr. Lee and her lab employees. She accepted none of the praise and gave it all to those around her. How like Lily.

When she returned to the table, he stood and held her chair. She fingered her award as the next person's name was called. After that winner returned to their seat, Lily stood and said, "Excuse me."

Lily hadn't returned by the time the last award had been given. With those done, his father took the stage and said all the right things, then made his announcement.

Still there was no Lily.

* * *

Max didn't waste any time explaining anything to his parents. He exited the ballroom and headed straight for the restrooms. A woman assured him Lily wasn't there. His gut told him she'd left. Ordering his car brought around, he headed straight to Lily's house. He should have known when she excused herself, she wouldn't be back.

There were no lights on in the house when he pulled into her driveway. Her car was there, so she was, as well. He had to talk to her. Tonight. The next morning, he was headed back to New York. He'd promised to fill in for another doctor the next week. Those plans, he had to honor.

But leaving before talking to Lily wasn't possible either. He had to explain.

Max pushed the doorbell. For the third time. Still no lights. No sound of feet. Nothing.

Could she really be that stubborn? Of course she could. Hadn't she stayed away from conferences because she couldn't face him?

He huffed and started around the house to her bedroom window. Now he was acting like a stalker. Like a desperate man. He rapped his knuckles on the window. Still nothing. He tapped again.

Finally, the shadow of Lily appeared in the window. "What're you doing?"

"I'm trying to talk to you. Let me in."

"Go away."

She wasn't making it easy on him. Not that he had expected her to. "Lily, we need to talk."

Lily pointed toward the front. She had him wait on the porch long enough he feared she wouldn't open the door. Relief washed through him at the sound of the lock being released. Lily didn't bother to turn the lights on. Not even a small welcome.

With the only glow coming from a distant streetlamp, he could still see she'd been crying. A lot.

He'd been the cause of those tears. He'd promised Ivy he wouldn't make Lily cry. His promises, he took pride in keeping. This time he'd failed. Somehow, he had to fix this. "Lily, I know you're upset, but I need to explain. Can I come in? Please."

She looked around him as if concerned about her neighbors. Her lips formed a tight line as she pushed the door wider and stepped back.

It wasn't an enthusiastic welcome, but he would take it. He entered and closed the door behind them. "It didn't happen the way you think it did."

Lily stood, her arms crossed over a knit tank top and shorts that showed the full length of her legs. Everything about her stance screaming "closed." "I'm not thinking anything."

He knew better than that. Lily was always thinking. "Do you mind if we turn on a light, sit down and talk like two rational adults?"

Lily growled, "That might be possible if I was feeling like a rational adult."

Max reached for her. She backed away. "Please, can we just sit down and talk this out?"

He couldn't remember another time in his life, except for when he'd asked his father to listen to him when Max said he was going into medicine, that he'd pleaded with someone to hear him out. He'd certainly never begged a woman he was interested in to give him a chance. Truthfully, he'd never had to or wanted to. So why did it matter so badly that Lily did?

Because he loved her.

"Okay. Have it your way. We'll do this standing and in the dark. I'm sorry you feel like you've been betrayed. My father did ask me to talk to you about packaging the products. He's always wanted me to go into the company and I saw this as something I could do for him that would help his business. I thought he might finally accept I went into medicine instead of his company. That I could offer something to his life's work. I guess what it comes down to is for once I wanted him to be proud of me. I hate that I even have to say that.

"I'm a grown man in a profession where I save lives and I'm good at my job, but I still need my father's acceptance. Medicine was never good enough for him, and this was one time I thought I could mesh the two. You got caught in the middle. I hadn't intended for that to happen."

Lily glared but still said nothing.

"I know you think I used you, betrayed you, especially after my Dad's insistence on announcing that his company would be packaging Vseal and Skintec together. It especially looked bad since you had only agreed this afternoon."

Lily put her hands on her hips and leaned toward him. "You mean to tell me that you didn't call and tell him of our agreement the second you left my house?"

"I didn't."

"Then, you must have been pretty sure of yourself or your father was of your abilities to seduce me into agreeing," she spat. "Did your father tell you to do anything you could to make it happen? Even take me to bed!"

"Hell, no! You make it sound like he's my pimp. Do you think I only made love to you because I wanted to get you to agree to a deal? That doesn't flatter me and it certainly degrades you."

"Well, what should I think?"

"Has it ever occurred to you that maybe I care about you? That I love you?" Saying the words out loud were a shock to him, but he realized he didn't care. They were true.

"You have a funny way of showing it!" Lily retorted.

"Or maybe you don't let anybody in enough to recognize it. You stay all tied up in your little shell, worried that you might not be in control of your world. You can't let go enough to let them show you love. Even with Ivy, you hold on so tightly it gives you an excuse not to take a chance or have some adventure."

"How dare you?" She took a step toward him, her eyes snapping. "The Casanova of the liver transplant world is telling me what it's like to really care about somebody. It's laughable. The best I can tell, you've spent your adult years caring only about yourself. The minute you have an opportunity to have a woman in your life who cares about you, the real you, the giving, caring you, you do nothing but use her. Now, I'm done here."

"How like you. Every time something goes wrong or it gets hard, you run off. Just like tonight. You just up and disappeared when you thought you might have to face conflict. You quit going to conferences because you didn't want to face you might be less than perfect. I'm not letting you hide this time."

"I'm not hiding from anything!"

A dry chuckle came from Max. "You've lived in Miami your entire life and have never been to the Everglades. You work all the time, and you never go to the Cuban area when you love the place. From what I can tell, you don't even have a hobby. You hold on to that image of the lonely girl with the mentally challenged sister like it's a lifeline. Ivy lives in a wonderful place where she's protected and taken care of and, most of all, happy. She has a full life, yet you still live behind the protective wall you built."

Lily glared at him. "She's like a child."

"In many ways, you've even held her back. She can do more than you let her do. If you let go some, she might surprise you. The only problem you'll have is how to fill the void with something. And that scares you. You cared for your patients. You take care of your sister. But what do you do for you?"

She staggered backward until she hit a table. Her hand gripped the edge. "I guess you got what you wanted. You made your father proud."

He said softly, "That might be what I thought I wanted. But not anymore. I want you."

She huffed. "You've made that clear. You want me so I'll sign on the dotted line in a business proposition. You're going to get what you want. I'll honor what I said. You send me the papers and I'll have my lawyer look at them. You can make your father proud then. Your job is done here."

"Lily, you don't have to agree." Could she make him feel angrier or more horrible?

"I said I'd do it, and your father made the announcement. I wouldn't dare pull out now. What would that do to his reputation and mine?"

Max took a step toward her. "See? There you go, not standing up for what you want."

She shook her head and put up a hand. "Why're you arguing with me when you got what you came after?"

"I'm going to say this one more time. It wasn't like that. All my father requested me to do was ask you. I did not pursue you with that in mind."

She crossed her arms again. "If I remember correctly, I was asked more than once."

The discussion had moved in a circle. Lily walked to the door and opened it. "You've told your side. I've said and heard all I want to. If you have anything else to say to me, make it through your daddy's company and my lawyer. You need to go."

Max stepped out on the porch. "Lily—"

She closed the door firmly between them.

CHAPTER TEN

LILY SLEEPWALKED THROUGH the next week. The only time Max wasn't at the forefront of her thoughts was when she was in surgery or seeing a patient. All she had done was go through the motions. How did a heart as broken as hers keep beating?

She made every effort to keep her life as normal and on track as possible. Those things she could handle. Could react and act as if everything in her world remained the same. Nighttime brought on its own set of problems. She crawled into bed as soon as she got home. When she was busy, she could breathe, but when she entered her bedroom, she missed Max with a power that had become physical. She of people thought being lovesick was a myth. After she'd closed the door on Max, she soon found out differently. She wrapped her arms tightly around herself and pulled her legs up until she formed a ball. Still, she couldn't keep the pain at bay.

Why, oh why had she let him into her life? Her bedroom? The pain of losing Max far surpassed the hurt of Jeff dumping her. It was so intense it consumed her. Life had become a hollow shell of what it once was. Those blissful days of Max were but a blur. She feared she'd never truly be happy again.

She didn't want to think about Max anymore. Yet she wanted to hear his voice, touch his face, kiss him…

His calls and texts pulled at her. The temptation to give in and respond was a constant shadow over her. If she did, what would change? It would just make the separation more painful. Leaving things as they were was the only way for her to survive. If what she was doing could be called that.

In an effort to keep her world as normal as possible, she picked up Ivy to come over to spend the night on Friday.

"Where is Max?" Ivy looked around the room.

"He had to go home. He doesn't live here. He lives in New York."

The expression on Ivy's face turned sad. "He was my friend."

"I know, honey. He is still your friend. You just won't see him every often." *Or ever*, Lily left off.

"Is he coming back?"

"No, honey, I don't think he is." Lily worked to keep the wobble out of her voice.

Ivy placed her hand on Lily's arm. "He made you cry?"

"No, I'm fine." Ivy became a misty blur.

Ivy continued to watch Lily. "You do not think that I see and understand, but I do."

Lily's shocked gaze met hers.

"You are crying. Max promised not to make you cry."

"Sometimes people can't help what they do." Max could have, but Lily wouldn't let Ivy believe anything but good about him. He'd been wonderful to Ivy, and Lily wouldn't take that away from either one of them.

"Do you like Max?"

"I did." No matter how he had hurt her, Lily still loved him.

"You can like him again."

Lily turned her back to Ivy so she wouldn't see the tears come to her eyes. "I don't think that's going to happen."

"Did you have a fight?"

"Yes, honey, we had a fight and he had to go home."

Ivy moved around Lily to stare at her face. "But you still cry. I am mad at him too. He promised."

Lily gave her a hug. "Thank you. I'm glad I have you for a sister. Now, let's talk about something else."

"But I miss my friend."

Lily needed to redirect Ivy to another subject. "What would you like to do tomorrow?"

"I want to learn to skate. A girl at the beach skated. Max told me I should learn."

Max would have. "Is that really what you want to do?"

Ivy nodded. "I want to try. Max said it's okay to fail. It's the not trying that's wrong."

Wasn't that what Max had been saying to her but in different words? Why hadn't she noticed that Ivy was more adventurous than her? Had she been hiding in a box she controlled, so she'd feel no pain from failure? "Okay, then we'll try. I've never done that before. It's time we learned."

Ivy nodded with enthusiasm.

Had she prevented Ivy from experiencing all she could because Lily had such tight guardrails around Ivy? At least Ivy was willing to try. Lily had pulled into a parking spot and stayed there until Max had come along. She'd become so regimented in her life she couldn't move. Afraid of being hurt. She couldn't trust anyone.

Max had proven he was a good guy. That he cared. He didn't need to go get Ivy, show her attention, do things she would enjoy. In surgery, in an emergency, Max had been supportive and helpful. He'd shown her tender care in and out of the bedroom. So why had she doubted him when he explained what had happened with his father? Had he really deserved the treatment she'd given him?

It was time she broadened her horizons. She'd been so caught up in her narrow life it was time to shake it up. She'd give up this morose existence she'd been living in and start making some changes. It was time she approached the world with a sense of wonder. "Ivy, is there anything else you'd like to learn to do?"

"I want to ride a bike. My friend knows how to. He rides around all the time. I could ride with him."

"I'd like to do that too. When you learn, we could bike down by the beach."

"Could we?" Ivy's excitement was infectious.

"Sure. You have been wanting to work off the compound. Do you still want to do that?"

"You mean at the shoe store?"

"Yes, I believe that's the place." It would take more fortitude for Lily to let her do it than Ivy would need to do the work. Facing fear was difficult.

Ivy nodded deeply. "I want to work at the shoe store."

"Okay. I'll talk to the director on Monday about you getting hired there." Lily's look turned stern. "But you have to promise me you won't ever run away again."

"I promise." Ivy gave her a long look. "You are different, Lily."

She felt changed but was surprised Ivy noticed. "How's that?"

"You were happy when Max was here. You are sad now, but you will be happy again."

"Yes, I will be." Lily said with more confidence than she'd felt in a week. She hugged Ivy. "We'll both be happy."

Max shifted in an uncomfortable leather chair in the reception area outside his father's office. What he needed to discuss with his parent was business, so he'd made an appointment instead of talking to him at home. His father had always listened marginally better at his office to anything Max had to say. For once, Max wanted a man-to-man discussion, not a father-to-son one. Max would be saying things the man wouldn't want to hear. Difficult things for Max to say and even more so for his father to listen to.

When Max left on Sunday morning to return to New York City, he'd thought about driving by Lily's house first. But then he really would've looked like a stalker. Instead, he decided to give her a few days to calm down, and then he would try to contact her.

He hadn't done anything wrong, but what he hated was it didn't look that way to Lily. Her past experiences made her believe she couldn't trust a man. Her ex had certainly let her down when he'd tried to use her. Max's stomach roiled. To Lily, it looked as if he'd done the same thing. Max had to make sure Lily understood he hadn't taken their relationship to a personal level because he wanted to get her to agree to the packaging.

He'd called daily after he'd left Miami. All he could do was leave a voicemail message, but Lily never returned any of them. He tried texting, but there was silence from Lily. Just as she had done before, Lily had gone into hiding. When he finished his business with his father, Max was headed back to Miami. He had to make things right between him and Lily. He couldn't accept less. If he'd learned anything in the last miserable week, it was that he needed Lily to make his life complete.

His father's assistant said, "You may go in now."

Max pulled the modern floor-to-ceiling door open and stepped into the spacious glass-and-wood space. It was much like his father: sleek, clean and minimal. His father sat behind a large desk in the center of the room.

Shock rocked through Max when his father stood and hurried around his desk. Instead of offering his hand, he hugged Max.

"Come in. Come in. You did a great job getting that doctor to agree to the packaging."

Everything his father said went against Max's grain. Max's body tensed. He pushed away. "Her name is Dr. Lily Evans. Lily."

His father didn't miss a beat. "Yes, yes, Dr. Evans. You did it."

"Yeah, I did it," Max mumbled. But he wasn't proud of how it had all panned out. Lily felt used and that's the last thing he wanted to have happen. He'd lost more than one night's sleep because of it. It didn't help that he missed having her in his arms.

"Your mom is glad to have you home," his father continued as if he didn't recognize Max's lack of enthusiasm, which Max was sure he didn't. "Tell me what's so important that you felt the need to come all the way to Chicago to talk to me so late on a Friday evening."

His father returned to his seat behind the desk, and Max took a chair in front of him.

Max inhaled deeply and let his breath out slowly. This

is the moment he'd been preparing for since he'd made the decision days earlier. "We need to get a few things straight."

His father's brows rose. "In regard to…?"

"Mine and Lily's merger. I have some stipulations I want to include in the contract."

His father's look turned to stone. He placed his hands across his chest in a defensive manner. "Such as?"

"The first is you will agree to a ten-year proprietary ownership period instead of the usual twenty years."

His father's chair creaked when he sat forward so quickly.

Max didn't pause. "I'd also like for my share of the profits to be designated to go to the Palm Plantation in Miami along with one third of the company profits directed to go to the Liver Foundation."

"I don't think I—"

Max pushed on. "That's how it has to be if I'm going to sign the contract. Otherwise, I'll take Vseal elsewhere."

His father stood. "You'd do that to my company?"

"I don't think I'm doing anything to your company. You'll have the prestige of being the one to put the package out. And the income. That should lead to more business for you."

"Why're you doing this?" Disbelief covered his father's face.

Max shrugged. "It's the right thing to do."

His father sat again. "Mmm, I think there's more to it than that. You're doing it for that doctor. You fell for her."

Max's jaw tightened. His father remained so focused on his work he still made no effort to remember Lily's name. Even when he'd been reminded a number of times.

"I'm in love with Lily." Max emphasized Lily's name.

"Is that so?"

"Yes, it is. What I did to her was unforgivable." Max intended to make her understand he couldn't live without her.

"What did you do? I thought all you did was ask her to let us package your products together." There was more interest in his father's voice than expected.

"I did, but you made the announcement after she'd just told me she would agree. Lily feels she has been manipulated."

His father huffed. "How do you manipulate someone into making millions?"

"Lily is more interested in helping people than she is in the money."

His father's look of disbelief was typical. "What do you mean? We develop our products to make money and increase business."

Max moved to the edge of his seat as if preparing to leave. "In that case, maybe Lily and I need to take our products elsewhere."

His father waved his hand. "I don't want you to do that."

"Then you agree to my stipulations?" Max fixed his look on his father daring him not to approve.

"You aren't leaving the company much of a profit margin, or you either."

Max shrugged. "Lily has a mentally challenged sister who lives at Palm Plantation. I want there to be constant funds for the upkeep of the place for Ivy and the other residents, with or without the ability to pay."

"Is that all?" His father voice was a cross between frustration and admiration.

"That's all for me. Lily may have more demands when the time comes. I don't know."

"You're not giving me a choice, are you?"

Max shook his head.

His father watched Max over the top of his hands. "What's all of this about?"

"This is about me trying to make up for a wrong. I got so wrapped up in trying to prove myself to you that I hurt someone I care about."

"Trying to prove something to me?" His father's voice went higher with surprise. "What do you mean? You don't have to prove anything to me."

"I know you weren't pleased with me when I went into medicine instead of joining the company. When you came to me and asked about talking to Lily, I thought if I got the packaging contract, then it might make it up to you. Instead, I hurt Lily with my selfishness." Disgust welled in his gut.

"I didn't ask you to hurt her. I thought you might know her. I just thought it was a logical step to ask you to contact her."

"I know that. I'm the one who let it get out of hand." He met his father's gaze. "Just as I've let other things go on too long. I should have said this long ago. I love you, Dad. I do. I'm sorry I disappointed you by not wanting to work at The James Company, but I'm good at my profession. I save lives. I'm well respected for my abilities. It's time for me to stop being that kid who's always trying to please his father. Those days are gone. I hope you can accept my life decisions, but if not, that's for you to deal with."

"Of course, I hoped you'd want to work in my company, but I never said I wasn't proud of you."

"No, but you've made it clear in every way possible. In fact, you even implied that if I didn't approach Lily about contracting with you, then I might be the cause of your company having financial trouble."

"I think you misunderstood."

Max sat straighter in his chair. "No, Dad, I did not."

His father waved a hand as if what Max said meant nothing. "All I've ever wanted was to share my business with my son. But that doesn't mean that I'm not proud of you. Of course I've heard of your good work. You do save lives. I recognize the importance of that. I may not have said it in the past, but I am proud of you."

Max's breath caught. He'd just heard something he'd never heard before.

"Who wouldn't be proud of that glue you developed? I was confident you were a chip off the old block. I do have to admit I hoped you'd give up practicing medicine and start working on medical developments for me. But I quickly figured out that wasn't going to happen."

"No, it isn't," Max said in a firm voice.

"I'm a businessman, Max. You've always known that. I see the bottom line."

"Yeah, Dad, that's the one sure thing about you." Something Max couldn't always agree with.

"That doesn't mean I'm not proud of you. I didn't want to, but I admired how you stood up to me and found your own path."

"You did?" Max had no doubt his shock rang out clearly. "Thanks for that. It means a lot."

His father came around the desk as Max stood. The older man took Max into a hug that Max returned. "I'll make your demands work somehow. Are you going after… Lily?"

His father had used Lily's name correctly for the first time. "I am. As soon as I leave here, I'm headed to Miami. I hope I can convince her that I want whatever she wants."

"Then, start by blaming it on me." His father grinned.

Max chuckled. "I'll do that, but I do have to put some responsibility on myself."

"The one thing I've learned with your mother is that eating humble pie can go a long way toward easing the problem."

Max and his father had rarely shared this type of interaction. It felt good. "Thanks, Dad, I'll keep that in mind."

"Your mother said she thought Lily might be that special one by the way you looked at her."

Max smiled. "Mom would notice."

"Yeah. She also reminded me that I'm a father first and a businessman second. And for me to keep that in mind when dealing with you. Forgive me if sometimes I forget that."

"Already done. I love you, Dad."

His father looked a little taken back, but he responded, "I love you too."

Ten days had gone by. Lily had counted every one. It was the same amount of time Max had been in town. The last had been far more painful than those before them. They seemed like years instead of days.

Despite her disappointment in Max, she'd taken some of what Max had said to heart and had already started making some changes in her life. She'd set work hours, and she stuck to them, not lingering at the hospital because she had no other place to go. She used the time she gained to join a yoga class, where she had started meeting people who had nothing to do with the medical field. One evening she spent in a chair in her backyard beneath a banana tree, reading a book just for fun.

Max might've broken her heart, but he'd made her take off the mask she'd worn and face her need to move forward. She planned to do something new every month, even if it was just walking around a part of her neighborhood she'd never been to before. She shouldn't have been, but she was surprised how much adding something new and simple affected her world. Like the pop of a champagne bottle, her life had been released to flow freely and bubble.

The only problem was she had no one to share her newfound life with. As much as she enjoyed it, she still missed Max with every fiber of her being. She dreamed of him each night and reached for him every morning. All those beautiful memories she'd thought she'd have they were there but didn't hold her and nestle her against a warm body.

The second Tuesday afternoon after Max had left, a large envelope was delivered to her office. The James Company logo in the corner gave away who it was from. It would be the contract papers she'd been expecting. The ones that would tie her and Max together forever and not in the way she wanted.

Lily opened the package. On top of all the legal papers lay a note with Mr. James's letterhead on it.

Dr. Evans,
It was a pleasure to meet you. I think that you will find you will like working with The James Company.

I have enclosed the contract and particulars that

will cement our relationship. As you read through, you will see some out-of-the-ordinary stipulations. Max would not agree to his part without them.

Please contact me if you have any questions.

Later that evening, Lily pulled one leg up beneath her as she settled on the cushion in the chair in her backyard. She opened the book she'd been reading. Over the last few hours, she'd thought of nothing but the odd but pleasantly surprising demands in the contract from The James Company. She would let her lawyer review it, but she had already decided to sign it. Max had once again taken care of her and Ivy.

Lily had already figured out she'd been wrong about him and the contract confirmed it. She wished her happily-ever-after could be that easily achieved. Would Max forgive her for thinking the worst of him? The longer time went on, the harder it would be to face Max, but she was going to have to. Tomorrow, she would call him. By then, she would have her nerve up.

What he'd said about her hiding kept running through her mind. Wasn't that what she was doing again? That, too, had to stop. She wouldn't wait to call him tomorrow. She would do it tonight. Thank him. Apologize. She needed to do it right away. Ivy asked about Max every time they were together. Maybe by Friday night when she came to stay, Lily could give Ivy an update on Max.

Lily opened the book. She'd read a while, fix a salad and then make the call. It was time to face her mistakes.

The sound of a car door closing reached her ears, but she didn't give it much thought. It was the time of day most of her neighbors were coming home for the evening. It wasn't until she sensed someone watching her that she looked up.

She gasped. Her heart raced as her book fluttered to the ground. *Max.*

He stood at the corner of her house.

Lily tried to move but couldn't. All she could do was stare.

"I tried the doorbell." He sounded unsure.

The confident, charming and always-quick-with-a-humorous-quip Max James acted as if he didn't know what to say or do next. She shouldn't have been surprised after their last meeting. Hadn't she slammed the door between them? Worse, not taken his calls or answered his texts. The amazing part was that he'd even bothered to come see her. "Max, what are you doing here?"

"Uh, may I join you?" He shifted his feet.

Was he nervous? "Sure." She straightened and indicated the other chair beside her, her hand shaking. Her heart fluttered. Max was actually here.

Lily feasted her eyes on him as he strolled toward her, soaking in his every detail. He looked ruggedly handsome with a five o'clock shadow covering his jaw. His dark hair had grown, and a lock hung over his forehead. He wore a floral shirt with a brightly colored birds-of-paradise pattern, and tan cargo shorts. Brown sandals protected his feet. He was all she'd ever wanted and more.

"It's good to see you, Lily." He took the chair next to her.

"Max, I—"

"No, Lily. I need to go first." He took a deep breath. "I came to tell you how sorry I am. I promise I didn't spend time with you, make love to you or have something to do with Ivy just to get your agreement. I told my father

I wasn't participating in any more of his deals. In fact, I told him a number of things I should have said long ago. I hurt you, and I don't want to ever do that again."

"It was my fault—"

He put up a hand. "Let me finish. You should have received the contract. Sign it or don't, that is up to you. I want you to be pleased with it. That's all I ever want is for you to be happy."

Her eyes narrowed. "Did you come all this way just to tell me that?"

Max shrugged. "That and other things. But they can wait until we work the business out." He paused. "I didn't mean for things to happen the way they did."

"I know."

His eyes widened. "You do?"

"Yeah. I figured it out not long after you left. But I couldn't bring myself to tell you that. I've been putting my issues with Jeff, or really my lifelong issues of having control, making sure Ivy wasn't hurt and me, as well, off on you. You were right. I keep a protective wall around me. But somehow, you climbed over it. It has taken me years, but because of you, I now know that to have happiness, sometimes you must accept the pain of loss. I can't protect Ivy all the time, or myself either.

"I've made assumptions about you based on hearsay and that wasn't fair to you. Over and over, you have proven to be a stand-up guy, one I could depend on. I couldn't have asked someone to be nicer to Ivy than you have been."

"I like Ivy. I've enjoyed getting to know her."

"I know that. I knew it last week. I'm sorry about how I treated you. I was just scared."

"Of me?" Max looked horrified.

"Yes, no. Of my feelings. About how much you mattered to me."

Max's stance eased.

Lily went on, fearing she might not get it all out if she didn't. "But we live so far apart. How can we ever have a real relationship when we're in different parts of the country? It would just end one day anyway. I didn't want it to hurt any more than it already did to have you leave. I was planning to call you tonight and tell you all this, and you showed up. I really am sorry I didn't trust you. You didn't deserve that. The stipulations you put in the contract prove that."

Max took her hand. "We both messed up. Do you think we can start over?"

"Yeah," she nodded. "I would like that."

"Friends?"

Lily was hoping for more, but she'd take that over nothing. Her hands tightened on his. "Friends."

"I like the sound of that," he said thoughtfully. "It has a nice ring to it. I'm not known for having women friends. Casual relationships, yes, but I don't want those anymore and especially not with you." He gave her a sheepish look. "You've changed me, Lily Evans. For the better."

She had?

"I'm crazy about you, Lily. You have shown me what I want out of life. You make my days easy and my nights amazing. I know what acceptance is because of you. I want to have you with me forever. I want to help you see about Ivy and be the brother she has never had. I want—I need—you always. I love you more than I can say."

Lily's eyes swam with moisture, blurring the wonderful man in front of her. These were tears of happiness instead of pain. She rose and threw herself into Max's arms.

"Whoa, that must mean you feel the same."

She kissed his neck, his cheek before her lips found his. "You bet I do."

Max gathered her to him, pulling her legs to the side so that she sat across his lap. Lily continued to kiss him, running her fingers through his hair. His hand slid over her back and up to slip under her hair. He took the kiss deeper, making her moan with delight. She'd missed him so much. Having Max's kisses again was like finding home.

He pulled back but continued to hold her close. She looked into his beautiful blue eyes. He wiped the moisture from her cheeks. "You need to stop crying. I promised Ivy I wouldn't make you cry."

"These are good tears. Tears of happiness. I've missed you so much."

"Honey, I've missed you too." Max kissed her tenderly.

She pulled away. "I need to tell you something."

"What's that?"

"I love you."

"I love you, too, with everything in me. I know this has all happened pretty fast, but I have something else I want to discuss with you." His lips brushed her cheek. "Dr. Lee offered me a position in your department. What would you think about me moving to Miami?"

Lily's mouth fell open. "You are relocating here?"

"Only if it's okay with you. I don't want to do anything that you don't agree with."

"Of course I agree with it. I can't think of anything more perfect." Lily wrapped her arms around his neck and kissed him soundly. Max eagerly returned her embrace. She pulled back. "I need to warn you that I've started making some changes in my life."

"You have? I hope they don't exclude me."

She grinned. "Never. I agreed to let Ivy start working at a shoe store off the compound. She's only been there a couple of days but loves it. From what I can tell, the owner is pleased, as well. She and I learned to roller-skate the other Saturday. She wants to learn to ride a bike."

"That's great."

"I've started keeping regular hours at the hospital and—" she reached for the book and placed it on the arm of the chair, "—I'm taking time to read a book."

"You are making some changes. I'm proud of you. I'll try to add to your fun when I can." His hand slid along her bare leg as he gave her a wicked grin. "My plans are to move down here as soon as I can, date you for a while, maybe move in if invited, then I'm going to ask Ivy if I have permission to marry you. Then I want to give you that baby you want."

Lily's gaze met his. "Do you mind if I tweak the plan just a little?"

Max's eyes filled with concern. Was he still worried she'd not forgiven him? "I think the moving here as soon as possible sounds great, but I think you should move in here when you come. As for marrying you, I'm ready for that whenever you are. As for having your baby, I can't think of anything that would give me more joy."

His look had brightened as she spoke. "Me, either, except for maybe having two."

"At the same time?" she squeaked.

Max shrugged. "Twins or singles—I just want to make a family with you. And for Ivy to be an aunt."

"It sounds like a life I won't run from."

He kissed her tenderly. "If you do, I'll come find you."

Lily kissed him deeply. "You are all I'll ever need. You are more than enough."

Max looked into her eyes a moment as if he were taking in her words and holding them close. "Thank you for saying that." His hand slipped under her shorts to cup her butt cheek. "Do you mind if we get started on that baby right away? I have missed you. And I want to show you how much I love you."

Lily stood and Max followed. She went up on her toes and kissed him. "I love you."

"And I love you. With you, I am whole."

* * * * *

SECRET FROM THEIR LA NIGHT

JULIE DANVERS

MILLS & BOON

To Madeleine P. and Crazy Joe,
the best morning writing partners ever.

CHAPTER ONE

It wasn't even ten thirty, and Dr. Emily Archer had already seen three patients. A torn rotator cuff, an injured meniscus and a case of tennis elbow made for a productive morning, and she was just getting started. She looked at the appointments filling her schedule for the afternoon with a mixture of relief and excitement. Six months had passed since she and her best friend Izzie had left their steady, secure jobs at Denver General Hospital to start their own private practice in sports medicine. Izzie had been worried that they might not have enough patients to support a full-time practice, but Emily had felt certain that if other doctors made it work, then she and Izzie could do it, too.

And now, things were finally beginning to pick up. Their reputation as an orthopedic practice was spreading, and they were starting to get referrals from physicians who worked with professional athletes. She might have a busy day ahead of her, but it was nothing compared to the expectations she'd faced at the hospital, where pressure to see increasing numbers of patients meant working ten- or twelve-hour days, cramming as many patients into her schedule as possible without enough time to spend with any of them.

Private practice was a different world in comparison to the hospital. Emily had been able to see her three patients that morning at a leisurely pace, carefully outlining each treatment plan and talking over any obstacles that might interfere with healing. In addition to the reduced pressure, she felt far more confident in herself as a doctor, knowing that she'd had the time to thoroughly review and plan for each case.

She'd been certain that going into private practice was the right decision, but it had still been a risk. Even more so because she'd taken Izzie along with her. It had been one thing to put her own career and livelihood on the line, but with Izzie counting on her, too, Emily couldn't allow their practice to fail. And now, it appeared that her worry had been unfounded: their clinical caseloads were filling, and she and Izzie could relax, just a little.

It seemed like just the right time for a quick coffee break and a congratulatory moment with Izzie. Emily paused to gather the waves of her unruly mahogany-brown hair into a ponytail before heading into the receptionist's area to see if Izzie was between patients. But when she walked past Izzie's office, it was empty, and there was no sign of her coat or bag in the reception area.

"Has Dr. Birch arrived yet?" Emily asked the receptionist.

"Not yet," Grace responded. "She's twenty minutes late for her first patient."

A chill settled in the pit of Emily's stomach. It wasn't like Izzie to be late, especially with a patient scheduled. A hundred different worst-case scenarios raced through her mind. But just as she fished her cell phone out of the pocket of her white coat, a commotion at the door stopped her. Izzie was trying to make her way through the front door on crutches, her foot in a walking cast and her arms weighed down by her handbag and lunch container.

"Izzie!" Emily cried, lifting the handbag from her friend's petite frame while Grace held the door open. "What on earth happened to you?"

"Lateral malleolar fracture," Izzie replied, her face grim.

"Oh my God! You broke your ankle? How?"

"It happened last night, on my way home from work. That's what I get for biking after dark." She glanced at Emily, as though expecting an *I told you so*, but Emily held her tongue. A former triathlete, Izzie rode her bicycle every chance she could get, including to and from work. Emily had often expressed her concern that cycling home in the dark could be reckless, but she wasn't going to chastise Izzie now. It wouldn't help matters, and the last thing her friend needed was a lecture on top of her injury.

"Did you get hit by a car?" she asked.

"Not exactly. The car was parked—I just ran into it. The driver was getting out and opened the door without checking for bicycles. I managed to avoid running into them head-on, but only just. I spun out and caught my ankle on the edge of the door."

"You shouldn't've come in today. You should be at home, resting."

"I can't take time off now. Today's the first day since we opened that I've had a full schedule of appointments. The practice can't afford for me to cancel them all."

Emily tried to suppress the pang of guilt that stabbed at her heart whenever the topic of money arose. If Izzie still had her job at the hospital, she could be at home resting, knowing that she had paid time off and other doctors who could cover her patients.

"Oh, don't look like that," Izzie said. "I know what you're thinking, and I do *not* regret leaving the hospital. Sure, I probably could have taken today off if I still worked there, but what about the next day? What about the endless weeks of too many new patients and no time for following up with the old ones? This is better."

Izzie's words eased her discomfort, but just a little. "Maybe I can see some of your patients for today."

"A generous offer, but not necessary." Izzie rolled her eyes at Emily's worried expression. "Look, I know you feel responsible for everyone and everything, but I actually am capable of making my own decisions. I'll be fine seeing patients today."

"Are you sure? Because I can find a way to fit them onto my schedule somehow."

"I know you would if I needed you to. But I've got this. And…" She took a deep breath and bit her lip. "You might not be feeling so generous when you hear the favor I have to ask of you."

Oh, no. The realization of what Izzie's injured ankle would mean for the next several weeks hit Emily with full force. The World Youth Dance Championship. It was taking place in Los Angeles next week, and Izzie was supposed to be part of the competition's medical staff.

They'd planned for Emily to maintain the practice in Denver for six weeks while Izzie was gone. Not only had Izzie been looking forward to it for months, but they'd both hoped that being on the medical team would be a good way to form connections with colleagues in the sports medicine world. If all went well, they could build their practice's reputation, gain more patients at the professional athlete level and earn a place as medical consultants for other major sports events. The dance competition was supposed to be their gateway to bigger things. Now, it looked like those bigger things would have to be put off for a while.

Unless Emily went instead of Izzie.

There was almost nothing Emily wouldn't do for her friend…except return to Los Angeles. For a dance competition, of all things.

Emily had grown up in Los Angeles and started dancing when she was six. She'd quickly demonstrated a talent for it. She'd never felt more herself than when she was dancing, connecting her feelings to movement. But her pure enjoyment of dance quickly turned into something else. Her dance instructor was friends with an actor who knew a producer, and before long Emily found herself cast in a breakfast cereal commercial. And then the casting director had known lots of other people who needed a child to dance and to do a little acting in commercials, and he thought that Emily would be just right for that kind of work.

Emily missed dancing just for fun, but her mother explained that she had to keep performing, because they needed money, and this could be Emily's way of helping. How could she say no? Her father had just left, and if her mother said they needed money, then Emily couldn't let her down.

A whirlwind career as a child performer followed. She spent most of her childhood and teen years dancing in stage productions and taking acting roles on a few television shows. She had to dance the way others wanted her to, and memorize lines, and she had to do it over and over again, even if she was tired or had school the next day. But by the time she was a teenager, Emily noticed that even though she was working hard and bringing in a steady income, it never seemed to be quite enough for her mother.

At fourteen, she'd started to suspect their constant lack of funds had something to do with the acrid smell of alcohol and the empty bottles that cluttered the bureau in her mother's room. It had been a relief when a knee injury at twenty had finally given her an excuse to tell her mother that she was done with performing. For the first time in her life, Emily was able to focus on herself. She threw herself into her college coursework, and as she healed from her knee injury, she discovered she had a passion for medicine. When she eventually left Los Angeles, she'd promised herself she would never go back.

Except that Izzie needed her. The hope in her friend's eyes clawed at Emily's heart. But LA?

"I can't, Izzie."

"Please? It's only six weeks. Everything's arranged—the hotel accommodations, the flight, the scheduling. All we have to do is swap places."

Emily grasped desperately for an escape. "But they'll be expecting you. You're the one who applied for the position. You're the one they approved to be on the team."

"Nothing that a few phone calls can't fix. We'll simply explain to the administrators that we're in practice together and that they're getting a physician with the same training and qualifications as they would have had with me. I'm sure they'll be glad to have an immediate replacement instead of having to run around looking for someone just days before the competition."

Izzie looked at her with pleading eyes, and Emily once again felt a wave of guilt wash over her. When the two of them had left their jobs at the hospital, she'd promised Izzie she'd do whatever it took for their practice to be successful. Was she really going to let her friend down now, after Izzie had shown such faith in her? The competition could give their reputation a boost that would put them months ahead of schedule. Maybe they could even think about hiring another doctor to provide backup for times like this.

But Los Angeles held so many memories, none of which she was ready to face.

"I know it's a big ask," said Izzie. "Your mother..."

"Won't even know I'm there, if I can help it."

A glimmer of hope returned to Izzie's eyes. "Does that mean you'll go?"

"It means I'll think about it." Even as she said it, Emily knew that letting Izzie down was out of the question. Her friend was counting on her.

For the first time in ten years, she was going home.

A week later found Emily sitting at a hotel bar in West Hollywood, just a few blocks from the high school she'd attended as a teen. She'd walked by the hotel a thousand times while growing up, but she'd never seen the inside of it. It felt surreal to be in a place so close to her childhood and yet so utterly unfamiliar to her. The barroom was elegant but cozy, with gleaming dark wood countertops and leather chairs. More importantly, it was empty of any other hotel guests.

Or nearly empty. A man had arrived shortly after Emily, and he sat just a few bar stools away, nursing a drink. Emily tried to keep her attention on the medical journal article she was reading, yet she found her gaze returning to the man again and again. Dark, wavy hair that was on the longish side, and a pair of deep-set brown eyes. He had the kind of face that could have gotten her into trouble years ago. Before she became a respectable doctor.

She tore her gaze away from where Brown Eyes sat down the bar and tried to focus on her journal article. She hoped the man hadn't caught her staring; she didn't want to attract his interest, and she didn't want to have any more uncomfortable conversations than she'd already had that day.

He was attractive, though. Too bad she had zero interest in meeting anyone. If Izzie were here, she'd have groaned and told Emily that Los Angeles was wasted on her.

Poor Izzie had been looking forward to all the excitement that LA had to offer, but Emily had no such plans. Her intentions were to spend the next few weeks working, reading up on medical journals in her spare time and perhaps taking in a stage show if the mood struck.

The only reason she wasn't in her room now was because her memories were too loud in the silence.

Even at the height of her career as a child actor, Emily had only ever been moderately famous. She'd had a few roles on television shows that didn't get picked up beyond the first season, and she'd been in one movie. Still, she'd noticed a woman staring at her when she checked in, as though trying to make out who she was.

And then, on the way up to her room, she'd run into that same woman, who appeared to be traveling with her daughter, a child of about six. Emily recognized all the signs of a mother and daughter on their way to an audition: the mother's face, anxious and tight-lipped, the little girl's glittering dance costume, far too neat and unwrinkled for a child that age.

The woman squinted at Emily. "I hope you don't mind me asking, but...didn't you used to be Emily Archer?"

Emily wasn't sure how to answer such a question other than to give a small smile and a nod.

"I loved watching your show when I was my daughter's age...the one about the ballerina who ran the lost-pet detective agency? I was devastated when it was canceled." She nudged her child's shoulder. "Maybe if Samantha's audition goes well today, it can happen for her, too. Any advice for a budding actress? Sammie's very talented. She's quite a little dancer, and she sings and plays piano, too."

Emily felt her smile stiffen. She hadn't expected to be recognized so soon, and the woman's attention left her feeling exposed, uncertain. The little girl looked up at her with a nervous gaze, and suddenly all Emily wanted to do was to reassure the child that no matter what happened at her audition, she deserved to feel proud of herself. But the moment was bringing up too many memories that she wasn't ready to deal with, and too many feelings that she didn't know how to articulate. "Just be yourself," she managed to say as the elevator doors finally opened.

For a split second, the woman looked disappointed. "Thanks," she muttered, shuffling her daughter off the elevator. Perhaps she'd been expecting to hear something more profound, or some sort of industry insider advice that would make her daughter a shoo-in at her audition.

Be yourself. Such a simple phrase, yet she'd been trying to follow it for most of her life—with a dubious amount of success. When she got to her own hotel room, the woman's question was still swirling in her head. *Didn't you used to be Emily Archer?*

If she was no longer Emily Archer, then who was she? And why had she returned to a place where people felt so comfortable pointing her out, as though she were a celebrity rather than a person? This hardly ever happened in Denver. But of course, on her first day back in Los Angeles in over ten years, it had happened almost the moment she arrived. That was the Los Angeles she remembered. If you were even remotely recognizable, you couldn't walk down Sunset Boulevard without someone mentally calculating where you ranked on the scale of fame. Yet another reason she'd hoped to never come back.

She couldn't bear to stay in her hotel room, alone with her swirling thoughts. The face of the little girl, nervous and hopeful, had brought back memories of Emily's childhood that felt as fresh as though they'd happened yesterday. She desperately wished she had someone to talk to so she could take her mind off things. But she didn't know anyone else in LA; all her friends from the old days had moved, and anyone she hadn't kept in contact with didn't need to know she was here.

At a loss for what to do, she'd brought a medical journal down to the hotel bar and tried to concentrate on it while nursing a gin and tonic and avoiding the gaze of the dark-haired man in the corner.

Now *he* was the one staring at her, she was sure of it. For a fleeting moment, she wondered if he might possibly be attracted to her, but then her brain immediately supplied a number of reasons for why that couldn't possibly be true. Her entire body was hunched over the journal, she was wearing her university sweatshirt, her hair was in a messy ponytail and a highlighter hung from her lip.

She'd been so eager not to be alone in her room that she hadn't thought much about her appearance before coming down to the bar, and unless the man was drawn to medical school chic, he probably wasn't looking at her *that* way.

Why, then, was he staring? She quickly tore her gaze away and caught a slight movement of his head as he tried to maintain eye contact. He was definitely looking at her.

Well, if that were the case, then she needn't be wary of looking at him. She peeked over the edge of her journal. His wavy hair fell just past his chin. Olive skin, facial hair that was more than stubble but less than a lumberjack-style beard. He was wearing a white shirt that was somewhat rumpled, probably from traveling, and left open at the collar. Emily didn't date much, and the few relationships she'd had had all fizzled out after just a few months. But when she did date, she usually went for the brooding type, and the way this man's eyebrows hooded his eyes gave him an expression of intense thoughtfulness.

Or maybe he looked that way because he was deep in thought. Maybe he'd come to the quiet bar to sit with his thoughts, just as she'd come to get away from hers. For all she knew, the only reason he was looking at her was because she couldn't seem to stop staring at him.

Why *couldn't* she stop staring at him? It wasn't as though she'd never seen a good-looking man before.

Maybe it had something to do with those brown eyes of his. Somehow, they seemed richer and warmer than other men's eyes. She forced herself to look away again.

He spoke to the bartender, who began walking over to her. Probably to tell her that she was making his sole other patron uncomfortable, and to politely ask her to keep her eyes to herself. She turned back to her reading, cursing herself for being ridiculous. What did she think was going to happen, that the man in the corner would buy her a drink, they'd strike up a conversation and then have a passionate night in his hotel room? Most likely, he just wanted to be left alone.

The bartender approached, placing another gin and tonic in front of her. "From the gentleman," he said, nodding his head toward the man.

The highlighter fell out of Emily's mouth as her jaw dropped in surprise. The man waved to her and raised his eyebrows, the question apparent on his face.

She should probably return the drink to the bartender and call it a night. Even if she'd been looking for a date—which she wasn't—coming back to LA was hard enough without adding any romantic entanglements.

But then a germ of an idea formed in her mind. Perhaps Brown Eyes over there wasn't interested in romantic entanglement. Perhaps he might be more interested in...whatever it was that people went looking for in hotel bars.

It had been more than a decade since *she* had gone looking for anything, or anyone, in a hotel bar. But then, it was a decade since she'd been back in LA, and she was having a rough reentry. Whatever Brown Eyes' intentions for the evening might be, she knew one thing for certain: she was grateful for that gin and tonic he'd bought her.

She locked eyes with him and took a long, slow sip of her drink.

"Daniel Labarr," he said moments later, when he'd come over from his corner to introduce himself. "And you?"

She took another sip of the gin and tonic. "Apparently, I used to be Emily Archer." She watched to see how he would react, but he showed no sign of recognition. She relaxed her shoulders a bit. At least he hadn't been staring just because he recognized her.

He smiled, clearly bemused. "How can you *used* to have been someone?"

She put her highlighter down and did a little jazz hands motion. "Veronica Lawson, Girl Pet Detective?"

His face remained blank. "I have no idea what you're talking about."

"That's the first piece of good news I've heard all day."

"Damn. And here I was hoping that me buying you a drink might count as good news."

"Well. It certainly didn't go amiss."

"You didn't answer my question, though. How can you *used* to have been someone?"

"I wouldn't have thought it possible, either, but I was informed just this afternoon that I'm a 'used to be.'"

"You don't look like the kind of person who lets other people tell you who you are."

"Oh? And how can you be so sure?"

He gestured toward her journal article, with its many highlighted passages. "It's a Saturday night in LA, one of the most exciting cities in the world, and you're alone in a bar at 7:00 p.m. Even though you're in an elegant hotel filled with fascinating people, you'd rather read than take advantage of your surroundings. In fact, you've nearly highlighted this entire page. You're clearly not one to let your environs determine your actions. If you want to sit at a bar and read, then, dammit, that's what you're going to do."

She couldn't help smiling. "Fascinating people, hmm?"

He shrugged. "I couldn't resist a little self-promotion."

His shrug made him appear even more disarming and

had the added benefit of drawing her attention to his shoulders for the first time. Broad, sturdy shoulders. The kind that might make a man particularly good at holding someone.

A small voice in the very back corner of her mind was telling her she should bid Daniel a prim farewell and go to bed early so she could be refreshed for her first day on the job tomorrow. The other ninety-five percent of her was noticing how the waves of Daniel's hair fell against his eyes, tempting her to push it back.

She pushed a lock of her own hair behind one ear instead, trying to regain her focus. She still couldn't quite believe this was happening. More than anything, she'd dreaded going back to her lonely hotel room. And now, here was an excuse not to be alone. A handsome, reasonably conversational, practically gift-wrapped excuse.

"You're not from around here, are you?" she asked him.

"What gave me away?"

"For one thing, you look way too relaxed to be from LA." He did, too. Something about his posture held a certain grace; the way he calmly filled the space in front of her made her suspect he was used to feeling at ease in nearly any environment.

"How could someone *not* feel relaxed in LA? The mountains, the beaches...it's paradise."

"It's beautiful here. No one can deny that. But there's no substance."

"How can you say that? There's so much history to Hollywood. Look at this hotel—Judy Garland used to stay here all the time."

"The problem with Hollywood history is that it's all about what looks good to the audience. It doesn't necessarily tell you the whole story. Judy Garland is the perfect example—gorgeous on the outside but troubled underneath."

"Spoken like someone who knows there's usually more to a situation than meets the eye. Or the camera." He inclined his glass toward her. "Here's to what's beneath the surface."

She clinked her glass against his. "Cheers."

"You're right, by the way," he said, after they'd both taken a sip. "I'm not from LA. I'm only in town because—"

"Wait." She put a finger to his lips to stop him. His lips were light and feathery, and touching him made her feel a bit tingly, in a way that was more than just the gin and tonic kicking in. "Let's make a deal. We're two ships passing in the night, and nothing more. We don't need to know anything about each other beyond our names."

He raised his eyebrows, which made the rich brown of his eyes even more apparent. "If that's what you'd prefer. Although I have to admit I'm disappointed not to have a chance for us to get to know each other better."

"Let's just get to know each other for tonight, instead." She couldn't believe how forward she was being. Part of it was her reluctance to face the loneliness in her room, but there was something about Daniel that was drawing her, as well. Physically, he was on the muscular side, but the way he spoke, and the way he stood before her, calm and steady, with his shirt collar just open, gave him an air of vulnerability. When she'd touched his lips just a moment ago, she'd felt the faintest quiver go through her. She couldn't help but wonder what it might be like to let herself put her hands around the back of his neck, to feel herself pulled close to him.

She hadn't been pulled close to anyone for a long time. She'd never dated anyone seriously. She'd tried, but dating never seemed to go well for her. Her longest relationships over the past few years had all gone up in flames after a few months. It felt like ages since she'd been held, and she didn't think she'd mind being held by Daniel at all. And faced with the option of choosing between a man she barely knew and a lonely first night back in LA… Well, Daniel seemed nice, and he was certainly enjoyable to look at.

He put his hand over hers, very lightly, where it rested on the table. "Just for tonight, then," he said. She felt her hand come alive with the warmth of his, and the memories that clamored for her attention grew quiet as she gazed into the rich brown depths of his eyes.

The next morning, Emily woke with a jolt as her cell phone alarm went off. She grappled for the phone on the hotel room nightstand, stabbing frantically at the screen to silence it.

She blinked her eyes against the sunlight that peeped through the curtains, glancing around the unfamiliar room. Next to her, someone was snoring gently. Daniel.

She'd been right about him. He'd been funny, charming, interesting and had provided exactly the distraction she'd hoped for.

But now it was time for her to leave.

She couldn't believe what she'd done. It had been more than ten years since she'd had a one-night stand. But it had taken her less than twenty-four hours in Los Angeles to jump right back into old habits.

She tucked the waves of her hair behind her ears, trying to keep it out of her face as she gathered her clothes from where they'd been haphazardly thrown about the floor. Somehow her bra had landed underneath the credenza. How enthusiastic had they been for it to end up all the way over there? She wondered if one-night stands were as rare for him as they were for her. She hadn't asked. Getting to know him, after all, hadn't really been the point.

The last thing she wanted was to wake him and engage in any awkward morning-after conversation. As far as she was concerned, they wouldn't see each other again. Hopefully he'd understand that the moment he woke up and saw that she had gone.

She felt a twinge of guilt at the way she was leaving, slinking out without so much as a goodbye. He'd been nice enough that he deserved at least some acknowledgment of his existence. But what could there possibly be to say? They barely knew each other. If she woke him, then at best, they might exchange some false promises about calling one another, and she didn't need yet another person in her life who made promises they didn't intend to keep. She'd experienced more than enough of that, starting in her mother's old bungalow, a mere fifteen-minute walk from this hotel.

I am not that girl anymore, she thought fiercely, as she pulled her jeans on and threw her shirt over her head. Her cheeks burned, which made her even more glad that Daniel was asleep and unaware of the identity crisis she was undergoing as she scrabbled about the room for her belongings. For years, she'd built a life based on trying to be the exact opposite of the woman she'd been in her early twenties. She prided herself on being responsible. Professional. Steady. But then she'd run into Brown Eyes over there in the hotel bar, and somehow, her resolve to spend her time in Los Angeles focusing on work had melted.

Last night was just a fluke. It doesn't have to mean anything. It doesn't have to be a slippery slope back into old patterns. She'd simply had a moment of weakness, brought on by loneliness and old memories, and she'd given in to temptation. With time, she could forgive herself for that. But first, she needed to find her shoes.

Ah. She spied the pointed toe of one ballet flat poking out from beneath the bed. She gathered up her shoes, not bothering to put them on. Her own room was only a few floors away, and it was early enough that the halls were still empty. She turned the doorknob; the door creaked as she opened it, and she slowed so it would open quietly. At least she hadn't lost her silent creeping skills. And hopefully she hadn't lost her ability to perform the walk of shame with panache, if she did happen to run into any other hotel guests or staff on the way back to her room.

As she stepped out, Daniel turned over in his sleep, and her heart rose in her throat. His snores paused, and for a moment she was certain he'd woken up. But then she relaxed as his breathing returned to a slow, even pace. He really was very attractive, with his dark, tousled hair and his barely shaven stubble. But great hair or not, she needed to put last night behind her. Daniel, fun as he had been, represented a past she had tried her best to forget, and the past was where he needed to stay.

One brisk shower later, Emily was back in professional mode. She was determined to forget all about the night before. She'd come to Los Angeles to focus on work, and despite last night's interlude, she had every intention of spending the rest of her time in the city doing exactly that. She felt a tingle of excitement. As reluctant as she'd been to enter the dance world again, working on the medical staff for the contest was sure to give a boost to her and Izzie's practice. All Emily needed to do over the next six weeks was demonstrate her professionalism, make a few friends in the sports medicine world and do her best work as a doctor. That shouldn't be too hard, especially if she made sure that events like last night didn't happen again.

She took a cab to the convention center and found the right conference room a few moments before orientation was scheduled to begin. She was the last one into the meeting, but only just; a few other stragglers were still hanging their jackets when she arrived. She took the last seat available, next to a dark-haired physician who turned to greet her.

Her stomach dropped.

His brown eyes widened.

Emily was completely tongue-tied, but somehow, he was able to speak.

"Dr. Daniel Labarr," he said, holding out one hand. "I do believe we've met."

CHAPTER TWO

As a doctor, Emily knew it wasn't physically possible for a person's stomach to turn to ice. But when Daniel turned to introduce himself to her for the second time in twenty-four hours, she felt a cold sense of dread seize her entire midsection.

Desperately, she scanned the room. About twelve other medical staffers were settling into their seats. Every other chair was taken, aside from the one right next to Daniel.

The orientation was due to start any minute. How was she supposed to sit next to him for the entire day? The very thought was torture.

Daniel looked at his outstretched hand, which she hadn't taken, and then pulled it back. "I guess we've moved beyond the usual opening pleasantries, haven't we?"

Her cheeks burned as she glanced nervously around the room. No one else seemed to have heard Daniel's comment. Most of the team were absorbed in separate conversations as they got to know each other...because, of course, most of them probably hadn't met each other yet. Or at least, they didn't know each other on quite such intimate terms as she and Daniel did.

She realized she hadn't yet said a word to him. She'd

been too busy trying to overcome her shock. When she'd left his hotel room a few hours earlier, she'd hoped to avoid awkward morning-after conversation, but this was an entirely different level of hell.

She'd wanted to put last night's mistake behind her, not stare it in the face for the next six weeks.

Especially when that face held brown eyes with whorls of copper in their depths and dark, wavy hair that brushed against a firm jawline.

She swallowed, forcing herself to regain her composure. Her acting skills might be rusty, but she needed to rely on them now if she were going to pull off the role of Extremely Professional Medical Colleague with No Regrets from Last Night. She'd spent her entire childhood as an actress, hiding her true emotions both on and off the stage. She'd thought she didn't have to do that anymore. But she was back in LA now, and the ghosts of her past were haunting her in all sorts of unexpected ways.

She put on a bright, professional smile and said, in a low voice, "Well. This is certainly a surprise. I didn't realize that you were here for the dance contest."

"I tried to tell you last night, but as I recall, we got distracted pretty quickly."

"Shh." Her eyes darted around the room, and she dropped her voice to a whisper. "Dr. Labarr, please. I hope you'll understand that I don't want news of our… interlude…to become general knowledge among our colleagues."

She hoped he wasn't feeling snubbed by her hasty departure from his hotel room that morning. After all, they'd agreed from the start that they'd have just one night together. Neither of them could have predicted this situation.

Or was that entirely true? He had been about to tell her why he was in town when she'd put a finger over those soft, feathery lips of his. If she hadn't been so impulsive, they could have realized much sooner that they were co-workers. This whole situation was her fault.

Unfortunately, she had absolutely no idea what to do about it.

All she knew for certain was that she would give anything to prevent the news from getting out among the medical staff. The entire point of working on the contest's medical team was to connect with other colleagues in the sports medicine world and have the chance to demonstrate her skill as a physician. In order to build the kind of practice that attracted high-performance athletes, they needed chances like this contest, where they could showcase their competence and their professionalism.

She didn't want her colleagues to make any assumptions about her based on last night. Last night had been about escaping her loneliness and her memories of the past.

A small corner of her brain piped up that even though she'd acted impulsively, she had still enjoyed her night with Daniel Labarr. But that wasn't the point. The point was that she was here to work, not to have a fling with a coworker she barely knew. And she needed to explain that to Daniel, as quickly as possible, though she didn't know how to have that conversation with twelve of their colleagues in the room.

"Listen… Daniel," she began, with absolutely no idea of how to continue. What could she possibly say that would be both quiet and discreet and would not attract the attention of others around them?

She was saved from blurting out whatever words were

rising to her lips as an older doctor with large, bushy brows approached the whiteboard at the front of the room and addressed the staff.

"Good morning, all, and welcome to the medical team of the World Youth Dance Championship. I see some of you are already getting to know one another, and I hope we'll all become quite close over the weeks ahead. For the next four hours, we'll review some of the most common presenting injuries for our contestants. Now, if you'll open your orientation packets to page three..."

Four hours. And she hadn't even had time to pick up breakfast on the way in, as she'd been so worried about finding the convention center. Four long, hunger-filled hours next to a man whose bed she'd crept out of earlier that morning.

Half of her wished to speak to Daniel privately, while the other half wanted to run from the room and never see him again. But, of course, running wasn't an option. She'd been seeking an escape last night, and look where that had gotten her.

She flipped open her orientation book. She still didn't know what she was going to say to Daniel, but at least she had time to think about it.

Daniel was having a hard time keeping his mind on the orientation. Dr. Hammersmith droned on at the front of the room about radial fractures and hip impingements, but Daniel's thoughts kept drifting back to the woman next to him.

He could imagine how she must feel. He'd been shocked to see her here, though now that he thought about it, he realized that there'd been clues she might be a doctor. Still, even if he'd picked up on those clues, plenty of doctors traveled to Los Angeles all the time. There'd been no reason to think they would end up working together.

She hadn't fooled him one bit with that thousand-watt smile of hers, charming as it was. Beneath the smile, her shock and anxiety were all too apparent. If she was trying to appear calm, then she was a terrible actress. He might not know much about her, but he could tell that she was worried.

She needn't be, of course. Did she think he was someone who would kiss and tell? She might, given that she didn't know him at all. But that had been her doing. Right from the start, she'd avoided any kind of personal conversation. And the way she'd tiptoed out of his room that morning sent a clear message that she was interested in nothing more than exactly what they'd agreed upon: a single night together.

But working together was going to make things complicated. Daniel never got involved with his colleagues, although he rarely had any regular colleagues to speak of. He'd spent most of his career as a cruise ship physician, sailing around the Caribbean and then up and down the Baja Coast. When he wanted a break from the ocean, he took temporary jobs on medical teams at sporting events. The itinerant lifestyle suited him. He spent his days surrounded by beautiful people and places, and if he ever grew bored or restless in one spot, he could always travel somewhere else.

Frequent travel meant that he rarely worked with the same colleagues for more than a few weeks. There were others like him; friends he'd made who'd chosen the same medical nomad lifestyle. But for the most part, he was constantly meeting new people. He liked it that way. And he was used to it. As the son of a diplomat, Daniel's childhood had been a series of moves from one country to another. When he was a boy, he'd longed for a place that felt like home, where he could keep a dog or cat and make a few friends. But his parents had been dismissive of his feelings: How could he complain when they provided him with the best nannies, the best toys and the best education? Besides, they said, he had his brother, David, for company. David, though, was six years older. He was a good older brother, but the difference in their ages meant that they didn't have much in common as children.

With no way to change his situation, young Daniel began to feel that perhaps his parents were right. He stopped trying to make friends each time his family moved to a new country, because he knew he'd be gone in a few months. He told himself there was no sense in longing for a dog he would never be able to care for anyway. He did have many fine things, things other children might have been jealous of, if he had known any other children well enough to invite them over to play. He tried to focus on what he had rather than what he wanted.

And it worked…for a while. But as a teenager, Daniel began to notice girls more often…and they noticed him, too. He tried to tell himself there was no point in getting close to anyone. But then, when he was sixteen, his father was briefly stationed in Switzerland, and he'd met Sofia, who was somehow just *different* from all the other girls he'd met. Her eyes were a rich brown, and her hair had strawberry highlights. But it was her laugh, like tinkling bells, that had won his heart.

They'd had a whirlwind romance for two weeks, and then his father had announced that they were moving to San Francisco, and that was the end of his time with Sofia. Daniel had tried very hard to keep his relationship with Sofia alive. There were many texts, letters and promises to visit. Through a series of carefully planned moves, Daniel managed to get his hands on the family's emergency credit card without his parents' knowledge and secretly bought a plane ticket to visit Sofia in Switzerland. But when he called to tell her of the plan, she'd told him not to come. Her parents were encouraging her to end the relationship. It wasn't practical, they said, for Sofia to invest so much time and energy in an adolescent relationship that had only lasted two weeks. And Sofia thought that perhaps they were right. Maybe they should simply appreciate the time they'd had together rather than trying to force their relationship to become more significant than it was.

Daniel had been devastated at first. He'd thought that Sofia would work just as hard as he to ensure their love crossed the globe. When she'd ended things, he'd decided to give up on relationships. What was the point of getting emotionally involved if relationships inevitably had to end? He'd finished college and then attended medical school in the Caribbean. When he'd learned that cruise ships required a physician aboard, the work had immediately appealed to him—after all, a nomadic lifestyle was all he knew.

He'd never forgotten what Sofia had said—that they could simply appreciate the time they'd had, rather than trying to force their relationship to have more meaning. They were words he lived by. He had gotten on very well over the years by limiting his romantic encounters to flings with cruise ship tourists and locals at various ports of call. He avoided dating colleagues, because the world of traveling medics was small, and there was too much of a chance of running into someone again after a year or two. He'd made some good friends that way, but when it came to dating, it was less painful for all involved to make a clean break. Expectations and commitments only served to set people up for heartbreak. It was far better to enjoy short-term flings for what they were, not make them into something more.

And then life, as it so often did, became far more complicated.

It began with the birth of Daniel's nephew. The moment tiny Blake's fist curled around Daniel's finger, he knew he was undone. He didn't want to be in Blake's life once in a while, only able to visit if the route of his cruise ship happened to put him ashore near his nephew. He wanted to see this boy grow up. Which meant that at the very least he needed to live on land.

Beyond, that, though...he wasn't certain how the details would sort themselves out. Was he going to live in the same place for the rest of his life? He couldn't fathom what that would look like. He'd signed on to the medical team for a dance contest in Los Angeles that would give him a few weeks of work, but after that, he had only a nebulous idea of what his future held. His brother, David, a respected physician in nearby Costa Mesa, had offered to help him find a job at one of the local hospitals. But Costa Mesa was where David's life was. Daniel wanted to be near his brother, but he didn't want to live the same life. Which, naturally, led to a crucial question: What *did* he want?

He thought about Emily, who was clearly uncomfortable sitting next to him. Her discomfort was the perfect representation of what he didn't want. All this tension between the two of them was exactly what came of extending a relationship beyond its limit—and in their case, that limit had been exactly one night. Twenty-four hours ago, they'd both been perfectly happy, but now, with the complication of working together, seeing each other every day, relying on each other—romance simply didn't mix well with those things.

Just because Daniel was ready to settle down somewhere on land didn't mean that he was looking for a relationship, or a family of his own. Far from it. Being an uncle was terrifying enough. From the moment Blake was born, Daniel had known he would do everything in his power to ensure that he felt loved and cared for every minute of his life. The weight of that responsibility was huge. He couldn't imagine how much more he might have felt it with a child of his own. He didn't know how David could bear it. Especially with the role models they'd had. He and David had grown up amid opulence, but their parents had never been especially good at the everyday tasks involved in raising children. Daniel couldn't remember a single emotional conversation he'd had with either of his parents.

He'd told David that he didn't think he could ever have a child, knowing that such a small and vulnerable life was completely dependent on him.

"You're overthinking it," David had replied. "When it's your child, you don't try to add up all the pieces as though it's some math problem that you're trying to set up just right. You just dive in and trust your instincts."

Every one of Daniel's instincts was telling him that he wasn't cut out for family life. If he couldn't handle dating for more than a few weeks, then he definitely couldn't cope with parenthood. But he might be able to handle finding a job somewhere on land and staying in the same place for a while.

He wondered if he'd approached Emily last night in part because he'd wanted to prove to himself that things weren't going to change. When he'd noticed her at the bar, he couldn't help buying her a drink, just to see what would happen.

The way she'd been reading had caught his attention. She was furiously attacking each paragraph with a highlighter. It reminded him of moments in medical school when he'd been trying and failing to keep his mind on a subject. He'd try to focus his attention by marking passages, but he knew from experience that this strategy didn't help if one highlighted the entire page, the way she was doing.

If she was trying to concentrate, he didn't want to bother her. But he could swear she was glancing at him, too. Purely on impulse, he'd bought her a drink. She could simply send it back if she wasn't interested.

But Emily had been very interested indeed. And he'd been all too eager to accept her suggestion of a single night together. It had provided him a hope, of sorts, that things wouldn't change too much. That brief romantic encounters were just as easy to come by on land as they were at sea.

But it seemed there was one rather significant drawback to not being able to simply sail away the next morning. A movement caught his eye; Emily was twining her mahogany-brown curls around her fingers as Dr. Hammersmith's orientation lecture dragged on and on. He'd always loved hair of that rich shade of brown.

He didn't regret his night with Emily. He just wasn't certain what she'd expect of him, if anything, now that they'd learned they were colleagues. She'd been perfectly clear that she wasn't interested in more than a night together. But that had been yesterday, when they thought they'd never see each other again.

She sat next to him with her spine straight, arms folded. He might not know her well, but he knew body language well enough to tell that she was fuming.

They needed to talk, and soon.

He scribbled a quick note on the margin of a page from his orientation packet, tore it off and passed it to her with the tip of his pen. *Break coming up soon. Coffee?*

Her gaze was wary, and she pushed the note back without a response. He couldn't believe it. She'd been all too eager to jump into bed with him last night, but now she was hesitant to trust him?

He underlined the word *coffee* twice and pushed the note back to her. She crumpled it into a tiny ball and dropped it back on the table.

This was getting ridiculous. She must know they needed to talk. Or did she think he had other intentions? Maybe he should clarify.

He tore off another section of paper and quickly wrote, *I just want to talk about how to handle this. Privately. Just a strategy session, nothing more.*

She regarded this with pursed lips, then turned the note over and began scribbling a message of her own. She passed it back to him.

What if it looks suspicious?

Suspicious? They'd simply be two colleagues getting coffee together. Clearly she was more anxious than he'd thought. He wrote back, *Not if we go during lunchtime. We're all supposed to get to know one another. It'll look stranger if we're the only two people here who don't talk to each other.*

She nodded, slowly, and he hoped she saw the reason

in that. The two of them were going to have to find a way to communicate over the next six weeks. If her goal was to hide their "interlude" from the staff, then they'd have to interact from time to time. For good measure, he took the note back and wrote, *Our secret is safe with me.*

"Ahem." As he slipped her the note, he realized that Dr. Hammersmith had stopped his lecture and was staring at him. "Dr. Labarr? Is there something on that note to Dr. Archer that you'd like to share with the rest of the orientation class?"

Daniel was at a loss for what to say until Dr. Hammersmith continued, "Just teasing, of course. But in all seriousness, if we could all keep our attention focused on the matter at hand, we'll get done that much faster."

Emily glared at him. Daniel didn't even know if she'd seen his final note. He spent the rest of the lecture with his eyes forward, which was just as well, because he didn't think he could have withstood a glare like that much longer.

Emily could feel her stomach rumbling as Dr. Hammersmith wrapped up his morning presentation at an agonizingly slow pace. Ironically, he'd ended with a half-hour lecture on policies regarding romantic relationships in the workplace, which were not forbidden, but also not recommended.

When he finally allowed them to break for lunch, Emily was so hungry that she almost didn't care that this meant she would have to figure out what to say to Daniel. She'd be fine talking to him for hours if it meant she could get a cup of coffee and something to eat.

"Let's get out of here," he muttered in her ear. "There's

an outstanding coffee shop across the street. What do you say I buy you a cup?"

"Thanks, but I can buy my own coffee. Will they have food?"

"Best croissants ever."

"Perfect. Let's go."

She thought their conversation was innocent enough, but as they rose from their chairs, she was nagged by a feeling of exposure. It reminded her of how she'd felt at auditions as a child: as though every eye were on her and everyone knew exactly how nervous she was and why.

It's just your imagination, she told herself. *No one is staring at you.*

That wasn't entirely true. A doctor who'd been sitting a few rows ahead of them was staring at her now. His name tag read Dr. Reyes. "Hang on," he said. "Didn't you used to be an actress?"

Oh, God. She would give anything for this not to be happening right now.

"Yeah," Dr. Reyes continued. "You were on that show about the gang of teenage werewolf hunters, weren't you?"

She tried to smile politely. "That was a long time ago. I gave up acting for medical school, and I've been a practicing physician for the past five years."

Now everyone was staring at her, including Daniel. Great. She could add having to explain her former life as a child actor to the schedule for their upcoming conversation.

"I remember that show," one of the nurse practitioners piped up. "*Natasha the Werewolf Hunter*, right? I was bummed when it got canceled after just one season."

"So Natasha grew up and became a physician? That's fascinating," said another of the nurses.

Emily cleared her throat and forced a smile. Everyone was trying to be friendly, she reminded herself. They couldn't know how uncomfortable their attention was making her. "It's Dr. Emily Archer, actually. It's been years since I was in front of a camera. I've been working in Denver for the past five years, and my friend Isabelle Birch and I just opened our own practice, specializing in high-performance athletes."

There. Izzie would be proud; she'd seized the chance to mention the private practice. With any luck, she'd be able to bring it up more often over the next few weeks, and by this time next year, she and Izzie would be swimming in new patient referrals. The satisfaction she felt in taking this opportunity almost made up for her embarrassment.

And the discomfort was only momentary, as most of the staff responded with friendly nods and smiles and began to file out of the room. Everyone was probably just as focused on lunch as she was. But her heart sank as Dr. Reyes stood in her path, a contemplative expression on his face. "You know, I've got a ton of *Natasha* memorabilia at home," he said. "Maybe you could sign a few things for me to sell online. A signed copy of the Blu-ray set would probably pay for a nice dinner and some movie tickets."

Emily's mind was racing, but in her hunger-fueled fog, she couldn't think of an escape. "I, um, don't do a lot of signings anymore."

"Oh, it'll be no trouble. I can have my assistant bring a few things down tomorrow. It would probably only take you an hour or two to get through everything."

An hour or two? How much memorabilia did he have? And how was she going to say no to someone so forward, without being rude herself? She couldn't think of anything she felt less like doing than signing memorabilia from one of the worst television shows she'd ever worked on.

Dr. Reyes showed no sign of relenting. "How about a quick selfie together before lunch?" he said. "My friends will never believe that I work with Natasha now." Before Emily could respond, Dr. Reyes leaned in front of her and snapped a photo with his phone.

"That's enough, Reyes," Daniel interrupted. "Dr. Archer is here to work, just like the rest of us. Surely you're not so hard up for cash that you can't afford a few movie tickets."

Dr. Reyes stepped aside, clearly affronted. Emily felt bad, but also relieved: she was starving, and the man hadn't been able to take a hint.

"Sorry if I jumped in inappropriately," Daniel said as they headed across the street to the coffee shop. "But I know how Reyes is. He was here when I worked at this contest two years ago, and he hasn't changed a bit. He's completely oblivious to anyone's feelings but his own. I can't imagine how he's made it this far as a doctor—he's a good physician but terrible at patient rapport."

Emily knew the type. The profession was full of good doctors with terrible bedside manners. She wasn't surprised to learn that Reyes fit that mold, as he hadn't noticed her discomfort or backed down until Daniel stepped in.

"No need to apologize for that," she replied. "I couldn't think of a way out of the situation—probably because I was so hungry." She gave a long sigh. "So, I suppose I should explain about the whole *Natasha the Werewolf Hunter* thing."

"I'd love to hear the explanation, but I think I've already got the gist of it. I gather you had an acting career when you were young, and then you decided to become a doctor."

The way he said it made it sound so matter-of-fact. "Most people think it's unusual."

He shrugged. "Most of us have things we're good at when we're young, but then our interests change as we get older. That seems normal to me. It must have been unusual to grow up in the public eye, though."

She nodded. "That part was definitely weird. But people hardly ever recognize me anymore."

"I'll bet you hate it when they do."

"How do you know?"

"Because now that Reyes spilled your secret, I'm starting to put together a few things from yesterday. Like how relieved you looked when I didn't recognize you, when you said you 'used' to be Emily Archer. You don't want to be noticed."

She gave him a small nod, still a little unnerved by Dr. Reyes's pushiness—and also slightly surprised that Daniel had noticed her discomfort. Most of the time when people recognized her or learned of her former career, they bombarded her with questions about what it had been like to be a child actress. But Daniel seemed more interested in how she felt than in having his questions answered. And as much as she didn't want to be beholden to Daniel for anything, given their complicated situation, she was grateful that he'd helped her navigate away from Reyes. She wasn't used to having someone else look out for her that way.

"You're right," she said. "Offstage, at least, I never did become comfortable with attention. I've tried to learn to fake being okay with it, because most of the time, people mean well. They're excited to see someone who's been part of something they love. But every so often, there's someone more pushy, like Reyes."

"And then your real feelings leak through."

"I suppose. Let's just say that there are some times when it's harder to be a good actress."

A deep frown clouded his face. "Reyes is an ass. Anyone with an ounce of sensitivity should have been able to see that you were uncomfortable. Anyone who was paying attention, anyway."

She shrugged. "That's show business. You get used to it."

"Is that what made you decide to quit acting?"

"Not exactly. Dance was always my passion, but acting brought in more money, so my mother pushed me toward acting roles. I'd wanted to quit show business for a long time, but I couldn't bring myself to make the decision. And then a torn anterior cruciate ligament made it for me."

Daniel winced. "Dancing is hard on the knees. That must have been traumatic."

"You would think. But then I became fascinated by how my doctors were treating my injury, and I realized that I'd never had the chance to explore other interests."

"Sounds like you must have been under a lot of pressure as a kid, if it took such a severe injury to open up some other options for you."

"You can't even imagine. My mother was a classic stage mom. She used to forge doctor's notes claiming I was sick because I missed so much school going to auditions."

"Wow."

"My whole life was about performing. It was all right if I was dancing in a stage show, because I loved to dance. But I hated acting, and once I was injured, I realized that my entire life was structured so that performing was all I had. If I ever became unable to dance, acting would be all that was left for me—I didn't have any other skills. I'd never had the chance to see what else was out there. The knee injury was almost lucky, in a way, because otherwise I don't know if I'd have ever considered going to medical school."

She was surprised by how much she was revealing, but somehow, she found Daniel easy to talk to. He had a way of staring intently as she spoke, as though he wanted to catch every word.

They reached the coffee shop and placed their orders. As they sat down, he said, "So. We have a lot to talk about. I'm not even sure where to start."

She took a deep breath. "Maybe I should start by apologizing. The way I left this morning, before you were even awake… I could have at least said goodbye."

"It's okay. Actually, I was awake."

"What?" Dammit, she'd been right. She'd thought he'd stopped snoring just before she left.

"I heard you opening the door."

"And you were just going to let me leave without saying anything?"

"And you were just going to leave without saying anything?"

A fair response. She was the one who'd left his room, sending a clear message that she didn't want to linger over an awkward goodbye. So why should she feel as though he'd been the one to abandon her?

"The fact is, neither of us planned to see each other again. And yet, here we are."

She smiled. "Truer words. What do we do now?"

He twisted the edge of his paper coffee cup. "I'm not sure. But if you're worried about the news getting around to our colleagues, don't be. I don't have any regrets about last night, but as far as I'm concerned, what happened was nobody's business but ours."

A wave of relief washed over her. "I appreciate your discretion. I hope you mean it."

"I do. And I know we don't have much basis for trust yet, but I hope that in time you'll see that I keep my promises."

"In that case, I wonder if we can promise each other that in addition to not mentioning the past, we'll also be strictly professional with one another from now on. I just think it would be good to establish that as a rule, so we're both aware that situations like last night will not be happening again."

"I think that goes without saying," he replied.

"Good," she said, feeling her shoulders drop in relief. "I just wanted to make sure we were on the same page."

"Of course. I absolutely agree that we can't let the events of last night happen again. In fact, I'd prefer it that way."

"Oh." She couldn't help feeling a bit snubbed. He was taking all this exactly as she'd hoped he would, but did he need to agree with her quite so readily?

"Last night was a very welcome, enjoyable distraction," he continued. "But it was also completely meaningless to me. As I'm sure it was to you, as well."

She supposed she should feel relieved, but the words *completely meaningless* continued to replay themselves in her mind. "Good," she said, because even though his words were blunt, Daniel was saying what she'd hoped to hear. "As far as I'm concerned, we're in a great position to have a fresh start."

He gave her a warm smile that made her feel as though the sun had come out in her heart. "A fresh start sounds great to me."

Later on, she would find herself thinking about that smile. Remembering how it brought out a spark in his eyes. For now, she simply found herself noticing that even though Daniel was a colleague, he was also one of the most attractive men she'd ever seen.

But since he was off-limits, she'd have to spend the next six weeks being careful not to reveal just how attractive she found him. She could only hope she was a good enough actress to pull it off.

CHAPTER THREE

EMILY ASSUMED SHE would feel better after her conversation with Daniel. It should have been a relief that they'd both clarified their expectations. Yet three days later, she found that she was still thinking about their conversation—with some frustration.

Last night was a very enjoyable distraction...but it was also completely meaningless to me. As I'm sure it was to you, as well.

Completely meaningless?

Why did his words bother her so much? She'd felt the same, so why were his words stuck on replay in her head?

Because they were a huge blow to her ego, of course. That had to be it. She chided herself for being so shallow. Still, even though she didn't want anything more than one night with Daniel, it was frustrating to find that he could dismiss their time together so easily. He was right: their night had been a one-off. But had he really needed to stress that it was *completely* meaningless?

It should have been a relief to know that he didn't harbor any deeper feelings. Neither of them had gotten hurt. But his words kept gnawing at her.

She told herself she was being childish. She wanted to

keep things professional and so did Daniel. But she still felt a flash of indignation at his bluntness.

Perhaps his words bothered her simply because she was lonely. She decided to call Izzie and update her on how things were going. As much as she didn't want to tell anyone about what had happened with Daniel, she needed Izzie's advice. She only hoped Izzie wouldn't blame her for putting the practice's reputation at risk with her impulsive behavior.

She needn't have worried.

"Oh my God, *this is so exciting*! I'm so jealous. If it weren't for this stupid ankle, I'd be the one living the high life in Hollywood right now."

"It's hardly the high life, Izzie. Work keeps me really busy. I've been in medical mode so much that I'm starting to diagnose random people's knees as I'm walking down the street. And dancers get some really nasty infections in their toes."

"As disgusting, and fascinating, as that may be, I'd much rather hear more about this Dr. Labarr who's had such an effect on you."

"Oh, Izzie. I don't know what to do. It just felt so surreal to be in LA again, and I didn't know how to handle a night on my own. If I hadn't been so impulsive—if I'd taken even two seconds to find out anything about Daniel—I could have avoided this whole mess. You know I'd never intentionally do anything that would put our reputation at risk."

"I do know that, Em. Which is why I think there's something about this guy that must be a little bit different. Because you're addicted to responsibility. So if he got you to be impulsive and let loose, then those brown eyes you told me about must be something special."

"I just worry that it could reflect badly on the practice if word ever got around about it. People might take us less seriously as doctors."

"Doctors need to have fun, too. Look, I'm not worried about it. I know that with you out there representing our practice, other doctors will see your professionalism and the great work you do, and we'll start getting our names out there. I'm actually a whole lot more worried about something else."

"What?"

"I'm worried that you'll miss an opportunity to go after something you want because you're so busy feeling responsible for everything. It's one thing to put your career first, but happiness is important, too, right?"

Happiness. What a concept. Emily hadn't thought about happiness since the moment her plane landed in Los Angeles. But Izzie's words also touched on something else that had been worrying her.

"Are you suggesting that Daniel has something to do with my happiness?"

"It's not what you're saying so much as how you're saying it. Are you aware that you've been talking about nothing but him for twenty minutes?"

Emily sputtered. "That isn't… That doesn't mean anything. I'm just worried about our business, that's all."

"Is that so? Because it seems to me as though you don't have much to worry about now that you've drawn lines and agreed to keep things professional. You said you think he's not likely to spread the information around, right?"

"Yes, I got the impression he'll be respectful, but…"

"But what? You had your night together, and now it's

done. Yet he's still on your mind. Which suggests, to me, that perhaps you like him."

"Like him! No offense, Iz, but you're way off base. I will admit that he is *attractive*, but even if we were interested in each other—which we aren't—this isn't going to go anywhere. I'm trying to make a good impression on all our other colleagues. I don't want anyone to think I'm viewing this contest just as a chance to have a good time."

Izzie gave a long, drawn-out sigh. "You know, it is possible to have a good time *and* be an excellent doctor. Back before we both became respected physicians, we used to know how to have fun. Remember fun, Emily? It was a regular experience for us until we got jobs at the hospital and started working seventy-hour weeks. Isn't that why we went into private practice in the first place, so we could have time for a little more fun in our lives?"

Izzie was right. Not about Daniel, of course, but that there was more to life than work. "Hey, I'm still fun," she said. "Remember that time I brought cookies to work? That was fun. Grace loved them."

"Yeah. That settles it, Em. You need to aim a little higher in the thrills department. As soon as you get back, we're taking a girls' weekend. My ankle will be all better and we can let loose."

"Is that a threat?" Izzie's idea of an exciting weekend usually involved thrusting Emily into situations where she would meet men and then watching Emily fumble her way through.

"It's a promise."

Emily decided to change the subject. "How's the practice doing?"

"Things have slowed down since you left, but that's to be expected. With only one doctor here, we're only seeing half the patients that we normally would. But I know we'll pick right back up again as soon as you get back."

Emily nodded, trying to ignore the rumble of anxiety in her stomach. She reminded herself that they'd always known it would take a year to eighteen months to fill their practice, and they'd committed to a slow and steady approach.

"We'll get there, Em. But in the meantime, keep letting as many people as you can know that we're open and that we need patients! And remember that not everything rides on this contest. There are a few medical conferences coming up next year where we can network, too. The contest is just a good way for us to show our skills in a practical setting. And I know you don't like being recognized, but look at the bright side—every kid and their parents are going to go to you first when they need medical advice."

"I know. It's already been happening." As the contest began and she'd met most of the coaches and parents, she'd been delighted that so many of them had approached her directly with questions about limb-strengthening exercises and injury prevention. There seemed to be a strong preference among the parents to seek information from her, far more so than from the other doctors. But then she'd abruptly realized why: the parents seemed to think that by getting to know her, they'd formed some sort of connection in the entertainment industry. No matter how many times she explained that she hadn't spoken to an agent or casting director in more than ten years, the parents still thought she could reveal some sort of knowledge as a Hollywood insider. It was frustrating to begin a conversation with a parent's questions about health care and then suddenly shift to questions about her own career as a performer.

"But that's great news," Izzie said. "It sounds like things are going better that we could have planned."

"I suppose. But we're supposed to build up our reputation as medical professionals, not as the practice that has a former child star on staff."

"Don't worry about it. All publicity is good publicity, right?"

"Now you sound like the one who grew up in Hollywood. I'd better hang up—I've clearly been a bad influence on you."

"Wait, before you go. Just one more thing. This Daniel guy."

"What about him?"

"Em, I know how responsible you are. It's one of the things that makes you such a good friend. I know I can always count on you."

"Aw, Izzie."

"But the thing is, you don't have to *only* be responsible. You don't have to deprive yourself of something good. And I don't know if Daniel is something good, but…try be open to the idea that maybe the fate of the world doesn't rest on your shoulders."

Emily smiled as she hung up the phone. Izzie meant well, but as far as she had ever known, the fate of the world *did* rest on her shoulders. With the exception of Izzie, people did let her down. It was a hard fact of life, but something she'd come to terms with from a young age.

When she was six, her parents had divorced. Her father had promised to visit, but his appearances were rare, and his phone calls were rarer. His absence from her life was something Emily gradually learned to accept, because acceptance was less painful than holding out hope that her father would fulfill any of his promises to her.

Emily's mother had said that with her father gone, the two of them would have to work together to make ends meet. They'd need every dime Emily earned from performing in order to keep a roof over their heads. Young Emily had taken her mother's words seriously and took on as much work as she could handle, because the thought of moving away from her home and losing all her friends at school had terrified her. It wasn't until she was much older that she began to question why they always seemed to be in such dire financial straits, even though she'd been working hard for much of her childhood.

Emily knew that her mother tried very hard to be warm and supportive—when she was sober. But much of the time, she wasn't sober. By the time Emily reached her late teens, she'd started to go to auditions and rehearsals by herself, because she couldn't trust her mother not to be drunk on set. Her mother spoke of how they had to work together, but Emily often felt that she was doing most of the work herself. She was the one who'd made sure the bills were paid each month and who took care of her mother when she stumbled home after a night at the bar. Emily was used to being responsible for her mother and herself, because if she didn't take care of the two of them, then who would? She didn't have anyone else she could count on. As far as she knew, relying on other people was simply asking to be let down.

Her knee injury at twenty had been a blessing in disguise. For the first time in her life, she was faced with something she couldn't fix. All she could do was rely on her doctors to care for her and follow their advice. And to her utter surprise, her doctors had come through for her. They'd been completely honest about her prognosis, explaining that she could be healed, but she might never dance professionally again. No one made any promises they couldn't keep. They did their best to avoid any complications, but they couldn't make any guarantees.

Emily had known then that she wanted to be a doctor. Her injury had left her feeling so vulnerable. Trusting the doctors who cared for her had required a huge leap of faith, but they hadn't let her down. And they'd been straightforward about what she could expect, telling her the hard news instead of what they thought she hoped to hear.

It was a value she tried to stay true to in her own practice. There was nothing she loved more than telling patients that they would make a full recovery. But sometimes she had to tell patients some difficult truths. In those cases, it was important to her to be as honest with them as her doctors had been with her, because she knew how much it hurt to be disappointed.

Emily loved her life as a doctor, and she'd made friends like Izzie whom she could count on. Izzie was one of the few people in Emily's life who looked out for her—although even she wasn't right all the time. For example, her assumption that Emily liked Daniel was completely off base. Of course, Emily thought, it would be just like Izzie to confuse attraction for something more. But Izzie was wrong this time. Daniel was undoubtedly handsome, but he'd made it clear that he wasn't interested in her. The best thing Emily could do for herself was to ignore her attraction to him and focus on work, as she'd planned all along. And while she was at it, she'd do her best to forget about his brown eyes and the way they'd looked when he'd said their night together had been completely meaningless.

To Emily's relief, she saw little of Daniel over the next few days. He seemed to be keeping his distance: when she entered a room, he inevitably remembered some important chart work he needed to take care of right away. If she needed a colleague to consult with and he happened to be near, he'd defer to one of the other doctors and quickly extricate himself from the conversation. She might have become annoyed by his avoidance of her, except that she was so immersed in the hubbub of the contest. The constant need to wrap knees and examine sore muscles gave her little time to think about anything else, let alone Daniel.

She'd been afraid that working at a dance contest would bring back painful memories, but instead, she was reminded of the parts of performing that she'd loved. The costumes, the excited chatter of her young patients and the artistry of the choreography awakened a part of her that she'd thought was gone forever once she'd torn her ACL. She realized how much she'd missed the freedom of expression that came through dancing, the ability to convey an emotion through music and movement that words alone could never express.

She'd taken to watching rehearsals from backstage while she was on call between patients. With more than a hundred teams from around the world competing, there was always some sort of practice going on. Many of the dancers were extremely talented, and Emily felt herself enveloped in a kind of magic as she watched. Others were still developing their abilities, and Emily watched these dancers with a professional interest, noting where some might benefit from additional exercises to strengthen stabilizing muscles or stretch certain ligaments.

She liked watching from backstage, where it was quiet. Most of the coaches and parents preferred to stay in the seating areas, which made the backstage area ideal for watching in solitude. She was so absorbed in the rehearsal of a group of Canadian teens that she jumped a little when she sensed someone come up beside her, and she almost jumped again when she realized it was Daniel.

"What are you doing back here?" he said. "Wouldn't you get a better view from the audience?"

"Actually, no," she replied. "From here I can see all the things the dancers don't want the audience to see. All that the choreography is supposed to hide. I can get a better sense of some of the things our young charges might need to stretch or strengthen."

"But there are hundreds of them. You can't design a physical therapy regimen for every single dancer in the contest."

"No, but I can get a general idea about what needs to be worked on. I'm seeing lots of weak ankles across the board. The way some of the contestants are performing jumps, I can see there's plenty of risk for patellofemoral pain syndrome. That's nothing new in the dance world, of course, but I'll know what to keep an eye out for when the dancers and their coaches come to us for consultations." She nodded toward one of the dancers. "Look there. Her ankle's wobbling on the arabesque."

"I have no idea what that means, but I'm impressed. Here I thought you'd snuck back here to take a break, and yet it turns out you're hard at work after all." He smiled, and she felt an unexpected flutter in her stomach.

"Is that why you snuck back here? To take a break?"

"Actually, I came back here because of you. I had to know what you were so focused on."

She rolled her eyes. "Be serious. Did you need me for something?"

"I can't come by just to talk?"

He'd been keeping clear of her for days, and now he wanted to talk? He must have read the doubt in her expression, because he quickly added, "Work's kept me busy for a few days."

"Oh. And here I thought you were avoiding me."

He looked just the tiniest bit shamefaced. "I've been trying to give you space so we could keep things professional, as we agreed. But keeping my distance was getting a little complicated. We have to be able to communicate as colleagues, after all. So I thought, maybe instead of avoiding one another, we might try to be friends."

Friends. Emily had never in her life been friends with someone she'd slept with. But Daniel was also a colleague, and she did tend to become friends with her coworkers. And he was right: they needed to be able to communicate freely and easily if they were to work together effectively.

True, she was attracted to Daniel, and it could be hard to be friends with someone she was so drawn to. But if she got to know him a bit, perhaps the attraction would wear off over time. Right now, she only knew him as a handsome pair of eyes and a charming smile—but he was offering her a chance to get to know him as something more. Maybe if they became friends, that bothersome flutter in her stomach that arose when he smiled would settle down.

"Friendship wasn't my only motive in coming back here," he added. "I really was wondering what had you so absorbed. As you were watching, you seemed so… enthralled. I had to know what could hold your attention so completely."

She turned back toward the stage, feeling herself pulled toward the spell cast by the combination of music and movement. "Shh. Not too loud. We don't want to disturb them."

They watched the rehearsal together for a few more moments, and he said quietly, "Do you ever miss it?"

"I miss this part. The discipline, the precision. And the way the music and the motion come together to make something totally unique, every single time."

"Aren't they just doing the same moves over and over again? I thought that was the point of rehearsing."

She smiled, warming to the topic. "To the untrained eye, that's what a rehearsal looks like. But I've never done the same dance move twice. Each one represents everything going on in that moment. The condition of my body, the mood I'm in, the music I'm listening to. The effect the environment is having on me. All those things are going to create subtle differences in how I move, so that each step of a dance is completely new, every time, even if I've done it a hundred times before."

They turned toward the stage again, and Emily pointed out one of the teens. "See how she's doing that pirouette? I've been noticing a lot of those unsteady knees across different teams. We might want to put out some general information for the coaches about exercises to strengthen hip muscles and stabilize knees."

"I'd never have noticed that on my own. What's the move supposed to look like? Show me."

She didn't know what on earth possessed her, but she did a quick plié, a small jump and then a pirouette. It was the first dancing of any kind she'd done in years, yet it came back to her as naturally as breathing. Perhaps that was why she didn't feel embarrassed. Or perhaps it was the utter sincerity in Daniel's face. She'd thought he might laugh, but his face was completely devoid of any mockery.

"That was amazing," he said.

"Oh, come on. I barely did anything."

"No, it was impressive. It was so...graceful."

She searched his face again, looking to see if he was laughing at her, but he didn't seem amused at all. She wasn't certain how to read his expression, but it felt as though he were looking at her anew.

"Do it again," he breathed.

"I don't know," she said, suddenly self-conscious.

"Please? Just once more. I don't know much about dance, but I've never seen anything like that."

But before she could consider Daniel's request any further, they were interrupted by a crash and a scream from the stage.

It felt surreal for Emily to run onto the stage. For a moment, she almost expected the spotlight to find her. But she put her memories aside as she rushed out with Daniel close behind her.

A group of teens crowded around one of the dancers, who lay in a crumpled heap on the floor.

"Back up, please," said Daniel, motioning for the teens to back away. "Let's give her some air."

"What happened?" asked Emily.

"Ainslee fell from up there," said one of the teens, pointing to an aerial hoop that hung about sixteen feet above the stage. "It all happened so fast. We've practiced that move a dozen times in rehearsal, and she's never fallen before."

Two women came racing up the auditorium aisle. "Looks like mother and coach are on their way," she told Daniel.

"Good. Why don't you start a top-to-toe exam, and I'll get a quick history and keep them calm?"

She nodded. The teen was conscious and groaning, which was a good sign. Emily took her penlight from her pocket, shining it into the girl's eyes. Pupils were equal and responding. All good. She could hear Daniel's conversation as she palpated the girl's limbs.

"Is she going to be all right?" one woman asked. "I'm her mother. Her father's going to kill me—he didn't want her doing any aerial acrobatics without a net, but Ainslee begged us to let her try it."

"I'm sure Ainslee's father will just be relieved that you're here to take care of her," Daniel said.

"Was the hoop not secured properly?" asked the coach. "The stagehand checked and checked."

From the floor, Ainslee groaned, "My fault. My hand slipped."

"Lie still," Emily said. "Let's not worry about blame right now. Let's just try to see where you hurt."

"It's my arm," the teen replied, and Emily noted the telltale swelling along the girl's wrist. She traced the arm, very gently. "Don't try to move it," she told the girl. "You're probably looking at a broken wrist."

"What's going to happen now?"

Daniel squatted down next to the girl, his face reassuring. "The good news is that Dr. Archer and I are going to give you some medicine to make the swelling go down. You'll be in a lot less pain in just a few minutes. Then you'll need to go to the hospital for some X-rays and a cast for that wrist."

"A cast?" Ainslee half raised her body from the floor, exchanging glances with her mother. "For how long?"

"It depends on how bad the break is, which we won't know until we see the X-ray. But it'll probably be at least six to eight weeks."

Again, Ainslee exchanged a glance with her mother. There was something about those glances that made a wave of discomfort wash over Emily. Their expressions were all too familiar to her. She recognized the look of an athlete who wanted to push herself, and a mother who was all too willing to let it happen.

As if on cue, Ainslee said, "But what about the contest? Can I still dance with a broken wrist?"

"Right now, your focus needs to be on healing," Emily said.

"Agreed," Daniel added. "I know it's a huge disappointment, but we need to see what's going on with that wrist and get it on the path to healing before we can make any recommendations about future activity."

"But I have to dance. I've come all this way. Mom, tell them I can still do it. I won't do any of the aerial stuff. But I can still be in the contest, can't I?"

Her mother said, "Ainslee's worked so hard to prepare for the contest. She's had her heart set on performing here for months. Wouldn't there be some way to make it not so painful for her to perform? Just to get her through the next few weeks?"

Emily knew where this was going. Working in sports medicine, she'd heard such requests before. Athletes sometimes asked for painkillers to power through their discomfort instead of taking the required time to heal.

She always denied the requests. As a doctor and as a former performer, she knew that simply masking the pain wasn't what was best for the patient. Daniel, however, seemed surprised.

"What exactly are you asking?" he said, his eyes narrowing.

Ainslee's mother seemed flustered, as though no one had ever challenged such a request before. And perhaps no one had, because she said, "Dr. Stanek, back home... he never has a problem with prescribing some painkillers whenever Ainslee needs to perform through an injury. He knows she knows her limits. And Ainslee takes dancing very seriously. She'll be so upset if she can't perform."

Daniel's eyes blazed. "I'll want to have a few words with Dr. Stanek, because it sounds as though he's been completely negligent in his care. In the meantime, you can expect that Ainslee will need to take at least the next two weeks off from dancing."

There were disappointed gasps from Ainslee and the teens around her, but Daniel was adamant. "A broken wrist is nothing to mess around with, and we want to make sure it heals completely. I know it's upsetting, but the best thing you can do for your daughter is support her through her disappointment, not let her push herself and risk serious injury down the road."

"Of course," Ainslee's mother said meekly. "I would never put my daughter's health at risk. I only wanted to ask about her options. But you're right, Doctor." She looked at Ainslee with renewed firmness. "This is just one contest, dear. There will be others. The priority right now is to make sure you're all right."

Something in Emily's stomach twisted at hearing those words. For a second, she felt herself transported back in time, to another dance contest, another moment with a different doctor. Her own mother, pleading, saying, "Emily has an important audition coming up next week. She can do physical therapy later. For now, can't you just prescribe something to get her through the pain?"

The doctor had refused, but her mother had cajoled her into going to the audition anyway. A week later, she'd torn her ACL.

Tears threatened to flood her eyes. She tried to hide them, but Daniel glanced at her at just the wrong moment, and she knew he'd seen her expression.

"Hey," he muttered, as Ainslee and her mother argued, with her mother insisting that she take the next few weeks off. "You okay?"

"I'm fine." She wiped at her eyes furiously.

"If you need a minute to yourself, I can take care of things here."

"No, I shouldn't leave."

"It's okay if you need to, though. This isn't a two-doc job. It's just a matter of getting the ambulance here and getting the patient to the hospital for a cast."

She knew he was right, but as much as she wanted to be alone so that she could let the tears fall, she also couldn't bring herself to go. "I can't leave a patient I've cared for," she said. "I have to see her off to the hospital."

He nodded. "All right, but let me deal with the mom."

"You don't have to. I can handle it."

"I know you can. But you don't have to." He gave her that smile again, the one that felt like warm hands around her heart. And then he said the words she longed to hear but could never trust: "You don't need to worry."

CHAPTER FOUR

DANIEL WAS STARTING to wonder if he should go in search of Emily. It had been over an hour since Ainslee and her mother had been safely packed off to the hospital, and the tearful teens had dispersed to review their new choreography without their star performer. He'd seen no sign of Emily, and he was worried about her.

He knew that something had hit her hard, and he could tell she'd been trying to hide her reaction with every fiber of her being. She'd made a noble effort, but Daniel had noticed the stray tears that had escaped her furious attempts to blink them back.

He didn't know what she'd been so upset about, but he had a feeling it had something to do with his conversation with Ainslee's mother. It was always difficult to have to confront a parent and let them know that they'd been pushing their child too hard. He was glad Emily had allowed him to take over after the initial crisis had passed. She clearly felt a strong responsibility toward her patients, but there was no need to have two doctors on the scene for a broken wrist. And no need for her to push herself through an emotionally difficult situation when she clearly needed a moment alone.

But as the minutes passed, he felt uneasy at the thought

of leaving Emily entirely alone. It was one thing to give her space, but he didn't want her to feel abandoned in her hour of need. After all, they'd agreed to be friends.

In truth, he'd surprised himself by bringing up friendship. He was very aware of his attraction to her, and he'd spent the past few days doing his best to put that out of his mind. She'd been right during their conversation backstage: he had been avoiding her. Given his attraction to her, he felt that was the best way to deal with the situation.

But then he'd gone backstage, where he'd temporarily stored a case of bandages and other medical supplies in the large open area. As he'd shifted around music stands and set pieces in search of it, his gaze happened to light upon where Emily stood, watching the dancers from her corner.

The light fell across her in a way that enhanced the highlights in her hair, and he saw that among the brown strands, her hair held notes of dark auburn. Her expression was enraptured; she seemed completely caught up in the dancing. He leaned forward so he could see the dancers on the stage. As far as he could tell, they were simply doing the same moves over and over again. Emily was clearly looking at them in a way that he couldn't, appreciating something he didn't understand. As he watched her, he was struck once again by her concentration. He'd never seen anyone study something so intensely, the way Emily was studying the dancers. He had the feeling that she might not give her time or attention easily, but that once someone had it, she gave it all. He felt a twinge of envy toward the dancers. He wanted someone to look at him that way—breathless with concentration, her focus completely absorbed.

He couldn't resist anymore. He had to go and talk to her. He needed to know what she was seeing in those dancers that had her so captivated.

He'd been surprised when she'd danced a few steps for him. He hadn't expected it at all, but her spontaneity had delighted him. He'd noticed over the past few days that though she was a quiet person, she wasn't invisible. She had a presence that made people notice when she walked into a room. He hadn't been able to put his finger on exactly what it was that caught people's attention, but there was something there. And as she demonstrated the sequence of dance steps, he realized what it was. There was an unusual grace to her movements. The way she bent her legs or arranged her arms was always done with precision and care, yet at the same time it seemed to happen so naturally that she didn't even seem to think about it. He supposed the way she moved must be the result of years of dance experience, but he was struck that she could convey such emotion with just a few sweeping movements of her body.

Daniel had never been good at conveying emotion in any shape or form. It was something he had very little practice in. He did, however, know how it felt to hold back strong feelings. And even though he was inclined to leave Emily alone with her thoughts, a nagging instinct kept tugging at his mind, making him question whether space was really what she needed.

He decided to wait until she reappeared, but she never returned to the auditorium. He wanted to go in search of her, but he wasn't certain what he would say. What if she *did* want space? Then he remembered what she'd said about their night together—that she'd been alone with her memories and had wanted a distraction. What if she was alone and unhappy now?

He'd been pleasantly surprised when she'd agreed to his offer of friendship. Talking to her, seeing her passion for dance and for the athletes in her care had been invigorating. Now that he'd gotten to know her, he didn't want to botch their tenuous connection, especially as things had felt so easy between the two of them only moments ago.

He wished he could be more like his brother, David. When they were children, David had had the benefit of six years of additional wisdom. He always knew just what to say to help Daniel feel better. Thinking about David settled it: as a child, even when he'd thought he wanted to be alone, knowing that David was there had always made him feel better. He decided that he would check on Emily, just to see if she wanted to talk.

He formed a plan of attack. He might not know what to say, but in his admittedly limited experience, troubled friends responded well to food and drink. He bought two hot chocolates from a kiosk outside the auditorium and began searching the medical team's exam rooms, drinks in hand. If Emily didn't want to talk, he could always tell her he'd just stopped by to give her some hot chocolate and then leave.

He found her in the farthest exam room, her head in her hands.

"I come bearing gifts," he said, pushing the chocolate toward her.

She accepted it—eagerly, he noticed. She did seem to love hot drinks. He tried to look elsewhere as she frantically wiped tears from her eyes.

"Thanks," she said. "Sorry about leaving you with the patient."

"It was no trouble at all. The crisis was over. Mom and patient are probably both on the way to the hospital by now. They're fine. I was just worried about you."

She took a long sip of her hot chocolate, her hands trembling a bit. "I'm so embarrassed. I can't believe how easily I fell apart back there."

"Do you, uh, want to talk about it?"

"That's kind of you, but… I'm sure you have better things to do than listen to stories of my tragic past."

"Not really. We're almost done with work for the day, and I'm happy to listen if you need to talk." He realized he meant it, too. He might not have much experience discussing feelings with anyone besides David, but it grieved him to see Emily so upset, and he wanted to help if he could.

She hesitated. She seemed to be going through some internal struggle, and Daniel wondered if she was just as unused to emotional conversations as he was. For a moment, he thought she might have decided not to speak at all. But then she said, "I suppose it's obvious that your discussion with that patient's mother had an effect on me."

"With Ainslee's mother?" He could certainly understand why Emily would be upset. "It's always hard when a patient's parent is pushing them too hard. Fortunately, it doesn't happen very often."

"It used to happen all the time to me," she said.

"I'm sorry."

"It's in the past. I didn't think it could hurt me anymore. But then, when I heard Ainslee's mother pushing you to prescribe painkillers, suggesting that her daughter could power through her injury to keep performing, it brought back some strong memories. It all came flooding back. I couldn't handle it." Her eyes began watering again, and she quickly wiped at them with one sleeve. "I just needed a moment."

"I understand. Maybe not about that exact situation, but I can definitely relate to feeling shaken up by something that happens with a patient. And confrontations with patients and their parents are always hard, especially when they get pushy."

"But I didn't confront anyone! I didn't say a word. You were the one who stood up for the patient. You were the one who got her mother to back down."

"So what? As long as one of us said something, what's the difference?"

"I should have been the one who said something, because I know what it's like to be in that position. I know what it's like to have your mother cajoling doctors to prescribe painkillers and to feel like you have to keep going, even though you know, deep down, that your body's had enough and it needs to rest. But I didn't say a thing back there. I was paralyzed."

His jaw clenched in anger on her behalf. He knew that child performers could face lots of pressure. But parents were supposed to serve as a child's support system, not become part of the problem.

"Fifteen years ago, that could have been me," she continued. "My mother did the exact same thing. She'd try to convince doctors to clear me for performances, even if I was injured. She'd push me to perform, even if I wasn't feeling well."

"Didn't any of your doctors try to stop her?"

"Most of the time, they'd tell her no. But no one ever

acted shocked. No one ever stood up to her the way you stood up to Ainslee's mother. And so she never stopped pushing. She never backed down, never asserted that my health was what really mattered." She took another sip of her hot chocolate. "I suppose it's silly to cry over it. It's not as though I ended up addicted to painkillers. My doctors refused her, which is why I respect most people in our profession. But I wish that just *once*, my mother had said what Ainslee's mother did—that my health was the priority. Only it never was."

He frowned. "Some parents aren't cut out to have their kids in the spotlight, even if their child is talented. It's got to be difficult for you to be back in an environment like this."

"Actually, I was surprised at how well things were going, until this afternoon. Being here has reminded me that there's a lot I used to like about performing, mixed in with the memories of everything I hated about it."

"I'm glad it's not all bad. And you don't have to go through this alone. You can let me know anytime if working with a patient gets to be a little too much."

Her back stiffened. "I don't want anyone on the team to be under the impression that I can't handle anything."

"It's not like that. I just meant that I'm here to help, if you ever need it. If you ever want a break, for any reason. Just let me know. I'll jump in for you."

"I appreciate that you're trying to help, but it's not necessary. Honestly, it might be counterproductive." Even as she refused him, her shoulders relaxed a bit; he could see that she was calming down. "You see, I have ulterior motives for working at this contest. My friend Izzie and I left our jobs at a hospital to start a private practice a few months ago."

"That's fantastic. And very impressive. Starting your own practice is huge."

"Yes, but in order to get work, we need patients. And in order to get patients to come to us, we need to build our reputation."

"Ah. So you're hoping this contest will give other sports medicine bigwigs the chance to see you in action, and they'll send referrals?"

"Exactly. And that's not going to happen if I fall apart and turn to you every time I get slammed with an unhappy memory. Of which there are many in Los Angeles."

"Yes, I recall your deep love of LA. I believe you mentioned your passion for this town on the night we first met." She laughed, and he was heartened to see that she appeared to be somewhat cheered. He was even more glad that he was able to make a passing reference to their night together without the mood becoming awkward. Maybe he wasn't so bad at emotional conversations after all. Or perhaps they weren't as hard as his family had made them out to be.

He was encouraged even further when Emily said, "I do feel a little better now. Thanks."

"No problem. After all, even when things are at their worst, happiness is just around the corner."

She fixed him with an evil glare. "You did not just say what I think you did."

"What, 'happiness is just around the corner'? But it is, isn't it?" His eyes were wide and innocent. After their encounter with Dr. Reyes on their first day, he hadn't been able to resist the urge to look Emily up on the internet, and he'd discovered that *Veronica Lawson, Girl Pet Detective* was a children's cult classic. He'd never seen the show as a child, but he'd learned that the phrase *happiness is just around the corner* was something that Veronica said in nearly every single episode.

"You looked me up online, didn't you?"

"Guilty."

She smacked his arm, but without heat. He could tell she wasn't really mad. She hesitated a moment, as though thinking something over. Then she nodded, as though she'd made her decision, and said, "Would you like to get out of here? It's after five, and I think we're going to need something stronger than hot chocolate for the rest of this conversation."

Ten minutes later, they were sitting across from each other at a noisy bar in West Hollywood that offered an impressive array of cocktails and organic smoothies.

"Isn't combining alcohol and health drinks rather strange for a bar?" he'd said when she brought him in. "It seems like they're sending mixed messages."

"Not at all. From what I recall growing up here, everyone in LA is either actively destroying their bodies or completely health obsessed. Nothing seems to have changed in the past fifteen years. There's no middle ground. This bar caters to both crowds."

Emily wasn't sure why, exactly, she'd suggested they go out for a drink. She could have simply thanked Daniel for listening and sent him on his way.

But once again, she hadn't wanted to be alone with her feelings. This time felt different than her first night in Los Angeles. Back then, she'd wanted to escape her thoughts entirely. Tonight, she wasn't trying to avoid her memories. They were there, making themselves known, loud and clear. There was no escaping them. But somehow, they weren't quite as painful with Daniel around.

It was a good thing that he had happened to be there with his hot chocolate. But that wasn't quite right, she realized. Daniel hadn't shown up by accident. He'd bought that chocolate for her, he'd come looking for her, because he'd seen that she was upset, and he'd cared about how she was feeling.

She wasn't used to people caring, aside from Izzie, and so she hadn't quite known what to say at first. She hadn't wanted to burden Daniel with her bad memories of her mother, but her guard had been down and the words had come spilling out. And once they were out, she found that she didn't feel quite as bad. Izzie was always telling her that she didn't have to go through things alone. Now, apparently, Daniel had joined in with the same message.

She'd have to make sure the two of them never met or they'd browbeat her into an emotional puddle. Not that Daniel and Izzie were ever likely to run into one another.

Daniel was looking over the drinks menu. "This is convenient. The menu boasts whiskey as well as hangover tonics. I could pick up a few bottles of wheatgrass juice to bring home for tomorrow."

"Enough about wheatgrass juice. Let's talk about the reason we're here. You looked me up online and started quoting my own catchphrases at me."

"I'm sorry. I couldn't resist."

"It's not a big deal. I know anyone can watch old episodes of *Veronica Lawson* or *Natasha the Werewolf Hunter* online with a few clicks. Fortunately it's been such a long time that most people outside LA don't even recognize me. Or if they do, they rarely say anything. Not everyone's as forward as our friend Dr. Reyes."

"Has he been bothering you again? Do you need me to talk to him?"

The look she gave him was bemused. "Why would *you* talk to him?"

"I just… I thought…that maybe you could use some help."

"I can handle Reyes." She had handled him, too. Reyes had decided to follow through with his idea of having his assistant bring a van full of *Natasha* merchandise to the convention center. He'd begged her to sign each item. Although she hated to refuse a colleague, she'd had to tell him in no uncertain terms that she wouldn't be signing the merchandise under any circumstances. Not only was it outside her role as a medical professional, but it also would have taken hours. Reyes's collection was extensive. To smooth things over, she'd offered to let him to take another selfie with her—that, at least, had only taken a couple of minutes.

"Are you sure?" Daniel was looking at his phone. "Because that photo you took with him is one of the first things that comes up if you type your name in a search engine."

"Give me that." She lunged for his phone, then thought better of it. "Actually, no. Never mind. I don't want to see what else is out there."

"But you were asking me about it just a second ago."

"Yes, because I want you to tell me what you found. But I don't want to *see* it. I don't think I can handle looking at pictures of myself."

"Can I ask you something? Was there ever anything you liked about being famous?"

She thought for a minute. "I mean, I was never that

famous. I think we can say I was a pretty solid B-list celebrity at best."

"But still... B-list or not, you get to use the word *celebrity* when you describe yourself. Isn't there a little bit of fun in that?"

"I don't know if I'd call it fun. It was hard to make friends at school, because other kids only wanted to talk about the shows I was in. I could never tell if they were really interested in me. I did get to skip all the lines at a theme park once. That was fun. And sometimes kids my age who I didn't know would recognize me and get really excited. That was fun, too. But mostly it was a lot of work. I enjoy being a doctor much more than I ever enjoyed being semifamous. And there's so much weirdness on the internet today that I don't think I could have handled staying in the business. A few years ago, someone took an awkward *Natasha* photo and turned it into a meme. That was so embarrassing."

"The internet is a weird place. But if it makes you feel any better, aside from that photo with you and Reyes, there's hardly anything that comes up. There's all the old episodes of your show, and a couple of old *Natasha* message boards, and that's about it."

"That doesn't sound so bad."

"It's really not. Although I don't know why Natasha gets so much attention. Veronica Lawson was clearly your finest role."

"Most people prefer Natasha. She has a much bigger fan base."

"But Natasha didn't make any sense as a character. She's supposed to be a werewolf hunter, but she's this thin little wisp of a teenage girl?"

She laughed. He couldn't know it, but he was voicing thoughts she'd had as a teenager, especially when she'd gotten notes about her body from the network and the director. It had been her first role as an older teen, and she hadn't been ready for so many frank comments about her weight, or for the revealing costumes Natasha was notorious for.

"Her magic was supposed to boost her abilities, so she could punch and kick werewolves even though she was a wisp," she explained. "And I guess her magic also made it so that a midriff T-shirt and miniskirt provided all the armor she needed to defend herself from supernatural enemies. I was actually relieved when the show was canceled. As an adult, I look back and feel as though it's a miracle I didn't come out of all that with serious body image problems."

"It's a tough culture. No wonder you've got issues."

She raised an eyebrow. "I beg your pardon? I've got issues?"

"Of course you do. Everyone has issues." His smile was so disarming that she couldn't possibly take offense.

"Okay, then what are your issues?"

He thought for a moment. "I have major commitment problems."

Emily gave a laugh that was half a snort. "Of course you do."

"What's that supposed to mean?"

"Daniel. We slept together the first night we met. We had a night that was, as you put it, 'completely meaningless.'"

He winced. "Was I really that blunt?"

"I'm afraid so."

"Sorry."

"I graciously accept your apology. But based on our

history together, it's not exactly a surprise to hear that you've got commitment issues. I'm sure we both do."

"You, too?"

"I don't know if you noticed, but I was the one who suggested we spend the night together without sharing any personal information whatsoever. I think that probably screams 'commitment issues.'"

"You're pretty up-front about it, huh?"

"Well, I can always blame mine on my tragic Hollywood upbringing. What's your excuse?"

He gave a low chuckle, but his face grew serious as he considered her question. "I moved around a lot as a kid. My dad was a diplomat, so we were constantly traveling. My brother and I grew up in various different boarding schools across Europe. We never had time to get close to anyone. You know how you were just saying that everyone recognized you as a child? For me, things were different—I was completely invisible. I was always the new kid in school, so no one ever knew who I was. As soon as I made a friend, it was time to leave for another country. I could always find new people I liked being around, but I never really had any close friendships. We moved so much that after a while, it started to feel like there wasn't much of a point to having more serious friendships…or, later on, more serious relationships. So I stopped trying."

She thought she could relate. She'd often felt as soon as she started to rely on someone, they disappeared. So she'd simply stopped relying on people.

"I know you don't like Los Angeles, but at least you have a hometown," he continued. "At least you come from somewhere. Whenever I started a new school as a kid, people would always ask where I was from, and I had no idea what to say. When you've lived everywhere, you don't come from anywhere."

"So why keep moving? If you disliked it so much, why not find a place to settle down right away?"

"That's what my brother, David, did. He's six years older, and he's always been better at figuring his life out than I am. He picked Costa Mesa because he liked the weather and stayed because he found a job and a wife. But I can't do it that way. I don't want to just pick somewhere at random and build a life there. I want a reason to be somewhere. I want an actual home, where it matters if I'm there or not. And since there's never been anywhere like that for me, I decided I'd rather just keep sailing. Until now, of course."

"Until now? What's happened?"

"Blake Labarr is what happened. Six pounds, seven ounces."

Her heart plummeted to her stomach. "You have a child?"

"No, a nephew. He's just a few weeks old, but it's true when they say about children—they really do change everything. And the second I saw Blake, I knew that I couldn't keep up with the itinerant physician lifestyle. It's been fun, but I want to find a stable home base somewhere. Maybe not in California, but at least somewhere on land. That way I'll know when I can visit him, instead of being on a cruise ship's schedule."

She thought for a moment. "Would you ever want a family of your own?"

He shook his head vehemently. "I want to be there for Blake, but family life…it's not for me. For most of my childhood, my parents barely spent much time in the same country, let alone the same room. I don't know the first thing about being a family man. I can't even picture it." He frowned, thinking. "It's one of the worries I have with Blake. My brother, David, was always there for me, but I've never had to be there for anyone. What if I can't do it? What if I let him down?"

"Hey. I'm sure you'll be a great uncle. And you might be better at being there for people than you think. Look at the way you came to my rescue with that hot chocolate. I feel loads better now."

"Hot chocolate is just one small step, though. If I had to become a steady, reliable family man tomorrow, I'm pretty sure I'd fail miserably."

"You're not alone in that. The last thing I'm looking for right now is a family."

"I'm surprised. The way you get on so well with the young athletes we work with…you seem to really enjoy children."

Her heart gave a strange twinge. She'd always thought concepts like home and family were nice in an abstract sense. They were perfectly fine things, for other people. She'd seen from her patients how comforting they had the potential to be. Families could offer support during times of illness or strife. But she also knew firsthand just how painful it could be when things went wrong—when relationships were difficult and the support just wasn't there. Or when children were depended upon to support their parents, rather than the other way round. Her own mother could barely be depended upon to be the same person from day to day.

She'd decided long ago that she just wasn't meant to have a family. It had been hard enough to get through her own upbringing, and she couldn't bear the thought of the mistakes she could make while raising children.

What if a child of her own felt unloved or unsupported? What if she didn't know how to provide love and support? And whom would she rely on if she were a parent? She'd never had a relationship that had lasted longer than a few months. In her experience, people left as soon as things got hard, and she knew there were plenty of things about parenting that were hard.

"I do like children," she said. "But I didn't exactly have the best role models for parents. I've always been afraid that I wouldn't be good at it, since I'd feel as though I was starting without a good example to follow up on. And parenthood isn't something I'd want to mess up. It's such a huge responsibility. Besides, in order to have children, I'd most likely want to have a relationship first. And as we've both mentioned..." She gave a small shrug. "Commitment issues."

"And here all this talk of family life was starting to make me think you were a hopeless romantic."

"My friend Izzie would laugh so hard to hear you say that. She knows I don't believe in love, so she's constantly trying to set me up with people in order to prove me wrong. She means well, but it isn't going to happen."

"You sound pretty convinced."

"I mean, you can't hold out hope for something you don't believe is real. The best you can do is be pragmatic. I like my life in Denver. The practice Izzie and I are building is everything to me. I'd rather just appreciate what I have instead of wishing for anything more."

He gave her an odd look. "Someone else said something like that to me once. I don't think she believed in love, either."

Emily was aware that their conversation had grown

far more serious than she'd planned, but she couldn't stop herself from asking, "And what about you?"

"I don't think so," he said. "My brother, David, and his wife are very close. But what they have is built on something different than what we usually think of as hearts-and-flowers love. It's very real, and I'm not sure how they got there. I'll have to ask him sometime."

"So you've seen it happen."

"I have. But seeing isn't believing. It's not enough for me, somehow. I think love might exist, but I don't believe that everyone has a chance at it. I think what happened to David was a fluke. It was just fortunate that he found the right person for him. But luck isn't love. And there's no way for me to know if I'll ever have that kind of luck. I may not be able to have it all, so I might as well focus on doing what I can with what I have, instead of chasing after love, which might not even be real."

"Now that is a very honest answer," she said.

"Are you sure?" he replied. "I was worried it might be cynical and depressing."

Emily considered this. She didn't think Daniel's views on love were cynical at all. If anything, she found his words to be a refreshing contrast to what she typically saw in movies and books. Hell, she'd acted in films that promoted a hearts-and-flowers, happily-ever-after view of love.

But she'd never seen it in real life. Not outside movies or books. And it was oddly comforting to learn that Daniel saw things the same way. His skepticism about love made her feel safer with him. It meant that he wasn't the kind of person who made false promises or tried to put an overly positive perspective on things, all the while knowing perfectly well that he wouldn't be able to follow through.

Daniel might be commitmentphobic. But he was also honest. A quality that had been startlingly absent from most of the men in her life. She felt more comfortable with him than she'd felt with anyone in a long time.

"It's what you really think, and that's the most important thing," she said. "Goodness, if I'd known our discussion was going to get so philosophical, I'd have ordered a few more drinks."

"Did you want me to get you another drink?"

"No," she said. "I want to take you to my favorite place."

CHAPTER FIVE

THE SUN WAS just beginning to cast a dim golden haze over the tops of the palm trees lining the street when they arrived at the entrance of Griffith Park. Emily kept such a quick pace that even with his long strides, Daniel had to hurry to keep up with her.

"Is it necessary to go so fast?" he asked.

"Yes. Hurry up, or we'll miss it."

"Miss what?"

"The sun's about to set. And when it does, you'll have a chance to witness something very beautiful and very rare—something I actually like about Los Angeles."

"You mean there really is something you like about this town? Impossible. I'll believe it when I see it."

"Pick up the pace and you will. I can't believe I didn't think of doing this earlier. This was one of my favorite ways to spend an evening when I was younger."

It took them about twenty minutes to hike up a steep path, surrounded by sage scrub and oak trees. As they ascended, the huge dome of a white art deco building loomed ahead.

"Is that where we're headed?" asked Daniel.

"Yep. Griffith Observatory. It's the best place in Hollywood to see the stars. Or the sunsets, if we hurry."

They finally reached the top of the trail. A few stray tourists milled about the building's entrance, soaking in the day's last rays of sunlight. "Come on," Emily said, grabbing Daniel by the hand and leading him to a terrace.

She'd always felt as though there was something magical about Griffith Observatory. All the expectations she faced, all the responsibility that had been thrust upon her shoulders, seemed to melt away when she gazed at the sky from the observatory's terrace. When she took in the view of the Hollywood Hills, the towering high-rises and the bustle and life of Los Angeles that sprawled all the way to the ocean, it felt to her as though she existed in a world without limitations. She'd imagined herself as a bird, flying over those hills, free of responsibility, if only for a moment.

Of course, the view wasn't always perfect. The ocean only came into view on exceptionally clear days, and today the city spread before them was enveloped in a wreath of feathery clouds. Still, the clouds had a beauty of their own, lit up as they were by the setting sun.

"This is gorgeous," Daniel said. "I've been to LA so many times, but I can't believe I've never come up here."

"People say that all the time. But I'm glad this place isn't overrun with visitors. I used to hike up here at least once a week when I was younger, partly because the park offered some solitude. It's a special place."

She wondered why she hadn't thought to visit the park sooner. She'd been in Los Angeles for more than a week, and in all that time she'd been so focused on the memories she wanted to avoid that she'd neglected to recall any of the things she used to enjoy there. She couldn't believe that she'd forgotten about Griffith Park.

Something about spending time with Daniel had

shaken a memory loose and made her recall that she didn't hate everything about Los Angeles. She'd had good times here, as well. She'd simply been dreading her return so much that she hadn't stopped to think about whether there were memories she'd enjoy revisiting. But she'd been struck by the note of longing in Daniel's voice when he'd talked about how much he'd wanted a home as a child. He'd even sounded a bit envious of her for being from LA. And he was partly right, she thought. As hard as it was to remember some parts of her childhood, there were good things about it, too. If Daniel didn't have his own hometown, then she could at least share a little bit of the best part of hers.

She noticed Daniel was smiling at her, and she quickly looked away. Although things had become more relaxed between the two of them, she still felt a small electric jolt in her stomach each time he smiled. That was the price one paid for having attractive coworkers, she supposed. It was just as well that she and Daniel were becoming friends. The sooner she got used to seeing that smile, the sooner she'd be immune to its effects.

"What are you thinking?" he asked.

"Oh…just that I've never brought anyone up here before."

"Then I'll consider myself honored to be your first guest."

Emily gazed at the city skyline. As a girl, when she'd come to the park to take in the vast expanse of the city and the stars, she hadn't had to act, or pretend to feel a certain way, or worry about anyone else. She could just be.

But in those moments, she'd always been alone. Now, Daniel was here, and she was painfully aware of him standing next to her. It occurred to her that as eager as she'd been to share this with him, taking in a sunset together might not be the best way to defuse her attraction to one of the handsomest coworkers she'd ever had.

Too late to do anything about that now. Daniel had extended a hand of friendship, and it would be rude of her to offer anything but friendship in return. No matter how much the setting sun brought out the flecks of gold in his brown eyes.

"Is something wrong?" he asked. "You've been quiet for a bit."

He made it so difficult to hide things from him. She'd only known him for a few days, but he always seemed able to pick up on her feelings. No one she'd ever dated had had that knack for knowing when she was feeling something strongly, nor did she expect anyone to. If she said she was fine, people usually didn't question her further, even if she was clearly upset. Most of the time, she hid her feelings, and no one ever noticed. And now that someone finally noticed, he was off-limits.

She had to tell Daniel something, because she didn't think he'd accept "I'm fine" as a response. "I'm just cold," she said, which wasn't entirely untrue. With the sun setting, the breeze in the air felt slightly sharper than it had when they'd first arrived at the observatory.

Immediately, he took off his dark blue bomber jacket and set it around her shoulders.

"Oh, you don't have to..." she began but then trailed off as she felt the warmth of the sleeves around her. The jacket smelled so good. There were traces of his aftershave, almond and lemon. Unbidden, thoughts came to her mind of the last time that scent had wafted over her.

"I insist," he said. "There's no reason for you to be without a jacket when it's chilly out."

She felt grateful for the jacket as the sun set faster, casting an ombré of gold tones over the city before finally fading from view. She and Daniel continued to stand on the terrace, even though there was nothing to see but darkness now. She was aware of him standing close to her, she was enveloped in the smell of him, but he might as well be miles away. She couldn't touch him; she couldn't show him how she felt. They were standing in the same spot, but she was as alone as she'd ever been with her feelings.

Thoughts of their night together raced through her mind. She couldn't forget the heat that had come from his skin, or the way his hands had made her feel, running over her body and through the tangled curls of her hair. She recalled the compact feel of him as she'd come to rest, briefly, in the nook of his shoulder. She'd allowed herself to rest there for just a second, that night, because that feeling of lying in someone's arms, secure and held, wasn't meant for one-night stands. That was for relationships, for people who knew each other. But she hadn't been able to resist letting her head rest on his chest and feeling herself encircled by those arms.

She wondered if he'd thought about that night very much over the past few days. He probably didn't. She'd asked that they keep things professional, and he'd done so. Quickly, efficiently, without protest. As though it hadn't been much of a struggle for him at all.

"Are you sure nothing's bothering you?" he said.

"It's nothing. I'm just...very tired all of a sudden. Maybe we should go call it a night."

"But we just got here. Don't you want to watch the stars come out?"

She did. But she was well aware that her motivations weren't entirely pure. Her attraction to Daniel was growing stronger by the minute, and she was having a hard time wrestling it to the ground. The best thing for their friendship would be to return to the hotel and go to bed early. In separate rooms. "We have to be up early tomorrow," she said. "We should make sure we get enough sleep."

He seemed disappointed, and she could understand why. The observatory held a great deal of natural beauty, and she felt bad that they weren't taking more time to explore it. But she also didn't think she could handle being in such close proximity to him for much longer. Daniel had held to their agreement, and she wanted to respect that. And if she spent much more time wearing his jacket, she wasn't sure she'd be able to.

She was relieved that Daniel was unable to read her thoughts. *You're being completely silly*, she told herself. *You're friends. He's not interested in you. You already had one night of passion, and look how complicated that made things. Nothing's going to happen again.*

Nothing *could* happen again. The two of them were both planning to leave the city after six weeks, she for her practice in Denver and he for whatever kind of home he was hoping to find after all his years of travel. Obviously, neither of them was in a place where they were looking for a relationship. She concentrated on putting one foot in front of the other on the hiking trail and tried to ignore the thoughts of Daniel that swirled in her mind.

The path they walked was shrouded in shadows; they had to pick their way carefully down the hill. Emily had forgotten how dark the path could get after sunset, as it was purposefully kept unlit for the benefit of stargazers. She was just about to warn Daniel to watch his step at a particularly rocky turn when she felt him slip.

It happened in an instant; she reached out instinctively to help him, and they both tumbled off the path together, rolling a few times before they came to a stop amid crushed patches of sour grass and clover. He'd made a shield of his arms, protecting her as they rolled, and she'd landed on top. As Emily took a moment to orient herself, she was very aware of the sensation of his body against hers, the pressure of his fingers where they gripped her tightly.

They were both breathing heavily. "You okay?" he asked.

"I think so. You?"

"Nothing seems to be broken, but I'll need to sit up to check."

She tried to rise, but he was still holding her against his chest. She waited a moment, expecting him to let go, but he held her longer. They both lay still in the darkness. All was silent but for the sound of their breath.

Finally, Emily said, "You'll need to let go of me if I'm going to get up."

"I know," he said, but he continued to hold her.

Maybe it was the fact that he didn't let go that left her feeling emboldened. Or maybe, pinned as she was to his chest, surrounded by the scent of his aftershave and the smell of nearby sweet clover, she was finally unable to resist her own instincts. Whatever the reason, she made no effort to end their awkward embrace. She lowered her forehead to let it just barely touch his. She could almost feel his eyelashes flutter against her cheeks.

"Daniel?"

"Yes?"

"You know what we were saying earlier, about how neither of us believes in love?"

"I remember."

"Well, I was thinking about the other part of what you said, about not being able to have it all, but doing what you can with what you do have."

"And?" His voice was low. He made no sign of letting go; his arms encircled her as tightly as ever.

"I just wanted to tell you that I think it's a very good idea. Making the most of what you have. I think everyone should do that."

"Do you think *we* should do that?"

She couldn't see his expression, because it was dark, but she could feel the warmth of his breath against her cheek.

"I think maybe we should," she whispered, and then he was kissing her, his mouth drinking her in, his arms pressing her close. She tried to wriggle off his body, because surely it must be uncomfortable for him to have her pressing against him like that—but then he pulled her firmly against him, and suddenly she couldn't think anymore. She was lost in the sensation of her body against his, his mouth enveloping hers, his tongue demanding entrance at her lips. She opened her mouth to his, and her body burned for more as she yielded to let him in.

She could have stayed like that forever, lost in his kiss, but everything stopped with a sudden jolt as he gave a cry of pain. She disentangled herself from him quickly, and this time he let her up.

"What is it?"

He sat up and pulled one knee forward. “Damn. I think I must have twisted my ankle when I fell.”

Ankles. They were turning into the bane of her existence. “Can I take a look? It’s too dark for me to see much, but I could at least feel around to see if anything’s broken.”

“No, don’t bother. It doesn’t feel broken. I think I’ve just twisted it. There’s not much we can do for it until we get some light.” He tried to flex his ankle and swore softly.

“Does it hurt much?”

“No, it’s not that. It’s just the terrible timing of it all.”

“Or not so terrible.”

“Oh,” he said, and the hurt in his voice seemed to have nothing to do with his ankle. “I thought things were progressing rather nicely, but if I was mistaken, I’m sorry.”

She couldn’t let him think she hadn’t enjoyed their kiss. The very thought wrenched at her heart. “Things *were* progressing nicely,” she said. “Very nicely indeed. But isn’t that the reason we needed to stop? We’re working together, and if we become much more than colleagues, things could get very complicated very fast.”

He gave a heavy sigh and began probing his ankle. “You’re absolutely right. I was out of line. Don’t worry, it won’t happen again.”

Now there was a disappointing thought. But she didn’t have time to dwell on it. They needed to get Daniel back to the hotel so they could see to his injury. She stood up and held both hands out to him. “Can you stand? Let’s see if we can get you on your feet, and we’ll go from there.”

Daniel was several inches taller than Emily, but by holding her hands for balance, he was able to push himself up onto one leg. He pointed out a sturdy-looking walking stick that another hiker had left alongside the trail. By putting one arm around Emily's shoulder and using the stick on his other side, they were able to shuffle downhill to the road at an agonizingly slow pace.

Emily tried not to think about how it felt to have Daniel leaning on her, the same arm that had embraced her moments ago now draped across her shoulders for support. She wrapped one of her arms around his waist to steady him further. His body was lean and compact. She hadn't appreciated how tall he was until now, when he had to bend down to lean against her. She could tell he was trying not to put his full weight on her.

"Lean on me a bit more if you need to," she said. "I'm not as fragile as I look."

"Too bad we don't have Natasha's magic powers about now. She'd make short work of getting my ungainly bulk back to the main road."

"Well, you'll have to settle for me instead. The good news is, I've got something even more powerful than Natasha's magic—a medical degree. The sooner we can get you back to the hotel to take a look at that ankle, the better."

He tested his foot on the ground, then winced as he brought it back up. "Don't try to walk on it," she said. "We'll take things slow and steady all the way down. Do you want your jacket back?"

"Don't even think about it. You're keeping that jacket on until we get inside, out of the cold. It's the least I can do after you've allowed me to use you as a human crutch."

Eventually, they reached the main road, where Daniel called a cab to take them back to their hotel. They reached the lobby and nearly collapsed into an elevator.

"I can probably hobble into my room from here," he said.

She frowned. She hadn't anticipated ever seeing the inside of Daniel's hotel room again. But he was injured. She couldn't just leave him by himself. What if his situation was worse than they'd realized?

"I'm coming in with you, and we're going to take a look at that ankle together," she said in her firmest no-nonsense voice. He started to protest, and she gave him a look that brooked no further discussion.

They entered his room, Daniel performing an odd hop-shuffle onto the bed. He rolled back the leg of his slacks.

"You really don't need to do this," he said. "I'm a doctor, too. It's not as though I've never bandaged an ankle before."

"Just let me take a look. It's my fault you got hurt—if I hadn't brought you up there at sunset, you wouldn't have been hiking in the dark."

"Emily." He caught her hand, which had begun to unlace his boot. The way he said her name made her stomach perform the same jeté it had been doing since he'd first smiled at her earlier that evening. "This is not your fault. Accidents happen."

She nodded, trying to believe him.

"Besides, I had a good time. Well worth a little ankle pain." He unlaced his boot and eased it off his foot along with his sock, groaning.

He was sitting on the edge of the bed. She pulled up a chair and sat in front of him. "Here. Give me your leg."

"I'll be fine. I don't need examining. It's probably just a sprain."

"So it's true that doctors make the worst patients. Let me take a look right now so we can make sure it's nothing more serious." He hesitated, and she said, "If it is just a sprain, then you've got nothing to worry about, have you?"

Reluctantly, he stretched out his leg. She held it aloft with one hand and used the other to palpate the ankle, looking for any swelling or discoloration. "Relax your foot."

He did, and she began to test the ankle's range of motion, stopping when he winced. "You were right," she said. "It's just a sprain. Baby it for a few days, but put a little weight on it every now and then to stimulate blood flow, and you'll be good as new."

"I know what to do for a sprain. You'd think I never went to medical school."

"Then you'll know you should be elevating this. Come on, scoot back on the bed."

"I don't need anyone fussing over me," he protested.

"I'm not fussing. I'm just going to get you situated and put that leg up before I leave. Do you have any ibuprofen?"

"There's some in the duffel bag on the bureau, along with some bandages and an instant cold pack. But I can tape it up myself."

She gave him a firm look and retrieved the pain relievers, along with the bandages and the cold pack. Daniel swallowed two of the pills dry as she bandaged his ankle. His skin was hot against her fingers. As she finished bandaging, thoughts of the last time she'd been in this hotel room, and in this bed, threatened to overtake her mind. Those had been very different circumstances, indeed.

As she finished, he sat up. "Hey," she said, "Lie back down. You're supposed to keep that elevated." She squeezed the cold pack—a bag of water and ammonium nitrate—to activate it and then placed it against his ankle to keep the swelling down.

He flexed his foot a tiny bit. "I think you've put it in very good shape to heal up nicely. I can barely feel it at all anymore."

"Still. You should lie down."

"If it's doctor's orders, then I suppose I can't argue."

He lay back down, and Emily set the bottle of ibuprofen next to a glass of water on the nightstand. "Take two of these if you wake up at night, otherwise, just take them in the morning if there's any pain."

She knew it was time to leave. She'd taken care of his ankle, and there was nothing else she could do for him. But she couldn't bring herself to turn away. The memory of Daniel's kiss still burned on her lips.

He'd said it wouldn't happen again. Promised her, in fact, that it wouldn't. Because he knew she wanted to keep things professional, and for some reason, it seemed that what she wanted mattered to him.

It was a good thing he didn't know what she wanted right now. She was using every ounce of effort to prevent herself from trying to finish what they'd started in the park. The best thing for both of them right now would be for her to turn and leave.

But somehow, she couldn't bring herself to do it.

He caught her hand and held it for a moment. "Thanks."

"For almost getting your ankle broken?"

"For showing me something that was special to you."

He was still holding her hand. She knew she should let go, but something stopped her. She could still smell that scent of lemon and almond aftershave. Half an hour ago, he'd held her as her body practically melted into his during their kiss. They'd had their arms around each other for the entire trek down from the park to the main road. And she was still wearing his jacket.

"I should give this back," she said, taking it off. Without thinking, she brushed a few strands of hair out of his eyes. As she brushed them away, he caught the palm of her hand and held it against his cheek.

His face burned with a question. She hadn't been able to see his eyes when they'd kissed in the park. It had been too dark for her to see him at all. That kiss didn't really count, she thought, because it had happened almost by accident, after they'd tumbled off the path together. She didn't want an accidental kiss. She wanted a real one. But he'd promised her that it wouldn't happen again.

At least, it wouldn't happen again because of him. But the question in his eyes and the intensity of his gaze told her that she might be able to prevent that kiss in the park from being their last. If she wanted to.

There was only one way to find out.

She leaned in and pressed her lips against his, softly at first, and then more deeply as she ran her fingers through the long, wavy hair that she'd been longing to touch since their first night together. His hands went to her shoulders, then cupped her face, as though he were drinking her in.

He broke apart from her kiss, searching her eyes, to be sure, she knew, that she wanted this. "Is this a good idea?" he asked, his voice coming out in a ragged rasp.

"Probably not," she replied and leaned forward to kiss him again.

He responded with equal intensity, pulling her farther onto the bed so that she was nearly on top of him, his tongue once again demanding entry to her mouth. She yielded readily, relishing the feeling of his mouth on hers.

He was reaching above his head for something on the nightstand—protection, she realized. But as he reached, he winced again.

"Is your ankle all right? Do you need to stop?"

"Not on your life," he replied and pulled her to him again, his mouth enveloping hers.

He unbuttoned her jeans and slipped her waistband down her hips, peeling away her underwear. She kicked off her jeans and her hands flew to his belt buckle, shimmying his trousers down and off.

She lay next to him, nearly on top of him, and could feel him growing ready against one thigh. He moved his hands along her waist, then up to her breasts, where he gently grazed her nipples with his thumbs. She couldn't help emitting a small gasp, her nipples stiffening as he traced them lightly. His hands moved over her more firmly, and she moaned as he stroked and tugged, while an ache from deep within her threatened to become stronger by the minute.

She began to unbutton his shirt, her hands trembling from the growing want within her that was quickly becoming a need. He broke away from their kiss again in order to lift her T-shirt over her head. She finally managed to get his shirt open, and he tore it off with an urgency that made her wonder if he had been longing for this moment as much as she had.

He pulled the straps of her bra down and released one breast, and she cried out with pleasure as he laved her nipple with his tongue. He reached behind her and unhooked her bra so that both breasts fell before him. He cupped them both and looked up at her, breathless.

"My God, you're beautiful," he said.

There was something about this that was so different than their first time together. Now that she knew him, everything had changed. She liked him, respected him…his opinion mattered. She was still attracted to him, more than ever. But just as caring about him turned up the intensity of their heat together, it also made her feel as though the stakes were somehow higher than they had been when they'd first met. After just a few days of knowing him, there was an intimacy to what they were doing that she wasn't used to.

He opened the square packet and sheathed himself, and then reached to cup her bottom as she lowered herself onto him. He thrust forward and entered her with dizzying speed, and for a moment she thought she might shatter as he pushed himself into her, again and again. His movements were forceful, matching the intensity of her yearning, and as her body responded to his thrusts, their hips moved together and they found their own rhythm within a timeless dance.

It *was* like a dance, and despite the short time she'd known him, their movements felt as graceful as any pas de deux she'd ever performed, their bodies seeming to know exactly what to do. Only in this dance, she felt as though she were about to be lifted to a height she'd never been, and she wasn't certain if her feet would ever return to touch the ground.

His movements came faster now, and suddenly she was transported to that place beyond thought, where there was only the sensation of her body and his, their breath intermingling, their bodies intertwined. She felt herself shatter, over and over again, as he surged inside her and cried her name until, finally, breathless, she collapsed next to him.

She allowed herself to nestle into the crook of his

arm, and he held her against his chest, nuzzling his nose into her ear.

"I've been wanting to do that all week," he muttered.

"Me, too." She was glad to hear that he'd felt the same as she had, although what they'd just done had left her with little doubt about that. Still, it was nice to hear him say it. Their first night together might have been meaningless, as they hadn't known anything about one another and hadn't planned to see each other again. But tonight was…what, exactly? Not meaningless. But not a lifetime commitment or a star-crossed love affair, either.

She felt him tighten his arms around her. They could talk about what they were to each other later, she decided. This time, there would be no escaping that conversation. But for once, she didn't dread the morning-after talk. She might not have known Daniel for long, but she knew he would make her no false promises. She nuzzled more deeply into the crook of his shoulder as her eyes closed. Tomorrow would take care of itself. For tonight, she wanted to make the most of what she had.

CHAPTER SIX

EMILY SLIPPED OUT of the bed quietly in search of an early breakfast. Over the past few days, she'd been plagued by stronger-than-usual PMS symptoms. She'd found that having some food in the morning helped to ease things: a few bites of dry toast and a cup of tea gave her stomach something to focus on besides cramps.

Once again, she found herself tiptoeing across Daniel's hotel room, trying to leave without waking him. Only this time, she brought his key card with her so that she could get back in when she was done with breakfast. She'd only be a few minutes, and she really didn't want to disturb him just to tell him she was stepping out for a moment. His alarm was sure to go off within the hour to wake him up for work, and he'd need as much rest as he could get to help heal his ankle injury.

Getting rest certainly hadn't been on his mind last night. As complicated as their situation had become, she couldn't help smiling to herself. At least this time, she didn't have to worry about what Izzie might think. Izzie had made it clear that she wanted her to seize the moment, and Emily had certainly followed through on that advice.

But as she waited for her toast in the hotel dining

room, she knew that she and Daniel wouldn't be able to avoid facing up to the consequences of what they'd done. And the biggest part of it would be figuring out what they were to one another—if anything at all.

He'd said last night that he didn't believe in love and that he wasn't looking for a long-term relationship. She liked that he'd been so up-front about his feelings. It made her trust him more. She'd dated plenty of men who'd spouted off nonsense about how much they wanted a serious relationship, only to stop hearing from them after a few dates. She'd eventually realized that those men were simply saying what they thought she wanted to hear.

Daniel, however, had been clear about what he wanted. He might be looking for a home, but he wasn't looking for a relationship. Emily wasn't looking for that, either. And she already had a home, in Denver. She had friends and a medical practice that she'd built through her own efforts. Her life now was quiet, stable and secure. For so long, she'd focused on building a life that was as different from her childhood as she could make it. And now, with her life in Denver settled and her practice growing, all her plans were coming to fruition. What more could she possibly want?

She'd given up on any hope of a relationship long ago. On the rare occasions when she'd had deepening emotions for anyone she'd dated, she'd been let down. It happened over and over again. There'd been the guy who wanted an open relationship but had had an unusual interpretation of the word *open*, which only seemed to apply when he was interested in other women. There had been the man who was more than happy to spend time with her and take her on lots of dates—as long as she was the one paying. And there was the guy who—after a tempestuous, emotionally intense month with her—had left her apartment in the dead of night, along with a large sum of money from her wallet.

Her string of bad experiences had led her to believe that even though she might want a long-term partner, she probably wasn't going to find one. And since dating wasn't working out for her, she might as well resign herself to being happy with what she had in Denver: her practice and her friends.

And if she sometimes wished for something more—someone to love, perhaps, or a family—she simply reminded herself that if her role models for relationships were bad, her role models for parenting were even worse. She didn't know how to be a parent any more than she knew how to have a long-term relationship, and so it was best for everyone, really, if she simply ignored any desire for either of those things.

After their conversation of the night before, she was certain that Daniel wouldn't have any designs on deepening their relationship, either. Which was fortunate. If she'd met him at a different time in her life, she might be in serious danger of falling for him. It wasn't just her attraction to him, she realized. It was who he was as a person. Izzie was right—she *did* like him. Usually, the more she got to know someone, the more red flags she found. But the more she got to know Daniel, the more she felt he was being honest with her.

Maybe that was why she felt none of the frantic worry she'd had the morning after her first night with him, when she'd abruptly learned they were coworkers. She knew him now. Trusted him.

The question was, what would he do with that trust?

She was always uneasy whenever she began feeling

anything more than a surface-level attraction. Getting attached was a guaranteed way to get hurt, and she'd always thought it was best to avoid that by keeping men at arm's length. If she didn't get close to anyone, she didn't have to worry about them letting her down later on.

But if she and Daniel didn't have any expectations of one another, then neither of them would be let down. If commitments led to disappointment, then maybe they could avoid that by taking commitment out of the equation.

The germ of an idea began to form in her mind. She wasn't certain how Daniel would feel about it. But they needed to think of something to do about their situation, and as she sat munching her toast, she thought she might have come up with something that could work.

With a start, she realized she'd been away from Daniel's room for longer than she'd expected. He'd understand that she was coming back...wouldn't he? She hoped he wouldn't think she'd slunk out of his room without intending to talk.

Then again, she hadn't left him a note or any indication that she was returning.

What if he was awake, wondering where she was? What if he assumed she'd left because she didn't want to talk about what had happened, the way he'd assumed she hadn't been enjoying their kiss after his fall last night?

Suddenly, she realized that she really wanted to get back to his room before he woke up. She headed toward the elevator, picking up speed along the way.

Daniel's cell phone buzzed insistently from the nightstand. He rubbed his fingers into his bleary eyes, trying to orient himself. He was usually an early riser and had a standing alarm set for six in the morning, but last night had kept him up later than usual. A dull throb came from his ankle, which turned into a quick shot of pain when he tried to flex it. Even though it still hurt, it wasn't nearly as bad as it was the night before. Emily had done an excellent job of bandaging it.

Emily. He sat up in the bed, feeling the empty space next to him. She was gone. His heart sank. Last night he'd felt as though they'd finally reached a new level of understanding after days of tiptoeing around one another. But once again, she'd slipped out of his bed before they could talk about what would happen next.

Maybe he shouldn't be surprised. Emily was such an unusual mix of contradictions. She seemed so vulnerable at times, yet in an instant, she put on a toughness that was probably born from years of looking out for herself. He wondered what it had been like for her, growing up in the public eye, yet without anyone in the background to watch over or protect her.

He thought about their conversation at the bar, when she'd talked about how much she liked her life in Denver. She'd said that the private practice that she and her friend were building was everything to her. She seemed to have exactly what he'd been searching for for most of his life—a place that felt like home.

He wondered if she ever wanted anything more. He'd gotten the distinct impression, during their conversation, that she was just as antirelationship as he was. For some reason, the thought was upsetting to him. Perhaps it was because of the fleeting look of vulnerability he'd glimpsed crossing Emily's face at times. The same look that had drawn him in as she was watching the dancers from backstage. It was one thing for him to be cynical about love, but Emily… Somehow, he found himself wanting more for her.

But it seemed she didn't want more for herself. He sighed, pushing back the bedcovers. Even though he and Emily hadn't done much talking last night—and he couldn't help feeling a wry smile cross his face at the memory—he had assumed that they were due for a frank and heartfelt conversation this morning. But she'd slipped out of his room even more quietly this time than the last. True, they'd both made their feelings about relationships perfectly clear last night. Still, he would have thought that they owed each other a conversation. Whatever this was, they were more to one another than just a one-night stand at this point.

At the very least, he wished he had some way of knowing how she felt after last night. Having to guess was absolute torture. Because it wasn't as though he was about to sail away to some other port of call. He and Emily still had over a month left to their time in LA. More than a month to figure out how to coexist at work, if nothing else.

He wondered if he cared so much because for a moment last night Emily had reminded him of Sofia. *I'd rather just appreciate what I have instead of wishing for anything more*, Emily had said.

Sofia had said words to the same effect when she'd cut things off with him. They'd only been teenagers, and that wound had healed long ago. But there was a bittersweet lesson that he'd kept with him and applied to every relationship since then: *don't reach out for more.* If a short-term fling was all he could have, then he should try to appreciate that rather than stirring up disappointment by wishing it could be something else. When he thought about it, he realized he'd actually applied that philosophy to the rest of his life, as well. If he couldn't find a home or a place he belonged, then he'd make the best of sailing from port to port. Wanting more only led him to feel sad about what he didn't have, so why not focus on the good things in his life, instead?

He'd tried explaining his view to David once and had been surprised when his brother disagreed. In fact, David had told him that he was being absolutely absurd and that if he didn't reach out for the things he really wanted, he'd never get them. But everything always seemed to come so easily to David. He couldn't understand that things had been different for Daniel.

Emily, he thought, might understand. He wondered if the very fact that she wasn't here right now was proof of that. She seemed just as cautious as he was about wanting more from relationships. And that was probably why he felt so disappointed that she'd gone.

A click at the door startled him so much that he nearly fell out of bed—and then, to his utter surprise, Emily came in, holding a coffee in her outstretched hand.

"Oh, you're awake," she said. "I was hoping to get back before you were up. I just needed something to nibble on. I wasn't sure how you took your coffee, so I grabbed a handful of things."

"Just a little sugar is fine," he said, taking the cup from her and enjoying its reassuring warmth. She really had come back. She was actually here.

"Why are you looking at me like that?" she asked him.

"Like what?"

"Like you're shocked to see me. Did you think I'd given you the slip?"

"Maybe," he admitted. "But I'm glad you didn't sneak out this time."

"Well, this time is different, isn't it? We know each other. We're friends, we're coworkers and we're…" She waved her free hand in a motion that included the bed, their bodies and the rumpled sheets. "Whatever this is."

"I suppose we ought to have a conversation about what *this* is."

She gave him a smile that seemed a little sad. "I think we're long overdue for that. In fact—" she sighed "—maybe last night would have been the best time to have that conversation. Before we got carried away."

Was that what had happened? He'd felt caught up in passion, transported somewhere new. There was an openness he felt with her that he'd never had with anyone else. But she'd felt they'd gotten "carried away." What had last night meant to her?

"Do you regret getting carried away?" he asked tentatively.

"I don't have any regrets about last night," she said, and his shoulders, which he hadn't realized were tensed, relaxed in relief. "Do you?"

"Just one."

She looked surprised, then hurt, and before she could misunderstand, he quickly added, "My only regret is that you might get hurt. If we turn out to want different things."

"I see," she said, her eyes clearing. "So it's not so much a regret as a worry about the future."

"It's a worry about protecting us both."

"Because we're coworkers."

He hesitated. Somehow, that fact that they were working together didn't entirely sum up his reasons for wanting to be cautious. He thought again about that look of vulnerability he'd seen cross her face. The desire it elicited in him to protect her, to be there for her, even though he knew she didn't need his protection.

"That, and because I care about you," he said. "I wish there were some way to sustain this without either of us having to risk getting hurt."

"Spoken like a true commitmentphobe," she teased. "Actually, I have an idea on that score."

"Oh?"

She took a deep breath, clearly nervous. "As we're both well aware, we have a little over a month left here in Los Angeles."

He took her hand, hoping to ease her nerves. That vulnerability was present in her face again, along with a resolute expression that he was learning meant she was going to say whatever she needed to say, no matter what.

"Suppose we were to…make the most of that month?"

"And how do you propose we do that?"

"Well, I think it's fair to say that we both enjoyed last night immensely. At least, I did. And I hope you did, too."

He certainly had, but it was nice to hear Emily affirm it. He hadn't realized how much he'd been worrying over it until that moment. "Agreed. I enjoyed it very much indeed. But when you say we should 'make the most of this month,' are you suggesting we allow the events of last night to repeat themselves?"

He could feel her hand trembling a little, but her gaze was steady. "If you'd like. On a time-limited basis, of course. When the contest is over, we go our separate ways."

It was the perfect proposal, he realized. Neither of them was looking for a commitment. Both of them were planning to leave LA after the contest, she for Denver and he for whatever home he was looking for. Six weeks together was perfect for two people who had learned not to reach for more. It was exactly what he wanted: to be with her, with no expectations or commitments. And therefore no risk of disappointment.

But he needed to be certain they were both on the same page before moving forward. The last thing he'd ever want to do was hurt Emily.

"Are you sure about this?" he asked. "It's a big change from our first agreement. You remember, the one where we agreed to keep everything professional between us?"

"I think it's safe to say that keeping things professional didn't work out very well." She laughed, but he could hear the undercurrent of worry in her tone. She was still nervous, he realized.

"I think it's an excellent idea." She visibly relaxed at his words. "If neither of us wants a relationship, and we can't seem to just be colleagues, then this is the next best thing. We'll have a few weeks together, and then, at the end…" he kissed the hand he was holding "…we'll say our goodbyes."

She nodded. "That's the idea. We stay together while we're here and enjoy each other's company. But what happens in LA stays in LA. No strings attached."

"Now who's the commitmentphobe?" he said, but he smiled so she would know he was only teasing.

"Takes one to know one," she shot back.

He took a sip of the coffee she'd brought him and set it on the nightstand. "This plan of yours sounds incredibly intriguing," he said. "But I'll need you to be more specific. When you say that we'd 'enjoy each other's company,' what exactly would that look like?"

"Hmm. Perhaps instead of talking about the specifics, I could simply show you what I mean instead."

"Right now?"

"Oh, yes. Right away. No time like the present."

He had to fight his way out through the tangled sheets as he leaned toward her for a kiss, and then neither of them talked much after that.

The more time Emily spent with Daniel, the more satisfied she felt with their no-strings-attached arrangement.

As far as she was concerned, there was no downside. It had been nearly a week since they'd struck their agreement, and since then her days had become a satisfying blur of finding her stride at work and enjoying LA with Daniel during their off hours.

Now there was a strange idea: *enjoying* LA. She'd never thought she could actually feel happy in her hometown, yet somehow, exploring the city with Daniel made her see it in a new light. She'd always known, of course, that there was more to the urban sprawl of the city than faceless buildings and chain stores, but it had been years since she'd really considered whether LA could offer her anything she hadn't seen before. And to her surprise, it could—especially when she was with Daniel.

Perhaps spending so much time on cruise ships had given him a permanent tourist mind-set. He certainly knew how to explore a city, even one he'd been to before. Emily had thought she might take him to see a few of her old haunts from her adolescence, but she found it was far more fun to try things that were new to both of them. In the ten years since she'd been to LA, an entirely fresh crop of restaurants and music venues had sprung up, and she and Daniel found something new to do every day, whether it was visiting a small neighborhood taqueria or going to see an impromptu performance from an up-and-coming musician. And, of course, they had plenty of time to themselves… Emily was seeing almost as much of Daniel's hotel room as she was of LA's beaches.

It was an ideal situation, she thought, because it prevented either of them from getting too attached to one another. She'd always thought that it was best to avoid getting hurt by keeping her distance. If she didn't get close to anyone, she didn't have to worry about them letting her down later on.

But with Daniel, she could indulge her feelings for him. As they both knew they'd be leaving one another in a few weeks, neither of them had any expectations of one another afterward. It was a relief not to have to feel anxious about whether someone would eventually disappoint her.

Everything would have been going along very well indeed were it not for one nagging feeling.

Her PMS symptoms had gone on for a bit longer than she'd thought they would, with no sign of a period. At first it was simply a minor annoyance. She'd always had a rough time with PMS, and it wasn't so unusual for her periods to be a day or two late. The past few weeks had been something of a whirlwind, and she'd been distracted by all that had happened—her unexpected trip to LA, meeting Daniel and adjusting to the flow of working at the contest. Still, she would have thought that her period would have arrived by now. Instead, the vague uneasiness of her cramps persisted.

But she was so busy at work that she didn't have time to give the situation much thought, until Helen, one of the nurse practitioners, gave her a casual compliment.

"You're great with kids," Helen said after Emily had finished helping her with an especially anxious patient, a teen girl who'd been reluctant to disclose the extent of her knee pain at first, for fear she'd be cut from the competition. Emily had reassured the girl that the sooner they treated the pain, the less likely she was to have to withdraw due to injury. "Does it come from experience?"

"I suppose," Emily replied. "I did several pediatric rotations in training."

"Oh, no," Helen laughed. "I mean, do you have any of your own?"

"Any children? Goodness, no, I don't—" And then, halfway through her response, Emily froze.

Helen's question had made her consider her cramps of the past few days in a new light. When had she last gotten her period?

She'd never have considered it seriously if she wasn't a doctor, but—what if she was pregnant?

The idea was absolutely ridiculous, of course. She and Daniel had been extremely careful every time they had sex.

Emily realized Helen was still staring at her. "Sorry, just realized I've forgotten something."

Helen gave a sympathetic smile and moved on.

Emily made her way to the ladies' restroom, reviewing symptoms in her mind. Lots of women mistook very early signs of pregnancy for menstrual cramps. It wasn't that unusual for her own period to arrive two or three days late, but now it had been…four days? Five? She wasn't certain. She'd been so busy lately.

She reviewed the symptoms as she ducked her head into the women's restroom to make sure it was empty. Breast tenderness. Sensitivity to smells. Gingerly, she felt her breasts. Everything seemed normal. She hadn't noticed any unusual reactions to smells lately. She looked at herself in the mirror, feeling like a stranger in her own body.

I've got to be overreacting, she told herself. *I'm just a few days late, that's all.*

If there was one thing being a doctor had taught her, it was that human bodies were infinitely varied. A few days of cramps and a missed period could mean anything. There was no need to jump to the worst-case scenario just because things were a little out of sync. A good doctor would know that.

A good doctor would take a pregnancy test, just to be on the safe side. Of course, that was also true. If any patient had come to her with the same symptoms, she would immediately want to rule out pregnancy. The only difference in her case was that she was almost certain she could not be pregnant.

"If that's true, then there's nothing to fear, is there?" she said, looking her own reflection straight in the eye. Saying the words out loud settled her resolve. She was sure she wasn't pregnant, but just to be on the safe side, she would simply head down to the drugstore a few blocks away from the convention center, buy a pregnancy test and take it. When the results confirmed she wasn't pregnant, she could put the test out of her mind and put her ridiculous worries to rest.

It only took a few minutes to retrieve the test from the drugstore. She paid at the self-service kiosk, grateful that she didn't have to face any nosy cashiers. The store was mercifully empty; she didn't have to worry that one of her colleagues might appear with questions.

Once back in her own building, she headed toward the

women's restroom and sat down in a stall. Hands shaking, she began to open the dreaded box––and then stopped.

There was no need to take the test after all. The familiar faint spotting was confirmation of that. Her period had arrived. It was late, but it was there.

True, there was the slim possibility that it could be implantation bleeding, but that, she felt, was unlikely. Her periods had always been fairly light, though the severity of her cramps more than made up for it. And since she'd had no symptoms besides a late period, and now her period had arrived…she obviously wasn't pregnant. Taking the test at this point would be overdoing it. She stuffed the box back into her purse, feeling completely foolish. The afternoon had been an emotional roller coaster, and it was entirely her own fault. She couldn't believe she'd allowed her imagination to carry her so far from reality.

The emotional intensity of the past few minutes had taken her by surprise. As much as the idea of a baby terrified her, she'd also felt an unexpected surge of hope. Imagining a baby to love, a small child on whom she could lavish all the care and tenderness she'd never received…it was as though a need was awakening. A longing that she'd never allowed herself to indulge in, except for brief moments in dreams.

She'd told herself for years that she didn't want children. But the last few moments had revealed quite a different side of her. Apparently, all it took was for her period to be a few days late to get her fantasizing about an entirely different life.

How ironic, she thought. Daniel had been clear that he had no interest in relationships or in starting a family. Until this afternoon, she would have thought they were in perfect agreement on that matter. She couldn't believe she'd convinced herself she was pregnant in such a short amount of time, with such flimsy evidence. She was a doctor, for goodness' sake. She was supposed to stay calm and rational.

Wishful thinking, said a small voice in the back of her brain.

She dismissed the thought with a shake of her head. Her arrangement with Daniel was working perfectly, largely because they had no intention of seeing each other after their time in LA was over. She and Daniel would never be more to each other than what they were now. There was no point in fantasizing about anything else. And if a small part of her did, secretly, hope for more, then she would do what she did every time she wanted something she couldn't have. She'd take that part of herself and put it high up on a shelf, where it was useless to try and reach for it, and she'd do her best to forget that it was there.

And she'd make sure that Daniel never, ever found out about it.

As she headed out of the stall to wash her hands, she wondered what she should do with the test. Throw it away? She reached into her purse and put her hands on the test, considering. It was unlikely that anyone would notice a discarded pregnancy test, but there was still a chance that someone could find it, and that might invite unwanted gossip. At that moment, the restroom door swung open. She jumped, startled, and shoved the box deep within her purse.

"Dr. Archer, there you are." One of the physician assistants had come looking for her. "Sorry to intrude, but I just wanted to let you know you have a patient waiting. She's asking specifically for you, and I couldn't find you in any of the physicians' offices. Just wanted to let you know she was there."

The PA left, and Emily was alone. Relief flooded through her—if she'd decided to throw the test away, she'd have been caught red-handed the moment the PA opened the door. She decided to leave the test at the bottom of her purse for the present. She'd throw it away once she was sure it was completely safe to do so, even if that meant waiting until she got back to Denver. For now, it could stay buried in the depths of her purse, along with her foolish dreams and her runaway imagination.

CHAPTER SEVEN

DANIEL LIFTED THE baby from the bassinet, his heart warming at his nephew's smile. Then he quickly handed the baby to his brother, as the smile was followed by a gurgle and an abundance of spit-up.

"Here, I've got the hang of it by now," said David, deftly turning the baby so his face lay against the cloth draped over his shoulder. David gently bounced little Blake and patted his back, and Daniel marveled at how big his nephew had gotten in just a few weeks.

David's specialty was oncology, and he was highly valued and respected by the staff at the large research hospital where he worked. Daniel sometimes wondered if the careers he and his brother had chosen were their way of showing that they weren't like their parents. Perhaps they'd both wanted to do something good for humanity instead of following in their father's footsteps.

Daniel had never really understood his father's career in politics. Until he was an adult, he'd thought that much of his parent's work involved hosting dinner parties for the rich and famous. How well-known someone was, and how wealthy they were, was of the utmost importance. His parents had reacted with utter surprise when David had chosen to go to medical school, and their response was similar six years later, when Daniel did the same. But he and his brother had both felt a desire to work in a field where they could help others, even though their parents seemed baffled by the notion. They treated medicine almost as though it were an unusual hobby their sons had picked up, rather than a calling.

David's house in Costa Mesa was a stark contrast to the environment he and Daniel had grown up in. Although it was a respectable, tidy house, it was also clear that it was home to two new, overwhelmed parents and an infant. Toys were in evidence, and the dishes from several days ago were still in the sink—Daniel noticed at once and took care of them when he arrived, to give David and Trina a much-needed break. It was a far cry from the way Daniel and his brother had been raised, with maids to attend to every household chore, and his mother's obsessive standards of cleanliness. Daniel thought the biggest difference between David's house and the ones they'd grown up in was that it was clear that a child lived here.

That child reached over to bat a curled fist at Daniel's face. He traced the tiny fingers, fascinated by their delicacy.

"Trina and I are so glad you're thinking of settling down somewhere on land instead of continuing on the cruise ship circuit," David said. "Even if you don't end up in the Los Angeles area, it'll be so great for you to be able to visit regularly. We won't have to worry about whether you've hit a storm, or whether your schedule's been changed because someone got sick and the ship had to be diverted to Mexico."

"That only happened one time," Daniel replied.

"Yeah, but over the holidays. The worst possible time. It'll be nice to know that if you want to visit, all you have to do is book a flight. Or get in the car, if you end up staying in California. We'd love for you to settle somewhere nearby."

"I know, but... I'm just not sure California is for me."

"Are you joking? Between the mountains and the beach, what else are you looking for?"

Daniel mulled this over. His thoughts drifted to Emily, as they so often did these days. He'd never met anyone who seemed to have her life figured out the way she did. She'd walked away from a career in show business and built something better for herself. Her life in Denver mattered. Not just to her, but to her patients and colleagues. The practice she was building with her friend mattered. He wished there was a place on earth where he mattered as much as she did.

He tried to voice his thoughts to David. "I don't want to just plunk down in some random place. I want to be somewhere where it matters whether I stay or go. Somewhere people need me."

David spread his arms to indicate the house around them. "We need you! Look at this place. It's a total zoo. Mom would lose it if she saw what a mess our house is."

"Well, unlike Mom, you don't have twenty maids at your beck and call to help clean it up. And as much as I love you and Trina, I don't think you'd be very happy with my services as a live-in housekeeper."

"That's not what I meant. If you're looking for a place where you're important to people, we're right here."

"I know, I know. But I can't spend my life following in your footsteps. I already became a doctor because you went through medical school first. No offense, but I don't want to live here just because you do as well. And more importantly—" he nuzzled Blake's chubby neck with one finger "—I want to be the fun uncle. I want Blake to get excited when I visit. If I live too close to you, I'll have to be too involved with the hard stuff. I'll have to help you out with discipline and homework time. That's too much responsibility for me."

David rolled his eyes. "You haven't changed a bit. Do you really think you'll be able to settle down in just one place? Between the cruise ships, the dance contests and the sporting events, I think you move around now almost as much as we did when we were kids."

Daniel's face grew long, remembering the many different schools he'd attended. Thanks to the constant need to move, he'd often felt as though he'd had to give up friendships nearly as soon as he'd made them. He hadn't liked moving around so much, but he hadn't known anything else. "I'm not sure if I even know how to stay in one place. How do you do it?"

"You get used to it. Especially if you find a place that feels like home. We didn't get much of that growing up. I don't think our houses ever really felt like homes. Maybe more like museums."

That was an accurate description, Daniel thought. His mother never noticed if either of them had had a bad day at school, or if they were struggling with homework or feeling lonely. But she never failed to notice if a single tchotchke on the mantelpiece was a quarter inch out of place. He smiled again at the toys strewn about David's living room floor. Their parents would have hated it.

David and Trina weren't struggling for money, but they also didn't live in the ornate style that he and Daniel had grown up in. Their parents had cut David off when he married Trina, feeling that Trina's family didn't have the right connections and wasn't wealthy enough to move in the same circles as their son.

Daniel wasn't certain what his parents had expected David to do when they'd announced that he would be cut off from his inheritance if he went through with marrying Trina. His parents weren't the kind of people who had emotional conversations. Instead, they used their money to control their children. If they'd known David at all—if they'd ever taken the time to have even one meaningful conversation with him—then they'd have known that using their money as a manipulation tactic wouldn't work. Daniel hadn't been surprised at all when David had gone right ahead with the wedding. His brother's decision to forgo the family fortune and marry Trina was one of the most impressive, principled things he'd ever seen, but knowing David as he did, he also wouldn't have expected anything else.

His desire to stand with David had put even more strain on his already difficult relationship with their parents, but they hadn't disowned him, as they had David. Daniel had offered to split his inheritance with his brother, but David had brushed him off.

"We don't need it," he'd said. "Being a doctor might not make me rich, but it pays well enough that Trina and I can be independent. Besides, we have no way of knowing what Mom and Dad will do with their money. I don't want my financial plans to be dependent on anyone else, even someone I trust as much as you."

His brother had a point. Daniel assumed that his parents would leave some of their sizable fortune to him, but it wasn't a certainty. It was entirely possible that they could make a last-minute decision to bequeath their money to one of the many art institutes or political foundations they supported. Not that there was anything wrong with that; it was their money, and he made enough to support himself. After growing up amid wealth, no one knew better than he did that money couldn't buy happiness. But his parents viewed money as a means to control, even though it was ironic, Daniel thought, that their attempts to maintain control led them to lose so much.

For example: they had never once visited Blake, their anger at David's defiance superseding their chance to get to know their only grandchild. It was baffling to Daniel how much his parents' desire to have their own way seemed to take priority over everything else, including their relationship with both of their sons and now their grandson.

Despite the family turmoil they'd all gone through, David had never once seemed to regret his decision. Now, as Daniel watched David bounce the baby on his shoulder, he wondered if his brother really had managed to get everything he'd wanted—not just a home and a family, but love.

"Can I ask you something?" Daniel said. "How did you know that this life was what you wanted?"

"I guess it was more that I knew what I didn't want. I didn't want to recreate the childhood our parents gave us, with all the security but none of the warmth. I suppose I couldn't have predicted what it would be like on a daily basis. But I love all of it. The sleepless nights, the chaos around feedings, the unpredictable schedule when you're trying to balance your life with the needs of a tiny human. It's all worth it. It's everything."

"What about..." Daniel hesitated, not certain how to ask. "What about love?"

"What about it?"

"Is it real? Do you think it exists?"

Daniel burst out laughing. "Look who you're asking. A man happily married, holding his newborn son. What do you think I'm going to say?"

"Honestly, I was hoping you'd tell me whether it's really possible to have it all."

"Personally, I believe it is. But if you asked our parents, you'd get a different response. Dad would say there's no way to prove or disprove a concept as abstract as love. Mom would say that basing a relationship on love isn't practical, that it has more to do with what you have in common. And, of course—" he gave a brief snort of derision "—whether you come from the same background.

"But I think, little brother, that you're asking me a different question. I think you're asking whether I believe love is possible for *you*. And I think you know that you're the only one who can answer that question for yourself." David was silent for a moment. Then he added, "Why are you asking me this now?"

Daniel regarded Blake. "I guess you having a child has just got me thinking about it."

"No, that's not it."

"Excuse me?"

"You're not asking me about children. You're asking about love. Is there someone I should know about?"

Daniel was about to protest when he suddenly stopped short. He *had* been thinking about Emily. Probably would never have broached the conversation had he not been thinking about her. There was something about her that brought these questions to mind and got him wondering about what it was, deep down, that he really wanted.

Maybe that was because she seemed to be the kind of person who pursued the things that she really wanted.

He wished he could be that way. The trouble was, he so often didn't know what he wanted.

"Well…there is someone," he said.

"I knew it."

"But it's not what you think. Neither of us is interested in anything serious right now."

"Is that so? Because you're asking me some pretty pointed questions about love."

"Only on a theoretical level."

"Little brother, there's nothing about love that's theoretical. You feel it in your bones, in your gut and in your heart. Love's something you feel with your body, not something that makes logical sense in your mind. You talk about being tied down by obligations and expectations, but that's not how love works. It's not an equation that you have to solve. It's something that you realize in an instant."

Fine words from his brother, but Daniel didn't understand it. How could there be love without expectations and obligations? And how could there be love with them? To him, relationship meant rules, and responsibilities, and the potential to let someone down.

He looked at little Blake, who gazed back at him with wide eyes. He couldn't imagine anything worse than letting Blake down. He vowed it would never happen.

But the responsibility of a relationship? Of a child of his own someday? He couldn't envision it. If anything, his visit to his brother had confirmed to him: he wasn't a relationship man. Or a family man.

If anyone could understand that, he thought, it was probably Emily. Commitment terrified him because he couldn't stand the thought of letting down the people he cared about most. It was exactly why he and Emily had their agreement in place: so that neither of them would risk disappointing the other.

He tucked one corner of Blake's blanket back underneath his chin. He was glad he'd visited David. It was good to see him so happy. But he couldn't fathom how his brother withstood the responsibility of fatherhood. Blake was precious cargo. He was so vulnerable, so helpless, and it was David's job—and, to a lesser extent, Daniel's—to help him grow. To protect him from potential dangers, to worry constantly about all the perils of childhood that couldn't be prevented. Looking at David now, Daniel realized that to be a parent was to sign on for a life of constant worry. Thank God, Daniel thought, that he was only an uncle. He'd never be able to handle having a child of his own.

Emily thought her arrangement with Daniel was going quite well, despite her thorough embarrassment at how carried away she'd been by the idea of being pregnant. Aside from the pregnancy scare—which she was determined Daniel would never learn about—their arrangement was working well for both of them. They'd spent a few evenings wandering the city. She'd shown him some of the familiar haunts from when she'd grown up there, and he'd surprised her by knowing about a few spots she'd never heard of.

She was looking forward to going out with him again as her shift neared its end and was packing up to leave when one of the coaches arrived in her office. Three teen dancers were behind her, two of them supporting a girl who tried to stand between them.

"What seems to be the trouble?" Emily asked the coach.

"I don't know," the coach replied. "Hannah was going

through a rehearsal on the main stage when she got dizzy, and then her legs just folded under her."

Emily motioned for them to bring the girl in so she could sit down. "I don't feel so great, either," said one of the girls supporting Hannah. Emily's ears perked up in alarm. "Can you grab another chair from a nearby cubicle?" she asked, and when the coach did so, she had the other girl sit down as well.

Hannah's skin was flushed and hot. "I think I'm going to be sick," she said.

Emily pulled a small wastebasket out from under her computer desk and handed it to the girl. "Use this if you have to."

She noted the girl's rapid breathing and took her pulse, which was fast. "Do you feel faint?"

The girl nodded. "Head hurts."

The other teen, seated in the chair her coach had retrieved, seemed dizzy, too.

Emily was about to check the girl's temperature when two more teens appeared at the front of her office, lightheaded and weak.

"What's going on?" she said. She told the two girls to sit on the floor just outside her office, as her small cubicle couldn't hold them all. As she looked down the hall, she saw Daniel quickstepping toward her office, around small clusters of dancers milling dazedly through the medical hallway.

"Something's gone wrong during a rehearsal in the main auditorium," he told her. "Multiple dancers are collapsing. They're all going down fast and without warning. I'm not sure what to think. It could be a gas leak somewhere, but all the coaches and parents seem fine—it's only affecting the dancers."

She noticed he was perspiring heavily despite the air-conditioning in the hall. "Is it hot down there?"

"As blazes."

"You said the dancers are rehearsing. Is it a full dress rehearsal? Are the stage lights on?"

He smacked his forehead with his palm. "Of course. Burning full blast, and it's over ninety-five degrees outside. They're all going down with heatstroke."

"How many dancers down there are affected?"

"At least twenty. With more dropping as I was running up here for supplies. Shall we round them all up and bring them to the medical hallway?"

"No," she said, looking up to see more contestants straggling in. "They'll crowd the hallway and escalate the situation. Run back down and keep everyone on the main stage. Get the lights turned off. We'll set up ice buckets, misting fans and damp towels and treat them all down there."

As Daniel returned to the auditorium, Emily recruited the coach to help her gather supplies. She spoke to two other nurses who were out in the hallway assisting teenagers weak with heat exhaustion, updating them on the plan. Within ten minutes, the main auditorium had been turned into an emergency cooling station, with weakened athletes lying about the stage surrounded by cool, wet towels.

The next few hours were a blur, as Emily and Daniel tried to keep ahead of their patients. Heatstroke cases usually came on hard and fast, with few symptoms until patients suddenly found themselves ready to collapse. Emily wasn't surprised that the dancers, caught up in their rehearsal and used to intense performing conditions, hadn't noticed any signs that they needed to slow down.

"That's enough for one day," she said to a boy of about fifteen, who had been walking toward the stage and then stopped, his knees slowly sagging beneath him. She supported him as he sank to the floor and then leaned him against the wall in a seated position. Daniel was a step behind her with a large basket of ice packs, which they put around the boy's neck and shoulders. Emily peered into the boy's eyes and listened to his breathing, then handed the boy a water bottle. "Sip this every few minutes, and don't leave until a medic has given you the all clear, understand?"

The medical team had to keep all the affected contestants in the auditorium for the rest of the afternoon. The sun was setting by the time most of the dancers had revived. Emily took her own seat on the floor of the stage, her back pressed against a wall for support. She looked out upon the auditorium with a sense of pride. Not one single patient had suffered from any complications or escalating symptoms once the medical team had reached them.

Daniel approached and sat down beside her. "Looks like you saved the day," he said.

"*I* saved it? How?"

"No one else thought of heatstroke right away. I was guessing that it was a gas leak, or maybe food poisoning. We only had a small window of time to put the right treatment to the right symptoms."

She gave a small smile. While she could hardly take credit for something that had clearly been a team effort, it was nice to hear a compliment. "You weren't so bad yourself," she said. "If you hadn't coordinated with the parents and coaches to keep all the kids down here, we might have ended up with mass confusion."

As the last few athletes recovered and made their way from the auditorium, a few other doctors and nurses passed by and gave her a nod. "Good call today," one of them said in passing. Emily couldn't keep her face from glowing with pride. It was nice to know she'd completed a job well done and that she was recognized for it.

But as everyone else began to file out, Emily felt a jolt of anxiety in the pit of her stomach. She grabbed Daniel's arm.

"What is it?"

She pointed to the doorway, unable to articulate any words.

"What's wrong? You look as though you've seen a ghost."

She almost had. She could have sworn she'd seen the back of a familiar sleek, blond bob disappearing out of those very doors. "For a moment I thought… I thought I saw my mother."

"Your mother? But why would she be here?"

"I don't know. She can't possibly know I'm in Los Angeles. I haven't spoken to her in years."

One of the nurses came back into the auditorium. Emily thought that perhaps she'd forgotten something, but then she continued walking toward her.

"Dr. Archer? There was a woman here, just a moment ago, and she left this note for you."

She handed Emily a slim white envelope. Emily took it with trembling fingers. "Thanks, Helen."

She turned the envelope over in her hands.

"Are you going to open it?" asked Daniel. "Maybe it's nothing. Maybe it's not from her."

"Oh, it's from her."

"How do you know?"

"I just do." Even if she hadn't caught the glimpse of blond hair disappearing out the door, Emily could see the color of the ink where the light shone through the envelope. Purple ink. Her mother always wrote in purple ink. It was more fun, she'd always said, and her mother was lots of fun, until she wasn't.

"Do you want to be alone right now?"

She considered this. As much as she didn't want to drag Daniel into the messy world of her personal life, she'd already revealed so much to him. More than she usually did to most people. There was something about him that made her feel…safe. She wished she could put her finger on exactly what that thing was.

She thought about crumpling up the letter, or shredding it and throwing it away, unread. But her curiosity was too great. And as difficult as her mother was, there had been warm moments, as well.

And not that she would reveal it to Daniel, but her recent pregnancy scare had made her curious about her mother. Her parents' failures had been the source of her own fears of parenthood for so long. She'd been worried that she couldn't be a good mother precisely because she didn't feel she had good role models to follow up on.

In those first moments when she'd learned she wasn't pregnant, she'd been surprised at the strong sense of loss she'd felt. But as the days went on, that feeling of loss had been replaced with relief. She wouldn't have to face the challenge of trying not to make the same mistakes as her parents. She wouldn't have to worry about a child of her own growing up feeling as scared and alone as she had.

She was deep in thought, smoothing the envelope with her thumb and forefinger over and over again. A letter from her mother. There were so many questions Emily wanted to ask her, and yet she wasn't sure she'd be satisfied with any of the potential responses.

Daniel's voice startled her out of her reverie.

"You could just throw it away," he said.

"No. I have to read it. I just don't want to read it alone."

He nudged his shoulder against hers. "In that case, I'm right here."

Emily carefully tore the envelope open. She couldn't help smiling at her mother's trademark purple ink. It had been so long since she'd seen it.

The letter read,

Dear Emily,

I know that if I call you won't answer, and you don't have to explain why. Some of my greatest regrets are the mistakes I made as a mother. I'm at a place in my life where I'm trying to make amends to the people I've hurt. I wanted to tell you that I'm so proud of the doctor you've become, and I wish I could hear all about you and the work you're doing. I know it's a lot to ask, but I would love it if you'd visit while you're in Los Angeles. I'm still at the old house. Drop by anytime.

Love,
Mom

Make amends? What did that mean? Was her mother getting sober?

"Wow," said Daniel. He'd read the letter over her shoulder; pushed up next to her as he was, it would have been impossible for him not to see the words. "Has she ever reached out to you like this before?"

"Never." Anytime her mother had mentioned sobriety in the past, it had always been in passing, as though she were talking about needing to get to dusting the shelves someday. She had certainly never expressed any regret over Emily's childhood, or any awareness that it might have been difficult.

All her life, she'd felt as though she had two mothers—the fun mother and the alarming, unpredictable mother. But this letter seemed to come from a third version of her mother that she'd never met. One who could admit her mistakes and who seemed genuinely interested in Emily as a person.

There were still some things about the letter that she didn't understand. Most importantly, how had her mother known to give her the letter here? "How did she even know I was in LA at all?" she wondered aloud.

"I think I know," said Daniel grimly. "Reyes."

"What?"

Daniel took out his phone and fiddled with the screen. "Remember how I told you that Reyes posted that selfie he took with you online?" He tilted the screen toward her and clicked on the picture. Comments were posted underneath. She scrolled downward through the comments with the tip of one finger. It wasn't long before she arrived at one that read, "That's my daughter! I'm so proud of her." The username left on the comments was EmilysMom983.

Well, whatever other life changes her mother might be going through, she clearly hadn't lost her tendency to announce her status as Emily's mother in any situation. In a way, it was comforting to know that she might have changed but could still be counted on to be the same person Emily remembered. With the same problems.

"I'm going to kill Reyes," said Daniel. "I can't believe him."

"It's not his fault. He couldn't have known this would happen."

"Still. He should have asked your permission before posting that picture."

"It's not a big deal. Do you know how many pictures of me have been put online? It's not Reyes's fault that posting this one happened to have unforeseen consequences. I'd rather just focus on what I'm going to do next."

"Are you going to visit her?"

"I don't think I can."

"What if you had some moral support?"

"What do you mean?"

"What if I came along with you? That way you don't have to spend all that time in anxious anticipation by yourself. And I'll be right there when the visit's over, so you won't have to be alone. We can even plan something fun afterward."

"Another hike?"

He flexed his ankle experimentally. "I don't know if I'm ready for another hike just yet. I was thinking we could take in a movie. That way, if your visit goes well, you'll enjoy having something fun to do even more afterward. And if it doesn't go well…then at least you have something good to look forward to."

She thought about it. The idea of visiting her mother after so many years apart was daunting, but doing it on her own made her even more nervous. Daniel's offer to go with her was tempting. At least she'd have someone to talk to afterward, especially if it turned out to be a difficult visit.

But the idea of relying on Daniel for support made her nervous as well. She wasn't used to depending on anyone. What if he saw how messy her personal life was and he went running for the hills?

Then again, they were already planning to part ways in a few weeks. Daniel knew that, yet he was offering to be there for her.

"Come on," he nudged. "What have you got to lose?"

She realized that as much as she didn't want to get close to Daniel, she was also glad that he was here. There was something about his presence that was so comforting. There was a warmth about him. She'd seen him in action as a doctor; she knew his patients sensed it. And right now she could sense it, too.

She felt a surge of gratitude for the agreement they'd made. Six weeks. She couldn't fall for anyone in just six weeks. So she didn't need to worry that she was in any danger of falling for Daniel. She could just be glad of his support.

Perhaps it might not be too much of a risk to let herself rely on him, just for a little while. Izzie would probably agree. She hadn't forgotten her advice during their phone call after her first night with Daniel. Izzie had told her the real danger was that she could focus so much on doing the right thing, the responsible thing, that she forgot to let herself have something good. Well, Daniel was good for her. She was starting to become sure of it. And even though their time together was limited, he was here now. And he was offering to help.

She took his hand, interlacing her fingers in his. “Yes,” she said. “It would be great if you could come along.”

CHAPTER EIGHT

EMILY STOOD OUTSIDE the door of her mother's small West Hollywood bungalow. From the outside, it bore the semblance of a quiet, cheerful house. Her mother had painted the door red in a burst of energy when Emily was eight years old. Despite her mother's frenetic painting, the door had come out well, providing a whimsical contrast to the stucco exterior.

Unfortunately, Emily's memories of her childhood home had never matched its pleasant facade. When she'd come home from school or work, she'd felt sick to her stomach, never knowing what to expect when she opened the door. Her mother might be in a fine mood, full of energy and humor, or she might spend the entire day in her bedroom, drunk or sleeping off a hangover. She never knew which version of her mother would greet her. Emily could recall a hundred times when she'd stood outside, debating whether or not she'd go in.

Those times, she'd been alone. Now she had Daniel beside her.

Even though she'd been nervous about bringing him along with her, she was glad he was here. She had no intention of allowing herself to become dependent on his support, because she knew it couldn't last forever. But it was nice to have him here right now, when she had no way of knowing what she might be facing on the other side of that door.

He cupped her elbow. “You know, you don’t have to do this if you’re not ready. If you want, we can just leave for an earlier showing of our movie right now. I’ll get us popcorn.”

It was a tempting offer, but she couldn’t take him up on it. Ever since the pregnancy scare, ever since she’d been faced with the possibility that a helpless, vulnerable child might be depending solely on her, she’d burned with a question: *How* could her mother have let her down so badly?

Emily knew from her medical training that there were many factors that played a role in addiction. She’d sat through seminars in school and taken notes while her professors had lectured about genetic predispositions, about social and emotional contributors to alcoholism. But learning about addiction was a far cry from living through it. Even after her training in the complex nature of addiction, Emily couldn’t help reacting emotionally to the way her mother’s drinking had affected her as a child. Had her mother loved drinking more than she’d loved Emily? How could she not have realized how much Emily needed her?

It had only taken her one brief flash of worry that she might be pregnant to get a sense of the enormity of what it would mean to be a parent. She hadn’t even turned out to be pregnant, and yet amid all the fear and uncertainty of that moment, she’d felt that no matter what happened, she would make sure her child felt wanted and loved. Hadn’t her mother ever felt the same way?

But she couldn’t explain this to Daniel. The last thing

she wanted to do was let him know that her decision to visit her mother had anything to do with her fear that she'd been pregnant. Instead, she simply said, "It's just something I have to do." He nodded, and she was relieved that for once he took her explanation at face value, without suspecting that she felt more than she was willing to reveal.

Still, she stood in front of the door with leaden feet. Somehow she couldn't bring herself to take two steps forward and knock on the door.

"Do you want me to knock?" he said.

"No. No, I have to do it myself. I just need a minute."

"I understand. We can take as long as you need."

She searched for the right words, trying to explain. "I want to do this, but I also don't. I know it doesn't make sense."

"You don't have to explain. You just want to see if there's a way for you to be in each other's lives."

"Maybe. But even more than that, I need to know if it's possible for her to have changed. If she hasn't, I don't know if I'll be able to handle it. And if she has..." Emily paused. If her mother could stop drinking, then that would be a dream come true. She'd made half-hearted attempts at sobriety in the past, but something in her letter made it sound as though this time she was more serious. But how long would her mother be able to follow through with a commitment like that? How long before it became too hard for her to stick to sobriety? Assuming she was, indeed, sober?

She shook her head. "I don't know if I can trust her. I don't even know what version of her I'll see when we go in."

"Then before we go in, we should work out a signal.

Just in case things get too intense. If you start to get upset, then you give me the signal, and I'll come up with some excuse for us to leave immediately."

"A signal. I like that." Bringing him had been a good idea. She'd never brought anyone along for backup when visiting her mother before, but it was turning out to be useful. "Maybe I could tap my chin. If you see me do that, it means you've got to find a way to get me out of there."

"Sure. A chin tap at any time means I get you out. And I'll set an alarm on my cell phone for thirty minutes from now. When my phone rings, I'll act like I'm answering a call. You can nod, and I'll know you want to stay a little longer. Or you can tap your chin, and I'll say there's been some emergency and we have to leave."

She rubbed her forehead.

"What's wrong?"

"I'm just embarrassed that we have to set up such an elaborate plan. If I have to do all this just to visit my mother, maybe it's a sign that I shouldn't be here at all."

"How long has it been since you've seen her?"

"Ten years." Emily had sworn off any future visits to her mother's home after a particularly disastrous holiday dinner involving far too much alcohol and far too many recriminations from both of them. Since then, there had a been a few scattered, terse phone calls, but those had petered out, and it had been years since Emily had returned any of her mother's voice mails. Things were much easier that way.

It wasn't that she didn't miss her. She missed the mother who could be warm and fun. But again, she never knew which version of her mother would pick up the phone if she called. Just as she had no idea which version she was about to face now. Would her mother be happy to see her? Or would she deny that she'd sent Emily a letter inviting her to visit? If she'd been drunk when she dropped the letter off, she might not even remember doing it.

But her mother's note had suggested that she was trying to get sober, and that made Emily curious. And no matter what she was walking into, she wasn't alone. She had Daniel beside her.

She steeled her resolve. "Okay. I'm ready. Let's do this."

Five minutes later, she was sitting on her mother's old divan, with a cup of tea and her favorite almond cookies from her childhood.

Her mother was thrilled to see her. She was eager to meet Daniel and shot a significant look Emily's way as he introduced himself. Emily shot a look back, hoping she would take the hint not to ask too many questions.

It felt surreal to be back in her mother's living room. There were so many bits and pieces of her childhood within view: medals and certificates that she'd won from dance contests on the walls, a mantelpiece crowded with pictures of Emily. But there were pictures of other people and places, too, which was a change. When she'd been a child, the house had felt like a shrine to the two things her mother loved: drinking and Emily's career. But now there were photos on the mantelpiece of her mother hiking, a tennis racket in one corner and a table at the end of the room covered with oil paintings and art supplies. It seemed as though her mother had taken on some other interests since Emily had last seen her.

Daniel leaned in for a closer look at one of the oil paintings. "Did you do all these, Mrs. Archer?"

"Please, call me Tabitha. And yes, I did all three of them. There are a few more hanging in the sunroom."

"I'd love to take a look. It'll give the two of you a chance to catch up privately." He looked at Emily, who gave him a small nod. She didn't want Daniel to go, but he'd just be in the next room. And as much as she wanted support while talking with her mother, she also knew that there were certain things they could only discuss while alone.

She wasn't sure where to begin, so she simply said, "Since when do you do oil paintings?"

"I started a few years ago, as part of my recovery." Her mother took a deep breath. "When you stopped returning my calls, I started to realize that I'd made some serious mistakes. And even though I couldn't take any of those mistakes back, I knew that I was the one who needed to deal with them. Not you. So I got into a program and started doing the work. In fact, I'm almost three years sober."

Three years? Emily couldn't hide her surprise. When she'd gotten her letter, she'd thought, at best, that her mother might be making an attempt at sobriety. In her wildest dreams, she'd imagined that perhaps she had been sober for a month or two. But three years? It was more than she could possibly have hoped for. It was almost more than she believed.

"I know," her mother said, registering Emily's reaction. "Who would have thought that I could actually get sober, let alone stick to it? It was hard at first, but it got easier as time went on. Especially because I have lots of support."

"What kind of support?" She was still trying to wrap

her mind around the idea of her mother maintaining sobriety for so long when she'd never been able to do it before.

"I started going to therapy, and I've been working on developing more hobbies. It's all part of my program. I'm trying to do lots of things to stay active. I have an art class I go to every week, and a hiking club where I've met a few people my age."

Therapy? An art class? Emily knew she should be glad her mother was finally turning her life around, but she couldn't help feeling a wave of bitterness. When she was a child, her mother couldn't be relied on to pick her up from school, but now she could commit to a weekly art class?

"I'm sure it's hard to believe," her mother said, echoing her thoughts. "But it's really because of you that I've made this change at all."

"Because of me? But we've never talked about this at all. Not seriously." On the rare occasions the two of them had openly discussed Tabitha's drinking, Tabitha had responded with denial, or by lashing out at Emily.

"When we stopped talking, I thought there was a good chance I'd lost you forever. And then I realized that if I kept going on with things as they were, I might push everyone away, and then I'd be alone forever. I got very close to that point. And even though it's difficult for me to open up to other people, and to let myself rely on others, I didn't want to be alone. And so I got into recovery, and I started filling my life up with as many people and activities as I could."

This was a side of her mother she'd never seen before. As a child, she'd often felt as though *she* was the one who had to give her mother's life meaning. Tabitha had derived great pride from Emily's career, but Emily couldn't remember her mother having many interests of her own. Yet the photos and the artwork in the house told the story of a woman with a very full life indeed.

Her eye fell on a picture on the mantelpiece. It was a photo of her mother in hiking clothes, stopping to pose at a scenic overlook, next to a man who had his arm draped around her shoulders.

"Who's that, Mom?"

"Oh, that's Brandon. A very close friend. Boyfriend, actually. We've been together for about a year and a half."

Emily raised her eyebrows. Her mother had never dated anyone for more than a few months as far as she could recall. She supposed they had that in common.

"He's in recovery, too."

"I'm glad you haven't been lonely," Emily said, and she found that she meant it. "Have you heard from Dad?"

"Not for years."

"Me neither."

"Just so you know, I'm done blaming things on him. That's been part of my recovery as well."

Emily felt as though she was meeting someone new. She'd been so worried about which version of her mother she would encounter: the chaotic one who loved to have fun but who quickly let things get out of control, or the warm one, who was kind but difficult to rely on. She didn't know what to make of this new, introspective aspect of her mother.

"This is all so unlike you," she said.

"It hasn't been easy," her mother replied. "I go to a lot of support group meetings, which was hard for me at first. I've discovered that I have difficulty letting other people in, which may not surprise you. Mostly because of how my own parents treated me when I was young. You never got the chance to know Grandma and Grandpa, but they didn't tolerate emotions very well. If I was happy, I was too loud, if I was sad, I needed to stop complaining. I wasn't allowed to have feelings. But I don't blame them, either. They were only doing what they knew."

"So nothing's anyone's fault," Emily said, unable to hide the bitterness in her voice. Part of her wanted so badly to be happy for her mother, and to support her. But she couldn't help feeling resentful. If her mother really had been able to maintain her sobriety for three years, why hadn't she tried harder during Emily's childhood?

"That's not what I meant. I've had to take ownership of the mistakes I've made. And I've had to learn how to let people in."

Emily gave a small smile. "I guess trust issues run in our family."

Her mother sighed. "I guess they do. And I'm sorry for the part I've played in yours. I know I wasn't the mother you needed me to be. And I want to take accountability for that. I'm trying as hard as I can to change, but it doesn't erase the mistakes I've made. I can only hope that you and I have a chance to move forward, despite all that's happened in the past."

Emily was silent, trying to understand the emotions swirling within her. Part of her had dreamed of a moment just like this. For much of her life, she'd longed to have a real conversation with her mother. But now her mother was finally sober, finally trying to have a better relationship with her. And even though Emily wanted to be happy, she didn't know if she could trust that this was a permanent change. One conversation wasn't enough to be certain that her mother was a different person.

"I'd like to give you a chance, Mom," she said slowly.

"But I hope you understand that I have to be careful. I love that you're in recovery, but I don't know if I'm ready to let you back into my life yet."

"I understand. And the truth is, I didn't get sober for you. I did it for myself. And I don't expect anything from you. I can understand why you'd feel cautious about letting me into your life, after what your father and I put you through."

There it was: the invitation she'd been waiting for. Those words were an acknowledgment of how difficult her childhood had been. Her mother sat next to her, one arm on Emily's shoulder, and her expression told Emily that if she wanted to, she could ask the question that had burned within her as she stood outside the front door: *Why?* Why hadn't her mother been there for her?

But the question stuck in her throat. They hadn't had many heartfelt conversations. This was new territory for both of them, and Emily wasn't sure where to start.

Her mother seemed to guess her thoughts. "It's not easy to talk about these things," she said. "All I'm asking for is a chance to earn your trust."

Emily blinked back tears. She wasn't ready to cry in front of her. Not yet. Her mother was saying everything she'd always wanted to hear, but she had to proceed with caution for her own protection. "Trust takes time," she said, regaining her composure.

"I know it does. But I've been working hard on being patient. We can take all the time we need."

Patience. If her mother could work on it, so could she. When she'd stood outside this house, she'd felt as though she needed to confront her mother, demand an explanation for how she could have left her so alone. But she hadn't expected her to admit to her mistakes so openly, and to ask for the chance to build trust.

Maybe, Emily thought, she didn't need answers to her big questions today. Maybe there was a chance that she could take her time getting to know this new version of her mother.

She wanted, more than anything, to believe that they could make the most of that chance. From everything her mother was saying, it did seem as though she was taking sobriety seriously. In the past, her mother had never gone to meetings or socialized with other people in recovery. She'd never been involved with friends or hobbies. But now she was making a serious effort, with support and resources. She'd certainly never heard her talk about taking accountability before.

She had reason to hope. And she'd never know if her mother really could change unless she gave her a chance.

Daniel came back into the living room, his cell phone buzzing. He looked toward Emily, and she gave a slow, deliberate nod.

Emily and Daniel spent the next several hours at her mother's home. Tabitha regaled Daniel with stories about Emily's performances, which Emily found embarrassing, but not as much as she would have expected.

Dusk had fallen by the time they left. As it was far too late to see the movie they'd planned upon, they ordered a cab back to their hotel. Emily's mother had offered to let Emily stay in her childhood bedroom, but she declined. The visit had gone well, and she was glad to see that her mother was on the path to recovery, but she wasn't ready to stay under her roof again. She did, however, promise to visit at the holidays.

"That'll be strange," she said to Daniel as the cab dropped them off at the hotel. "It's been a long time since I spent the holidays with her. But it'll be a good chance to see if she's continued sticking with her recovery."

"It must be a relief to see her sober, though. And for so long. Has she ever been able to go a full year without drinking before?"

"Never. The longest I ever saw her sober as a child was a few days. Maybe a week at the absolute most."

"The program she's in must be doing something for her."

Emily wondered about that. Something had been nagging at the back of her mind since they'd left. She'd been surprised by how glad she'd been to see her mother, especially now that she was doing well. She hadn't realized how much she'd missed her. But in some ways, her mother was so very different—and who was this Brandon fellow who went on those hikes with her? Her mother had referred to him as a boyfriend, said they'd been together for a year. But her mother's relationships tended to be short-term, low-commitment affairs. Much like the ones that Emily tended to have.

When Emily was younger, her mother had been obsessed with her career. She'd put enormous pressure on her to succeed as a dancer and actress. One of the reasons it had been so difficult for Emily to stop speaking to her was because her mother hadn't seemed to have much else in her life besides Emily. Yet now she was dating, active, even artistic. She'd spoken with pride about those oil paintings. Something didn't add up. Tears sprang to her eyes as uneasiness overtook her.

"What is it?" said Daniel.

She turned her face away from his, knowing that if she tried to speak, she'd burst into tears.

"Hold on," he said, pushing an elevator button. "We're almost to my room. You can tell me then." He put an arm around her and held her until they reached his floor.

Once they were in his room, Emily let the tears fall. She couldn't have held them back any longer if she'd tried. Daniel waited patiently, holding her close to his chest.

"Sorry," she said as she began to recover.

"For what? You've just seen your mother for the first time in years. Anyone would have a reaction to that. I'm surprised you didn't break down sooner, honestly. I don't think I could have made it that long."

"I just feel as though I should be stronger. As though it shouldn't bother me so much."

"What? Seeing your mother?"

"Seeing her like this. Seeing her sober."

"But that's a good thing, isn't it?"

Emily felt the tears building, knew they were ready to fall again. "But why couldn't she get sober for *me*?" she burst out. "Why couldn't she have done this years ago?"

Daniel held her again while she cried. Far in the back of her mind came the persistent thought that she shouldn't allow herself to depend on anyone, shouldn't expect anyone to be there for her. But Daniel was here now. She buried her face in his shoulder and let herself go.

When she was ready, she came up for air and dried the last traces of tears with her sleeve. He still had his arm around her and wasn't letting go.

"I know I should just feel happy for her," she said. "But I can't help thinking, why wasn't I good enough for her to get sober when I was young? Wasn't I worth it?"

He paused for a long moment, thinking it over. "You know, I may not know your mother very well, but I understand what you are saying. My own mother wasn't so great at having feelings, or talking about them, or even really acknowledging them. I used to blame her for it, but now I think that maybe she just didn't know how to have those kinds of conversations with me. It wasn't that she didn't care about me. She just had no idea how to talk to me. I've never seen her have a deep conversation with anyone."

"So you think my mother just didn't know how to get sober?"

"I think that's exactly the case. It wasn't that you weren't good enough, or not worth it. She just didn't know how to change."

Emily nodded, her tears finally dry. "She's changed now, though. That woman you met this evening—she's worlds different from the mother I grew up with. She was relaxed and easygoing and actually seemed interested in us. The mother I grew up with just wanted to be left alone with her addiction. It's a remarkable change. I just I wish there was some way of knowing if it's permanent."

"And if it isn't?"

"I guess I'll have to wait and see what happens. I think I can give her a chance, though."

"I think that's all any of us can ask for."

She turned her face up toward his, and he gave her a slow kiss. It was a kiss meant to reassure, but it quickly turned into something more.

"I think we're well past the time when we could possibly make it to a movie," she said.

"Oh, I think I can come up with some ideas about what else we can do," he replied. And he did.

* * *

Late that night, so late that it was more accurate to call it early morning, Daniel woke with a pounding sensation in his head.

He shifted his body slowly so as not to wake Emily. After their lovemaking, she'd nestled into the crook of his arm, and he'd held her until she'd fallen asleep. Now she was snoring gently.

He loved watching her sleep. When their paths crossed during the day, they both were usually in professional mode. But in sleep, that unguarded, vulnerable expression slipped so naturally across her face. All he wanted to do was protect her.

A bad headache, however, did not leave him in his most protective mode. The dry air of hotels had always given his sinuses trouble. He rubbed his forehead, wishing he had something for the pain. He wondered whether it would be worth it to seek out a twenty-four-hour drugstore.

He thought back to when Emily had given him the ibuprofen for his ankle. She'd taken it from his duffel bag. Had either of them ever put it back? His bag was still on the bureau where he'd left it. He didn't want to risk waking Emily by turning the light on, so he got out of bed and carefully made his way to the bureau. He stretched his hand out blindly, patting the surface to feel for the duffel bag—and then cringed as something crashed to the floor. Not his duffel bag. He'd knocked over Emily's purse, and from the sound of things, a number of items had spilled out of it.

He could still hear Emily's gentle snores, so he knew she hadn't woken. He began to quietly scoop items back into the purse. The light was so dim he could barely make out any of them, which was just as well; he knew that looking inside a woman's purse was an invasion of privacy, and he wasn't trying to snoop. He shoveled what he supposed was probably a fairly standard collection of things back into the bag—a hairbrush, a wallet, some lipstick—when suddenly his eye fell on a box. In the dim light from the window, he could just see a brand name he recognized. A pregnancy test.

He could tell the box had been opened, though he wasn't sure if the test had been used. It took every ounce of willpower he possessed to push the box back into the purse and set everything back on the nightstand. His intention to look for ibuprofen was forgotten; the shock he was feeling was strong enough to distract from the pain in his head.

What was Emily doing with a pregnancy test in her purse? When had she bought it? And more importantly, why hadn't she said anything to him about it?

Suddenly, it was as if a complete stranger was sleeping next to him. Despite their short acquaintance—more than a month now—he'd felt as though he and Emily knew each other deeply. Now, it seemed they were worlds apart.

Why hadn't she told him? Didn't she trust him?

Maybe that was an unfair thought. Why should she trust him? His mind replayed every time he'd told her that he didn't believe in relationships, didn't want the responsibility or complications of a family.

But he'd never given a second thought to voicing those feelings. For one thing, they were true. And for another, he'd believed that she felt the same way.

It was taking all his strength not to wake her and ask her to explain what was going on. But he knew he couldn't. For reasons of her own, Emily had decided not to tell him why she'd bought the test, and he'd violated her privacy by looking in her purse. There could be some perfectly innocent explanation. And if there was, waking her in the early dawn hours to tell her that he'd looked in her purse without her permission, and would she mind explaining about the pregnancy test he'd found there—he couldn't see that conversation ending well.

His mind swirled with possibilities. For all he knew, the test had been negative. But if that was true, why did she still have it with her?

Perhaps she hadn't bothered to take the test at all and had never gotten around to taking it out of her purse. But that still didn't explain why she'd bought one in the first place. Or why she hadn't told him about it.

Perhaps she'd bought the test for a colleague or a friend. But then why had the box been opened?

Perhaps she'd taken the test, and it was positive, and he was going to be a father.

But they'd been careful. And Emily would never keep a secret of such magnitude from him. At least, he didn't think she would. They barely knew each other, after all. That had been the whole point of their arrangement, that they'd keep things physical and not get too close. But that couldn't mean that Emily would keep something like this a secret.

If there even was a secret. He reminded himself, again, that he didn't know the whole story. There was no use catastrophizing.

And a baby, he thought, would be an absolute catastrophe. He was still trying to find a place in the world for himself where he mattered. How could he possibly handle the enormous responsibility of providing for, protecting and caring for a child when he didn't even have his own life in order? A child needed a home. He should know that better than anyone, having spent so much of his childhood being uprooted from place to place. If he'd never been able to find a home of his own, he didn't know how he could provide one for anyone else.

You're getting ahead of yourself, he thought. *It's probably all a huge misunderstanding. Relax.*

He just needed to stay calm until he and Emily could sit down and talk this through. He was sure she'd have some explanation that would clear everything up.

Since there was absolutely no chance of his returning to sleep, he eased himself out of bed. As eager as he was for Emily to wake up, he didn't want to disturb her. If she woke now, there would be no way he could avoid confronting her about the test and revealing that he'd snooped. But he'd have to find a way to bring it up somehow, unless she did first.

Which led him to wonder if Emily had ever planned to tell him about the test. Perhaps she'd meant to tell him but simply hadn't gotten around to it yet. But he couldn't imagine her keeping such a secret from him. On the other hand, maybe she thought that it wasn't his business to know. Their relationship was never meant to be anything more than a fling, after all. Had she not told him because she didn't want it to become anything more? He shook his head. The possibility of a pregnancy added a whole new layer of complications that neither of them had ever though to consider.

He couldn't stand the thought of staying in the room any longer, and he knew he needed time to compose his thoughts before he spoke with her again. He wrote her a quick note saying that he'd gone out for an early-morning jog and would see her at work and left the room while she was still snoring.

CHAPTER NINE

EMILY WOKE WITH a start, the bed cold beside her. Daniel must have left some time ago. She noticed his writing on the nightstand and leaned over to read the note—apparently, he'd gone for a jog and then straight to work.

That wasn't surprising. Daniel had offered her so much support yesterday. It was only natural that he might want a bit of time to himself. And she appreciated that he'd let her sleep. She checked her phone—there was enough time for a quick shower and some toast.

She showered and began to put on a set of clothes that she'd moved down to Daniel's room, to save herself the trouble of running back to her own room every time she needed to change. And that was when she noticed.

The blouse she was trying to button was one she'd owned for years. She was familiar with the way it met the contours of her body. But it had never made her uncomfortable, as it did now.

She prodded her breasts, gently, and was met with a jolt of pain. Come to think of it, they'd been pretty tender all morning.

But breast tenderness, on its own, wasn't necessarily a symptom of anything significant. Not unless it presented with additional symptoms.

Such as a late and light period, which she'd initially dismissed, because her periods were usually light. And then there were the cramps that had lasted longer than usual. And now breast tenderness. All early signs of pregnancy.

You never did take the test, she thought.

No, she hadn't taken it. Because she'd been positive there was no need. She'd felt so foolish when she'd gotten her period—or what she'd thought had been her period. She'd been so certain that she was overreacting to the signs.

Now she was feeling foolish for a different reason. What kind of doctor noticed extended cramps along with a late period and didn't bother to take a pregnancy test?

The kind of doctor who didn't want to believe she was pregnant, of course. The kind of doctor who didn't want to admit to herself that the idea of having a child filled her with fear.

She didn't have the faintest idea of how to be a parent. A child was vulnerable, helpless. She knew from experience how much children needed someone responsible to rely on. And she didn't have many role models to draw from. Her father had left when she was very young. Her mother might be trying now, but that didn't erase the long, lonely years of Emily's childhood. What if her child needed her and she didn't know what to do? What if her child was depending on her and she let them down?

Let's back up about twenty steps, she thought. *You still don't know for sure that you're pregnant.*

She needed answers. She was going to have to take a pregnancy test, immediately.

Fortunately, she knew exactly where to find one. The test she'd bought just a few weeks ago was still stuffed in the bottom of her purse. When she'd decided not to take it, after her first pregnancy scare, she hadn't wanted to look at it again. So she'd left it in there, out of sight and out of mind, planning to dispose of it once she got back to Denver before Izzie could find it and ask questions. Now, she was glad to have it available. It was one thing to make a trip to the drugstore while telling herself the entire time that she was overreacting. It would have been quite another to make that same purchase while showing strong signs of being pregnant.

She took the test and dialed Izzie's number while she awaited the results. She could barely keep the phone steady in her hands.

Izzie picked up on the first ring. She tried to understand Emily's stumbling, incoherent speech.

"Wait, calm down," she said, her tones soothing through the phone. "We'll figure this out together."

"Daniel and I were so careful. I don't see how this could have happened."

"Let's worry about that later. For now, let's just focus on the next step. What does the test say?"

"I can't figure out the instructions," Emily cried.

"That's because you're scared. Trust me, you're a doctor, I promise you can figure out a simple pregnancy test. You're just overwhelmed. Take a few deep breaths."

Emily breathed slowly in and out until the room stopped spinning around her. "Okay," she said. "I think I can at least talk now."

"Good. Talking is good. So how long have you been having symptoms?"

"Just a few days. But I didn't think anything of it at first. And now—oh, God, Izzie, I'm so scared. I can't do this. I can't be a mother. I don't have the slightest idea how to be one."

"Let's take it one step at a time. Does the test show results yet?"

"I can't look."

"You can. No matter what it says, I'm here for you."

Emily forced herself to look at the test. One thin red line had appeared, to show the test was working. And next to it, another red line, faint but unmistakably present. She was pregnant.

"It's positive," she said to Izzie. "I'm going to have a baby."

"Oh my God. Are you okay?"

Was she? There were so many questions swirling in her mind, and seconds ago, all of them had seemed incredibly important. But now there was only one fact that held any significance for her. She was going to have a baby.

"Emily? Are you there? Are you okay?"

"Yes. It's just a lot to process. I'm trying to get my mind around it."

She was going to be a mother. In nine months, an infant would be in the world because of her. She would have a baby to love and protect and to show the world. And she'd be able to shower her own child with all the love and warmth she hadn't had while she was growing up.

"I know it's a lot, Em. This is such big news. Are you ready for a change this huge?"

"I'm going to have to be, aren't I? In nine months, I'm going to be a mother." As she said the words, an unexpected sense of calm settled over her. She was going to be a mother. "I'm glad, Izzie. I'm really glad."

And to her surprise, she was. All the fear of a few moments ago had changed into something new. Or rather, she had a better understanding of it. Yes, having a baby left her feeling vulnerable, but the second she'd seen the positive test result, she'd known what she wanted. She might not have had the best role models for parents, but she knew she didn't have to worry that she might not be up to the responsibility of parenting, or that she would let her child down. Because there was nothing on this earth that would stop her from being there for her child when they needed her. Her child would never question for a second whether they were wanted or loved.

And it started with this moment.

"You're going to be an auntie, Izzie."

"Oh my God. I'm going to have to start buying little outfits right away."

"Um… Izzie?"

"Yeah?"

"Thank you so much for being here. I don't think I could have gotten through that without you. But I think I need a little time on my own to process what's happened."

"I completely understand. Take the time you need and call me back later. Oh my God, this is so exciting!"

Emily hung up the phone, feeling alone in the room without Izzie's voice. But she wasn't alone, she realized. Just below her heart, a little life was forming.

How had this happened?

She and Daniel had used protection every time. She counted back through the weeks. In order for her to have a positive pregnancy test now, it had probably happened on their first night together. She'd been pregnant with his child for nearly the whole time they'd known each other.

She looked at herself in the mirror. Such a monumental change had happened in the space of only a few minutes, and yet she looked the same as she had that morning. Maybe there was a little more fullness to her body. No, she had to be imagining it. It would be too soon for that. Wouldn't it?

Her hand went to her abdomen. She knew how pregnancy worked. And yet the life growing inside her felt like a complete mystery. What would her baby be like? What would she be like as a mother?

Ready or not, it was time to find out.

She'd been so preoccupied with her fears about motherhood that she hadn't had much time to think about the exciting side of it. There was the fascination of watching a tiny person grow and develop, the thrill of helping a child learn something new. There was the warmth and love that she planned to shower this child with.

She knew from her own experience just how much things could go wrong. But didn't all parents make some mistakes? With luck, hers would be significantly smaller than those of her own parents. She was so glad that she'd visited her mother and agreed to take a chance on their relationship. She wanted her child to grow up in a world where change was possible, where people could have second chances. And she'd have Izzie for help. Single motherhood would be a challenge, but people did it all the time. Families came in all shapes and sizes.

And she would be a single mother, she was certain. She could no longer avoid her thoughts of Daniel and how he might react to the news.

Daniel had told her, flat out, that he didn't want children. They'd both told each other that they didn't want a relationship. He didn't even believe in love.

In fairness, she'd thought she felt the same as he did. But now everything was different. Now, even though she didn't believe in love, she wanted to, because she wanted her child to grow up in a world where love was possible.

But believing in something, and wanting to believe in it, weren't the same thing. Her relationship with Daniel was never supposed to be anything more than a fling.

And now there were only a few days left to their time in LA, and she was pregnant.

She had no idea what to tell him, but she had to think of something.

She knew the kind of man Daniel was. He might not want children, but faced with a child of his own, he would do the right thing. He'd changed his career because his nephew was born. She was certain he would want to be involved with the baby. Just how involved, she couldn't say.

A series of images flashed through her mind. Daniel teaching a child to ride a bicycle, reading a bedtime story, brushing teeth together. Family life.

But that was unlikely to happen, she knew. After their time in LA was over, they were supposed to part ways. Neither of them had brought up the idea of trying to make things work, either long-distance or otherwise. He'd given no sign that he was interested in anything more. And she hadn't considered it, until now, because she'd actually found comfort in the time limit around their relationship. She'd felt relieved that she didn't have to form any expectations around him, because that meant she wouldn't have to be disappointed when he let her down, the same way nearly everyone else had.

Except that as she'd gotten to know Daniel, she'd had to challenge that belief. In their short time together, he'd been there every time she'd needed him. He'd kept their secret and respected her boundaries when she hadn't wanted their relationship made public knowledge. He'd stood up for her at work when Dr. Reyes got too pushy. He'd been there for her when she'd visited her mother.

Every step of the way, he'd shown her that she could count on him.

True, a few weeks wasn't much time. But she thought they'd been close enough, intimate enough, that she knew who he was. He was someone she could trust.

But trust and love were different things. While she might be able to trust him as someone who would take care of their child, she had no reason to believe that he was interested in something more with her.

The past few weeks had been a lovely escape. But that wasn't real life. It was nothing more than a fantasy. They were trying to have all the benefits of a relationship with none of the commitments or responsibilities. And if a part of her was grieving because that fantasy was over, it didn't matter. That would have to go high up on the shelf, where she couldn't reach for it, because no matter what his involvement was in their child's life, Daniel was never going to feel anything more for her.

And so if she was falling for him, even just a little bit, it still didn't matter. Daniel had been adamantly clear that commitment wasn't for him.

Yet the ache in her heart grew stronger when she thought about telling him she was pregnant. For one wild moment, she allowed her imagination to run completely free. She pictured him delighted, filled with excitement, eager to start a new life with the baby and with her. Thrilled at the idea of moving to Denver and spending every day together.

But that went against everything he'd ever shared about himself. If she brought up the possibility of extending their relationship, she was sure he would tell her that while he'd be there for the baby, he wasn't interested in continuing things with her. She tried to imagine herself saying the words:

Daniel, I'm pregnant. Also, I'd like the two of us to stay together and see where our relationship can go, although I'm already reasonably certain I'm in love with you. What do you think?

She couldn't throw all that at him at once. He'd be reeling from learning she was pregnant. And what if he didn't want them to stay together? She imagined him trying to let her down gently, all while trying to absorb the shock of her words. Or, worse, he'd try to make a go of it with her out of a sense of obligation, even though he didn't have any feelings for her. That would be even worse than rejecting her outright.

She needed to put away her fantasies. The best thing for the baby, and for Daniel—for all of them, really—would be for her to show Daniel that she was perfectly fine ending their fling, just as they'd agreed upon. That way he could offer to be there for the baby without feeling any kind of obligation to her, which would just make things far more complicated for everyone.

Maybe, she thought, she could tell him about the baby after the contest was over. She could keep it secret for just a little longer. She'd have to tell him eventually, of course. But she could always send him a letter after she got back to Denver.

She didn't like the idea of lying to him, but keeping a secret wasn't the same as a lie, not really. And there were only a few days to go before they both left. Wrapping things up at work was sure to keep her busy; she just needed to avoid him until then.

Her heart ached in protest. *It won't be that hard*, she told herself firmly. It was the same tone she'd taken with herself when she'd had to take on acting roles she hadn't liked. *You can do this. You have to do this.*

And she did. She had to accept that whatever she'd had with Daniel was now over, whether he knew it or not. And since they'd both agreed not to have any expectations of one another, then he shouldn't mind if she avoided him now. In fact, it was only natural that things might cool off between the two of them as their time together came to an end. Since there was nothing real between them, it shouldn't bother either of them that much.

And if it bothered her a lot…well, that didn't matter. Those feelings were packed away where she couldn't reach them. Where they needed to stay, for her child's sake. And, most likely, for her own.

Daniel could swear that Emily was avoiding him.

More than a day had passed since he'd found the pregnancy test, and he hadn't been able to get the thought of it out of his mind. There had to be a reasonable explanation, and he was sure that if he and Emily talked, all would become clear. But he never seemed to have a chance to get her alone for a private conversation.

Whenever he came by her exam room, he found her with a patient or chatting with a colleague. She'd never seemed to be such a social butterfly, but today it seemed that at every spare moment she was talking with someone else. He'd sent some texts and suggested they get together after work, but she replied that she was very busy wrapping up chart notes, as they had only a day or two left in Los Angeles. He could understand that; he'd had to stay late with some chart work of his own. Still, he felt as though she could have found a way to meet if she really wanted to see him. He'd come by her hotel room a few times, but she never seemed to be there.

It was as if she was deliberately keeping her distance.

Finally, he realized that he wasn't going to find a moment alone with her unless he made it happen. She and Helen were chatting over a cup of coffee when he knocked on her door.

"Sorry to interrupt, but could I have a minute with Emily?" he asked. "There's just something I need to go over with her."

Emily raised her eyebrows but motioned for him to come in. "Sorry, Helen," she said as the nurse practitioner left. "We'll finish catching up later." She turned toward Daniel. "That was abrupt."

"Would you mind shutting your door? I need to speak to you in private."

She raised her eyebrows again but complied. "What's this all about?"

"Is there anything you want to tell me?"

The look of surprise on her face filled him with a cold sense of doom. She was hiding something, he knew it. But surely she wouldn't hide something as big as a pregnancy. Not from him. Not after they'd grown so close over these past few weeks. But had they grown close? This was only supposed to be a brief affair, after all. Not a deep emotional connection.

And yet, it had grown deeper. Or so he'd thought. None of his experiences with Emily had even remotely resembled the meaningless flings he'd had in his career as a cruise ship doctor, hopping from island to island. Every conversation with Emily was meaningful. He'd felt that they knew each other in a way he'd never experienced before. It had been her vulnerability, her openness, that had attracted him to her in the first place. Except for David, there'd never been anyone in his life with whom he'd had any sort of in-depth emotional conversation. Perhaps he'd had a hint of that, in his youth, with Sofia. And then for a long time, there had been no one. He'd been starved for emotional connection, he realized. Until Emily had come along. Emily might be a good actress, but when it came to big emotions, she wore her heart on her sleeve.

But had she been hiding something from him the whole time?

"Emily?" he probed again. "You look like you have something to say."

"What…what would I have to tell you?"

"I don't know," he said. "But it really does seem as though there's something."

"I can't imagine what."

"I know you're pregnant," he blurted out.

Her jaw dropped. "How did you find out?"

He stared at her, stunned. Until that moment, he hadn't fully believed it was true. He simply couldn't imagine Emily, vulnerable and genuine as she was, keeping such a secret from him. But now she'd confirmed it.

"I found the pregnancy test in your purse yesterday morning," he said.

"You looked in my purse?"

"No—I just knocked it over, and the box fell out. I wasn't trying to snoop. But it was pretty hard to miss. How long have you had it?"

"I bought the test more than three weeks ago, but—"

"*Three weeks?* You've known about this for longer than three weeks and you never said anything?"

"No. Daniel, listen. I bought the test back then because

I thought I might be pregnant. But then I got my period, or what I thought was my period, and I never took the test. Except that yesterday, I realized it wasn't a real period. Just breakthrough bleeding. So yes, Daniel, I am pregnant. A little over five weeks along, I would guess. But I didn't know for sure until yesterday, I swear."

"Why didn't you tell me at first, when you suspected?"

"Because I thought it was a false alarm! I felt incredibly foolish." Tears were streaming down her face. She wiped at them furiously, and he recognized the Emily he'd come to know over the past few weeks. The one who was scared but tough.

"I really wish you had told me sooner," he said. "There was no need for you to be alone with this." Even as he spoke, he was still trying to absorb the news. A baby. He was going to be a father.

"I was nervous. You'd talked about not wanting children."

"I suppose we both did. How are you feeling?"

He was relieved to see her smile. Her tears had stopped. "I know it's a big change. It's something neither of us expected, and it's going to be a huge adjustment. But honestly, I'm feeling good about it. I'm going to raise this child with as much love as I can give to it."

He took her hand. "Then we're going to have a very lucky child."

She seemed to be searching his face for something. Was it reassurance? She must be feeling so vulnerable, he thought. He realized he hadn't said anything about how he felt. In truth, it was such overwhelming news that it was still sinking in.

"Don't worry," he said, trying to find words that might reassure her. He thought back over their conversations, of how often and how openly he'd said that he didn't want to settle down, didn't want a family of his own. But now that it was happening, he felt an unexpected rush of emotion. Most of all, though, he didn't want Emily to feel as though she couldn't depend on him. He knew how sensitive she was to people letting her down, and he wanted to make sure she knew that despite his earlier words, he would always be there for their child.

And even though he knew it was hard for her to trust, surely, he thought, she knew the kind of man he was. As surprising as this turn of events might be, ensuring the well-being of his child would be his first priority.

"I want to make sure you know that our child will always be well cared for," he continued. "My family is very well-off, but even if they weren't, I have plenty of savings. I'll make sure out baby doesn't want for anything."

She withdrew her hand from his. "I'm not worried about money," she said.

"Even so, I want to support my own child. And I want to be in their life."

"Of course," she said, her face composed. "I wouldn't expect anything less of you."

She seemed cooler, somehow. More distant. The more he tried to reassure her he'd be there, the further away she seemed to get.

"I just want to be clear that I'll be there, no matter what it takes. I'm not going to let the baby down. I'll be there for our child."

"I know. I hear that perfectly well—that you'll be here for the baby."

She looked as though she was waiting for him to say something else, but he couldn't think of what it might be.

Then he realized that they hadn't yet discussed what the pregnancy would mean for their relationship.

Over the past few weeks, he'd watched Emily work with young patients. He knew that she would make an excellent mother. But that had nothing to do with whether she wanted to be with him.

Emily had been the one to propose they stay together for the duration of their time in LA. Would she want to continue seeing him after their time at the contest was over? Just because she was having his child didn't necessarily mean that she wanted to be with him anymore.

"There's plenty of time to make all the arrangements," she said, her tone brusque and businesslike.

"Yes, of course. But that's not all that I..." He faltered.

"Go on," she said.

But what about our relationship? he wanted to say. He tried to get the words out, but they stuck in his throat. Emily had only spoken about the baby thus far. Did she not want anything more from him? Did he not mean anything to her?

He couldn't, he thought. Her life was in Denver. They'd never planned on anything long term. But then again, the situation had changed considerably since they'd made their plans.

He was seized with a sudden urge to tell her he was moving to Denver, no matter what. It seemed that what he'd been searching for his entire life was there: a chance to belong to people, to matter to someone. If his child was there—and if Emily was there, then that was reason enough for him to make his life there. But if he told her that, she'd probably think he was crazy, making a major life decision on a moment's notice. And for all he knew, she'd prefer he stayed as far from Denver as possible. Although nothing would stop him from seeing his child. In fact, it was best to clarify that right now.

"I just want to be clear that I mean what I say about being involved with the baby," he said. "We'll need to talk about custody arrangements and visitation. And even though you've said you don't need money, we should sit down and go through all the financials at some point."

"So we'll be staying in touch strictly to talk about the baby."

That clarified things for him. She would stay in contact because she was thinking about the baby. But as for their relationship, Daniel was getting the distinct impression that Emily intended to stick to their original agreement.

If that was what she wanted, then he'd respect her decision. Even if it meant letting go of her. Which he realized, at that moment, was the last thing he wanted. He didn't want her out of his life. Quite the opposite—the past six weeks had only shown him that he wanted to be with her even more.

But if she didn't want the same thing…he couldn't ask her to offer more. And he couldn't tell her how *he* felt. Not without knowing if she felt the same way. Not when he suspected she didn't.

"Just to talk about the baby," he agreed.

"Perfect. It's what I think is for the best as well. There's no need to make the situation more complicated than it already is. We can work out the details of exactly what our arrangement will look like later, but I think the main thing for now is to be clear that we're strictly co-parents. Nothing more."

"I understand," he said quietly. "And even though it's a surprise, I think we know each other well enough to trust that we'll both do whatever it takes to make sure our child has the best life possible."

"Of course we will," she said, her gaze growing fierce. "I wouldn't expect anything else."

"And as for the two of us..." He'd been trying to play his tone off as casual, but he found he couldn't finish the sentence. The enormity of the situation was catching up to him. Having a child, yes, that was monumental. But the idea of things changing between him and Emily was almost unbearable.

He realized that he'd been allowing himself to exist in a blissful cocoon, without giving much thought to what would happen when their fling was over. He hadn't *wanted* to think about what would happen when their fling was over. He had, in fact, been avoiding thinking about it at all.

Because he didn't want to think about a time when he wouldn't be able to slip his arm around Emily's waist, or hear her laugh, or run his fingers through her long mahogany hair. He didn't want to think about when she wouldn't be around to make jokes, or for the two of them to have deep conversations about whatever might be on their minds.

Yet that time was fast approaching, and he wasn't ready for it, because he'd been pretending to himself that things could go on as they were between the two of them indefinitely. Because even though they'd only agreed to a fling, he didn't want to think about life without her. And if he'd brought up the idea of extending their time together, he might have to hear that she didn't feel the same way. So he'd remained silent, in order to allow himself to keep pretending.

But now she was pregnant, and within days of leaving LA, and neither of them could afford to pretend anymore. Emily was making it clear that she didn't want him in her life as anything more than the father of her child. His first priority had to be the baby, of course, but his heart ached as he realized that his time with Emily was over—just as he was starting to understand how much he wanted more.

"I think it will be best if the two of us remain good friends," she said. Was that a tremble underneath her voice, or was she just speaking quickly? "Staying on good terms will be the best thing for the baby. And I know that's what we both want."

He couldn't argue. Of course that was what he wanted, too. And yet, hearing her say it out loud reminded him of what he'd believed for years: that expectations in relationships only led to heartbreak. Ending things between him and Emily now was for the best.

But if that was true, why did he feel as though something he'd longed for was slipping just past his fingertips?

CHAPTER TEN

"AND THAT WAS the last time I saw her," said Daniel.

A week had passed, and he was back at David's house. He hadn't wanted to tell his brother about what had happened with Emily at first. David had been skeptical of his short-term relationship from the beginning, and Daniel was afraid that David would say he'd told him so.

There was something about being apart from Emily that left him with a feeling of…of *wrongness*. He couldn't articulate why. He just knew that during the few weeks he'd known her, he'd felt more like himself than he had in years.

But if she didn't feel the same way, there was nothing that could be done. He knew they were both determined to provide a good life for their child. But when it came to their relationship…he'd been too afraid to ask for more. Especially when he'd been so certain of rejection.

During their six weeks together, he'd thought they'd grown so close. He knew that trust was difficult for her, but he'd thought he had earned a place in her life as someone she could rely on. But maybe he'd misread the situation. Maybe she simply thought he'd let her down. Was that why she hadn't told him about that first pregnancy scare? He wished she'd told him what she'd been going through. And then, to keep the news of her pregnancy from him for a whole day once it was confirmed. The fact that she felt the need to hide was one more piece of evidence that she saw him as yet another person who would disappoint her.

But hadn't he proven that wasn't who he was? At least enough for her to give him a chance? Maybe not. Maybe Emily was too scarred by her past to let herself rely on anyone. It made him sad to think that she might always keep people at arm's length. He used to do that, too… until he'd met her.

He wondered if she'd even thought of him over the past week. He hadn't seen her since their last conversation, but he couldn't get her face out of his mind.

"Have you talked to her at all?" asked David.

"Not yet."

"What? Come on, man. It's been a week. This is the mother of your child. You want to be in the baby's life, don't you?"

Daniel glared at his brother, his eyes blazing. "Of course I do! Who do you think I am?"

"I know perfectly well who you are. But some people, Emily included, might not know you as well as I do. And might be inclined to make some assumptions about your ability to commit to taking care of a child. Based on, you know, just about everything you've ever said about not wanting to be tied down."

"I would never abandon a child."

"I know you wouldn't. But I've known you for your entire life. She hasn't. If you want to be involved, you're going to have to call her and make some practical arrangements."

"I don't think she wants to talk to me," he replied.

"Do you want to talk to her?"

"Of course I do! But I don't think I can say anything she wants to hear."

"Maybe it's time for you to stop trying to say what you think she wants to hear and start telling her how you really feel."

Daniel was taken aback by the sharpness in his brother's voice. "What do you mean? What else could I have possibly done? Our original agreement was that we'd only be together for six weeks. It was her idea."

"Oh, little brother. Don't you know that once a baby comes along, everything changes?"

"Are you kidding me?" He'd spent the past week feeling as though his life had been turned upside down.

Learning that he was about to become a father was the biggest emotional roller coaster he'd ever been on. He'd never pictured himself as a parent. He'd always assumed that since relationships weren't for him, then parenthood wasn't an option, either. But now that he was faced with the reality of it, he realized that he'd been so certain he *wouldn't* be a parent that he'd never considered whether he could be one. And the more thought he gave it, the more he realized that all he wanted was to love and protect his child.

But he hadn't yet been able to bring himself to call Emily to discuss the details. He would have to, and soon. But he'd been putting it off because their last conversation had been painful enough. The thought of talking to her again, knowing that she had no interest in him and that she was only communicating with him for the sake of their child, made his heart feel as though it was splitting in two.

"What else could I have done?" he asked his brother

again. "She clearly had no interest in continuing our relationship. All she would talk about was how we were going to get in touch to make arrangements about the baby."

"Did it ever occur to you that maybe she was trying to gauge how you felt? From what you've said, it sounds to me as though you gave her the same message."

"I was trying to follow her lead! She said it's best for the child if we don't complicate our relationship. And I have to agree. It's the right thing to do."

"It's a cop-out, if you ask me."

"Excuse me?"

"Look, Daniel, no one respects you more than I do. But it's my job as your older brother to tell you that I think you're making a huge mistake."

"By trying to do what's best for my child?"

"By hiding from your true feelings. Perhaps she only wanted to talk about the baby, but did you tell her what *you* wanted? You didn't put your heart on the line."

"Of course I didn't. What if she'd said that she didn't see a future for us?"

"Then you'd know, and you'd have to respect that. But what I can't support, little brother, is you convincing yourself that you can't reach for the happiness that's in front of you just because there's a chance you might not get it."

Daniel thought about this. "You didn't see her on that last day. She was so brusque."

"Perhaps. But we're talking about what you said and did. How you felt. Daniel, if this was just a fling, if this woman meant nothing to you, then why, a week later, do I know everything about her? I know that she was a child actress and uses vanilla-scented hand cream and that her favorite color is purple. It's an awful lot of information to know about a woman I've never met. And do you know why I know all this information, Daniel?"

"Why?"

"Because you won't stop talking about her! For the past six weeks, it's been Emily this and Emily that. This fling of yours seems to have gotten awfully serious long before there was ever a baby involved."

That was true enough. Even from the start, his relationship with Emily had been far different from his typical flings. Things had always been serious between the two of them. He simply hadn't admitted it to himself—or to her.

And even though he didn't know if she'd feel the same as he did, his brother was right. He needed to tell her how he felt. Not only to give their relationship a chance, but because learning that he was going to be a father had changed his perspective on love. He wanted to believe that it was worth taking a risk for love. For his child's sake, as well as for his own.

"David," he said suddenly, "do you think I'll be a good father?"

"I know you will," his brother replied. "You're amazing with Blake. You've got Trina and me for help. Your child will have so much love in their life. And you know what else, little brother?"

"What?"

"I have a feeling that you will, too."

Emily had settled back into her life in Denver, but nothing felt the same as it had before she left. She supposed that was to be expected. She was pregnant, after all.

But that wasn't the only thing that had changed. She

found herself constantly thinking of Daniel. Try as she might, she couldn't stop images of him from coming to mind. His eyes lighting up when he noticed she was in the room. His smile after she'd made a joke.

That was over, she reminded herself. Daniel wasn't interested in anything more than a fling. He'd be in her life as the father of her child and nothing more.

For a moment, during their last conversation, she'd thought he might be about to suggest that they try to make a relationship work. But of course he hadn't. The very thought was completely impractical. But it still hurt that he hadn't at least tried.

She hadn't expected him to offer to move to Denver with her. Or ask that she stay in LA with him. She knew it was unrealistic to think that he could have made such a big decision right away, especially immediately after learning she was pregnant. But deep in her heart, she had hoped for something, anything, that indicated that he was thinking about a future with the two of them together. The details weren't important. What mattered were his intentions and how he felt.

But his intentions, apparently, were to keep her at arm's length. And so she'd returned to Denver and tried to resume the life she'd left behind.

Izzie had been excited to have her back. Emily knew her friend was trying to hide how overwhelmed she'd been during her absence. Their phone had been ringing constantly with athletes who wanted to schedule appointments. Emily's work at the dance contest had paid off, and their schedules were finally filling up. Her relief at seeing the practice grow helped to offset her grief at everything that had happened with Daniel. It wasn't much, but it was something.

But despite the increase in their caseloads, Emily found it almost impossible to immerse herself in work. Thoughts of Daniel kept springing to mind.

"So let me get this straight," Izzie said. "You're absolutely certain he didn't want to at least try to make things work."

They were sitting in their practice's break room, rehashing everything that had happened for what felt like the hundredth time.

"I could tell he didn't," said Emily. "He made it very clear that our only involvement in each other's live would be to coordinate taking care of the baby."

"It sounds like he's taking that seriously."

"That's the kind of person he is. I know it's the best thing for the baby if he's involved. And I'd never stand in the way of him getting to know his own child. I want my baby to know their father. But…he doesn't want anything more. Not with me."

"Okay, but what about how you feel? Did you tell him?"

Emily squirmed uncomfortably. The trouble was, she hadn't been aware of how she felt until recently. And she'd been too afraid to explain her feelings to Daniel.

Seeing him again, but knowing that he didn't want to be with her, would be heartbreaking enough. Worrying that he might try to stay with her out of obligation would be even worse.

It was enough for her to know that no matter what, he would put the baby first. Just as she would.

All these thoughts ran through her mind as she told Izzie, "No, I didn't explain. But I didn't even know myself until it was too late. Both of us were afraid of commitment, but maybe I was even more afraid of it than he was."

"Hmm. You know what I think the problem is?"

"What?"

"I think this is one of those times when you're trying so hard to protect yourself from getting hurt that you can't see what's right in front of you."

"What's right in front of me?"

Izzie looked ahead, out toward the glass doors of the lobby. "Someone who's about six foot two, badly in need of a haircut, with—yes, I do believe you were right—a positively sparkling pair of brown eyes."

Emily sat straight up in surprise. "What are you talking about?"

"Hot stuff out in the lobby there. Why don't you go and say hello?"

"Daniel's here? In Denver? How did he even find us?"

"The good old internet, of course. Oh, and I helped."

"Izzie!"

"He found our practice number online and called about a dozen times to make sure this was the right place. He's nice. I like him, Em. I mean, not as much as you do, of course. But I don't think anyone likes him as much as you do."

"But how can I go out there? What do I say to him?"

"You know. Just say what's in your heart."

Emily approached the lobby with trepidation, still unable to believe that Daniel was actually there. But it was true. He looked a bit travel-worn, but his eyes were the same. And his smile was better than ever. Though maybe that was because she hadn't seen it for a while, so its effect on her was strong.

"I know why you're here," she said, mustering all her

resolve. She would have to be strong. If she and Daniel were going to coparent, she'd need all her determination to keep her feelings under control.

"You do?" he said.

"Of course. I appreciate you coming here, but you probably could have accomplished the same thing with a phone call."

"I doubt it," he said.

"You came because you want to talk about the baby. Don't worry, Daniel. I know you'll be a good father. We'll figure out a way for you to be in the child's life."

She was trying so hard to sound positive, but her voice sounded fake, even to her own ears. She wondered if he could tell.

"Emily," he said, reaching out to grasp both of her hands. "You're right that I'm determined to be in my child's life. I'll always do what's best for the baby. But that's not why I'm here. I came to tell you something very important."

She looked up at him, uncomprehending.

"When we last talked in LA, we agreed that our fling was over. We decided that ending it was the right thing to do. And I still feel that way. It was long past time for it to be over."

Her heart sank. Had Daniel come all this way just to crush every last vestige of hope that she had? It seemed unnecessarily cruel.

"Because the way I feel about you—the way I've felt about you for a long time—goes far deeper than a simple fling. It's much more serious than that. And for too long, I was afraid to admit that to myself. I let my fear of what might happen get in the way of my ability to see that I had something wonderful right before my eyes."

Tears began to gather in the corners of her eyes. It couldn't be possible. And yet Daniel was here, saying the words she'd longed to hear during their last conversation.

"And then you told me that you were pregnant. And I realized that if I was going to be a father, I couldn't keep hiding from myself. I had to tell the truth. And the truth is—" he swallowed and clasped her hand even tighter "—the truth is, I love you."

She stared at him, stunned. He loved her? She wanted to believe it with all her heart. She'd dreamed of this moment: of Daniel telling her that he felt the same way about their relationship as she did, that he wanted to give it a chance to work.

She knew what she felt for him, of course. But she'd never thought he could feel that way about her.

As usual, the hope left her feeling frightened. What if she let the walls around her heart down and she just got hurt, as she had been over and over again?

But if she never let those walls down, she'd get hurt just the same. Her conversation with her mother had shown her that. A conversation she'd never have had were it not for Daniel.

Tears were streaming down her face. He raised a finger to her cheek and wiped them away. "I know it's hard for you to trust," he said. "And it's hard for me to let people know how I'm really feeling. But part of the reason I came here today to tell you this in person is because I wanted you to have a reason to trust that this is how I really feel about you. And I wanted to give you a way to feel certain about that."

He took her hands and put them together, palms facing inward, still holding them in his own. She was mesmerized, unable to look away from his eyes.

"We're both doctors," he said. "But you're a dancer, too. You told me that every dance move reflects what's going on in a single moment. The condition of our bodies, the mood we're in." He put her right hand on his heart, keeping it pressed there with his own hand. "And the way we feel about each other."

He looked down at her hand. "So now we're in a new kind of dance. One where we need to be standing in front of each other in order for both of us to understand how we really feel. I wanted to be here in front of you when I told you I loved you, so that you could put your hand on my heart and know that I mean every word."

Her hand was on his heart now, and she could feel it, pumping away. The beat was steady and calm. His eyes, as he gazed at her, were warm and steadfast.

He was right. She had her answer. Not from his words, but from the steady drumbeat of his heart. She thought of how he'd shown her, repeatedly, that he wouldn't let her down. She knew the kind of doctor he was. She'd seen him stand up for his patients. And she knew the kind of person he was, because he'd helped her reunite with her mother, and he'd come all the way to Denver to make sure that she knew, in the only way she could trust, how he felt about her. And he loved her. She was ninety-nine percent certain that he really, actually loved her.

There was just one other thing she needed to do to be one hundred percent sure.

"Okay," she said, keeping one hand on his heart and wrapping the other around his neck. "My hands can only tell me so much. I'll need to make sure you mean it in one other way, too." She leaned close to him and gave him a long, slow kiss, her lips taking in everything she'd missed during their days apart.

Some time later, they broke apart. "I hope you got what you needed," he said huskily, and she noticed that there were tears in his eyes.

"I did," she said. "I've conducted a thorough diagnostic evaluation, and after that kiss, I can conclusively say that I have all the information I need to trust you with my heart. Which is a good thing, because I love you, too."

"Now that's a relief," he said and kissed her again.

A curt "ahem" caught their attention. Grace, the receptionist, was looking pointedly from them to the patients who had just arrived and were signing in at the reception desk.

"Ah, right," said Emily, blushing and smoothing her skirt. "We can't have anyone thinking we're unprofessional. The practice's reputation is at stake, after all."

"Of course," said Daniel. "And I'm about to go on the Denver job market. I can't become known as a doctor who goes around kissing his colleagues in public places."

"The Denver job market? Does that mean you're moving here?"

"I think it makes the most sense. You've spent a lot of time and effort building your practice in Denver. You can't leave now, just when things are finally getting off the ground. It wouldn't make sense. You're planning to stay and raise our child here, I'm sure."

She nodded—it had been what she intended.

"Then if my child lives here, I'll need to as well."

"But what about your family in Los Angeles?"

"I can visit them anytime. I only ever wanted to get a permanent job somewhere on land so that my schedule would be more predictable. It didn't matter where. I can get to Los Angeles from Denver as easily as anywhere else. There's absolutely nothing keeping me in LA and every possible reason to be here."

Her tears began to fall again.

"Oh, no," he said. "I hoped that would be good news. I thought it was what you wanted. But if I was wrong, it doesn't have to be Denver."

"That's not it," she said. "I'm just trying to believe that it really is possible to have everything I've always wanted."

He held her close and was about to kiss her again when he noticed Grace glaring at them. "Would it be unprofessional for me to kiss you again?" he asked.

"Most unprofessional. I think you should do it anyway."

"Doctor's orders. I'd better do as I'm told." And he did.

When they were done, she said, "You know, if you need a job, business is picking up at a certain sports medicine practice that I know of. We could really use a third doctor on staff for backup for the next time one of us breaks an ankle. I can take you on a tour of the place right now, if you like."

He slipped an arm around her waist. "I'd be delighted to take a tour. But we'll have to think about the job offer. I may have a conflict of interest."

She wrinkled her brow. "How so?"

"Well, I was planning to propose to the boss. Not right away, but soon. I need time to get to know Denver and plan something romantic. Maybe something involving hot air balloons or a candlelight dinner. What do you think? Do I have a chance?"

"More than a chance. In fact, I don't think you'll need the balloons or the candlelight dinner. If you love her, she's going to say yes."

EPILOGUE

One year later

"Oh, dear..." Emily rummaged through her luggage, unable to find the tube of toothpaste she was certain she'd packed when she left Denver. It was Thanksgiving, and she and Daniel were spending the holiday weekend at David and Trina's house in Costa Mesa. "Darling, have you seen the toothpaste?"

"I'm afraid so," he called from the hallway beyond the spare bedroom.

"Well? Where is it?"

"Everywhere."

"What?"

"Come see for yourself."

Emily went into the hallway, where Daniel stood holding their three-month-old daughter, Delphine, against his shoulder. The baby's cheeks were flushed, her eyes closed in slumber. Her hair was wavy, like Daniel's, and a deep mahogany brown, like Emily's. Emily marveled at her daughter's tiny, perfect hands, and the way her small stomach moved up and down with each breath. She still couldn't believe that she and Daniel had produced such an innocent, pristine creature. She kissed the top of Delphine's forehead, and then her eyes widened as she took in the chaos of the hallway walls, smeared with layers of toothpaste.

"Blake must have gotten into our luggage," said Daniel. Seconds later, David and Trina appeared, David holding an unrepentant Blake and Trina holding an empty tube of toothpaste.

"I think he thought it was one of his finger paints," Trina said. "I'm so sorry. I swear it was only yesterday he learned to walk, and now he's getting into everything."

"It's no problem," Emily replied. "I'm just glad we have a while to go before Delphine hits that stage."

"Personally, I can't wait until Delphine and Blake can start getting into mischief together," said Daniel. Emily raised her eyebrows, and Daniel added, "I didn't mean *mischief*, exactly. I just meant that it'll be fun when they're old enough to play together."

"I hope I can get this cleaned up before your mother gets here," Trina said.

At that moment, the doorbell rang.

Emily opened the door to see her mother and Brandon—now her fiancé—standing on the front step. She and her mother exchanged a hug, and then her mother reached out her arms for Delphine.

Tabitha was still sober. She and Emily spoke nearly every week, and her mother had continued to maintain her active lifestyle. David and Trina had wanted to make the Thanksgiving holiday a family affair, inviting Emily and Daniel as well as her mother and Brandon. For the first time in her life, Emily had felt excited to visit Los Angeles and see her mother. They'd grown even closer since Delphine's birth, and her mother was every bit the doting grandmother. To Emily's surprise, she found that she welcomed her mother's involvement, especially when her mother began sharing stories of how vulnerable she'd felt during Emily's own infancy. Caring for a child was every bit the awesome responsibility Emily had imagined it to be, but being able to talk to her mother about it helped more than she could have ever predicted.

Motherhood was full of surprises, but so far she hadn't faced any of them alone. Between her mother, and Daniel, and Izzie, and everyone else in their lives who adored Delphine, Emily had never felt more supported in her life.

A year ago, she couldn't have imagined herself feeling that way. Before she'd met Daniel, she'd believed that trusting other people was just another chance to get hurt. But in spite of all her expectations, he'd shown her something different. He'd made the choice to be there for her, and for Delphine, and every day he showed her that he would continue to make that choice for the rest of their lives.

She left her mother cooing over Delphine and went back into the hallway, where she found Daniel scraping toothpaste from the wall. "Need some help?" she asked.

"No, I've got this. Trina and David have their hands full keeping Blake from his next act of destruction, and you should go spend some time with your mother—it's been a while since you've seen her."

She slipped an arm around his waist. "But then who will *you* be spending time with?"

He smiled and clasped her hand to his heart. "I'm perfectly happy to be of use out here."

"Daniel, you're not upset that your parents didn't come, are you?"

Daniel and David's parents had politely declined their invitation to visit over the holiday, citing a previously booked cruise in the Maldives. Daniel had told her that he was neither surprised nor upset by this decision, yet now, as she saw him scrubbing furiously at the toothpaste on the wall, she wondered if he'd been more upset than he let on.

He stopped scrubbing, and Emily anxiously twisted her wedding ring, waiting for his response.

And then, to her utter surprise, he started laughing. He turned and gathered her into his arms.

"Daniel? What's gotten into you?"

"I just couldn't help laughing at the idea that I might be upset, when I don't think I've ever been this happy in my life."

Relief flooded through her. "Then you're not disappointed that your parents didn't come?"

"Are you kidding? We held the door open for them, but they have to decide to walk through it. And whether they do or not, I'm not going to waste a single moment feeling disappointed about it. Not when we have so many good things in our lives right now. Not when our home, and our family, are so complete."

She leaned against his chest, breathing in the scent of his aftershave. "We are happy, aren't we?"

He held her and she closed her eyes, so certain of his response that she didn't even need to hear him say it. The pressure of his arms around her, the warmth of his chest as she leaned against him, was answer enough. And the deep kiss he gave her as he stroked a lock of her hair with his fingers erased any doubts that might have lingered.

The moment might have stretched on indefinitely had Emily not heard Trina's voice from the other room. "Emily? Daniel? You're not doing the cleaning up, are you? I can take care of it myself in just a moment."

Emily jumped at the sound of her voice, and Daniel pulled her to him tighter. "What's wrong?" he whispered. "Afraid someone will see that we're in love?"

She smiled and placed her arms around his neck. "I think that secret's already out." She had just leaned in to kiss him again when a crash came from their bedroom. She and Daniel raced into the room to see that Blake had toppled the contents of their large suitcase onto himself. The toddler was surrounded by clothes, makeup and jewelry and was eagerly exploring the artistic merits of applying lipstick to Daniel's new white oxford shirt.

"This calls for a little teamwork," said Daniel. "What do you say—I'll take our luggage, you take our nephew?"

"On it," said Emily. She disentangled a protesting Blake from their belongings and handed him off to Trina, who could be heard chastising him all the way down the hallway, and then bent to help Daniel salvage their belongings, which Blake had been happily destroying for the past few minutes. "What was that you were saying earlier, about looking forward to when Blake would be able to teach our daughter all about getting into mischief?"

"I don't think that's exactly what I said, but nevertheless, I take it back. I want everything to stay just as it is, right now."

"Right now, surrounded by chaos and destructive toddlers?"

"Yes. Right now. Surrounded by family, with the love of my life by my side. I couldn't ask for anything more."

Emily held up his ruined shirt and smiled. "Not even a new shirt?"

"No. That one's perfect. I love it. In fact, give it here. I want to change into it right now."

She laughed and said, "Daniel, stop!" as he made to change into the lipstick-smeared shirt, but deep down, she knew that part of him was serious. He loved their life together, chaotic and messy as it was—and she felt exactly the same way.

A year ago, she'd doubted whether love existed. Now she knew that it did. She heard it in Daniel's voice when he sang to Delphine and saw it in his eyes when he laughed over the shirt that Blake had ruined. She read it in his face when he looked at her the way he was looking at her now.

But most importantly, she felt it in the way he was there for her, every day. Just as she would always be there for him.

She smiled, watching him fold his clothes and put them back into his suitcase—and then he stopped and looked at her with an expression of wonder.

"What is it?" she asked.

"I just realized that I must have packed my suitcase a hundred times. Maybe even a thousand. But this is the first time I've ever packed my suitcase in a place that feels like home. I mean, not our home in Denver, but..."

"I know what you mean." And she did. "Our home is where we're together. You, and me, and Delphine."

He nodded. "It doesn't matter if we're living out of a suitcase or a mansion, as long as we're together."

She gave him a warm smile. "Do you ever miss it, though? All that traveling you used to do? Seeing the world, exploring something new every day?"

"Where on earth would I want to go?" he said, leaning down to kiss her. "I've got everything I need right here."

* * * * *

MILLS & BOON

Coming next month

THE MIDWIFE'S MIRACLE TWINS
Caroline Anderson

The rest of the clinic was busy but routine, with no dramas or crises, and she ended her shift only an hour late.

She went into the locker room to change, found the pregnancy tests strips still in her pocket and put them in her locker, then changed her clothes, dropping the scrubs into the laundry bin. Then she pulled out her bag and a tampon fell out. She bent down and picked it up, then stared at it thoughtfully.

Was her period overdue?

She wasn't sure. Her cycle wasn't an issue, so she never really bothered to make a note, but her periods usually started on a Tuesday, and it was Thursday.

Her heart gave a dull thud and she stared at it for another moment, then put it and the test strips in her bag and shut her locker.

There was no way she could be pregnant—was there? Surely not.

But all the way home her heart was racing, and the first thing she did once she'd closed the front door was run upstairs to the bathroom to do the test.

How could a minute be so long?

She perched on the edge of the bath, staring at the little strip and not quite sure what she wanted to see, one line or two.

One appeared instantly, to show the test was working. Not that anything else was going to happen—

Another line? Really? And a strong, dark line, too, not some vague little shadow.

She got up, her legs like jelly, and walked slowly out of the bathroom, sank down onto the bed and stared blankly at the test strip.

How could she possibly be pregnant? Dan had said it was a tiny tear, and she and Mark had tried for years. How could she be? Unless they'd just been incompatible, but even so…

She slid a hand down over her board-flat tummy. Was there really a baby in there? Dan's baby?

Please, no.

Please, yes!

But…

She'd have to tell him. Not yet, though. It might have been a fluke. She'd do another test in a while.

And then another one, until all the tests were used up.

Four of them couldn't be wrong.

She started to cry, great tearing sobs welling up from deep inside her where the pain she'd hidden for so long had festered like poison, and then the tears died away, leaving only joy.

JOIN US ON SOCIAL MEDIA!

Stay up to date with our latest releases, author news and gossip, special offers and discounts, and all the behind-the-scenes action from Mills & Boon...

millsandboon

millsandboonuk

millsandboon

It might just be true love...